# Finding
# The Firefighter
Louisa Heaton

# MILLS & BOON

**Louisa Heaton** lives on Hayling Island, Hampshire, with her husband, four children and a small zoo. She has worked in various roles in the health industry—most recently four years as a community first responder, answering emergency calls. When not writing, Louisa enjoys other creative pursuits, including reading, quilting and patchwork—usually instead of the things she *ought* to be doing!

Visit the Author Profile page
at millsandboon.com.au for more titles.

Dear Reader,

The character of Addalyn (Addy) had been taking up space in my brain for years, but I didn't know too much about her, which story to fit her into or which hero would step up to take a place at her side. I was never ready to write her, and each time I had to come up with a new synopsis, I'd pull her character out, brush her off and take another look. Was I ready to write her?

Very often, the answer was no, LOL!

But this time, I began to see a little girl called Carys, who was being raised by a firefighter father—Ryan. And I saw these two, holding hands at the zoo, and from nowhere, Addy stepped in and scooped Carys up into her arms!

Addy was ready. All she'd needed was a little girl to love and a hunky fireman to keep her safe, even though she knew that Ryan represented a danger to her heart.

So, I hope you enjoy Addy and Ryan's story. It's been a long time coming, but for me, the wait was worth it!

Happy reading,

*Louisa* xxx

# DEDICATION

For Nick

# CHAPTER ONE

THIS WAS THE perfect place. To rest. To recharge after a difficult and complicated shout. Here, halfway up Abraham's Hill, there was a clearing amongst the trees and she could look down upon the people in the park. Families sharing picnics. Children playing, giggling, chasing one another. Young couples sitting on the grass. Older ones holding hands, or feeding the birds gathered around their feet. The perfect place to stop thinking about the awful situations people often found themselves in and instead bask in the peace and serenity of happy, content, *safe* ones.

Hazardous Area Response Team paramedic Addalyn Snow yearned for the serenity of happy, content people, but often felt it was a condition that would always somehow be out of her reach. She wasn't bitter about it. It was something she had become resigned to. Her life was filled with drama, both at work and unfortunately, these last few years, at home.

Biting into her chicken salad wrap, she found her gaze captured by a young boy and a girl chasing each other around, laughing, and she didn't notice a dollop of garlic mayonnaise escape from her wrap until it landed on her uniform. She swore quietly and used her finger to wipe it up, licked it, then reached for the wipes that she kept in the glove compartment of her work vehicle. She was just rubbing at her uniform, hoping and praying that the mayo wouldn't stain, when she received a call.

'Three one four, this is Control. We have a report of a situation occurring at Finnegan's Hole in Bakewell. Possible tunnel collapse with multiple casualties. Cave rescue and fire brigade en route. Can you attend, over?'

'Control, this is three one four. Show as attending. ETA…' she glanced at her watch '…fifteen minutes, over.'

'Thank you, three one four.'

Addalyn looked about for a bin to throw the last part of her sandwich into, but the one near her car was already overflowing. So she just stuffed the rest of her sandwich into her mouth, closed the car door and started up the engine, activating the blue lights. She would use the siren when she reached built-up areas and traffic.

She felt some trepidation in her stomach. Finnegan's Hole was a popular potholing site with a narrow entrance. She'd attended a job there once before, as a new paramedic, when a potholer had gashed his leg open on a sharp rock formation. She could remember standing there, looking down at the cave entrance, and wondering why on earth anyone would be crazy enough to do potholing as a hobby. She'd never been fond of enclosed spaces herself, but hadn't realised the extent of this until she did her three-day-long confined space training in her quest to become a HART paramedic.

HART paramedics received extra training. They specialised in providing first responder care in areas considered more hazardous than those a conventional paramedic would operate in, often working alongside multiple other agencies.

Addalyn had worked hard to become a HART paramedic and she loved her job. It meant she had to think carefully about each and every decision. Each and every shout was completely different and no two work days were the same. She often worked long hours, but the best thing about that was that when she got home, exhausted and tired, it meant she could fall into bed and go right to sleep. When she woke up the cycle would begin again, so she didn't have to think too hard about the spaces in between when she was finished for the day and when she had to clock on again. It meant she didn't have to notice how alone she was. Or who she was missing. Or why.

And if those thoughts did creep in she silenced them with food, or the TV, or loud music pumping through her ears as she exercised to retain her fitness levels.

She knew how to push herself hard. It was what

she had always done. Even as a child. And pushing hard, being determined not to let life beat her to a pulp, as it had tried in the last few years, was what kept her going.

Addalyn activated the sirens as she came upon traffic. There was always a lot of traffic in Derbyshire, even in rural areas such as Bakewell or Matlock. Her work covered the area of Derbyshire that contained the Peak District, and it was popular with tourists and walkers. And in this next job's case potholers. The Peak District had a lot of natural pothole formations. Nettle Pot, which was over a hundred and fifty metres deep, Poole's Cavern, a two-million-year-old limestone cavern, and the mighty Titan Cave, near Castleton, which was Britain's biggest cave.

She had to remain alert. Not all pedestrians saw the lights or heard the sirens. Nor all drivers. She had to be constantly alert for all the hazards that might come her way. It had become a learned skill. In life, as well as at work.

'Stay there…' she murmured to herself as a car appeared at a T-junction on her left, praying that the driver would see her and ease back to let her go past first. Thankfully, the driver saw her, and she raised a hand in thanks as she zoomed past.

Finnegan's Hole, her satnav instructed her, was halfway up a mountain on the other side of Bakewell. It was situated on the east face of Mitcham's Steps, another popular tourist attraction, because the hill there was like a stepped pyramid, with a viewing platform on the top. Finnegan's Hole had only been discovered in 1999, and from what she remembered reading, potholers were still mapping out its many caverns, twists and turns, deep into the earth.

A helicopter flew overhead and she became aware of other sirens ahead of her, and on one long stretch of road she saw the disappearing tail-end of a fire engine. It looked as if they might all arrive at the same time.

She radioed through to Control. 'Any update on the Finnegan's Hole job, Control? Do we know the number or types of casualties, over?'

'We do have an update for you. At least four trapped after a confirmed tunnel collapse. Mostly minor injuries, but one caver is said to be trapped beneath the rubble, over.'

'Any other information on that patient, over?'

'Patient is male and trapped about twenty feet beneath the surface, over.'

Addalyn shivered, imagining what that might look and feel like. Trapped beneath the ground, in the dark, in close quarters, dirt and muck in the air, maybe water… Torchlights flashing this way and that, sound echoing, reverberating around you. In pain. Trapped. Unable to move.

'Thanks, Control.'

Her thoughts immediately jumped back to her confined spaces training. She needed to be aware of the topography of the area they'd be working in, maybe find an expert on the tunnels if one was available. She'd have to think about the risk of further tunnel collapse, maybe gaseous emissions could be a danger, or an increase in water levels? Free-flowing solids? And all of this before she could even think about her patient. She knew nothing about him. He might have other medical conditions that she knew nothing about. A condition that would complicate her ability to attend him. And if he were trapped that far down, the big question was…would she have to go down there?

Her vehicle began to ascend the hill road on Mitcham's Steps, its engine roaring, easily taking her up the steep incline, smoothly and expertly. Some hikers were making their way down and moved to the side of the road to hug the verge as she passed.

She saw curious eyes and faces. Saw some stop to watch her pass, even one or two debating going back the way they'd come to watch the drama that was causing all these sirens to be heard, all these emergency vehicles to pass by.

*Finnegan's Hole. One mile*, she read on her satnav.

The sun was out, at least. It wasn't a grey, drizzly day. They'd have daylight and a bit of warmth to assist them.

When she arrived at Finnegan's Hole she parked and opened her boot to slip on her high-vis vest, her hard hat, and grab her equipment. As she closed the boot she became aware of a fire chief in a white hard hat approaching her. She recognised him. It was her father's friend Paolo. And seeing him walk towards her, in his fireman's garb, reminded her so strongly of how her father and brother had used to look that grief smacked her in the gut, as if she'd been swung at with a wrecking ball.

'Addy. Good to see you. Are you okay?'

She gave him a quick nod, not quite trusting herself to speak yet. It had been over a year, but it still felt so raw. Thankfully, Paolo seemed to understand, and he jumped straight to business.

'We've got seven in total, trapped from a tunnel collapse, and we have communications. Six of them are fine. Minor injuries, cuts, grazes, some bruises. But one potholer is trapped beneath the rubble. Attempts were made to lift off whatever rocks they could, but they had to stop because of risk of further collapse, and apparently there is one large boulder trapping his left leg. They say it doesn't look good. Almost crushed. Cave rescue is here, setting up, and we've got equipment going in right now to secure the cave roof.'

'Okay. Conditions down below?'

'Mixed. It's a tight squeeze, as I'm sure you know, but only a bare inflow of water. Trickles— nothing more. No gaseous emissions, so I don't think we need to worry about the risk of anything blowing up or catching fire. But they're panicking.'

'To be expected. Who have you got on your team that's good with small spaces?'

The chief smirked. 'You know they're all good.'

'What about Charlie?' She'd worked with Charlie before on an entrapment case.

'Off sick. But we do have Ryan Baker. He's new, but extremely good with stuff like this. Used to be in the army. Did a lot of tunnel work.'

'Then he's my guy. Get him in a harness and rope—he's coming in with me, once I've done the risk assessment.'

A new guy. That was good. He'd have no associations with her past.

The chief saluted and jogged off to talk to his team.

A tunnel guy. Army guy. Sounded good.

Addalyn went over to the mountain rescue team member who was co-ordinating his team with fire and rescue regarding the cave supports that were going in.

'How's it looking?'

'Nearly all the supports are in. Just setting up the lighting for you.'

'What can you tell me about this place?'

'It's pretty much what you'd expect. Lots of close quarters. Limestone, mostly. Some bigger caverns as you descend further. Atmosphere is moist.'

'Hazards?'

'There are some sharp rock formations. Stalagmites. Stalactites.'

'Biologics?'

'Nothing to concern you.'

'You're full of pleasant information.'

He smiled. 'I aim to please.'

'I'm going to lead the rescue. One of the fire crew is going in with me.'

'All right. We'll keep in touch with radio. You'll need one of these.' He passed her a hand radio that she slotted into her vest as he clipped her to a guide rope. 'Where's your other guy?'

'Here.'

She turned to give him a smile. A nod. To introduce herself by name, especially since they'd be in close quarters with one another. She liked firefighters. Had an affinity for them. Her father and brother had both been firefighters. She'd even thought that she would be one, too.

But Ryan Baker was not the sort of guy you just had a single glance at. He was not the type of guy you said hello to and then got on with what you were doing.

He was…different. Intense. Handsome.

Three danger zones that instantly made her heart thud painfully in her chest in an alert as his rich chocolate eyes bored into hers.

'Ryan? I'm Addalyn.'

She held out her hand for him to shake, aware

of a tremor in her voice just as she felt a powerful feeling pass through her when he shook her hand and then let go, his dark eyes barely meeting hers.

'Nice to meet you.' He attached himself to the guide rope with strong, square hands.

An army guy. A tunnel guy.

A *firefighter* guy.

No. She wouldn't think about that.

The mountain rescue man gave her the thumbs-up. 'Lights are in. I've got two of my team who will meet you at cavern two. The tunnel collapse is just ahead of them.'

'All right.'

'Just follow the guide rope down. There will be cameras for you to use when you near the tunnel breach. Go in feet first. There's a small cavern about ten feet down, where you can move around and begin to crawl deeper in.'

'Perfect. Thank you.'

She eyed the small hole in the earth, that basically looked like it was the entrance to a badger sett or something. It didn't look like anything humans should be climbing down into, but she and Ryan would have to go. It was dark. Shadowy. It gave her the shivers, but she knew she could deal with it.

She took a step forward, then felt a hand on her arm.

'I'll go first,' suggested Ryan.

She looked at him and nodded briefly. Her heart

was pounding so fast because of her claustrophobia, wasn't it? Nothing to do with him.

'I'll show you where to put your hands.'

She nodded. 'Thanks.'

He went in feet first, as instructed. Finnegan's Hole swallowed him up easily and he had no hesitation about heading into the dark. She watched him disappear.

People often joked that they wished the earth would swallow them up, but they wouldn't say it if they truly knew how it felt, she thought, following him down, her eyes taking a moment to adjust to the darkness. There were lanterns, as the mountain rescue guy had said, but they were spaced far apart and there were sections as they climbed down where the only light was provided by their head torches.

Her hands touched rock. Her boots found purchase on ledges and outcrops and her body scraped along the tunnel sides, where it got narrow. She tried to push images of this tunnel caving in on her away, knowing she needed to trust in the facts that she had been told: tunnel supports were in place.

Sounds began to carry towards her through the tunnels and caverns. Voices. Some shouting. Others trying to soothe and calm. The dripping of water. The echoes of everything.

Something skittered across the back of her hand and she yelled.

Ryan looked up at her. 'You okay?'

His concern for her was touching, but she was here to help someone. Not to be another person who would need rescuing. 'Fine.'

He squinted, as if deciding to trust that she was telling the truth.

'Honestly. I'm fine. Just not fond of spiders, that's all.'

'Stay by me.'

She had no plans to do anything else.

They descended into the cavern, with Ryan holding out his hands to help her down onto the cave floor. It was a decent size. About the size of her bathroom at home. Tall enough to stand up in. Ahead of them was a small crawlspace, lit with lamps.

*Have I got to go in there?*

'It shouldn't be far. Remember the mountain rescue guys are in the next cavern already.'

Addalyn nodded. Her mouth had gone incredibly dry, yet the rest of her was sweating, and her heart was hammering away in her chest. All she could feel was a sense of pressure all around her. The pressure that might be on the rock walls. The floor. The ceiling. And if she crawled into that space...

'Addalyn?'

She looked at Ryan.

'You can go back if you want.'

The temptation was immense. It would be so easy, wouldn't it? To just start climbing back in the other direction. Towards the surface. Towards the sunshine and the light and the fresh air. To space and freedom and peace.

But there was a man in trouble who needed her. A man who needed her medical expertise. She couldn't walk away from him, no matter what.

'No. I'm doing this.'

He nodded, a slight smile playing around his beautiful mouth, and that smile was enough. That smile said, *I believe in you. I'm proud of you.*

She thought of her father. Her brother. She was not going to die like they had. 'Let's do this.'

Ryan grinned. 'All right.'

He got down on his hands and knees and began to crawl into the tunnel. As his feet disappeared into the shadows she sucked in a determined breath and followed after him, trying to ignore all that she felt digging into the soft flesh of her belly, or the way her helmet would knock into the rock above her head. Her clothes were wet and dirty and her kit bag, being dragged behind her, must be in a terrible state.

They crawled for what seemed like an age, towards the lights and noises ahead, and then suddenly, in front of her, Ryan was getting to his feet and turning to help her up. His hand reaching for her. She ignored how it felt to take it. Then they were in the second cavern with two of the mountain rescue team.

'Ryan. Addalyn.' Ryan made the introductions.

'Raj. Max,' said one of the men, doing likewise. 'And this lovely gent down here, in need of your help, is John. John Faraday.'

John lay on his back on the cavern floor, his left leg trapped under an immense rock and some rubble. Around him sat the other cavers, two men and a woman. They all looked scuffed and dirty, muddy and frightened. John was pale, but conscious. He lifted a hand in greeting.

'We didn't want to leave him,' the woman said. 'We come down together. We go up together. That's our motto.'

'Sounds good to me,' said Addalyn. 'Now, let's see how we can do this. Ryan? Would you check these guys over whilst I look at John?'

'Sure.'

She knelt by John, took his hand and squeezed it. 'Hey, how are you doing?'

'I've had better days.'

'I bet. On a scale of one to horrible, do you want to tell me how much it hurts?'

'Surprisingly, not much.'

That was probably the adrenaline, keeping him numb.

'I'm going to get a line in to give you some painkillers anyway, just in case. You allergic to anything, John?'

It helped her to focus on her patient. It stopped her being aware of what was all around her, pressing down.

'Just my ex-wife.'

She smiled. She liked him. It took a lot to remain upbeat in a situation such as this.

'This should help.'

She gave him a shot of painkiller, then hooked up a bag of intravenous fluids.

Ryan knelt beside her. 'Just cuts and bruises on the others. They missed the worst of it because John, here, pushed them out of the way.'

'Hero, huh? We need them to go to the surface.'

He nodded. 'Agreed. What do we know about the three trapped behind the rubble?'

One of the mountain rescue guys spoke. 'They're okay. Just John got badly hurt.'

'Okay.' Addalyn stood, stretched her legs. 'I know these guys want to stay and help John, but we need them to go up. That way we can work better on getting John out and opening up the tunnel for the others too. Besides…' her voice dropped low '… I'm not sure they're going to want to see what comes next.'

Mountain rescue nodded. 'I'll get them out.'

Addy knelt back down to John, her gaze taking in his position, his leg beneath the rock, his foot sticking out on the other side. 'Can you wiggle your toes for me?'

'I'll try.' John concentrated and looked up at her hopefully. 'Did my foot move?'

'No. I'm afraid not.' Grim, she reached past

him, squeezing past the boulder. 'Can you feel me touching you?' She stroked just above his ankle.

'No.'

The boulder was massive. His leg beneath it had to be crushed and there would be no way to save it.

Loosening his boot, she tried to feel for a pedal foot pulse, but nothing would register and the foot was cold. She sat back on her haunches.

'John, what kind of support do you have at home?'

'I live with my girlfriend. She's a nurse. She's gonna be so angry with me about this.'

Addy gave him a sympathetic smile, then turned to Ryan. 'Any chance this boulder could be lifted quickly?'

'We could get equipment in, to either remove it or break it up into smaller manageable pieces, but it would take time.'

'How much time?'

Ryan shrugged. 'As much as I'd like to say it could be done quickly, in these conditions it might take time to manoeuvre it through those crawl spaces before we could get set up. But even if we removed it, wouldn't he be at risk for compartment syndrome?'

She was impressed that he would know about it. Compartment syndrome was a condition that occurred in incidents like these, when pressure within the muscles built to dangerous levels. That pressure could lead to decreased blood flow and prevent nourishment and oxygen reaching the tissues. Which, in turn, could lead to a build-up of toxins, so that when the pressure was removed, those toxins would flood the heart and cause the patient to go into cardiac arrest.

'I could do a fasciotomy, but that would just prolong the agony long term.'

A fasciotomy was an emergency procedure performed to try to prevent compartment syndrome. It involved making an incision along the fascia to relieve tension and pressure in tissue.

'Addalyn? You don't have to whisper. Just tell me straight,' said John.

She knelt beside him once again. 'Your leg isn't great, John. It has a severe crush injury with a lot of soft tissue avulsion and high levels of contamination. Your foot has no pulse, and it is also cold and does not move. Your blood pressure is low and you're the wrong side of fifty.'

Her patient swallowed. 'None of that sounds good.'

'It isn't. I'm sorry, but I'm pretty sure a doctor is going to want to perform an expedient procedure on your lower leg.'

She watched his face carefully, having avoided the word amputation, but knowing it was implied. No medic liked telling a patient bad news. But it was something she'd hardened herself to. She couldn't allow doubts and recriminations any room in her mind these days. She already had enough to deal with. So she steeled herself.

'Will it hurt?'

'No. The doctor would put you under. You won't feel a thing. And me and Ryan are going to help take care of you and get you back up to the surface afterwards.'

John looked at Ryan, then back to Addy. 'Have you seen many of these before?'

'Yes.' He didn't need details. He just needed to know this wasn't her first time. 'Everyone is going to do their best for you, John, okay?'

He nodded. 'Before they put me under…can I ask you to tell my girlfriend something? Just in case.'

'You'll be able to tell her yourself when you wake up in hospital. But sure… Just in case.' She leaned in to hear.

'Tell her that I love her and that she made my life the best that it ever could be.'

She looked him in the eyes. 'I will. But everyone's got you, okay?'

'Okay.'

Just then more of Ryan's fire crew arrived, this time with a doctor in tow. Addalyn apprised Dr Barrow of the situation, he confirmed the necessity for the procedure, and made quick work of removing John from his left leg, bandaging him and stabilising him for removal back up to the surface.

Dr Barrow went first, then Ryan took the front

of John's stretcher, whilst his crew mate Tom took the rear. Addalyn followed them up, keeping an eye on the monitoring equipment and hoping that John didn't choose to have a further medical crisis whilst stuck in a small tunnel. Thankfully, he remained stable all the way, and they all emerged on the surface, dirtied, muddied and relieved, before passing John off to an ambulance that would take him to hospital.

Addalyn turned to see Ryan heading back into Finnegan's Hole. 'Where are you going?'

'There are still people down there.'

'I know, but surely it's someone else's turn to go down?'

'That's not how this works.' He smiled, disappearing into the earth a second time.

Addy called through to Control and apprised them of the situation. 'One patient has been medically evacuated, but there are still three trapped behind the collapse. I've been informed that they don't have any serious injuries, but as this is still a multi-operational job, I'd like to stay on scene and be of some help, over.'

'Thank you, three one four. Received. Stay safe out there.'

'I will. Over and out.'

# CHAPTER TWO

IT TOOK THREE hours to dig out the tunnel safely and free the rest of the potholers, who were mightily relieved to see some friendly, helpful faces on the other side of the rubble.

Their cuts and bruises were as to be expected, though one of the potholers, a young woman, had a suspected fractured forearm. Ryan splinted it and then followed the others out through the tunnels and into the fresh air, where the sky was blue and the air was warm and welcome.

'Addy? I've splinted this lady's arm. I think she might have a fracture.'

'I'll take a look.'

He was glad to see Addalyn was still there, waiting for him to come out. There'd been no need for her to stay. After all the main casualty, John, had been evacuated many hours before, and the other patients had only mild injuries that wouldn't even require a visit to hospital. And there were other paramedics here. Other ambulances.

She could have left.

But she hadn't.

And he had to admit it felt quite good to see

someone looking so relieved when he emerged safe and sound.

He barely knew Addy. Had met her only today. But they'd been through something dangerous together and that bonded people in a way that no one else would be able to understand, so he knew he'd look forward to working with her in the future.

Finnegan's Hole would now be closed to the public until the tunnels and caverns could be confirmed as stable and safe.

Ryan checked in with his chief, then headed over towards Addy to thank her before he left. She was helping the lady with the injured arm into an ambulance, standing back as the doors closed.

'Thanks for staying.'

She turned to smile at him. A beautiful smile. 'It was my job.'

'Yes, it was, but even so… I appreciate you still being here now we've got everyone out.'

'*"We come down together, we go up together."* I think I heard that somewhere,' she said with a smile, repeating the words of one of the potholers. 'Besides, I have this thing about keeping an eye on firefighters.'

'Oh?' He gave an amused raise of one eyebrow.

She smiled at him. 'Long story.'

'Best ones are. Listen, I've just spoken to the chief and we're all heading to the Castle and Crow for an evening of decompressing, fine ales and a trivia quiz. You and your team are all welcome to join us.'

He thought she'd say no. He thought she'd say she'd think about it. Or she'd try to make it. Any of those excuses. But it wasn't as if he was asking her out on a date. This was a group thing. It had been a long day, and this last job had been a tough and exhausting one. All he wanted was to have a shower, some food and then an early night, but he also knew of the restorative power of a night out with his crewmates. Decompressing, destressing, having fun and laughing was crucial to help deal with their long hard days on the job. And tonight was a good night to do it. His daughter, Carys, was with his parents for a sleepover.

To his surprise, she said, 'Sounds great! I'll ask the others.'

'Perfect. I'll see you later, then.'

She gave him a nod and turned to head back to her rapid response vehicle. She was still in the clothes she'd been in when she'd gone below with him. The mud had dried out.

'Hey, listen...' He hadn't known he was going to say anything else until his mouth had opened up and begun to spurt sounds. He thought rapidly as she turned to face him again, a look of query on her face. 'You did great down there today. I know you weren't exactly fond of being in such a confined space.'

She smiled and nodded. 'I wasn't, but...thanks.'

He wasn't sure exactly how to end the conversation now. Nod? Say goodbye again? Give her a little wave?

*No, that would be weird. Why does it matter? What's got into you? Just walk away, Ryan.*

Why had he suddenly become tongue-tied? The last time he'd been tongue-tied had been ages ago. When, exactly?

He frowned, and when the memory came he felt bad.

He'd been tongue-tied when he'd watched his bride, Angharad, walk down the aisle towards him. She'd looked so beautiful in her stunning white gown, holding that bouquet of summer flowers before her as she'd walked to the sound of the 'Wedding March', and just seeing her had seemed to stop all his normal bodily functions from working. His mouth had gone dry, his brain had emptied of all possible thought and reason, and all he'd been able to get himself to do was continue to breathe and try not to cry.

Addy looked nothing like Angharad. She was muddy, rumpled, her hair sprouting loose tendrils around her tired face, but there was something about her…something that called to him. What was it?

*It doesn't matter. She's just a colleague. I probably won't see her again for a while after tonight. I can just enjoy her company and not think too hard about it.*

'I'll see you tonight, then?'

Another nod. Another smile. Her eyes were *stunning*.

'You can count on it.'

'Great. I'll…er…' He pointed in the direction of the fire engine. Saw the amusement in her gaze and laughed at himself as he walked away.

Addy pushed open the doors to the Castle and Crow. It was one of Derbyshire's tiniest pubs, situated in what had used to be the gatehouse to a castle that now stood in ruins. She'd been, oh, so glad to get the invitation—anything to keep her out of that empty and now silent house.

She wasn't a fan of that silence. It felt thick and heavy. It made the house seem…lifeless. And somehow, though she was the only one living, she felt like a ghost, haunting its rooms, looking for life to latch on to. She missed her dad. She missed Ricky. The empty spaces where they'd usually sat felt cruelly difficult. Dad by the window in the recliner he'd loved so much. Ricky stretched out on the couch, playing video games.

Gone.

Taken from her so quickly.

They'd been her whole world, her security blanket, her soft place to fall after all that horrible business with Nathan, and just as she'd begun to shine again…just as she'd begun to smile and laugh again…life had snatched them both away.

It hurt to be in the house.

Music greeted her as she pushed through the doors and then smiles and cheers as some of the ambulance and fire crew greeted her, insisting she join them at their table. She made the international gesture that said *I'll just grab a drink... anyone else want one?* by pointing at the bar before making her way back over to them armed with a gin and tonic.

Chrissie and Jools had a seat open next to them, so she sat there. 'Hi, guys.'

Chrissie was a paramedic and Jools was an emergency care assistant. On the table next to them were some of the fire crew guys. Paolo, Brewster, Tom and—her heart thudded quicker—Ryan.

She raised her glass to them all. 'So, what are we doing?'

'Pub quiz,' said Chrissie. 'Ambulance versus Fire versus everyone else, I guess. Thatch is in the loo, but he's going to help make up our four.'

Thatch was one of the 999 call takers who worked at Control.

'Great.' Addy took a sip of her drink. 'I always knew all that trivia Dad used to give me would come in handy one day.'

It had been her dad's thing. Every day at dinner he would present her and Ricky with a fun fact for the day. Even when she'd moved back in with them after her split with Nathan. Sometimes it would be hilarious, sometimes intriguing, but it always sparked conversation, and dinner times Chez Snow had quickly become her favourite time of the day.

Nowadays dinner was a ready meal heated in the microwave and eaten in silence in front of the TV. Addy would do her best and watch a quiz shows if she could, whilst eating, but it never quite took away the fact that she was eating alone and that the two seats that would normally be filled with two strong, hearty men were actually empty.

Paolo nodded. 'Ah, yes, Vic knew a thing or two. Where did he get his facts, Addy? Novelty toilet paper?' He laughed and took a sip of his pint, raising his glass in a mock salute to the dead and the lost.

She smiled. 'I don't know. He picked them up from somewhere.'

'Victor Snow?' Ryan asked.

Addy nodded.

'I've seen his picture in the fire station. Ricky's too. I didn't realise you were related. I'm sorry for your loss.'

'Thank you.'

A strange atmosphere settled around the table, with no one quite sure what to say to change the subject, or even if changing the subject was the right thing to do. They all knew what had happened. They all knew what she'd gone through. With maybe the exception of Ryan.

Thankfully it was broken by the return of Thatch from the toilets.

'I'd give the restroom a miss for five minutes, guys. I think I had a dodgy kebab at midday.'

Everyone burst into laughter and Thatch looked around him, not quite sure that his joke had been that funny, or original, but appreciative all the same.

Behind them, at the bar, one of the barmen switched on a microphone and notified them that the quiz would start in ten minutes and that someone would come round with paper and pens momentarily.

Addy took a moment to catch up with Chrissie and Jools. She'd not seen them since the job at Finnegan's Hole that afternoon, and she asked them if they'd had any other interesting shouts.

'A guy who thought he was about to go into a diabetic coma.'

'You got to him in time?'

'He wasn't even a diabetic, Addy! Not been diagnosed—nothing. His blood sugars were fine, but when we looked up his deets on the tablet we could see the guy is constantly visiting his doctor, day after day after day.'

'Health anxiety?'

She nodded. 'We had to check him over, though. The only thing we found wrong was a slightly elevated heart rate, but that was probably down to his stress.'

'Poor guy. Must be hard to live with a condition like that.'

'I think he's lonely, too. Lives alone. Has done for years. The place had a feeling of neglect, you know?'

Addy could sympathise. When she'd lost Dad and Ricky, she'd found it hard to keep up with maintaining the house. Especially because she'd worked as many hours as she could so that she didn't have to be in that empty house. And the more and more things piled up, the worse she felt. But this last year, on New Year's Eve, she'd made a resolution to get on top of things with the house. She'd put on some music, or listen to a podcast, or an audiobook, she'd told herself, and work for fifteen minutes.

*Today I'm going to tidy and sort that corner by Dad's chair.*

*This time I'm going to go through that wardrobe and get rid of the clutter at the bottom.*

It was easier in short, manageable bursts. Not so overwhelming. And there'd even been a moment, when the house had begun to look better, brighter, when she'd been proud of herself. The depression and the grief had lifted enough for her to see good things in life again.

It still didn't make it any easier to be home alone, though. She wasn't sure she'd ever get used to living that way.

'Welcome, everyone, to the Castle and Crow

quiz night! We've got some amazing prizes for our winners and our runners up. For the team that places second there is a lovely prize of six bottles of wine, donated by the Tutbury Vineyard, along with tickets to a wine-tasting evening. But for our winners—drumroll, please...'

The clientele all began a low drumming on their tables, building to a crescendo and stopping only when Natalie, the pub landlady, who had the microphone, raised her hands, laughing.

'For our winning team there is a prize kindly donated by the local zoo. Free tickets for six people alongside a zookeeper experience and a meal, drinks included, at their onsite restaurant, Reservation!'

Addy's friend Chrissie leaned in. 'A zoo? No, thanks. I get itchy just thinking about fur.'

Addy smiled.

'So, get your pens and pencils ready!'

Addalyn grabbed her pen and then happened to look up at the fire crew's table. Her gaze met Ryan's and she smiled at him before looking away. She would have quite happily sat at their table. The fire crew had long been a part of her family because of her dad and Ricky. And Ryan seemed nice. Dangerously nice. But he was a fireman, so that made him off-limits.

'First question! What is considered the most dangerous bird in the world?'

Most dangerous bird...? thought Addy.

Chrissie leaned in and whispered, 'Would that be a bird of prey, do you think?'

Addy didn't think so. It might be the obvious choice, but she felt sure she knew the right answer. She just couldn't think of it.

Jools added, 'An emu? They can hurt you if they kick you.'

And then the answer came like a bolt of lightning. 'It's the cassowary,' Addy whispered.

'The what?' Chrissie frowned.

'Lives in Australia. Claws like daggers. Trust me, it's the cassowary.'

'Okay, but if you're wrong, you owe me a glass of wine.'

Addy knew she wasn't wrong. She remembered her dad telling her. One of his fun facts for the day. They'd been discussing flightless birds, and the only ones she and Ricky had been able to come up with had been penguins and kiwis. The cassowary was apparently bigger and stronger and infinitely more dangerous to humans.

'Question two... Which planet has a pink sky?'

Addy looked blankly at Thatch, Jools and Chrissie.

'Mars is the red planet,' said Thatch. 'Could be that.'

'We don't have any other answer. Let's write it down.'

They continued on through the questions, with the quiz pausing at half-time for people to use the loo and order more drinks. Addy was waiting at the bar when Ryan came alongside her.

'Hey,' he said.

'Hey, yourself. How are your team getting on?'

'Not bad, I think. We may be in with a chance of winning.'

'Confident! I like it.'

He laughed. 'It's either confidence or arrogance. Take your pick.'

'Well, you seem like a nice guy to me, so I'll say confidence to be kind.'

'How's your team doing?'

'Good. Though Chrissie has to leave in ten minutes, because her babysitter is on a school night, and Thatch is too busy chatting up that girl in the green dress over there by the pool table, so I think the second half might be just me and Jools.'

'Ah. The fickleness of friends. Who knew the promise of a day at the zoo wouldn't be enough to hold people in their place?'

She laughed. 'A day at the zoo sounds amazing to me. I love animals.'

'Me too.'

He turned to smile at her. A genuinely warm smile. His eyes were bright with happiness and she felt it again. That punch to the gut...that pull in his direction. It disturbed her, so she distracted herself by trying to get the barman's attention to ask for an extra packet of crisps.

'Well, good luck for the second half.'

She grabbed her and Jools's drinks, gripped the crisp packet corners between her teeth, and walked back to her table, her heart still fluttering from having been in Ryan's presence.

He was easy to be with. Easy to talk to. He made her nervous, yes, but it was a *good* nervous. An exciting nervous. It was something she would have to be in control of, but she knew she couldn't avoid him. They worked in the field of emergency response—they would most likely meet lots of times now that he was with Blue Watch.

'Everybody ready? Okay... Question number sixteen... What object will a male penguin give a female penguin to try and romance her?'

There was some muted chuckling and whispered answers. One team shouted out a rude one, to a chorus of giggles, but Addy simply smiled and wrote down the answer—a pebble.

'How long are elephants pregnant?'

The questions got more and more intense, and when the quiz was done the answer sheets were collected in for marking.

Jools grabbed her coat and stood up. 'Well, I've got to go.'

Addy looked up at her in surprise. 'But we've not got the results yet! You can't leave me here alone.'

'You've got the fabulous men and women of Blue Watch to sit with.'

'They're the enemy!' she said, with a laugh.

'They love you. They're your family. Sit next to Ryan. There's space there. Ryan? You don't mind if Addy sits next to you, do you?'

He looked at her. Smiled. 'Of course not.'

That smile was everything. Drawing her in until her anxiety put up a wall.

'But what if we win?' she asked Jools. 'I think we're in with a good chance.'

'Then you go to the zoo and have your meal at Reservation! Zoos aren't my thing. They always leave me feeling sad. But, hey, if we're runners up I wouldn't mind having one of those bottles of wine.'

And with that Jools slung her bag over her shoulder, dropped a kiss on Addy's cheek and sauntered out through the door.

Flabbergasted, Addy turned and looked at Blue Watch, who made welcoming motions with their arms and invited her to sit with them. Nervously, she took her drink over to their table and settled into the seat next to Ryan.

'Thanks.'

'You're one of us by all accounts, anyway. An honorary fire crew member.'

Addy blushed even though he was right. She did still feel that these guys were her family. Paolo, the chief, had worked with her father for a long time. He had served with him and was now near retirement. He'd also been chief to Ricky. They'd all been close. She thought nothing of calling into the station to say hi, if she was passing by.

Nervously, she glanced at Ryan, and caught him looking at her. 'How long have you been a fireman?' she asked, knowing she needed to say something, and that was the only question that popped into her brain.

'About four years.'

'But you were in the army before—is that right?' she asked, recalling what Paolo had told her at Finnegan's Hole.

'Yes, I was.'

'What made you leave the army, if you don't mind my asking?'

'Not at all. I was married and my wife didn't like it. Said she felt isolated. Like she was a single woman. She didn't want to feel like a single parent when she learned that she was expecting.'

'Oh, you have a child?'

She could almost feel herself relaxing. If he was married with a child, then she didn't have to worry about whether he was attracted to her or not.

He smiled. 'Carys. She's five.' He reached into his back pocket and pulled out his phone and showed her a picture.

The little girl was the spitting image of her father. Same dark hair, same chocolate eyes. A wide smile. 'She's beautiful.'

'I think so, but then I'm biased.'

'Is your wife looking after her this evening?'

His eyes darkened slightly. 'No, she's with her grandparents for a sleepover.'

'Oh. Your wife didn't want to come out tonight?'

He shook his head, a grim smile upon his face. 'I'm no longer married to Angharad.'

*Single?*

'Oh?' She felt nervous again. 'I'm sorry to hear that.'

'She…er…wasn't cut out for motherhood. She thought it was something she wanted, but when Carys arrived she realised that being a parent was harder than it looked and that it required a significant amount of personal sacrifice that she wasn't willing to make. So she left.'

Addy stared at him in surprise. She couldn't imagine walking away from her own child. Being a mother was all that she'd ever wanted. Something she'd chased with singular determination at one point in her life. But nature had let it be known that she would probably never get her dream. She had been unable to get pregnant when she'd been with Nathan, and tests had not shown why. Unexplained infertility had placed a huge toll on their relationship and Nathan had sought solace in the arms of another. Someone who would give him the child that he wanted, leaving Addy alone and desolate and having to move back in with her father and brother.

'I'm sorry. How old was Carys when her mother…?' She didn't want to say *left*.

'About sixteen months.'

'Oh. That must have been difficult…'

How did any woman walk away from her child? Her own flesh and blood…made with the man that she'd loved? She tried to understand. Tried to imagine what might have made her leave. It could have been anything, and she was in no place to judge.

'It was. But I got through it, and Carys and I are good.'

'Does she ask about her mother?'

'Sometimes. She misses having one—I know that. I try to be everything that she needs, but… it's not the same.'

Addy wanted to offer him some comfort. Maybe place her hand on his in a show of compassion. But she was scared to do so. Her life might have been in his hands this afternoon, but she still felt unable to reach out and let him know that she understood his pain, and that she was sorry he was experiencing it.

'I'm sure she'll be fine.'

They were stopped from talking any more when Natalie switched the microphone back on and it made a high-pitched sound. Everyone winced.

'Whoa! Sorry everyone!' she laughed. 'The results are in!'

Addy took a sip of her drink. All of her team were gone except for Thatch, who was technically still there in the pub, just not with her. He seemed to have been successful in his wooing of the woman in the green dress, as they were now sitting together, drinking and flirting with one another.

'It was a close-run thing, ladies and gentlemen, with just one point separating first and second place!'

The crowd whooped and cheered, and when the noise had settled down Natalie gripped the microphone and said, 'In third place, with twenty-one points, we have Team Eclipse!'

There was another cheer and applause.

'And in second place, with twenty-five points, and winning the six bottles of wine with a wine-tasting experience at the Tutbury Vineyard, we have Team Blue Watch!'

Addy clapped hard and beamed a smile at them all.

'And in first place, with twenty-six points, and winning the family zoo ticket, the zookeeper experience and dinner and drinks at Reservation restaurant, we have Team 999!'

Addy gasped in joy and surprise as everyone began to applaud. Briefly she stood and took a bow, this way, then that, before Natalie came over and presented her with an envelope containing her prize.

'Has to be redeemed by the end of this month, I'm afraid,' Natalie whispered, before smiling and walking away, back to the bar.

'Well done, Addy!' said Paolo.

'Yeah, well done,' said the others in chorus, including Ryan.

'It was a team thing,' she said graciously, wondering what on earth she'd do with a family ticket to the zoo when she didn't have a family. Well, she had Blue Watch… Paolo had four grown-up kids, but the others were single. Except Ryan…

She held out the envelope to him. 'You should have this. You and Carys.'

Ryan looked at her in surprise. 'But you won.'

'I don't have a family to take to the zoo. You do.'

Hesitantly, he reached for the envelope, but as he held it he looked at her. 'On one condition.'

'What's that?'

'You come with us.'

# CHAPTER THREE

IT HAD BEEN the right thing to do, hadn't it? Asking Addalyn to go with them to the zoo?

It was a question that kept rattling through his brain the day before they were due to go, as he and Blue Watch raced towards a road traffic incident on the motorway.

The call had come through eight minutes ago. A multi-vehicle pile-up, after a tree had come down in the strong winds they were having.

Would Addy be there? She might be, if she was on duty today. He'd not seen her since the Castle and Crow pub quiz, when she'd very kindly gifted himself and Carys the family ticket to the zoo.

Carys had been so happy when he'd told her about the day out they were going to have at the zoo. His daughter loved animals! She particularly had an affinity for tigers, and had two cuddly toy versions that slept in her bed with her—Tigger and Joey. And if there was a nature documentary on the television she'd much rather watch that than any cartoon or movie. He loved her confidence and thirst for knowledge, and nurtured it at every turn. So to be offered tickets to the zoo, where

Carys could see tigers in real life and pretend to be a zookeeper...? Of course he'd accepted!

It had felt only right to invite the real winner of the prize along. Addy had said she had no family, but from what he understood she was an honorary member of Blue Watch because of her father and brother. So of course he'd insisted she go with them.

But it would only be as friends, even though he did feel attracted to her. How could he not? She was beautiful, inside and out. Dark, almost black, straight hair. Large chocolate-brown eyes, underlined by darker shadows that hinted at bad sleep patterns, and full, soft pink lips in a very pale face. The kind of pale that if you saw it in a movie, you'd imagine her as a vampire. Because even though she had an outdoorsy job, she looked as if she'd never gone out in the sunlight. Yet she was strong and funny and kind. Generous, clearly. Warm-hearted. And clever—he couldn't forget that.

She looked as if she needed a good day out, and he knew Carys was chatty and confident enough with strangers for it to not be awkward.

*'We're going to have a lady with us,'* he'd told her. *'Her name is Addalyn.'*

*'Addalyn? She sounds like a princess.'*

*'I guess she is, in a way. She looks after people. She's a paramedic, but her daddy and her brother were firefighters like me.'*

*'Is she pretty?'*

*'I guess so.'*

*'Is she your girlfriend?'*

He'd smiled at his daughter's questioning, before shaking his head.

*'Do you want her to be your girlfriend?'*

Carys had chuckled and snuggled into him on the couch, leaving him with a question that had been on his mind lately. When Angharad had left, he'd sworn never to be with a woman ever again. Especially one who wasn't committed. But would he one day be ready for a relationship? With his daughter in tow? He refused to expose Carys to any woman who wouldn't love his daughter as much as she loved him, and he just wasn't sure there were any woman like that out there. Or, more truthfully, any that he could trust. He'd already been burned, and he wouldn't do so again.

'Coming up on the site. Game mode, guys,' said Paolo from the driving seat of the fire engine.

Ryan looked through the windscreen to the accident site up ahead. Police were already there, blocking off traffic and sending it down the outside lane only, to help ease some of the tailback. Lights flashed, and on the side of the motorway he could see one or two people from various vehicles, clearly unhurt. Behind them he heard more sirens as ambulances approached, but he had no time to look as he fastened his helmet and clambered from the vehicle to receive instructions from Paolo.

He was to go and help secure a white transit van that was on its roof, teetering in the gale-force winds that were still blowing. Steam was issuing from its underside, where a radiator must have been broken, and the driver was still trapped inside. The vehicle needed securing so that the patient could be safely extracted without causing further harm to himself or to the other rescuers that were turning up on-scene.

He collected the wedges that would provide primary stabilisation for the vehicle, whilst his colleague Matt began to attach the struts. The winds were strong, and they didn't need the vehicle moving whilst they attempted an extraction.

And then he heard her voice.

Addalyn.

He turned to look, saw her with Paolo, organising the scene. She was saying who should go where, and triaging the remaining drivers and passengers with injuries as she strode towards the vehicle he was working on. She knelt down by the driver, who was unconscious and had a lot of blood dripping from his head onto the roof of his car. He was held in place by his seatbelt. She checked his pulse and called for a head collar from the paramedic who had rushed to her side to assist. Ryan watched her carefully attach the collar, talking all the time to her patient, explaining everything she was doing even though the man was unconscious.

He respected her for that. The trapped, injured man wasn't just a piece of meat, but a person, and whether he could hear her or not she clearly wanted him to know what was happening to him, just in case. Who knew what the unconscious mind retained? This man, if he survived, might have dreams years into the future of a woman's voice reassuring him in disturbing times and might later wonder what his dreams meant.

'Ryan? We need you to cover the spill from that motorhome and secure the gas canisters inside.'

He saluted Paolo and ran to attend to his next job. The motorhome was on its side, all passengers and the driver having escaped the vehicle. But these motorhomes had kitchens, with little gas stoves in them, and they needed to be fed from pressurised gas canisters.

Some motorhomes carried only one, others two.

And they were an explosive hazard that needed to be removed.

Addy looked up from her patient and watched as Ryan ran to contain the gas. A part of her wanted to reach out, grab his arm and haul him back. Say, *No, not you. You have a daughter. Let someone else go. I need you.*

She was shocking herself with her thoughts.

Someone had to go and contain the danger, and if it wasn't Ryan it would be another of the fire crew, so which one was more expendable if it were all to go wrong?

*None of them! I can't lose any more people.*

Ryan was a father. To a little girl who had already lost her mother. She didn't need to lose her dad too. And that was all this was, right? Concern for a little girl she'd never met?

But she had no time to think more deeply about it, because she needed to do a primary survey on this driver, trapped right in front of her. He had a large laceration to his scalp, many cuts embedded with glass on his face and hands, and a rapidly expanding forearm with distortion that spoke of a broken bone or two. The arm could wait to be splinted. It was his left arm, and she couldn't reach it from the roadside. But she could get his head bandaged to help control the blood loss whilst she performed her primary survey.

'Chrissie, can you get this?'

Chrissie, the paramedic with her and one of her team mates from the pub quiz, nodded and got to work.

Addy used her stethoscope to listen to the man's chest. He sounded a little bradycardic, but there were equal lung sounds, so that was good. She couldn't feel any depressed skull fractures and there was no way to ask the patient where he had pain.

She stood up as Chrissie placed an oxygen mask on the man's face and got the attention of Paolo.

'We need to get this man out as quickly as possible so he can be more fully assessed.'

'On it.'

Paolo got the attention of two of his crew mates and they began to cut open the vehicle after placing a protective blanket over her patient.

It was hard sometimes to stand back and wait. As a paramedic the urge to action was strong, but it was imperative that they do this right. This man's ability to walk and even have a future relied on their knowledge and training to know when it was right to stand back and wait and when to treat. When to go slow and when to act fast.

She looked up briefly, over to the motorhome. Where was Ryan? She couldn't see him, and felt some anxiety, but then he appeared as he came around the back of the vehicle and she felt a palpable sense of relief. Felt a smile appear on her face. Felt some of her tension leave her.

How strange that she should feel this way. And why? She barely knew him.

*He kept me safe underground.*

That was all it had to be, right? She owed him—that was all. And he'd been kind at the quiz night, even walking her to her car in the dark when she'd decided to go home.

They'd walked quietly, side by side, and she'd felt nervous about saying anything so had kept quiet before pointing her key fob at her car and hearing it unlock.

*'Well, this is me,'* she'd said.

*'Thanks for a great night. And for being so generous about the prize.'*

*'It was my pleasure.'*

And it had been. She'd felt good about offering him the tickets. A little girl would get more out of a zoo experience than she would. A family deserved the ticket and she didn't have one. She was alone, and most probably always would be.

Ryan had leaned in and opened her car door for her, like a gentleman. It had been nice. Thoughtful.

She'd clambered in. Put her key in the ignition.

*'Well, goodnight, Ryan. Get home safe.'*

*'You too.'*

And he'd let go of the car door.

She'd closed it, wound down the window.

*'See you at work, maybe?'*

*'And if not Saturday. Ten a.m. At the zoo.'*

*'I'll meet you there.'*

She was kind of looking forward to it. Having someone to go with. Spending some time with him. Him and his daughter. It would be nice. It meant not having to be at home alone, waiting for her next shift, trying to fill the hours with something, anything, so as not to be reminded that the house was so quiet because she was the only one in it.

The driver was out now. On a backboard. Addalyn let one of the other paramedics splint his arm, then assess him and whisk him away, so she could deal with the next trauma. There were a few lacerations. A degloving incident with a motorcyclist, who was sitting on the side of the motorway, cradling his bad hand. He'd worn a helmet and leathers, but not gloves.

'Let me look at that.' She examined him quickly. It would need surgery—that was for sure. She glanced behind her to quickly assess his bike. It was crumpled at the front. 'You ran into someone?' she asked.

'The red car. Threw me over the top.'

'Wait—you were thrown? Sit still.' She clambered behind him and held his head in place, whilst calling out for assistance.

Ryan came running over. 'You okay?'

'This motorcyclist was thrown over a car. He got up and walked over here, but I want him properly assessed in case of shock. Could you fetch me a neck collar and grab a couple more paramedics for me?'

'Sure thing.' And he ran off to do her bidding.

'I'm okay. It's just my hand,' the motorcyclist said. 'Nothing's broken. I just walked.'

'Your legs might be fine, but what about your neck? Your back? You were in a collision.'

'I don't feel anything else wrong but my hand, and even that doesn't hurt much.'

'Because you've not got any nerve-endings left,

that's why. It doesn't mean it's good. And it could be only adrenaline keeping you upright right now.'

'Honestly... I'm fine.'

'What's your name?'

'Miguel. Miguel Aguila.'

'Where's your helmet, Miguel? And don't move your head.'

'I have it.'

One of the women nearby showed it to her. The helmet had significant scuff marks across it that showed Miguel had slid across the road on his head, and there was even a crack. He might have a closed head injury.

'Can you tell me what day it is, Miguel?'

'Friday.'

Correct. 'And who's our king or queen?'

Miguel paused. 'Charles?'

'Are you asking me or telling me?'

'Telling you.'

'Who's the prime minister?'

There was silence. 'I don't know. But I don't follow politics if I can help it.'

'Wise man. What did you eat for lunch?'

'That's easy. I ate...' Miguel's voice trailed off and then Addy's sixth sense kicked in as she felt a shift in Miguel's condition. He slowly began to lose consciousness and keeled over, with her guiding him down as much as she could.

At that moment Ryan arrived with two more

paramedics, Cindy and Emma, pushing a trolley and carrying a head collar.

'LOC just moments ago. Helmet shows evidence of a substantial impact. Let's get him on the trolley. Em, can you get the oxygen on him, please? I'll do the collar.'

Miguel was still breathing. He had simply lost consciousness. The question was, why?

Addy examined his head and felt the shift of bone beneath her fingers in the occipital area. 'Damn. Let's get him blue-lighted immediately.'

As Emma and Cindy whisked Miguel away, Addalyn looked at the frightened onlookers who had gathered at the roadside.

'Has anyone else sustained any injuries at all?'

They shook their heads. They looked as if they were shocked at having been involved in something so momentous, and were hugely relieved to have escaped without significant harm. That tree might have come down on a car roof. Instead it had hit the road, causing the nearest car to swerve immediately, another to hit its brakes and then, like a domino rally, cars had shunted each other, spun each other and, in the case of the transit, flipped over, most probably due to an uneven load in the back.

'You okay?' Ryan asked.

'Of course. You?'

'I'm good.'

'Good.' She gave him a brief smile. 'I'd better

check in with Paolo. See if there's anyone else in need.'

'I think we were lucky. The rest of these people will probably get away with a bit of whiplash.'

'They'll feel it tomorrow.'

'Police have already started mapping out the site, and we're about to do clean-up so we can get the motorway flowing again. Life never stops, does it?' he asked.

'It can do. And for some people life is never the same again.'

Ryan nodded, understanding on his face.

She hadn't meant to be maudlin. Life might continue, but when tragedy struck, those affected often felt in limbo, marvelling at those around them who just seemed to carry on as if nothing significant had happened.

Time had stood still when she'd lost her father and Ricky in one fell swoop. One moment they were alive. Her father. Her brother. Two people who loved her and cared for her. Her inability to have children didn't matter to them. And then they were gone, in an instant, and she was left alone in a hospital waiting room with her father's wedding band in a small plastic bag and her brother's St Christopher medallion in another.

That was all that was left of their presence here on earth—a couple of bits of metal that had sentimental value.

And memories.

And the knowledge that she would never get to speak to them again.

What had been their last words to one another? She couldn't recall.

'I'll see you tomorrow.'

Ryan laid a hand on her arm and rested it there for just long enough before he disappeared for her to register how reassured and comforted his touch made her feel.

Acknowledged. Seen. Appreciated.

Yes. But also liked and cared for.

His touch had surprised her. Pleased her. Made her yearn for more.

She felt a little bereft when he ran back to help his crew, and she admired his form as he did so. He didn't shirk the gruelling work. He mucked in with his team to help clear the road of debris.

*He's a good guy.*

But she knew she couldn't get involved with him. And that tomorrow she would have to be careful. Keep her distance. Maybe focus on Carys? Make sure the little girl had a good day out?

Then she wouldn't have to worry about having any little moments with Ryan.

*Seems good to me.*

# CHAPTER FOUR

CARYS HAD WANTED to wear a pretty dress so that Addalyn would like her.

*'She's going to like you no matter what you wear,'* Ryan had told her that morning before they drove out.

*'I still want to look pretty.'*

*'But you're going to get a zookeeper experience. It might be better for you to wear your jeans and a nice tee shirt instead.'*

But Carys had insisted. And so here they were, waiting by the zoo entrance, with Ryan in jeans and a nice tee shirt and Carys in one of her party frocks—a beautiful pale green dress with soft white polka dots on it. She wore strappy white sandals and had even tried to paint her toenails, he noticed. In bright, bubblegum-pink.

He smiled, having managed to bribe her to wear a cardigan, too, and had bent down to kiss her on the top of her head when he heard a voice.

'Good morning! You must be Carys?'

And he watched as Addalyn knelt to be face to face with Carys and shake her hand, her face full of smiles.

Addalyn had chosen to wear a dress, too. A denim shirt dress, belted at the waist with a bright red belt. And her hair was down for the first time. Waves and waves of black hair that shimmered blue and indigo in the sunlight.

She looked beautiful.

'Hi, Addalyn,' said Carys, smiling. 'Thank you for winning the prize and sharing it with us.'

Ryan smiled. They'd practised that sentence in the car, with him telling his daughter it was a polite thing to say and do.

'Oh, you're very welcome. But you must call me Addy. All my friends do.'

Carys grinned. 'Addy.'

She stood and bestowed a smile upon him that gladdened his heart.

'Shall we go in?' she asked.

He nodded and stepped back, indicating that she should go first.

They entered the zoo and showed their prize ticket at the gate. The girl behind the desk beamed a smile at them and asked them to make their way to the giraffe house, where they would be met by the head keeper in fifteen minutes' time. She handed them a small map, pointed out where they were at the moment and showed them which path to take to find the location they needed.

'Thanks.'

Exiting the entrance building, they stepped out

into sunlight. It was going to be a lovely day. Blue skies. A gentle breeze. Not a cloud to be seen.

'Did you drive here?' he asked Addy.

'No, I took the bus. My car's at the garage, having a service. I drove it there and caught the bus from the stop outside.'

'They didn't offer you a courtesy car?'

'They did, but I don't mind taking the bus.'

Carys had noticed an enclosure coming up on their left and ran over to look at it. As they got closer, they saw it was full of meerkats, and that there was a group of meerkats perched on top of a fallen tree trunk, staring back at the crowds.

'Daddy, can you see them? They're so cute!'

Ryan laughed and nodded, lifting her up onto his hip for a better look. There appeared to be Perspex domes inside the enclosure, so that people could go underneath the ground and pop their heads up and be closer to the meerkats.

'Can we do that, Dad?' asked Carys excitedly.

'Maybe later, honey. We need to get to the giraffe house, remember?'

She nodded and slid back to the ground, looking for the next exciting enclosure and finding it when she saw chimpanzees playing on some ropes. She squealed with excitement.

'She loves animals,' he said, feeling he ought to explain to Addy.

'I do, too. I don't blame her.'

'What's your favourite?' he asked.

'I like tigers.'

'They're Carys's favourites, too.'

'Really? Then she and I are going to get on!'

He laughed, and watched as Addy followed his daughter to the chimpanzee enclosure and stood beside her, helping to point out the animals, watching them play.

Carys was being Carys. Chatty. Sociable. Laughing. Smiling. Talking to Addy as if she'd known her her entire lifetime, even though they'd only known each other for ten minutes. But his daughter was like that. Everyone said so. When she'd started nursery the teachers had said that she was a confident, clever and happy girl, who wasn't afraid to talk to anyone. And when she'd started reception year her teacher had been so impressed with her she'd awarded her a Buddy Badge, which meant that she was the girl anyone could go to if they felt lonely or had no one to talk to. Carys would make them her friend and find them more.

She got that quality from her mother. Angharad had always been a social butterfly, loving life and going to all the parties and events where they'd lived. She loved being with people. Becoming a mother had placed limitations on that, she'd said, when she'd left. It had kept her at home and she hadn't liked how that had made her feel. As if life was passing her by and all she could do was look after a crying, squalling baby that wouldn't settle when she tried to comfort her.

That had been a huge thing in their relationship. Angharad had had difficulty comforting Carys when she was a baby, and yet Ryan would come home, pick up his daughter and she'd stop crying instantly. He'd tried telling Angharad that she just needed to relax. That Carys could pick up on her mother's frustrations and fears. But his wife hadn't liked him telling her that, either.

He'd thought he was helping. He'd just made it worse. Angharad had thought he was criticising her, but he hadn't been. He'd been trying to give her some advice. Trying to help her bond with Carys, because he'd seen how apart from her Angharad was feeling.

It had been strange, because Angharad had loved being pregnant. Had sailed through her pregnancy. Had blossomed, in fact. And yet when Carys was born, his wife had changed. She hadn't been the mother he'd thought she would be.

So it was nice to see Carys interacting so well with Addalyn.

They made their way to the giraffe house and saw a sign for the zookeeper experience participants, telling them to stand by and wait. So they did.

'Have you ever seen a giraffe in real life, Carys?' Addy asked.

'No. They're meant to be really tall. Like really, *really* tall!'

Addy laughed. 'Taller than me?'

'Taller than a house!'

'Taller than a castle?'

'Taller than the moon!' Carys beamed and slipped her hand effortlessly into Addy's.

He watched as a look of pleasant surprise crossed Addy's face, and then a warm, happy smile.

It was nice to see. Very, very nice.

The door opened and a young woman stood there, in a khaki shirt and shorts and boots.

'Hello, everyone! My name is Macy and I'm going to get you to help me feed the giraffes today. So, who's going to be my special helper?'

'Me, me, me!' said Carys, her hand in the air, practically bouncing up and down on the spot.

'And what's your name?'

'Carys.'

'Well, Carys, that's a very pretty dress you've got on. We won't want to get it dirty, so we'll have to be extra-careful. Why don't you and your mum and dad follow me?'

Addy glanced at him when Macy said *'mum and dad'*, but Ryan simply shrugged and let the assumption stay. What did it matter if it was wrong? What would be the point in explaining to Macy? It didn't matter. Not really. It was nice, actually. Because he'd never had that. That feeling of being a complete family unit. And if he wanted to pretend for a bit, then why not? Who was it harming? Carys certainly seemed happy about it, and was holding on to Addy as if she never wanted to let go.

They climbed some metal steps, their shoes clanking, and came out onto a platform with a metal safety rail. The aroma of giraffe was pretty strong, and now he understood why. There were three giraffes looking directly at them. At head level! And off to one side was a big pile of leaves and branches.

Macy stood in front of them. 'Giraffes are traditionally found in Africa, and they are the tallest living mammals on the planet. Giraffes are considered to be ruminants. Do you know what that means, Carys?'

His daughter shook her head.

'It means that they're animals that get their food from grazing plants, such as grasses and leaves from trees. They then ferment that food in a special stomach before they can digest it.' Macy turned to scratch the head of one of the giraffes. 'This is Mabel. Next to her is her sister Ethel, and the slightly smaller one is Ethel's daughter, Clara.'

'Can I touch one?' asked Carys, her face filled with wonder.

'Why don't you grab a branch and offer it to one of them? She'll reach for it with her tongue and when she takes the branch you can stroke her.'

Carys chose a branch and held it out and the giraffe called Clara came forward to take it, her long, dark tongue wrapping around the branch to strip it of leaves.

Carys let go of Addy's hand to reach out and stroke the giraffe. 'She's so soft!' she exclaimed.

Macy smiled. 'These are what we call reticulated giraffes. They have quite a distinctive coat pattern with polygon markings. Do you know what polygon means?'

Carys shook her head.

'It means five-sided. If you look at the dark markings on her coat, you'll see each of them is five sided, separated by white fur—do you see?'

Carys nodded, her face awash with wonder and joy.

They all stepped forward with branches to feed the giraffes. Ethel, Mabel and Clara were clearly used to being fed this way by humans. They took a great interest in what was being offered to them and were not afraid to interact with them at all.

'Why do they have horns?' asked Addy.

'Both male and female giraffes have them, but you can tell the sex of a giraffe from their horns. If they are thin, and have tufts of hair, then you're looking at a female giraffe. If they're bald, then it's a male. They use them in combat, when they're fighting over food sources or females.'

'Oh…'

It was fun to feed the giraffes. They were quite gentle, with wide brown eyes and long, black tongues that they used almost like a tool.

'We have seven giraffes here in Tutbury Zoo, but Clara will be leaving us soon to become part of a new breeding pair down in Devon.'

'Won't she be sad without her mummy?' asked Carys.

Ryan felt his heart ache when he heard her ask the question. She often asked him what mummies were like, and why she didn't have one, and although he'd tried to answer her questions as truthfully as he could, they often made him feel he was failing her somehow.

How did you tell your own daughter that her mummy had felt tied down by being a mother? That she'd lost her freedom? That looking after a child who cried all the time had made Angharad feel that she wasn't cut out to be a mother? It would make Carys feel it was her fault, when it totally wasn't! Angharad's leaving had all been about Angharad, but Carys wouldn't see it that way.

And so he did his best. Told Carys that her mummy hadn't been able to stay. That some people thought they could be parents, but then found out that they just couldn't.

'She might be a little scared,' said Macy now. 'Especially with the travelling down to Devon. But then she'll be excited to be somewhere new, and to meet different giraffes and make a new family of her own.'

He could see that Carys was sceptical about this.

Addy crouched beside her. 'I'm sure her mummy will be sad to see her go, but that's what happens when you grow up sometimes. You move out and make a family of your own. I'm sure you'll do it one day.'

'And Daddy will be sad when I leave?'

Addy nodded. 'But you'll still be able to see him and you might not even move very far away.'

'What if I don't want to make a new family of my own?'

'Then that's absolutely fine, too. There's nothing in this world that says you have to. Lots of people don't have children.'

He looked at her then, and wondered. Addy was in her mid-thirties, if he had to guess, and she didn't have any kids. Was that a choice she'd made? He didn't want to ask.

But she seemed to like kids. Or she seemed to like Carys, anyhow.

'You can stay with me however long you like,' he said, to reassure his daughter.

Carys turned and smiled at him.

'Do you want to help me let them out into the main yard?' Macy asked.

Carys nodded.

'Okay. Follow me.'

They followed Macy back down the steps to a series of gates and levers. Macy showed Carys which lever to pull to open up the giraffes' enclosure to the outside yard. His daughter took a hold of the lever and pulled it down, and as she did so the metal doors slid open, revealing the zoo outside and the outdoor giraffe enclosure, and Ethel, Mabel and Clara turned to look, before slowly heading out.

'Okay! Now I'm going to take you over to the ape house, where I believe you're all going to help prepare their food and clean the house.'

'Are we going to see tigers today?' asked Carys.

'That's the last step on the tour,' said Macy.

'You like tigers, too?' Addy asked Carys.

'I *love* tigers!'

'Me too!'

'Yay!' Carys threw her arms around Addy and gave her a big hug.

Addy hugged her back, squeezing her tight, and Ryan couldn't help it. He felt great about how the two of them were getting on. He'd known it was going to be good, but he'd not imagined the two of them would click so well. Addy was giving his daughter her full attention. Listening to her. Interacting with her. Holding her hand as they walked and pointing out interesting things. Clearly Addy was having a great time, too.

At the ape house they went into a kitchen area where there were huge piles of produce waiting to be prepped. They spent a good half an hour chopping fruit, leaves, seeds, bark and eggs, and then mixed it with some special monkey pellets which looked like small biscuits. The keeper added an insect mix afterwards.

'We like to try and reflect what they might eat in the wild,' he said.

'I thought monkeys only ate bananas,' said Carys.

The keeper, Ian, nodded. 'Lots of people think that. They do eat fruit—as you can see here—but we don't give them too much of it. We've found that by reducing fruit we can improve an ape's dental health as well as their physical fitness. Fruit that has been commercially grown for human consumption is different to the fruit available to primates in the wild, so we're very careful with the amount they consume.'

Carys looked lost.

'They're just trying to keep the monkeys healthy,' said Ryan, realising that Ian might not know how to simplify some of the terms he used so that younger kids could follow. Perhaps he was new?

'Oh, okay… Like Miss Roberts tells me not to eat too many sweets?'

Miss Roberts was the family dentist.

'Exactly!'

'And the fruit here is like sweeties for the monkeys?'

'That's right.'

'Oh…'

They headed out into an empty enclosure and Ian told them that they should all try to hide the food around the compound as it would 'enrich the apes' living experience'.

Again, Ryan had to explain. 'It's like a game for them...so they don't get bored.'

Carys had great fun stuffing food inside a rubber tyre. She even climbed a rope onto a platform and balanced half a watermelon on a pole there. Addy held her arms out to help Carys down. Once they were done, they were able to go out to the viewing area and watch as Ian released some orangutans out into the open for them to go and forage.

'Look, Addy! They found my food!'

'They did! Aren't they clever?'

Ryan started taking pictures on his phone. Carys was pointing at the apes. Addy was kneeling down next to Carys, with her arm around her shoulder. He took one of Addy and Carys laughing so hard and so genuinely it almost looked like a mother and daughter photo. He stared at the photo, his heart captured by the sheer joy on their faces.

Was this what Carys needed? A connection with a mother figure? She certainly seemed to be enjoying it. Revelling in it, actually. And Addalyn seemed genuinely happy, too.

He looked up from his phone at the two of them, deciding to put his phone away and enjoy this moment with them. Stepping forward, he laid a hand on Carys's back and pointed at a mother orangutan with her fluffy-haired baby.

'Aww! They're so cute!' squealed Carys.

'Having fun?' he asked Addy.

'I really am. I wasn't sure how this was going to go, but I am loving it. Carys is great, you know?'

'Thanks. I think so, too, but I am biased.'

'It must be difficult, raising her alone and having to work, too?'

'It's been a juggling act, but it's easier now that she's at school full time.' He looked at her carefully, before he said, 'I love being a dad. And you're great with kids. You're clearly a natural.'

She smiled at his comment. 'Thanks.'

But she looked a little sad. He was going to ask her if she was all right, but she spoke before he could.

'Hey, Carys, have you seen that one up at the top of the platform? He's huge!'

Clearly she wanted to change the subject, which was fine. The subject of whether people wanted children or not could be tricky to navigate. You couldn't assume that every woman wanted to have a child. You couldn't know if someone had had problems trying to conceive. It wasn't a conversation that you just blundered into, and he didn't want to upset Addy. They were all having a good day.

They fed the penguins next, actually getting to go into the enclosure with buckets of tiny nutrient-rich fish that were loaded with vitamins. The keepers made them wear overalls and boots and gloves, so that afterwards they wouldn't smell of fish, and it was great fun feeding them, watching them dive into the water or waddle on land. They were quite noisy too!

After that they went into the elephant house and helped to give the elephants a bath, spraying them with water from hoses after using what looked like a garden broom to give them a scrub.

The two elephants they were working with— Achilles and Bindu—loved their baths and playfully squirted water over themselves and their keepers, and in turn Addy, Ryan and Carys! They tried to stay as dry as they could, but it didn't really matter because they were all having so much fun! After the elephants' baths they were able to hand-feed them, and Bindu in particular was most enamoured with Carys, using his trunk to constantly sniff the little girl, making Carys giggle continuously at his antics.

And then came the moment that he knew Carys and Addy had waited for and looked forward to the most. The big cats. There wouldn't be the chance for any personal interaction, but they were given a behind-the-scenes tour and were able to help clean out a couple of pens.

'This is Sierra. She's a Sumatran tiger—a species which is critically endangered. But we are very proud to say that she is expecting two cubs, and has only about another month before she delivers.'

'She's going to be a mummy?' Carys asked in awe and wonder.

'That's right,' said Sally, the keeper. 'Sumatran tigers are usually smaller in size than the other tigers you might know about, and can you see those white spots on the backs of her ears?'

They all nodded.

'They act as false eyes and make other animals think that they have been spotted from behind.'

'Nature's so clever!' said Addy.

'Their coats are unique to each animal, so when Sierra has her two cubs they will each have their own pattern. Sumatran tigers usually have stripes that are closer together and more orange and black than other tigers'. They also have webbed paws, which makes them very good swimmers.'

'It's not true that cats don't like water, is it?' asked Carys.

'That's definitely not true! Sierra loves sitting or bathing in her pond out in her enclosure.'

'Where's the daddy?'

'The father is Loki, but you can't see him today, because he's currently with the vet, having a dental procedure.'

'Does he need a filling?'

Sally smiled at Carys. 'Kind of. He broke a tooth and developed a little abscess. It's being cleaned out, so it doesn't make him ill. We try to keep high levels of good health for our animals as we want them all to survive and work within our breeding programme.'

'She looks so majestic,' said Addy, gazing at the tiger as she panted away on her bed.

'She is a beauty,' agreed Sally.

The tiger wasn't the only beautiful creature he could see, Ryan thought.

'Tigers are meant to hunt and kill other animals to survive, so…what do you feed them?' asked Carys.

'You're absolutely right. Tigers do like to hunt—usually at night—so we feed them a variety of meat that we hide in their enclosure, so they have to hunt for it, or climb, or work out how to get the meat that's hanging from the trees.'

Sally knelt down and looked his daughter right in the eyes.

'Have you ever touched a tiger tooth?' she asked.

Carys shook her head.

'Want to see one?'

'Yes, please!'

Sally pulled a real-life tiger fang from her pocket and handed it to Carys. 'This came from a male Amur tiger called Colossus. Do you know where Amur tigers live?'

'No…' Carys took the tooth and gazed at it in wonder.

'They come from Russia. They used to be called Siberian tigers.'

'I've heard of those! I've seen them on the telly.'

'You have? Then do you know how many are left?'

Carys looked sad. 'Not many.'

'That's why tigers such as Sierra are precious. We not only try to keep up their numbers here in captivity, we also work around the world helping to educate people about tigers, their habitats, and how we humans can help them survive in the wild.'

'How can we?'

'Well, we work with the communities near tigers. The people there help us watch them and count them. And because the locals take an active part in monitoring them, it helps us reduce poaching. Do you know what poaching is?'

Carys shrugged.

'It's when someone illegally hunts an animal and kills it.'

'Oh. That's bad…'

'It is.'

'Why do people kill tigers?'

'That's a very good question. Some people want their fur. Others believe that parts of the tiger can be used in medicine.'

'Can it?'

Sally shook her head.

'I want to help a tiger. How can I?'

The keeper smiled. 'You're so sweet to want to help. We offer adoptions here, where you can adopt any animal in the zoo. Or you can get your mum and dad to help you look online and see if there's an animal charity you want to support instead.'

Sally was the second person to mistake them for a family. The idea that he and Addy were married, was… Well, Ryan could see the flush on her cheeks, too.

'I'll think about it.'

Sally smiled. 'Good idea. You don't want to rush into anything. I think you're a very wise little girl.'

'I'm going to be a vet when I'm older.'

'Sounds perfect for you. Now, let me show you the ocelots.'

They had a great time looking around the zoo, learning a lot about all the animals, and when the morning was over they headed to Reservation, the zoo's restaurant.

The restaurant was very elegant. Soft grey decor, crisp white tablecloths and hyper-realistic animal art in graphite pencil all over the walls. It was like a mural of a jungle, lit by wall sconces and candlelight. Greenery cascaded down from multitudes of baskets above their heads, and the soft scent of hibiscus was barely there.

Ryan, Addy and Carys were seated at a table in a bay window that overlooked the flamingo enclosure. Lots of salmon-pink birds stood in the water, occasionally dipping their beaks to try and feed on whatever it was flamingos fed on.

Ryan would bet Carys knew what they ate.

'What are you going to have, Carys? Do you need any help with reading the menu?' Addy asked.

She was sitting next to his daughter and opposite him.

'What's this?' Carys pointed to the menu.

'Vegetable lasagne.'

'Oh, I love lasagne! Can I have that?'

'Sure,' said Ryan. 'What do you fancy, Addy?'

'I don't know. Having seen all those animals, I'm kind of glad that this restaurant doesn't serve any animal products at all. I'd feel weird eating them after that.'

'I agree. All of this sounds lovely, but I'm not sure what to pick.'

'I think I might start with the gazpacho...'

'I'll join you. What about a main course?'

'Erm... I think maybe the vegetable chana with pilau rice?'

'Hmm... I think I'll go for the Brazilian black bean chilli.'

They gave their choices to the waitress, who took their menus from them and then provided Carys with a tablet to play animal games on whilst she waited.

'This is so nice... I can't remember the last time I sat in a restaurant,' Addalyn said.

'Really?'

'Really. I think the last time was before I lost Dad and Ricky.'

'What was the occasion?'

Addy frowned.

'Why were you in a restaurant?'

'Oh! Hen night for a group of friends.'

'You don't have a significant other who takes you out for a meal? Just the two of you?'

'There was Nathan... But that was so long ago I can't even remember.'

'Nathan?'

'My ex. Obviously. We did go out to restaurants in the early days, but then our lives became so consumed with other stuff I guess we forgot to remember we were actually a couple.'

He could understand that. When he and Angharad had first met, everything had been wonderful. A whirlwind of romance and nights out on the town. But then, after they'd been together for a while, living together, then married, work had become a priority for him—especially after he'd begun to feel that he was failing her as a husband. Angharad had never seemed happy. No matter what he'd tried. And then she'd got pregnant with Carys.

Yes, it had been unplanned, but she'd seemed to love being pregnant, and he'd thought, briefly, that everything would be all right between them again. But it hadn't worked out.

'Life can get like that, sometimes,' he said.

'Maybe. But I often blame myself.'

'Why?'

She glanced at Carys, but his daughter was absorbed in a game where she could chase butterflies with a net.

'Maybe I neglected him.'

'Did he tell you he felt neglected?'

'No. Not directly. But eventually his actions spoke louder than any words he might have used.'

Ryan frowned, unsure what she meant.

'He met someone else,' she said in a low voice, looking awkward.

Oh. He hadn't meant to make her feel bad. Because they'd been having a lovely time here today and the day wasn't over yet! The obvious hurt in her eyes pained him.

'I'm sorry. I didn't mean to pry.'

She shrugged. 'It's fine.'

'No, it's not. You must have been hurt.'

Were those tears he could see forming in her eyes? He had tissues in his pocket. He always carried them. For Carys. But now he passed one to her and felt his heart soften at the way she thankfully took it and dabbed at her eyes.

'A little.'

He wanted to reach for her hand. To comfort her. But he felt that he couldn't with Carys right there next to them. He didn't want to confuse his daughter with what was going on between them. He'd already told her that they were just friends who happened to work together, and that was all.

Instead, he tried to show it on his face. With

his concern for her. His apology. 'I know what it's like to lose someone you once loved. To have them walk away and choose somebody or something else other than you.'

Addy gazed back at him. And then at Carys. She nodded.

# CHAPTER FIVE

SHE DIDN'T WANT to talk about Nathan. She'd closed that episode in her life long ago. One huge painful episode, locked away in a box. She'd once believed it would be the only painful episode in her life, and then she'd lost Dad and Ricky, further breaking her heart…

Now she had lots of pain locked away in the dark recesses of her soul, and she never intended to examine it again. She was trying to reclaim her enjoyment of life. Find meaning in her work. Saving lives. Keeping people safe. Giving other people a future. It gave her some meaning. A reason for being here.

She intended to find her life's purpose in serving others, because that was all she could foresee. Stealing moments for herself that she would savour in private and hope that it would be enough.

But today? So far she was loving her time with Ryan and Carys. Carys was the sweetest little girl. Enthusiastic, warm, clever. And best of all Carys had kept on holding her hand, wherever they'd been that morning. They'd shared some lovely moments feeding the animals, and washing the elephants had been so funny. Especially when that one elephant had trumpeted water everywhere. They'd got a little wet, but Addy hadn't minded at all. Her dress had dried quickly in the lovely sunshine and so had Carys's.

They'd all been laughing, especially Ryan, and just for a moment…for one brief second…she had allowed herself to imagine they were her family. That Ryan was her boyfriend or her husband, just the way Sally and the other keeper had clearly thought. That Carys was her daughter and that this was what love and family would look like. What it would *feel* like.

When had she last truly laughed like that? When had she last truly *belonged*?

And then that brief moment of joy had been followed by such a long, extended moment of hollow grief, in which she'd known that she was just borrowing someone else's family. That she was pretending and that none of this belonged to her. What was she doing? Believing in it? If she believed in it and enjoyed it too much, it would just make going home alone even harder than it normally was.

The tigers had perked her up somewhat. Getting so close to such magnificent animals. To Sierra, who was carrying the hope of two new precious lives.

Was she jealous of a tiger?

Having a baby had once been her entire reason

for being. Having Nathan's baby was all she'd ever wanted at one time in her life…

'I only lost a boyfriend. It must have been harder for you. Losing not only your partner, but the mother of your child,' she replied.

'It was a shock, yes, but that doesn't mean my pain was greater than yours. Everyone deals with pain, grief and loss in different ways. What could bring one person to their knees might not even upset another.'

'I guess…' She looked at Carys, still absorbed in her game. 'What was she like as a baby?'

'I have pictures.' Ryan got out his phone and scrolled back through a photo album before passing the phone to her. 'Just keep swiping left.'

Her fingers brushed his as he passed the phone, and she felt a frisson of something race up her arm and smack her squarely in the gut. Trying vainly to ignore it, she began to scroll through and saw the first picture was of Carys as a baby, being held by her mother, Angharad, in the hospital. Angharad looked tired, but happy. There was a BP cuff around her upper arm, a cannula in the back of her left hand.

Angharad was pretty. The kind of woman who didn't need make-up. She had long, luxurious hair. Honey-blonde. Elegant hands and long thin fingers and she wore a doozy of an engagement ring. It must have cost a fortune. Carys was scrunched up, tiny, with chubby fists and a shock of dark, fluffy hair. She looked perfect. They both did.

'She's beautiful.'

'She was eight pounds two ounces of perfection,' Ryan said with a smile at his daughter.

Addy loved the way he looked at Carys then. Full of love and adoration.

'Was she a good baby?'

She scrolled through many more pictures. One of Ryan holding Carys. One of the three of them together, as if a midwife had taken the photo for them, or maybe a visiting friend or family member. Carys swaddled in her cot at home. Carys having a bath. Carys crying as water was poured over her head to wash her fluffy hair. One of her lying on a changing mat. And then a swathe of professional baby shots, all artfully done in black and white as Carys slept. Swaddled within a circle of daisies. In a basket. On a pretend cloud...

And then there was a shot that almost stopped her swiping. Made her want to peruse the image a little more closely. Another black and white arty shot. Ryan and Carys. But Ryan had no top on. He was doing skin to skin, cradling his daughter, and all she could see apart from a perfect baby was a perfect guy. Muscled and fit, with flat abs and a small military tattoo on his upper arm.

She wanted to study him. Absorb him. But she also didn't want to be caught staring at him, so she swiped on and began to notice that Angharad was in hardly any of the photos now, and when she was she looked distant, as if she weren't truly present in the moment.

Did Angharad not know what a gift she'd truly been given with this perfect baby and wonderful man? How had she walked away from all of that?

'She was very good. The kind of well-behaved baby that makes you think you've cracked parenting and could easily have another.'

'You wanted another?'

'Of course I did! I always wanted lots of kids.'

Another reason she could not have him. Because she could never give him what he wanted.

'Wanted? Past tense?'

He shrugged. 'I *do* want more kids. Being a dad is the greatest thing in the whole world. But finding the right person who wants that too is hard.'

'I guess…'

'Plus, it's going to take a lot of time, you know? Meeting someone that's right for you. Meeting someone that's not only right for me, but someone who's also right for Carys. I mean, I don't think I've ever asked her if she would want to have a baby brother or sister one day.'

'I want a sister,' Carys said, having clearly been listening.

Addy smiled and glanced up at Ryan. 'See? You have your answer.'

He grinned. 'Maybe one day, honey.'

'If I get a sister, that means I also get a mummy, right?'

'That's true—though technically she'd be your step-mum,' Ryan answered.

'Ooh. Would I help choose her?'

'Er…actually, yes, I think you will help me. When that day comes.' Ryan managed to look a little uncomfortable.

'I'll help you too,' said Addy, leaning in towards Carys. 'It's going to take a strong woman to take on a fireman.'

'Why?'

'Because a fireman has a dangerous job and that can put a lot of strain on a relationship. It's got to be someone who will go into it knowing she could get a phone call at any time to tell her that her husband has been in an accident and is hurt.'

She didn't want to say *or worse*.

'Does that mean that I'm strong?' Carys asked.

Addalyn nodded. 'It does. You're very strong.'

'Cool. Then maybe I could teach my new mummy how to be like me.' Carys pressed 'play' on her game again and became absorbed, as Addy looked up at Ryan and smiled.

'You see? It's easy.'

'Is it?'

Ryan raised an eyebrow as the waitress arrived at their table with their starters—gazpacho for both Ryan and Addy and a small green salad with croutons for Carys.

The food was delicious, and after such a busy morning they'd worked up quite an appetite. The gazpacho was sweet and refreshing, a little peppery, and gone much too soon. But then their main courses arrived and Addalyn tucked into her chili hungrily.

'I wonder what we'll be doing this afternoon?' said Carys.

'I think we're free to roam around the zoo on our own now,' said Addy. 'Anything you want to see in particular?'

'I don't mind. How about you, Daddy?'

Ryan shrugged. 'I'm happy to just see where the path takes us. So, Addy, what do you normally do on your time off from work?'

The question surprised her, and she wasn't sure how to answer.

*This and that... I stay out of the house as much as I can... I waste time sitting in cafés or book-shops...*

'I guess it depends. Erm... I like going and looking around bookshops. I...er...do a little dressmaking on occasion.'

'Really?'

'Yes. I made what I'm wearing now.'

'You made that?'

She blushed as his gaze swept over her body. Clearly he was looking at her handiwork, the dress, but it felt as if he was looking at her body.

'Is it difficult?'

Her mouth was dry. 'It can be, sometimes. But I've been doing it for so long now I kind of know what to do.'

'Well, I think that's pretty amazing. I tried to make an outfit for Carys's Christmas show once. She was an angel, so all I had to do was sew a sheet and tie her waist with some tinsel, but I couldn't even do that.' He laughed.

'Maybe Addy could help you make my Halloween costume!' Carys piped up eagerly.

'What's this?'

Ryan groaned. 'Oh, she's been on at me to make her the costume of one of her favourite book characters. No one seems to sell it, as it's a little obscure, but I've told her I'll do my best.'

'What's the character?'

Addy was interested. It might be fun to make something for Carys, and it would give her something to do when she had to be at home. Plus, as a bonus, she would have to keep seeing Carys for fittings, and that meant also seeing Ryan. Whom she liked. A lot. Despite his being a fireman and totally on her list of forbidden things.

'She's a princess,' said Carys.

Addy frowned. 'That doesn't sound too hard.'

'And…?' urged Ryan, raising his eyebrows at his daughter.

'And the captain of a space fleet. Her name's Hattie.'

'A princess space captain? Hmm... Does this book of yours have pictures?'

Carys nodded.

'Then you'll have to show me, so I can get some sort of idea.'

'Okay!' Carys seemed thrilled.

'You don't have to. It's going to be a lot of work,' said Ryan, obviously trying to give her a way out.

'It's no problem. I'd be happy to help out. I've got, like, six weeks? That should be plenty of time to work around shifts and school.'

'Carys? Say thank you to Addy.'

'Thank you, Addy!' Carys threw her arms around Addy and gave her a big squeeze.

Addy laughed and hugged her back. 'You're very welcome.'

Seriously... Was there anything better than this?

Their second to last stop was the gorilla enclosure. Addy wanted to see the big silverback and there he was, in all his magnificent, muscled glory. Sitting in the middle of the enclosure, with his back against a tree, he surveyed his group of females and their babies. There were one or two juveniles playing around, swinging from ropes and tyres and chasing each other, but most of them were basically just enjoying the September sunshine.

The crowds were thick around this enclosure, watching from up high, looking down at the gorillas below. Plenty of people were taking pictures of the big silverback, especially when he opened his mouth to yawn and revealed an impressive set of sharp, dangerous-looking fangs. He was a proud beast, and Addy was impressed by his presence. The way he just seemed to know he was the most important of all and that he owned all that he surveyed. It was his territory, through and through, and no intruders were going to come after his near and dear ones.

Which made it so incredibly shocking when someone in the crowd suddenly screamed, off to the left. Addy looked to see what was going on and realised someone had fallen.

A child had fallen into the enclosure.

Instantly she whipped her head back to check on the silverback. He was already up and slowly making his way across the grass as his females scattered with their babies and ran to the other side of the enclosure, away from the child.

The child's mother was screaming, yelling, trying to distract the big silverback, and so was everyone else.

Addy looked at Ryan. Hoping her gaze told him everything.

*We need to move. We need to help.*

'Carys? Come with us.'

They began to run away from the enclosure, pushing through the crowds that had begun to gather to see what all the commotion was about.

'He's going to kill him!' Addy heard someone

scream, and she hoped that it wasn't true. That they wouldn't be too late.

They burst into the welcome centre and Addy grabbed a woman from behind the desk. 'Please look after her!' She knelt in front of Carys. 'Your daddy and I have some work to do, okay? We'll be back. I promise. Just stay with this lady.'

Carys nodded, looking frightened.

Addy saw a rush of employees heading to a door marked *Staff Only* and followed them, with Ryan close behind. Once through, they found a room with a bank of screens overlooking the situation. The silverback was just sitting there, only once lifting his hand to prod at the small child that lay motionless beside him on the grass.

Addy and Ryan identified themselves to the staff.

'We have the Dangerous Animal Response Team formulating a plan now,' they were told.

'And how long will that take?' asked Addy. 'You need to disperse the crowd around the enclosure, because all the screaming and noise could cause that silverback to react badly.'

'Thank you, but we know what we're doing.'

'Do you? Because I don't see anyone trying to control the situation. You need to disperse the crowd and then either tranquilise the silverback or see if he can be called back to his indoor enclosure. Will he do that?'

One of the men looked at her. 'Maybe. If we got Garrett to do it.'

'Where's Garrett?' asked Ryan.

'I'm Garrett.' A young man with a straggly beard stepped forward. 'Kitaana seems to like me.'

'We need to get all the gorillas out of there so we can attend to that child. Have you called for an ambulance?'

'Yes, of course we have.'

'Then you need to get those gorillas out of there. Get the females inside with the babies—that might bring Kitaana in, yes?'

'It might be safer to dart him,' said another zoo employee. 'It's policy if the public become endangered.'

'Get the dart ready, but let's try the other way first. There's no reason Kitaana should suffer because a member of the public made an error.'

They moved quickly, and Addy watched the staff as they began opening up the doors that would allow the gorillas to return to their inside enclosures. The females ran in quickly, holding their babies and looking panicked. Addy could see that they were frightened by this event, too, not understanding what had happened. They were used to being watched by the public. To having humans nearby every single day. But they'd never come up close to one who wasn't a keeper. They'd never come into contact with people whose faces and scents they didn't know.

And now one was with them, lying motionless on their grass.

'Kitaana! Hey, boy!'

Addy and Ryan stood behind the tempered glass, watching as Garrett tried to get the silverback away from the boy.

The boy still lay face-down on the grass, with Kitaana beside him. The silverback had made no aggressive moves at all.

Kitaana looked to Garrett, then back at the boy.

'Bedtime, Kitaana. Come on, now!'

The silverback looked around his enclosure. He saw that the rest of his group had gone inside and slowly stood up, leaning over the boy. He made a low rumbling noise, and then slowly began to walk towards the enclosure doors.

Addy felt a surge of relief that this seemed to be working, and that no further harm would be done to the boy by the gorilla, but that still didn't mean it was over. The boy had suffered a significant fall and might have all manner of injuries. He did look as if he was breathing, but that was all they knew about his condition.

'That's it, Kitaana. Good boy. That's it…'

The silverback entered his enclosure and Garrett slid the door shut. As soon as it was closed Addy grabbed the basic first aid kit that was kept next to it and, with Ryan, ran out into the gorilla enclosure.

It felt weird, knowing that moments ago a huge,

powerful animal had been present but that they were now safe. Rule one in any emergency was that before you ran into an accident site yourself, you checked that it was safe to do so.

'Get the rest of these people away—it's not a spectator sport!' Ryan ordered the staff as he followed her into the enclosure.

Addy settled herself beside the boy, glancing up briefly and meeting the gaze of the boy's mother before giving the boy a visual assessment. He had some cuts and grazes, and his left leg looked longer than the right, which suggested either a fracture or a dislocation. His right arm was bent in a way it shouldn't be, and she had no idea if he had any broken ribs puncturing organs inside. He could be bleeding internally. Every second was precious.

'What's his name?' she called out to the mother, up above.

'Leo!'

'Okay. Leo? Can you hear me? You're okay. We've got you. But if you can hear me, I need you to open your eyes. Can you do that for me?'

Leo's eyelids flickered, but didn't fully open.

So he was near consciousness. Maybe...

She ran her hands over him, checking his skull for any visible signs of deformity, feeling for the tell-tale signs of a possible skull fracture. Leo was unconscious, but he wasn't vomiting, and there was no bleeding from his nose or ears. There was no bruising behind his ears or beneath his eyes, so maybe he was just concussed? No one would know for sure unless he had a CT scan of his head, which wouldn't happen until he was in hospital.

Addy checked his neck. Ideally, she needed a cervical collar, but there wasn't one in the first aid kit and they were still waiting for the paramedics to arrive. His airway was clear, and without equipment she was reluctant to move him.

Leo groaned and began to cry. A good sign. In fact, it was a relief. Leo looked to be about five, maybe six years old. Skinny, though, so not much padding. When he'd fallen, he would have fallen hard.

'What should we do?' Ryan asked.

'Nothing until the paramedics get here with a collar and board. They'll get him on oxygen and insert an IV. Let's just keep him talking and awake, and be ready to roll him if he stops breathing.'

'You think he will?'

She shook her head. 'Children are strong. Resilient. And they can compensate for their injuries a lot longer than adults can. Leo? Sweetheart? My name's Addalyn and I'm a paramedic. This is Ryan and he's a fireman. You've had a fall, and I know you must be hurting, but try to stay still for me, all right? That's very important.'

Leo nodded his head.

'Don't move, sweetie. Don't nod your head. Just say yes or no, okay?'

'Okay…' Leo sounded incredibly frightened.

'Don't worry. We're going to look after you and you're safe. There are no animals here. All the gorillas are inside. It's just us and we're waiting for the ambulance to arrive.'

As if on cue, the sound of sirens could be heard as Addy finished speaking.

She looked at Ryan with relief. It was at times such as these that she realised just how much she depended on the equipment she usually had with her. She had nothing right now except for the few bandages and antiseptic wipes that existed in the first aid kit. It was designed for basic cuts and scrapes, not catastrophic falls. But having Ryan by her side was calming.

'They're nearly here. Tell me, Leo, what's your favourite animal?'

'G-G-Gorillas.'

She smiled. 'Well, the gorillas that you were with looked after you when you fell. They didn't hurt you. They were just curious. Even the big fella. The silverback. He sat with you and watched over you until we got here, so I want you to keep them as your favourite animal, okay?'

'O-Okay.'

'Good lad.' She stroked the side of his face gently, trying to provide comfort, keeping him talking until the arrival of the paramedics.

Apparently, he didn't like football, so couldn't tell her his favourite team. He preferred playing tennis. His favourite colour was blue, and his favourite ice cream flavour was triple chocolate chip.

She recognised the paramedics when they came running into the enclosure. Mikey and Jones. Good guys. Addy explained what had happened, and the results of her primary survey. She watched as together they splinted Leo's arm and leg, then gave him some painkillers, IV fluids, an oxygen mask and a collar, before they carefully, with perfect choreography, manoeuvred Leo onto a backboard. He cried out as they moved him, so they upped the painkiller before they got him on the trolley and wheeled him to the ambulance.

His mother was running alongside, crying and apologising as she went.

'I was filming the gorilla! I didn't see Leo climbing over the barrier to get a better look! I didn't see! I'm so sorry!'

Addy said nothing. She could feel the mother's distress and understood her position. You couldn't watch a child twenty-four-seven, and who wouldn't want to capture the perfect picture of that magnificent silverback? But at the same time she was meant to be responsible for her child. Her maternal guilt would beat her up about this incident more than anyone else could. Something like this would make the evening news, or at least the local newspaper, and plenty of people would have judgments to make. This mother did not need Addy's judgment. She and Ryan had simply been there to help.

With the ambulance gone, they were thanked by the zoo staff for their assistance and offered tea and coffee, which they turned down. They wanted to get back to Carys, who had to be frightened by events.

When they went to find her they found her in the staff room, munching on a biscuit and playing with someone's phone.

'Daddy!' She ran to her father and Ryan gave her a big squeeze. 'Is that little boy okay?'

'He will be, honey. He's at the hospital now, getting all the help he needs.'

Carys smiled, then looked up at Addy. 'Did you put him back together again? That's what Daddy says you do.'

'He was still in one piece, thankfully. I didn't have to do much mending.'

She didn't need to tell Carys about all the possible injuries Leo might have. Why frighten her?

'So, can we go home now?'

Addy looked at Ryan and he nodded.

'I think we've all had enough adventure for today.'

Ryan got Carys fastened into her car seat, then checked and double-checked the seatbelt before he stood up and closed the car door. Addy was standing there, waiting to say goodbye.

'Well, it's certainly been a day to remember,' she said, with a glorious smile.

'It certainly has. Can we give you a lift home?'

'I can take the bus.'

'Let me give you a lift. I know Carys would like it.'

Addy looked uncertain, but then she smiled again. 'Well, if Carys would like it…okay, then.'

She began to open the rear door.

'You can sit up front with me.'

'It's okay. I'd like to sit with Carys. Make sure she's okay.'

'All right.'

He got into the driving seat and started the engine, glancing into the rear-view mirror to check that Addy was seat-belted up. He couldn't help but notice the way Carys leant into Addy, looping her arm through hers and resting her head against Addy's arm. And he also couldn't help but notice the way Addy smiled. Her face was full of contentment and joy as she laid her head against Carys's.

The two of them had clearly bonded, and he wondered if he had held Carys's happiness back by not letting any women into their lives. He'd thought he was doing a good thing, not having a string of women coming and going through their lives. He'd certainly not been ready. He'd been afraid of how it might make his daughter feel, but also of how it might make him feel.

When he'd stood in that church and sworn to spend his life with Angharad he'd meant it. And he'd fought for his marriage. Fought to keep Angharad with them. His daughter had needed her mother. He'd wanted his wife. When she'd walked away, leaving them behind, he'd never felt pain like it. But he'd had to push it aside to look after Carys. There'd been no time for him to collapse, to wallow in depression. He had a daughter. And she'd needed her daddy more than ever now that she didn't have a mother.

The idea of letting another woman into his life when he'd so clearly failed with Angharad had left him doubting himself. Left him worrying about just what he had to offer a partner. He wasn't simple. He came with baggage. A child whom another woman would have to take on if their relationship ever got serious.

He'd often thought, even though Carys was confident and outgoing, that maybe she'd be different with a mummy figure—but look at her!

'Everything okay?' Addy asked, having caught him staring at them.

'Just thinking about how happy you both look.'

Addy smiled. 'She makes it easy. You must be very proud that you have such a wonderful little girl. You're doing a good job.'

'You think so?' He felt a warmth in his chest. Her words made him feel good. 'I often have my doubts.'

'Don't.'

He gave her a nod and then began to pull out of the car parking space. 'So, the big question is… where do you live?'

'Union Road. You know it?'

He raised his eyebrows. 'I do. It's two streets over from us.'

'Is it? Which road are you?'

'Thatcher Lane.'

'I know it well.'

'I can't believe we live so close to you.'

'Did you move into that small house on the corner?' she asked. 'The one with the large hydrangea bush in the front garden?'

'That's the one!'

Addy laughed. 'Wow. Okay…'

'Does that mean I can come round to your house and play?' Carys asked.

'Carys! You don't invite yourself to people's houses. You wait to be invited,' Ryan interrupted.

Addy raised a hand in protest. 'That's okay. I'd love you to come round one day. I don't have any toys or anything, though.'

'That's okay. I can bring mine. What do you like to play?'

'I don't know.'

'Do you like jigsaw puzzles?'

'I love jigsaws! I haven't done one in such a long time, though. I might not be any good.'

'That's okay. I can help you. Daddy has just bought me a five-hundred-piece one with tigers on it. I think it's going to be hard, but it would be fun to do together.'

'Okay! You're on.'

Ryan smiled and pulled out into the traffic. 'Beware, though…five hundred pieces…might take some time.'

Addy nodded and laughed. 'Sounds perfect. How about next weekend? Saturday?'

Carys beamed.

'She won't forget,' he warned Addy, with a smile.

'Neither will I,' said Addy, hugging the little girl once more.

It had been such a long time since he'd felt so content. Since he'd felt he was with someone to whom he could trust his heart. He could, couldn't he? He was wary of rushing into anything. And he didn't want to get hurt again. But the way Addy was holding on to Carys and enjoying her company reminded him of what he'd thought it might have been like if everything had worked out with Angharad. He'd hoped for these moments. Wished for them. Imagined them. And now he could see it in a woman with whom he worked. A woman who was not Angharad.

Was he ready to face these feelings? This overload of emotions?

One last glance in the rear-view mirror showed him that Carys had her eyes closed. Was she falling asleep? Snuggled into Addy like that? Most times he didn't mind her falling asleep in the car. He'd simply carry her out at the other end and place her in her bed. But they'd be dropping Addalyn off first.

'Which number Union Road?' he asked quietly.

'Four.'

'Okay.'

She gave him such a smile then, and it did even more crazy things to his insides. Today had been incredible. Crazy and scary at times, but he'd face any gorilla, any day, rather than have to figure out how Addalyn was making him feel.

Because what if this was serious?

He felt as if he was on a precipice and about to fall.

Did she feel the same way? He wasn't sure she did, because she looked so secure in herself. So happy. So content. Maybe he was reading too much into this? Maybe this was just a fun day for her? She'd bonded more with Carys than she had with him, and apart from her beautiful smiles he'd not noticed her sending him any signals.

*I'm wrong. I have to be.*

# CHAPTER SIX

THE CAR RIDE came to an end much too soon, and before Addy knew it Ryan was pulling up outside of her house.

It seemed to stare at her knowingly. Taunting her.

*When you come back in you're going to be alone. All alone! Again!*

Her day with Ryan and Carys was at an end. Her unexpected day. Her gift from the win at the Castle and Crow. And what a wonderful day it had been. Apart from the little boy, Leo, falling into that enclosure, the day had been wonderful and dreamy. Just the sort of day she would have imagined for herself if she'd ever been so lucky as to have created a family of her own.

It was so easy to imagine Ryan as her partner. So easy to imagine Carys as her daughter.

But they couldn't be.

Ryan was a firefighter, and she simply would not attach herself to another man who put his life at risk every day. She'd worried enough about her dad and Ricky and rightfully so, losing them both in one fell swoop in that building collapse. She could not be with Ryan and go through that kind of worry again.

Besides, he'd told her today that ideally he wanted more children, and she couldn't give him that. It hadn't worked with Nathan, and Nathan had left her, finding himself a woman who could give him the children he'd so desperately wanted.

And Carys? She wasn't her daughter. And she couldn't deny that precious little girl the chance to have a brother or sister. But she could pretend, at least for a day, that she was her mother.

'Here we are,' Ryan said, coming to a halt outside her property and pulling on the handbrake.

Addy glanced at the house one more time. She could envisage its empty rooms. Its quietness. The living space with its empty chairs. Dad's empty spot. Ricky's. Their faces smiling down at her from the photos she had framed and lined up on the mantelpiece, to keep them with her as much as she could. The neat, tidy kitchen, without the crumbs that her dad would leave behind every time he made himself a cheese sandwich. Without the knife perched over the edge of the sink in case he decided to make himself another. The empty bedrooms. The wardrobes still filled with their clothes. Clothes that, on occasion, she would still press her face into, to inhale their scent that was fading now.

Time was slowly erasing all evidence of them

and only her memories remained. Memories that could quite often be haunting.

'Thank you for giving me a lift.'

'You said your car's having a service?'

'Yes. It should be ready on Monday.'

'Need a lift to pick it up?'

'You're very kind, but I can walk it.'

Addy looked down at Carys, still slumped against her, fast asleep. She didn't want to wake her. Didn't want to move her at all. If she could stay here for the rest of her life in this bubble, pretending, then she would. Very happily.

'She looks so content. I don't want to disturb her,' she said quietly, stroking Carys's hair.

'She'll be okay.'

Addy nodded, trying to draw out the moment, but knowing she shouldn't. So, she leant down and kissed the top of Carys's head.

'Hey, sleepyhead. I've got to go.'

Carys mumbled and stirred, but didn't wake up as Addy moved away and undid her seatbelt. Every movement was torture, because she knew every movement was a return to her loneliness. Her solitude. It was probably a good thing that Carys didn't wake up, because it would have made it so hard to say goodbye. Even though they did have a jigsaw date next weekend.

Addy opened the car door and got out, closing it behind her gently, but firmly. Still the little girl didn't stir.

Ryan got out too. 'Nice house!'

She turned to look at it, forcing a smile. 'It's all right. I'll give you a tour when Carys brings over her jigsaw.'

'You know you don't have to honour that promise, right? A five-hundred-piece jigsaw? That's not something that gets completed in one visit.'

'I don't mind. She can come over as often as she wants. I like her. I like her a lot. And it's not a hardship to spend time in her company.'

'What about spending time in mine?' he asked.

Addy looked at him, her heart pounding in her ears. How to answer? Should she tell him the truth? That she liked him enormously? That she found him attractive? That she longed for more? For human contact? To be loved? But that he terrified her all at the same time?

'You're okay. Not as great as Carys, but…' She laughed.

Ryan laughed too. 'Of course not. Who is?'

'Honestly, it's fine. Besides, I made her a promise and I don't break my promises to children.'

Ryan nodded appreciatively. 'You're amazing. You know that, right?'

Addy laughed nervously. 'Thanks. Erm…so are you.'

For a moment they just continued to stare at one another. The air in the gap between them was taut as a bow, and neither of them seemed to know what to say or do next.

Would he step forward and drop a kiss on her cheek?

Would he step away and simply say goodbye, giving her a cheery wave?

Which would she prefer? The heat and excitement and danger of the kiss? Or the disappointment of him simply walking away from her? If he kissed her, what would it mean? A simple friendly thank-you? Or something more?

If he walked away that would mean he didn't see her as anything other than a colleague or a friend. And somehow, in that moment anyway, she really didn't want to be just a colleague or a friend, no matter what job he had. She wanted the excitement and danger of a kiss on the cheek. She wanted the wonder. She wanted the thrill.

She wanted to be seen and acknowledged.

'Well, I guess I'd better go…'

'Yes.'

'Thank you for today. It was an adventure.'

She nodded. 'It was.'

'You're back at work on Monday?'

'Yes.'

'Me too.'

'Great. Maybe I'll see you?'

'Yes. If not, what time would you want me to bring Carys around next Saturday?'

'Around eleven? I could do lunch, and then we can jigsaw in the afternoon?'

'Sounds great.'

'Great.'

Another moment of tension, and then suddenly he stepped forward, placed his hands on her upper arms and leaned in to drop a kiss to her cheek.

She sucked in a breath and closed her eyes, trying to absorb every exciting moment as his lips brushed against the side of her face. He was close enough for her to hold. To touch. To kiss back if only she turned and faced him.

But she wasn't brave enough.

Because she was much too scared to let this become something else.

To let Ryan become something else.

And then he was stepping away, walking back to the driver's side of the car, and Addy looked down and saw Carys looking at them both.

She was smiling.

# CHAPTER SEVEN

'Is ADDY YOUR girlfriend now?' Carys asked as he got into the car.

Carys had tricked them both. Making them both think that she was asleep. Or had she just been fortunate and woken to see her father kiss a woman?

He was so bamboozled by the question that he just laughed awkwardly and shook his head. 'No, of course not! We're just friends. That's what you do when you say goodbye to friends. You give them a quick hug or a kiss goodbye.'

'I don't say goodbye to my friends like that.'

'No? Well, that's because you're little. You will when you're older.'

'Why?'

'I don't know. You just do.'

He started the engine and glanced out of his window at Addalyn. She wasn't going in, but was standing there, waiting for him to drive away. To wave goodbye.

Kissing her goodbye had felt good. He'd dithered about doing it. About how to leave her. Not sure what they were. But at the core of his feelings was the fact that after today they were definitely good friends, and so he'd chosen to do what he always did with his female friends—politely kissed her cheek, thank her for her time and walk away.

Only it hadn't worked that way with Addy. It hadn't felt as casual as that. He'd sensed in her a yearning for a connection. As if she was a solitary castaway on an island who needed the comfort of another person, loaded with need. Her eyes had said it all, almost like she didn't want him to go.

The softness of her skin, her alluring scent and the sensual caress of her long dark hair as he'd pressed his lips to her cheek had sent his senses into overdrive. His mind had gone blank. He'd almost forgotten what he was doing...had allowed himself to pause as he breathed her in... And just before he'd pulled back slightly, tempted by the idea of a full-on kiss—one his daughter wouldn't witness because she was asleep, so maybe it would be okay—his logic and higher reasoning had jumped in to protect him and he'd stepped away completely.

*I'm not ready. I might not be good enough for her. What if she doesn't feel that way?*

And now he was back in the car with a curious daughter and he had to drive away.

*Why isn't she going inside her house?*

Addy continued to stand by her front gate, watching them drive away, one hand raised in a wave. From this distance she looked like a ghost, with her pale face and dark hair. He felt drawn to keep looking at her, to keep wondering. And then he knew he couldn't do it any more, so he took a turning he didn't need, just so he didn't have to keep looking back. To keep regretting. To keep being annoyed at himself for being so cowardly.

When she was out of sight he still didn't relax, feeling he would have handled himself better if given a second chance.

'Daddy?'

'Yes, baby?'

'Are you okay?'

He pulled over and stopped the car to turn and look at her. She'd never asked him that question before.

'I'm fine.'

'You look sad.'

He tried to laugh it off. 'I'm not sad.'

'Are you lonely? Madison, at school, she only has a mummy and no daddy, and she says that her mummy gets sad sometimes because she's on her own.'

'I'm not on my own. I have you. You're my everything. I don't need anybody else.'

Carys smiled. 'But don't you sometimes wish? Because sometimes I wish for a mummy.'

Her words touched his heart. 'I know you do. And sure... We all wish sometimes.'

'I like Addy.'

'I do, too.'

\* \* \*

The house felt so empty when she went inside. Quiet. Much too quiet. Devoid of life and warmth and joy. She dropped her bag by the bottom of the staircase and with a heavy sigh made her way out to the back garden, unlocking the French doors and swinging them wide, so that she could stay outside for just a moment longer and breathe freely. She felt stifled inside. The warmth of the day had made the house seem fusty on her return.

Addy gazed at the trees, their branches softly moving in the gentle breeze. At the flowers turned up to the fading sun. At next door's cat, George, perched on the fence.

Life was beautiful. It could be beautiful. But why did she only allow herself to enjoy it when she was with others? Why did she insist on beating herself up about coming back to this place? Would it be best if she moved?

*No. Their memories are here. If I moved away, I'd feel like I was losing them all over again.*

Addy knew she needed to find a way to deal with her solitude. To find a way to enjoy being in this house again. Perhaps she needed to decorate it? Make it more her own now that it was no longer her father's?

She turned to look back into the kitchen. It hadn't been updated or remodelled for at least a decade. Maybe if she breathed new life into it, she might feel better? If she worked on the house as much as she was trying to work on herself maybe that would make her feel better about being here?

She stepped back inside and walked through the kitchen to the lounge. She looked at the wallpaper on the feature wall. It was a soft mushroom colour, with a tree effect on it. It looked a little sad, but maybe she could change that? She went over and looked at it. Down at the bottom, a piece was curling free. She took hold of it in her fingers and gave it a big rip, tearing a huge strip away.

And she felt a real buzz of excitement, and a rush…as if more and more of the past was being ripped away.


A fire had broken out in a small marina. Originally a cooking fire, on one barge, the flames had spread to three other boats and now the thick black smoke billowed up into the sky.

Addy saw it as she raced towards the scene in her rapid response vehicle. There were two known casualties, suffering burns and smoke inhalation, but she had no idea if there were others.

On the scene, she quickly appraised the casualties and handed them over to the paramedics when they arrived. They'd get them to the local burns unit quickly. Then she began a conversation with the fire chief, Paolo. Blue Watch were on duty, which meant that maybe Ryan was here, too.

'What have we got?' she asked.

'Pan burning on the hob on this boat.' He pointed

at the burnt-out shell. 'Left by the first female casualty, who is suspected to have dementia. The
second female casualty had left her for a moment,
to deal with a mechanical issue down below. The
fire then spread to boat two, where we think it
rapidly burnt its way up the sail and mast, which
collapsed onto boats three and four, causing con-
siderable damage.'

'Any other casualties?'

'My crew are sweeping the boats now.'

'Any hazardous materials?'

'Gas canisters. Boat fuel. The usual. All have
been secured.'

'Have we established a perimeter?'

'Got the boys in blue on it.'

'Good. Keep me apprised.'

'Will do.'

She wanted to ask him if Ryan was one of the
firemen she could see fighting back the flames.
The blaze was furiously eating up the old wooden
barges. This marina in particular, she knew, was
an historic one, where tourists came to view the
older boats that sometimes took people out on
tours around the local canals. She'd been on one
of them herself, with Dad and Ricky, and enjoyed
it so much, she'd taken Nathan. But he'd hated
what he called 'the faff' of the locks and the slow
progress of everything. He'd hated that it took almost a day's sailing to get somewhere that would
take fifteen minutes in a car.

She watched the firefighters as they slowly covered the flames with water and foam, making their way forward slowly but surely. A sudden bang had her flinching and cowering in shock, her arm raised to cover her face, her heart in her mouth. When she turned around, she saw that something they'd overlooked must have exploded in the heat. The firefighters all looked to be safe, though, and were continuing their push forward.

Her heart thudded painfully in her chest. It simply reminded her of the call with her dad and Ricky. Watching helplessly, unable to do anything. Worrying about the two men whom she loved so deeply and hoping that they would be okay.

What if the firefighters had been closer to that explosion? What if they'd been blown into the water? What if, God forbid, they'd been hurt? What if one of them had been Ryan?

She could easily ask Paolo who he had fighting the blaze. Could easily check. But she refused to do so. Because asking would mean something, wouldn't it? If she asked him it would reveal, not only to herself but to everyone else, that she cared about Ryan in particular. And she could not admit that to herself, never mind anyone else.

So she stood there and waited, biting her lip and keeping her torturous thoughts to herself.

With the blaze finally contained, Ryan pulled off his helmet and ran his hands through his sweaty hair as he made his way across the marina towards Paolo and, behind him, Addalyn.

'It's under control now, boss.'

'No further casualties?'

'Thankfully, no. Looks like all the boats were empty, as they usually are at this time of day.'

'Good. Finish off and then let's clear the area.'

'Will do.'

He peered past Paolo as his boss stalked down the grassy verge towards the carnage, and smiled at Addalyn.

'Hey.'

'Hey.'

She smiled back at him. A shy kind of smile. A sweet smile. One that seemed to say she was mightily relieved to see he was okay.

'How have you been?' he asked.

She paused for a moment. 'Good. You?'

'Yeah. A bit hot, but I'm okay.'

He pulled off a glove and examined his wrist. He'd felt that blast when it had gone off. He'd been incredibly close. But adrenaline had kept him going. Until now. Now he could feel hurt and pain, and he wondered if he'd been caught by something.

Instantly she was by his side. 'Let me look at that.'

She took his arm in her gentle, delicate hands, turning his wrist this way, then that. 'Can you feel me touch you here? And here?'

'Yes. It's sore, though. It's not a burn, is it?'

'No, it looks like something hit you when that blast went off. Did you feel anything?'

'Not in the moment.'

'You should get it properly looked at. You have good range of movement, but there are so many little bones in the wrist... You might have fractured one.'

'I'll get it checked.'

'I can splint it for you in the meantime.'

'No, that's okay.'

He had to pull his arm free. It was distracting him. Her touch. The way she held him.

It had been a long time since someone had taken care of him. When he'd married Angharad she hadn't taken any interest in his injuries. If it wasn't gushing blood, or broken, then she didn't get alarmed or worried. And she hadn't thought he should. He wasn't a dainty snowflake. He was a strong guy who worked out. Who looked after himself. He had to, working for the fire service.

And all the scrapes he'd got into in the army meant he didn't worry about the little things either. Army medics in particular didn't mollycoddle you. They patched you up and sent you back out if it wasn't anything deadly serious.

But to see the concern in Addy's gaze now, the intensity of her examination and the soft way she touched him, as if she really cared about him, was disturbing.

'You need to get it checked, Ryan.'

'I will.'

'When?'

'Later.'

'You can't work with a broken wrist. You could jeopardise a rescue if it decided to give out on you during a shout.'

She was right. And he hated it that she was right.

'I'll report it to Paolo as a possible injury,' she insisted, but she was smiling, trying to show him that she was only doing this for him so that he didn't get into trouble, and not just because she wanted to be a thorn in his side.

He laughed. 'Okay, okay... Thank you for checking it out.'

'You're welcome. Are you still coming on Saturday with Carys? I thought I could get the measurements for her Halloween costume whilst she's there.'

'Sure. But only if you're still happy to do that?'

'Of course! Why wouldn't I be?'

He had no way to answer. Because he was very happy to go and spend time with her. He knew Carys would be happy, too. But it felt like something scary.

*I mean, what am I doing? What am I pursuing here? A friendship? Something more?*

He'd always known that someday there might be someone else. In fact, he'd hoped for it, not wanting the rest of his days to be spent in solitude once Carys moved out and started a family of her own.

But this soon?

His head was a mess. His logic was confused. The only thing that was perfectly clear was how attracted he felt to Addalyn Snow.

It took Addy four days to complete her renovation of the living room.

The old wallpaper had come off easily with a steamer. She'd sanded the walls and filled in the cracks, then bought new wallpaper in a soft duck-egg-blue and applied it to the walls after watching a few how-to videos online. It turned out she had quite a knack for wallpapering.

Next, she'd repainted, covering her doors and skirting boards in a fresh coat of glossy white paint and her ceiling in a matt white. Yesterday a new pair of curtains had arrived in the post, and she'd taken down her father's old brown ones and put up her own to match the wallpaper. She'd re-arranged a few photo frames, added candlesticks, put a new rug over the wooden floors and added some potted ferns she'd bought from the local garden centre and now the living space felt fully transformed.

She was happy with it, and proud to show it off when Carys and Ryan arrived.

'This is what you've been working on?' Ryan asked as he came in and admired her work.

'Yes. Just this room so far. Next, I plan to work on the bedrooms.'

'I can't believe you did all this in one week.'

'It's amazing what you can do when you put your mind to it,' she replied, not wishing to add it was also amazing what could be achieved when you had nothing else in your life and no one to help you procrastinate.

'Well, it looks fabulous.'

'Thank you.'

It felt strange to be proud of the house. For a long time she'd only felt haunted by it. Burdened. Now she was looking at it in a different light, and she had to admit she was already beginning to feel a little better about being here, with all her plans to modernise and make the house work *for* her instead of against her.

'So, what can I get the two of you to drink?'

'Whatever you're having is fine,' Ryan said.

'Could I have juice?' asked Carys.

'Sure. What kind? I have apple or orange and mango.'

'Orange and mango, please.'

'No problem. I'll just get that for you. Why don't you get the jigsaw set up on that table over there and I'll be right back in.'

Addy headed into the kitchen and Ryan followed.

'She's been driving me crazy all week, going on about today. She couldn't wait to come here and be with you again,' Ryan said, leaning against a counter, smiling.

And him? Had he been waiting to be with her again?

His casual presence here with her felt strangely exciting. She grabbed two mugs from the cupboard and began to make tea, before she grabbed a glass and filled it with juice from the fridge.

'I've been looking forward to it, too,' she said.

'There's not many people who'd look forward to spending time with an excitable five-year-old.'

'Well, then, there must be something wrong with the rest of them. Besides, Carys is great, so it's not like it's any hardship on my part. And kids in general are fun! They remind you of what life was like before you had any grown-up responsibilities.'

'Life certainly is easier when you're a kid.'

'Exactly! The world hasn't hurt you yet, or tainted your vision of life.'

Ryan nodded. 'It does do that... I'm not exactly sure if I remember being a kid all that much.'

'You don't? I do. My dad and Ricky were my whole world growing up. My brother and I used to play in this area of green belt land, making dens and bows and arrows, or paddling in the brook trying to catch sticklebacks, or making rope swings on the trees. When I think back all I remember is an endless summer...' She paused. 'With maybe one heavy snowfall.'

'Snowball fights? Making snowmen?' He smiled.

She nodded, her memories reminding her of happier times. Times when she'd felt surrounded by love. Never alone. Even without a mother she had never felt that something was missing, because her dad and Ricky had made sure that she didn't. They'd involved her with everything. Made huge deals of her birthday and Christmas.

In fact, the only time she'd wished she could have a mother had been when her periods had begun and she'd been scared. But, again, her dad had come to the rescue, sitting her down, providing her with the products she needed, explaining everything. Not once had she felt embarrassed about it. Plus, she'd had her friends at school...

But she'd ached for her mother at that point. Realising that all those other important milestones she might have as a woman—puberty, marriage, pregnancy, giving birth—would pass by without her mother at her side.

When she'd struggled with her fertility with Nathan, undergoing all that IVF, she'd wondered what it might have been like to have faced it with her mother to talk to.

That was why she identified so closely with Carys. Wanted to spend time with her. Because she knew, deep in her heart, that even if Carys didn't say anything to her father, maybe she missed her mother anyway. Maybe not too much yet, but as she approached puberty she would. No doubt about it. She'd grown up without a mother by her side and she knew how it felt. And Carys had no brother to carry her through it. Just her dad. Another fireman. And who knew if that spelt doom for her as it had for Addy?

'We made the best snowman, Ricky and me. We went full out. Borrowed one of Dad's hats, one of our grandad's old pipes. Stick arms. Carrot nose. Scarf!'

Ryan laughed.

'Has Carys ever made a snowman?'

'I don't think it's snowed enough yet. But one day we will. Maybe I'll take her skiing one year, or to Lapland at Christmas. Who knows?'

'You should do that. Before she gets too old to want to build snowmen.'

'Does anyone ever get too old to want to build snowmen?'

Addy thought about it and laughed. 'Probably not.'

She'd never been skiing. Or to Lapland. She'd dreamed, with Nathan, that when she got pregnant—when they finally had a baby—they would do all the fun things. Lapland for Christmas. America for all the theme parks. The Caribbean for the beaches. They would explore and have fun and live life after all the rounds of drugs and injections and procedures she'd had and being made to feel like their lives were not their own, but something owned by the fertility specialists who'd kept her on strict regimens.

Maybe they shouldn't have waited? Maybe if they'd had more fun together then Nathan wouldn't have left?

'How strong do you like your tea?'

'I don't mind.'

'Okay. Strong it is, then.'

She passed him his cup and poured some juice for Carys, eager to get back into the next room and spend some time with her.

They walked through into the living area and spotted Carys at the table, patiently holding on to her box.

'So, what is this jigsaw, then?' Addy slid into the seat opposite her and Ryan sat beside his daughter.

'The tiger one!'

'Oh, wow.'

It was a very pretty jigsaw. Three tigers, lying together among lots of brown savannah grass. The pieces were all going to look the same...this was going to be a challenge.

'You don't pick easy ones, do you?'

'If it was easy then we'd finish it too fast,' Carys said.

'Well, we wouldn't want that to happen,' laughed Ryan.

Carys opened the box and spilled out the pieces onto the table.

'Shall we pick out edges and corners first? Try and build the outline?'

'Let's do it.'

They began sorting the pieces. It was a slow process and took them a good half an hour, even with three of them, as occasionally someone would miss one and throw an edge into the middle pile, from where it had to be retrieved and found by someone else. But eventually they'd sorted them all and began constructing the edges.

Addy couldn't help but notice Ryan's hands. His fine fingers. Occasionally they reached for the same piece and would laugh, embarrassed.

'I can't remember the last time I did a jigsaw,' Addy said. 'When *do* adults stop playing games?' she mused.

'I'm not sure all of them do.'

She laughed. 'No. I guess not. But I meant like this. Board games. Jigsaw puzzles. Video games. Whatever it is they loved as a child, when do they drift away from all that and why?'

'I guess other pressures step in. Work. Bills. Socialising. Relationships.'

'Maybe…'

'Do you have a boyfriend?' Carys suddenly asked Addy, stopping to look up at her with a smile.

'Do I…? Erm…well…no, I don't,' she answered, feeling her cheeks fill with colour.

'Do you want one?'

Addy laughed nervously. 'Well, maybe one day.

I did have one, but things didn't work out, so I'm taking care that whoever I choose next is the right one.'

'What was wrong with the last one?'

'Carys, we don't ask our friends questions like that,' said Ryan, trying to give her an out.

But Addy wanted to answer. She didn't want to evade the little girl's questions. Felt it was vital to be as honest with her as she could.

'Well, Nathan and I were happy for a while, but then we had a falling out.'

'When I fell out with Ruby, our teacher Mrs Graves said we had to shake hands and make up.'

Addy smiled. 'Mrs Graves sounds like a very sensible person. But adult relationships can be a lot more complicated than that.'

'Why?'

'They just are. You'll discover that as you get older.'

'So you didn't shake hands and say sorry to one another?'

Addy shook her head. 'No.'

'Oh.'

She looked at Ryan and he gave her a look back that said *sorry.* He had nothing to apologise for. And she did feel she'd answered Carys truthfully, so that was good.

Soon Carys found the last corner piece, and then they were able to attach two longer edge strips to form a bigger corner. The jigsaw was going well, and now they were beginning to find pieces to work on the tigers' faces.

'Here's a piece of fang!' Carys said, with a huge smile.

'Anyone want another drink?' Addy asked, grateful for Carys being there, distracting her, keeping her focused, so that she didn't have to worry about being alone with Ryan.

'I'm fine. But maybe we should stretch our legs for a bit? Go for a walk?' Ryan suggested.

Addy looked to Carys, to see what she thought of that idea. A walk with Ryan would be wonderful! Alone, it would be risky. Too intimate. But with Carys there...? Easier.

'Okay!' said Carys.

It was beautiful out. Sunny, but not very warm. Lots of people were out, to take advantage of the late summer they seemed to be having as September wore on.

'When we get back to the house, Carys, I'll take your measurements and show you some of the fabric I have. You can pick what you want for your Halloween costume.'

'You must let me know how much it costs, though. You're not doing this for free,' Ryan said.

'Nonsense! It's a pleasure.'

'Pleasure or not, I know fabric isn't cheap. I'll pay for what you use.'

She smiled, knowing he wouldn't win that one. She had had no intention of taking payment for making Carys's costume. It was going to be fun. Something she would enjoy doing. Something for someone else. It would give her a purpose.

'I don't want to be that space princess any more,' Carys said.

'You don't? What do you want to be?'

'I want to be a tiger.'

'Oh. Well, I'm not sure I have any tiger fabric…'

'Let's go and buy some, then,' said Ryan. 'I'll pay.'

Decision made, they headed through the park towards the row of shops on the road that led towards the town centre. Halfway down was a fabric and haberdashery shop that Addalyn often used. When they walked in, it was busy, but Carys's face lit up at the sight of all the pretty fabrics on show.

'Ooh, Addy! Look at this one!'

Carys had lifted a corner of soft tulle, delicately embroidered with dainty flowers in pale blues, pinks and mint-greens.

'Gorgeous!'

Addy pulled out a longer strip of the fabric to look at the pattern and see how it repeated. Ideas were whirling in her head as to what she might use it for.

'You won't look like a tiger in that,' Ryan said.

Carys nodded and looked around for animal prints, spotting some at the far end of the shop. They made their way there.

'Now, do you want a cotton print, or fleece, or

fur?' asked Addy. 'Bearing in mind that when you wear this it will be the end of October, so it could be cold.'

Carys was touching all the fabric, but seemed most enamoured by the fur.

'This one! It's nice and soft.'

'Hmm…'

Addy tested it with her fingers to see if the many layers might be too much for her sewing machine to deal with. But it seemed light and thin enough not to be a problem, yet thick enough to keep Carys warm. And if it wasn't, then Carys could always wear some clothes beneath it.

'This could work.'

'How much will you need?' Ryan asked.

'Two metres? To be on the safe side. And— Ooh, what about this?' Addy pointed at some lace trim that she knew would work well as teeth.

'Get whatever you need.'

The lady who owned the shop wound out two metres of fabric and half a metre of trim, folded it all and placed it in a bag for them as Ryan got out his card and paid.

They headed back outside.

'Where to next?' asked Ryan.

'Can we see if my magazine is in the shop?' Carys asked.

Addy looked to Ryan. 'Magazine?'

'She gets this partwork… It's about all the birds

in the world. I think she's got about twelve issues. At the moment they're doing birds of the UK.'

'You like birds?' she asked his daughter.

'Yes! I do! My favourite is the robin redbreast.'

'They are sweet. They're pretty tame, you know? You can get them to feed out of your hand if you're patient enough.'

'Can you?'

This piece of information seemed to blow Carys's mind.

Laughing, Addy allowed Carys to slip her hand into hers and they headed over to the newsagent to see if they had Carys's magazine. They did, so they bought it and headed back towards the park.

'You know, I've got a few bits and pieces in,' said Addy. 'We could easily make up a small picnic in the back garden.'

'Oh, we wouldn't want to put you out.'

'You wouldn't be! It would be a pleasure,' she said, smiling, hoping Ryan would say yes.

She didn't know what it was. She knew she ought to be not getting as involved with them as she was. But she simply couldn't help it. She loved their company. Loved the way it felt to be with them. Loved the way she felt she was a part of something. And she didn't want it to end now that they were here.

At home, they did a bit more on the jigsaw and then, when they'd all begun to feel that they truly couldn't see any of the pieces any more, and progress began to be severely stunted, Addalyn went into the kitchen and began making sandwiches and putting little snacky things like sausage rolls and cocktail sausages in the oven to warm through.

'Please don't go to too much trouble. Carys and I will be happy with a sandwich.'

'It's no trouble. In fact, I like it! It's been such a long time since I got to take care of anybody.'

Ryan looked at her for a moment, then turned around to check to see where Carys was. The little girl was giving the jigsaw one last attempt.

'You miss your dad? And your brother?'

'More than words can say,' she said, feeling a wave of sadness creep over her.

'Do you want to talk about them?'

She did. And maybe he would understand? Being a fireman himself...

'You must have heard what happened to them?'

'I know there was a building collapse.'

Addy nodded. 'They got called to a fire in a block of flats. Twenty floors that needed evacuation due to what turned out to be a faulty electric bike charger. Someone had been trying to charge their battery overnight, but the item was faulty and it started the blaze. We didn't know that until after...'

She paused in her chopping of the strawberries she was working her way through and turned to face him.

'I was there too, helping co-ordinate resources

and the rescue with Paolo, who was newly in charge of Blue Watch.'

'My chief Paolo?'

She nodded. 'He'd worked hard to get his promotion. Had earned it. He and my dad were best friends, and though they'd both gone for the post my dad couldn't have been prouder that his friend got it.'

'He sounds like a good guy.'

'He was the best. Ricky and Dad were tasked with trying to get as many people out as they could. They were using the stairwells, because they were concrete and weren't burning, and for a while it was working. They rescued forty-one people that night, before the heat and the fire became too much. The fire grew out of control, despite their measures to contain and dampen it. Dad and Ricky were in flat twenty-three when a roof gave way and trapped them both. Ricky's leg was trapped beneath some masonry and Dad attempted to pull him out. But then the top of the building began to collapse and they got trapped in the rubble. They burned to death before anyone could rescue them.'

Ryan stared at her in silence. 'You watched it happen? You were there?'

She nodded, wiping a silent tear from her eye. 'I was.'

Suddenly he moved from his spot opposite her and embraced her, holding her tight. It was sudden and unexpected, and she forgot to breathe for a moment, so shocked was she to be in his arms and to be held. But then she let go of the breath she was holding and relaxed into him. She squeezed him back and just allowed herself to be comforted. Breathing in his unique, wonderful scent.

Ryan felt so good. So strong. She could feel the musculature of his body against hers and realised that for the first time in years she felt safe. Protected. Cared for.

It was a heady moment, and one that she didn't want to end.

'Can I have some more juice?' Carys's voice piped up behind them, and suddenly Ryan let her go.

Addy stepped away, wiping her eyes rapidly before turning to smile at Carys. 'Of course you can! Have you got your glass from before?'

She refilled the glass with juice and handed it to her. 'Why don't you go out into the garden with that blanket over there and pick a spot for our picnic?'

'Okay!' But then Carys paused and looked at them both. 'What were you doing?'

Addy froze, not sure how to respond.

Ryan came to the rescue. 'Addy was a little upset. She was telling me about how she lost her dad and her brother. I was comforting her, that's all.'

'Oh. Okay!' And Carys grabbed the blanket and headed out.

Addy looked over at Ryan. 'Thank you.'

'It was the truth.'

'No. For the hug. I hadn't realised just how much I needed that.'

He smiled back at her. 'You're very welcome.'

# CHAPTER EIGHT

HE'D HEARD THE story of the loss of Victor and Ricky Snow. How could he not have? He worked in their station. Their pictures and their names and their years of service were up on the memorial wall with the others who had been lost over the decades. But he'd not heard it from her point of view and he hadn't known that she had watched it happen.

He couldn't imagine how that must have felt. To lose a father and a brother at the same time was awful enough, but to be there, helpless, watching it happen, knowing she could do nothing to reach them, must have been an agony he could only hope never to experience. Would he have been able to hold himself together? He wasn't sure of it.

Addalyn Snow was a remarkable woman. Stronger than she knew. And being able to hold her in his arms like that and comfort her had meant more than she knew. He'd longed to hold her. Longed to make her feel better and take away some of her pain. But the feel of her in his arms…the heat of her…her softness… He'd longed to do more. Kiss her. Tell her she was special. Keep her in his embrace and never let go.

Only he couldn't do that.

He helped her carry out the food she'd been preparing and together they assembled their picnic. He felt as if he wanted to give her a reason to smile again. To be happy. Because he felt that he was the one who had reminded her of her sad past and he felt responsible. It had been eye-opening to hear her version of events, that was for sure. And now he wanted her to think of happier times, so he would make her smile.

Losing a crew mate at a rescue was a risk of the job. They all knew that. They all knew the danger, but did it anyway. And they honoured those they'd lost. Honoured their sacrifice in trying to rescue others or to stop a fire from claiming any lives. Lost crew were heroes. Addy's father and her brother were heroes.

'I'm starving!' Carys tucked into a sandwich and opened up a packet of crisps.

'You should try one of these,' Addy said, offering Carys a halloumi stick wrapped in streaky bacon.

'What is it?'

'A special kind of cheese. It doesn't melt when you cook it.'

Carys took a bite. 'Yum!'

Addy laughed.

This was nice, thought Ryan. Sitting in her back

garden, in the sunshine, eating a picnic together. A simple pleasure. This was what it was all about, right? Spending time with family. Enjoying being together.

Addy was going to make someone a wonderful mother one day.

'You ever thought about having kids?' he asked, feeling relaxed and casual.

He felt he could ask her now. They knew each other so much better, and he now knew she'd been in a relationship before, with Nathan, so surely she must have thought about it. Or they must. And he only asked because Addy got on so well with Carys that he couldn't imagine her *not* being a mother.

But he saw a cloud cross her face and realised his error much too late.

'Of course I have. I've always wanted kids. But... I can't have them.'

He stared at her, shocked and surprised.

And feeling guilty. Again.

He should never have pried. 'I'm sorry.'

'It's okay!' she said, clearly trying to say it with a smile. 'I've accepted it.'

'Are you...? I mean, have you seen a doctor about it? Or...?'

'Nathan and I were trying for a long time. We tried naturally, and when nothing happened after a couple of years we went for testing. They couldn't find anything wrong with us, so we began IVF. I had four rounds. Three on the NHS and a fourth that we paid for ourselves, using all our savings. But it didn't work.'

'I'm so sorry.'

'It's not your fault.'

'I know, but… That's twice now I've brought up something sad for you and I'm beginning to feel paranoid.' He tried to laugh it off, to make her feel more comfortable, and he could see that she appreciated that.

'Honestly, it's fine. It's good for me to talk about it. People should talk about infertility openly, so it's seen as natural.'

'I guess…'

'We did have some hope on the second round. I did a home pregnancy test and it was positive, and we were over the moon. But when the clinic did a blood test the HCG levels were so low. Not where they ought to have been. And a second blood test a few days later showed that the levels had dropped even more. So…that was a no-go too.'

'That must have been devastating.'

'It was. All those treatments. The drugs, the injections… You begin to feel like a human experiment, you know? Your life becomes ruled by it all. You can think of nothing else. And as a couple you either turn towards each other after each failure, or you go looking for comfort elsewhere. Like Nathan did.'

'How long have you been apart?'

'Four years now. Four and a half… Something like that. I came back here to live with Ricky and Dad and then I lost them, too. It's been a hard few years.'

'I'm sorry. And I know I keep saying that, but I really mean it.'

'I know. And thank you. It's fine. That's life. Bad stuff happens. We just have to go with it.'

'Of course—but maybe this means that you've had your share of the bad stuff and from now on it's only good stuff all the way.'

Addy smiled and nodded. 'Let's hope!'

They finished their picnic and sat in the sun. Then Addy remembered she had ice creams in the freezer, so they had those. He liked watching her laugh. Loved watching her smile. But more than anything he adored the way she interacted with Carys.

Carys had been his whole world for years, and he would give his life for his daughter. To see Addy loving and having fun with his little girl meant everything.

It made him think about the future. It made him think about what sort of happiness he might find some day. Would it be with Addy? They got on so well together.

But…

He wanted more kids. He always had. And if Addy couldn't have children, then…

*There's more than one way to have a family.*

Addy looked at him as she laughed with his daughter, and he felt, deep down, that he would be able to pursue those other alternatives if Addy was by his side. Suddenly his heart began to pound as he realised he was thinking about what it would be like to have a family with Addalyn! It scared him. Terrified him. Made him realise that maybe he thought more of Addy than he ought to.

But he simply couldn't tear his eyes away from her as his thoughts raced ahead. Because when he'd held her, comforted her earlier, there'd been a response. He'd felt the way she'd sunk into him. She'd even made a soft sound of gratitude...of affection, and neither of them had really wanted to let go. And she was spending all this time with him. With his daughter. And sometimes he saw a look in her eyes. Of query. Of hope. Of fear.

But mostly he felt she was as attracted to him as he was to her.

*Boy, we are both in so much trouble here!*

# CHAPTER NINE

ADDY RACED THROUGH the streets, sirens blaring, as she navigated the traffic towards her latest shout. An industrial accident… All she knew was that there were a number of workers involved with some sort of chemical spillage.

As she drove, she tried to think of all the things she'd need to be aware of upon entering the site. Getting details from whoever was in charge. Establishing safety protocols. Keeping herself and the other rescuers safe, so that there wouldn't inadvertently be even more casualties than there already were.

It was the number one rule as a first responder—make sure it's safe for *you* before you proceed to assist a casualty.

It was a thought that had been running through her mind a lot just lately. Keeping herself safe. Keeping her heart safe, especially. Because spending time with Ryan and Carys was wonderful and she didn't want anything to spoil it. It had been a long time since she'd felt this happy. And the last few times she'd felt happy life had thrown spanners into the works and ruined everything, taking away the source of her happiness.

Maybe Ryan was right? Maybe it *was* now her turn to have happiness?

She wanted to believe that, but she was scared of not holding back. Not giving her absolute all seemed to be the only defence she had, and if she kept it in the back of her head at all times that she could lose Ryan and Carys at any moment, then maybe she'd be prepared for it, if it ever happened? Just thinking about it even now, as she raced towards someone else's tragedy, made her stomach churn.

She'd only known them such a short time and they already meant so much.

She'd been having dreams of kissing Ryan. A couple of times they'd come close. Both times they said goodbye to each other after spending time together Ryan would kiss her cheek, but she'd been yearning to have him kiss her on the lips.

He had not. Because each time Carys had been there.

At least, she thought that was the reason why. Maybe at the weekend he'd not kissed her on the lips because she'd told him that she couldn't have children. She knew he wanted more. He'd told her that. He probably thought there was no point in pursuing anything with her.

But she dreamed of his lips. Of his mouth. The way it smiled. The way it might feel. All the possible things it could do and how they might feel. And she loved to listen to him talk. He was funny and kind. Empathetic and genuine. That was what she loved about him the most. You got what you saw. He put on no airs or graces. There was no pretence about Ryan. And she liked the way he looked at her. Interested. Content. Warm. He seemed happy in her company and she was very happy in his.

But it was all so difficult, because of what he was—a fireman. Maybe if he was still in the army it would be easier? Or if he was a travelling salesman? Or a postman or a truck driver?

*Why did he have to be a fireman?*

As she got closer to the location she became aware of more sirens, more blue lights, as other first responders raced towards the scene. It was on an industrial site, and as she weaved her way down the road she became aware of workers in high-vis vests and hard hats exiting the site in an orderly manner, as their own buildings' sirens sounded to indicate that an evacuation needed to take place. Up ahead was a singular fire engine, and behind her came two more.

She felt herself switch into full-on work mode as she searched for a place to park that was safe.

'What are we dealing with?' she asked as she got out of her vehicle, slipping on her own high-vis vest and attracting the attention of what looked like a supervisor from inside the building.

'Acetone production. Somehow a fire started in Block B. We've evacuated, but we're still doing a headcount.'

'Get those numbers to the fire crew as soon as, please. Any casualties?'

'A couple over there. Robert, I think. And Wendy.'

Addy turned to look at two people sitting on a grass verge, both with their hands wrapped in gauze. She used her personal radio to contact ambulance control, update them on the situation and order more ambulance crews. This could be incredibly serious. Then she headed off towards the first fire engine to liaise with Paolo.

'We've got an acetone fire.'

'I've just heard. I've ordered all the men to use their breathing apparatus. Do we have a number?'

'Supervisor is doing a headcount right now. I'm going to check on those two over there and establish a triage tent. Get any casualties brought to me after decontamination procedures, yes?'

They needed to be cleaned of any acetone before they got to Addy as a preventative. To stop any more issues.

Paolo saluted her and ran off to issue orders to his men.

She didn't have time to look for Ryan. Her mind was on her patients.

As she got to their side, she set down her bag

and evaluated them. 'Hi, my name's Addy. Can you tell me what happened?'

She started with questions because they were both conscious and breathing. Robert staring at his hands. Wendy looking away into the distance. A cursory glance told her they did not appear to have any blood-loss or broken bones. They were the walking wounded, and getting them to answer her questions would give her a good idea about their respirations and their ability to talk, and whether she needed to check their airways.

She would do that anyway. It was something always checked after a chemical spill. Some chemicals could burn throats and airways if inhaled, and though her knowledge of acetone itself was sketchy, she did know that high amounts could cause irritation to the mucus membranes.

'We don't know,' said the man, Robert. 'One of the machines had been making funny noises all morning, and we were waiting for Engineering to take a look. We were going to shut it down, but our boss Gregori told us to keep it moving. There was a flash. Sudden. Blinding. And we heard a bang. Next thing we know the room is on fire.'

'You have injuries?' Abby asked, indicating his hands as she slipped on her gloves.

'Burns. My hands hurt like hell, but Wendy says hers feel fine.'

That wasn't good. When burns didn't hurt, it

usually meant that the thickness of the burns was deep and had destroyed the nerve-endings.

'How did the burns happen?'

'We tried to stop the fire. Used the extinguishers. But we got too close. My clothes caught fire and Wendy tried to put me out…rolled me on the floor.'

'And then I slipped and fell into the flames,' said Wendy. 'I think I've burnt my hair too.'

Wendy turned to look at her. All this time she'd been turned away, as if staring off into the distance. She tried to smile. And that was when Addy saw the burns on her face.

*Damn.*

They went halfway up her face. Reddened and painful-looking. Some of her hair was gone, as were her eyebrows and no doubt her eyelashes. It looked bad enough that she might need a skin graft.

'Did you go through a decontamination procedure?' she asked as she rummaged in her bag to set up for a cannula. She needed to get fluids and painkillers into Wendy immediately.

'I don't think so…'

She couldn't let Wendy or Robert sit there with acetone still burning into their wounds. It might hurt, but she needed to wash the chemical off their skin before she applied new coverings.

Technically, she needed soap and some warm water to wash it off fully, but she didn't have soap, and nor could she get them to rub their wounds. All she could do was rinse and dilute the acetone as much as possible.

Chrissie had arrived, along with her partner Jake, to assist. Addy explained the situation and after she'd rinsed the wounds Jake and Chrissie began applying dressings, so Robert and Wendy could be transferred to hospital.

'How are you doing, Wendy?' Addalyn asked, feeling the woman was in a state of shock and disbelief.

'I'm okay, I think. Is my face all right?'

Addalyn took in her visage. No, it wasn't all right. But it would be. One day.

'You'll get the best doctors and sort it out in no time.'

'But I'm getting married in two months.'

Addy's heart sank. 'You are? Congratulations.'

'Thanks. Me and Brian are soul mates. Knew each other at school, but then went our separate ways. He got married, so did I, and then we both got divorced for differing reasons. We met each other again a year ago and it was like life said to me, *Here you go. Have some happiness after all.*' Wendy tried to smile. 'Do you have a mirror? I want to see.'

'I don't. But there's no point in looking at it right now.'

'Is it bad?'

How to answer?

'It looks very sore.'

'Brian loves my face. Tells me every day I'm beautiful. Will he still do that, do you think?'

Addy hoped so. She hoped that, whoever this Brian was, he was the type of kind, loving man who would see past the burns and the scars that might remain and still want to marry the Wendy he'd fallen in love with.

'I'm sure he will.'

'This is our second chance at happiness. If he doesn't… Well…' Wendy blinked slowly, her eyes starting to glaze over.

Addalyn looked up in time to realise that Wendy was about to pass out. She called to Chrissie for help and they caught Wendy and lowered her to the ground, placing her in the recovery position and applying an oxygen mask to her face. She might have just fainted. It might just be shock. But they would monitor her blood sugar, her BP and her airway, just in case.

Addy was pushing the fluids, squeezing the bag, when something exploded. Instinctively, protectively, she covered Wendy's body with her own.

The boom was deafening, and smoke and a horrific stench filled the air. Blinking, cowering slightly, she turned to check on her colleagues. They were fine, but shocked. All of them were as they turned to look behind them. Part of the factory had gone up in smoke and the fire crews were trying to beat back the fire.

*Ryan.*

But she had no time to worry about him. No time to run and make sure he was safe. She had her priorities. Robert and Wendy... Chrissie and Jake.

Wendy was slowly coming round, having missed the explosion completely. She groaned as she came to. 'I feel sick...'

'You passed out. But you're okay. Stay lying there. We're going to transfer you to a trolley and get you off to hospital.'

'Can you call Brian?'

'Of course. Once you're safely in the ambulance.'

'Is he okay?'

'I'm sure he is. Where does he work?'

'In the admin office.'

Addy was soon transferring Wendy onto a trolley, getting her strapped in for the switch to the ambulance.

'Whereabouts?' It was best to keep her patient chatting. It was also a good way to keep an eye on any neural issues.

'The admin office here.'

Addy stopped briefly. 'Here? Where you work?'

'Yes.'

Addy turned to look at the building. Half of it was a blackened wreck, with smoke and flame billowing from all window cavities. Was that the admin office? Or part of the factory? No point in worrying Wendy until she had to.

'Give me his number and I'll pass it on to the paramedics. They can give it to the hospital, and they'll try to contact him for you, okay?'

'Okay.' Wendy smiled, her gaze content and dreamy.

Clearly the strong painkillers were working well.

Painkillers and anaesthesia were a blessing. They took the pain away. The hurt. The grief. For a while you were blissfully unaware. Reality would always come crashing back in at some point, but in that moment they would feel fine.

Addy had no idea if Wendy's future had been eliminated or not. She hoped it hadn't been. She hoped that Brian had escaped the fire and that he would meet Wendy at the hospital and hold her hand through all her painful debridement and surgeries. That he would stand by her side at their wedding and tell her she was beautiful, as he always had.

But she couldn't know for sure.

In her peripheral vision, she saw someone waving madly. She turned to see Paolo, flanked by two other fire crew, carrying an unconscious fireman away from the smoke and flame.

Her stomach flipped and churned.

And she ran towards the casualty.

# CHAPTER TEN

THE FIREMAN STILL wore his oxygen mask, so she couldn't see who it was. She raced towards them, watched as they got clear of the danger and laid the man down on the pavement.

Addy fell to her knees at his side and wrenched off the mask, her heart thumping crazily.

*Please don't let it be Ryan. Please don't let it be Ryan!*

It wasn't Ryan.

Relief hit her like a tsunami—and then immense guilt. It shouldn't matter who it was. One of Blue Watch was hurt. Hank Couzens. She didn't know him all that well, but she did know he had a wife. Three kids. Two boys and a newborn baby girl. Any of Blue Watch or any first responder getting hurt was horrible.

But still, relief was her overriding feeling as she placed the oxygen mask back over Hank's face and began a primary survey.

'What happened?'

'He was caught in the blast. Got knocked backwards into a wall. He banged his head pretty bad.'

She examined his head and his neck. She

couldn't feel any depressions, nor any movements that might indicate a fractured skull, and Hank wasn't conscious to tell her if anything hurt. But she had to assume there were injuries she wasn't aware of, and so she wrapped a cervical collar around his neck to immobilise his head and spine in case of hidden injury.

Addy checked his arms and legs. Nothing seemed broken. His abdomen was soft, as it should be. Hopefully, he was just concussed. She radioed for one of the ambulance crews to make its way to her position and when it came helped get him onto a spinal board and into the vehicle that soon roared away, sirens blaring.

She let her gaze fall upon the burning building. The fire crews were still aiming their water hoses at it and she wondered which one of them was Ryan. How many more times would she have to stand there and wonder if he was okay? This wasn't meant to be happening to her any more. He was only meant to be a friend. And yet already she cared for him deeply.

*Maybe I need to put up bigger walls?*

*Maybe I need to cut off contact altogether?*

It had been a fierce blaze and Ryan was sweating thoroughly by the time he emerged from the site, his job done. All the flames were out and the site had been doused with enough water that no spark would survive, no matter what.

Wearily, he pulled off his helmet and lifted his face to the waning sun, grateful for the small measure of cool breeze upon his face. He stood there for a moment before moving forward towards Paolo, towards the rest of his waiting crew.

He saw Addalyn there, too, nervously biting on her fingers.

He couldn't imagine how difficult this shout must have been for her. It had been no picnic for those inside, tackling the blaze, but knowing now what she had gone through with her brother and Ricky, he knew watching any fire get out of control must be difficult for her.

'You okay?' Paolo asked as he got closer.

'Yeah. All done and dusted. I think the source of the fire was in the east wing of the building, but Investigative Services will figure that out for sure.'

With any big fire like this, the fire service investigated the cause and origins of the fire. It was useful in criminal or arson prosecutions to have their evidence and skill.

'Okay. There's water over there—get it down you and then we'll head back.'

'Cheers, boss.' He gave Paolo a small salute and grabbed a bottle of water, necking half of it before he drew level with Addy. 'Hey.'

She didn't look happy. She looked nervous. On edge.

'You're all right?'

'Yeah. Just tired. Smelly. Looking forward to

a good shower.' He tried to laugh. To make light of the situation.

She nodded. 'I bet.'

'I hope you weren't too worried about me.'

'About you? I was worried about all of you! I had to send Hank off to the hospital.'

'Hank? Damn. Is he okay?'

'He was unconscious. Caught in the blast.'

'I didn't know.' He felt bad then. Before, all he'd wanted was a shower. Now all he wanted was to go and visit his friend. Make sure he was okay.

'I thought it was you. When they brought him out he had his mask on. For one minute…' she breathed in, then out, steadying her voice '… I thought it was you.'

He stared at her, realising in that moment that she cared for him as deeply as he cared for her and how scary that must be for her. He felt guilty. As if he was somehow torturing her because of his choice of job. But what could he do? He'd never been the kind of guy to want to work in an office. He liked jobs that required the use of adrenaline. The army. The fire service. He couldn't imagine any other life. That wasn't who he was.

'It wasn't. I'm fine.'

She nodded again, not actually looking at him, and he could see in that moment that she was fighting tears. That she was fighting a huge torrent of emotion.

'I like you, Ryan. I do. And I adore your daughter. But... I can't do this again. I can't stand there and watch and wait for you to be brought out on a stretcher or in a body bag. I just can't.'

'Addy—'

'No. I can't. I'm sorry. I have to protect myself here.'

And she turned and walked away from him.

He watched her go, shocked. They were hardly in a relationship with one another—they were just friends. Very good friends. Maybe this job had been too much? Any of his call-outs had the potential to be fatal and some people couldn't handle that.

But what about *her*? What about *her* job? She was a HART paramedic—she put herself in danger, too! She might lose her life one day, doing the job she loved, and then *he* would be the one left without *her*!

Did she ever think about that?

Because he thought about it all the time. And being left alone again did not appeal at all!

# CHAPTER ELEVEN

LIFE WAS SO much better without Ryan.

At least that was what Addy kept telling herself every time she felt her thoughts wandering to him. Perhaps if she told herself enough times then it would be true. It would be like when someone kept telling you that you were ugly. After enough times, you'd begin to believe it. This had to work in a similar fashion.

*I don't need Ryan and life is so much better without him.*

So why was she sitting at her sewing machine, missing him like crazy, and working on Carys's tiger costume? The head-piece was like a hood, but she was trying to put ears in, and eyes, and create some teeth, so it looked perfect, and it just wasn't working.

*It's because I need to fit it on Carys. See exactly where the eyes and ears need to go.*

But she couldn't go to their house. Couldn't visit. Because she needed this space from him. It was better this way. Before either of them got in too deep. Addy had sensed where their relationship was going. Yes, they were fine as work colleagues, and great friends, but her own feelings had been heading in a totally different direction when it came to Ryan and his daughter. They were like the little family she'd always dreamed of having. The almost perfect guy and the perfect little girl. Of course she'd begun to fall in love with them. Put water in front of a thirsty person and eventually they'd drink it even if they were told the water could hurt them.

So she'd had to separate herself from the water. Tell herself she didn't need it.

*If only I could get these ears right!*

She wondered briefly if Ryan took his daughter to the park often. Maybe if she saw them she could pull the little girl to one side so that she could get her to try on the outfit, mark where the ears and eyes ought to be, and then scurry off back home?

*Did I just even think that? Stalking a little girl in a public park and pulling her away to some bushes? I'm losing it here.*

Addy got up from her sewing machine and began to pace the room. Maybe she should give up making the costume entirely? After all, she didn't owe it to anyone.

*Except I made Carys a promise.*

And that meant something.

Just because she couldn't be with Ryan, that

did not mean she could let down that wonderful
little girl!

*I'll just march around there, knock on the door
and ask for a fitting.*

Ryan was standing in the kitchen, busy making
pancakes, pouring his mix into the frying pan,
allowing it to spread, and then getting Carys to
count to three before he would try and flip them.
So far, one had fallen to the floor, the second one
had caught on the edge of the pan and ripped, and
now he was on the third.

'Are we ready? One…two…'

The doorbell rang.

'Three!'

He flipped the pancake and it landed perfectly.
Typical. But he didn't want to leave it on the heat,
where it would burn, so he shifted the pan off to
one side and pointed at his daughter.

'Don't touch it, okay? I'll be back in a minute.'

He wiped his hands on a tea towel and threw it
over his shoulder as he headed towards the front
door. He had no idea who was calling, but he was
waiting for a parcel delivery. Maybe it was that
and he needed to sign for it? He'd ordered Carys
a scooter—a special treat. He needed to feel good
about himself, and maybe get out of the house
more. Stop moping about Addalyn walking away
from their friendship.

Okay, so maybe it had become more than a

friendship. Even though, technically, they hadn't done anything romantic. But the thoughts and the feelings had been there. The wishes. The yearnings. The whole shebang.

He'd felt strangely upset after that factory fire, when she'd told him she couldn't be his friend any more. He'd understood why, but spending time with Addy had begun to bring him out of his shell again. He'd not been able to remember the last time he'd felt so happy. As if he were part of something special.

And damn straight they'd had something special—even if they hadn't kissed. Not on the lips, anyway. He'd kissed her cheek, and each and every time he'd wondered what she might do if he turned and kissed her on the mouth. But he'd not done it. Afraid to ruin what they had. That fledgling relationship. Both of them still cautious…both of them teetering on the edge of taking flight, not wanting to fall.

But fall he had. He'd fallen big time.

Buying his daughter a scooter was something he hoped would take his mind off the fact that he wouldn't get to see Addy again except at work.

He yanked open the door.

And his mouth dropped open.

Addalyn.

She stood there looking beautiful, despite the furrow in her brows, and despite the hardened, determined look in her eyes. She held a bag at her side and looked not at him but somewhere just over his left shoulder.

'I need to borrow Carys.'

Borrow Carys? Right. Of course. That seemed perfectly natural.

'Addalyn... Borrow her for what?'

'For a fitting. For her tiger costume.'

'Oh... Oh! You're still making that?'

'Of course! I'm not going to let her down when I promised.'

'She's just inside.'

He stepped back and watched in confused admiration as she stalked past him, then paused, awaiting instruction.

'She's in the kitchen,' he added helpfully, not sure how to proceed with what was clearly a tetchy woman completely on the edge.

'Thank you.'

'You're welcome.'

He followed her through to the kitchen, pausing a few steps behind her as she paused in the kitchen doorway.

'Hey, you.'

He watched as her entire demeanour changed when she saw his daughter. A wide smile crept across her face, and when Carys looked up and saw who it was she barrelled into Addy with an enthusiasm that made him smile from ear to ear.

Just as Addy did.

Addy scooped her up and hefted her onto a hip.

'You are getting bigger every day! It's a good thing I came round to check!'

'Are you here to play with me?'

'I'm here to measure you up for your tiger costume. I've made a start on it, but I need to keep checking it on you, just so I don't go wrong.'

'Okay! Can I see it?'

'Of course you can!'

Addy and Carys headed off towards the lounge and Ryan followed, not sure how to act or how to proceed.

'Can I...er...make you a drink?' he asked, feeling that hot beverages were safe ground to tread.

She looked up at him, her face losing its smile. 'I'm not stopping that long, so no. Thank you.'

He gave a nod and realised that he was not needed there, and that Addy would probably be much more comfortable if he disappeared and left them to it.

It was hard to leave them be. Especially since he'd been missing her. It had only been a couple of days, but already he'd begun to feel it. And Carys had been asking repeatedly when they could go back to Addy's house to continue with the jigsaw.

He hadn't wanted to lie to his daughter, so he'd simply said that he didn't know as he hadn't had a chance to ask Addy about it. Which was kind of true! He'd just not mentioned the other part.

The pancake lay cooling in the pan and he turned the cooker off and began to tidy up. Clearly

Addy was more important to his daughter than her lunch. He didn't want to interrupt them, but it was agony not being able to be with her. Just in the next room!

*How quickly Addalyn has become important to me.*

But this was what happened to him, wasn't it? He'd not been able to keep Angharad, either. She'd walked away. For different reasons, maybe, but if their love for one another had been stronger, would she have been able to walk away so easily? Maybe he'd not given her enough space? Maybe he'd not loved her as fiercely as he ought to have done? Maybe he'd put Carys first too much and she'd felt neglected?

But wasn't that what you were supposed to do as a father? Put your child first?

The feeling of failure as a man had hit him hard when his wife had left. He'd always thought of himself as a relatively good catch. A decent guy. Hard-working. Dedicated. Loyal. But maybe he'd given too much to his job and his daughter? Had Angharad felt neglected? She'd not been too thrilled about him being a fireman, either, though in the beginning of their relationship she'd viewed it as sort of a cool thing. Maybe when the reality of life with a fireman had hit, replacing the image of a hunky, half-naked man cuddling puppies for a charity calendar, she hadn't been able to handle it?

Like Addy.

But Addy had known the reality from the start. She'd never seen him or viewed him as anything else. He'd always been a risk to her, and maybe that was why she'd never got too close?

He pottered about in the kitchen for some time. Cleaning. Tidying away. Sitting at the table with his head in his hands until he got fed up.

In the next room he could hear laughter. Carys's perfect giggling. Addy's too.

He wanted to know what was going on. He felt left out.

*This is my home. Why am I hiding away in the kitchen?*

So he decided to make his presence felt.

Addy was so glad she'd come to do a fitting on Carys, because clearly she'd sewed one of the main seams on the outfit wrong and it was much too big, drowning Carys in reams and folds of tiger fleece so that the little girl could barely be seen beneath it.

'Grr! Roar!'

Carys tried to sound like a tiger from within the folds of fabric as Addy tried to locate the neckline, and when she did, and Carys's head popped out through the top, they both giggled with fits of laughter.

And then the door opened.

Addy swallowed and sucked in a breath when she saw Ryan standing there.

'How's everything going? It all sounds fun.'

She gave a polite smile, trying to control her breathing and her heart rate around him. It hadn't got any easier. In fact, since she'd walked away from him and told him she couldn't do this with him any more, it had seemed harder!

'I just need to take a few more measurements.'

'Great.' Ryan settled down onto the couch and picked up a magazine that happened to be lying there.

She glanced at it. It was a kids' magazine. Brightly coloured. It looked odd to see him reading it—because surely that wasn't his reading material of choice? Was he trying to act casual and normal around her?

Addy smiled at Carys encouragingly as she positioned her this way, then that, marking out her seams with carefully placed pins. 'That's it. Don't move for a minute.'

'When can I come round to yours to do more of the jigsaw?'

'Erm… I'm not sure.'

'What about this weekend?'

'Er…'

Ryan put down the comic. 'You're off to your grandparents' house this weekend, remember? They're taking you to visit Lara and Jacob, your cousins.'

'Oh.' Carys sounded as if that was the last thing she wanted to do.

Addy smiled at her. 'Sleeping at your grandparents' house will be fun! Think of how much they can spoil you! I remember going to my grandparents' house as a child and I loved it. Nan used to make this egg custard tart that was better than you'd get in any shop. And I remember she had this horse and carriage ornament that sat in their bay window… It was actually a music box, and I would sit and play with it, and open up its secret compartment, and every time my nan would have put something inside—like fifty pence, or a sweetie, or something else for me to find.'

Carys smiled.

'And they had this cute little white poodle called Toby. He was a bit smelly, but I used to love him anyway. Do your grandparents have any pets for you to play with?'

'They have a cat.'

'What's his name?'

'Munchkin.'

Now it was Addy's turn to smile. 'What colour is he?'

'Kind of black and brown.'

'He's a tortoiseshell,' Ryan added, drawing her eye. 'He's very rare, apparently. Most torties are female, so it probably means that…' He stopped talking, looking kind of afraid to say more.

'Means that what?' she asked.

Ryan looked away from her briefly, before closing the magazine and putting it back down on the table. 'It means that he's probably sterile.'

Addy stared at him.

'What's sterile?' asked Carys.

Now she looked at his little girl. At her curious face. 'It means he won't be able to give a female cat any babies.'

Carys thought for a moment. 'Aww! That's sad. Poor Munchkin. He'd have very pretty babies. Hey, Dad, can we have a kitten?'

And the subject was changed as fast as that.

Ryan was clearly blindsided. 'Er...not just yet, sweetie. A kitten takes a lot of looking after, and it wouldn't be fair to get a cat whilst I'm at work most days and you're at school. It would be all alone.'

He was right. Addy had often thought about getting a pet, to help her deal with being alone in the house, but it just wouldn't be fair. Unless she got a rescue cat? One that was older and already housebroken? A cat looking for somewhere to spend its golden years?

'You know, Carys, I've been thinking about getting a cat,' she told her. 'I couldn't have a kitten, for the same reasons as you and your dad, but I've thought about getting an older one. Maybe bringing it home when I've got a week off or something. I do have some holiday due. That way I could use the week to help it settle in, and after that it would be fine on its own. Maybe... I don't know.'

'Could I come and visit if you do?'

Addy glanced at Ryan. His face was impassive.

'Sure. I'll let you know if I ever do it.'

She helped Carys off with her outfit, making sure she didn't get pricked with any errant pins.

'Right. Well, I'd better be off. I should be able to make some headway with this now.'

'I'll walk you out,' Ryan said.

'Oh. Thanks,' she muttered, gathering her things and heading to the front door.

She stopped there and turned to face him. Looked past him to make sure he was alone.

'I'm sorry if I was a bit abrupt earlier. I didn't mean to be. I just felt awkward. But I hope—I really, really hope—that we can get along with each other if we meet at work or anything.'

She felt awkward. Felt as if she was rambling. But she knew she'd been harsh before, and that it was only because of how Ryan made her feel.

She was hoping that, with distance, it would get easier. But standing here, right now, in this moment, staring into his beautiful chocolate eyes and looking at his soft mouth and the slight hint of stubble, made her feel that maybe she was making a mistake. He looked so good in his dark jeans and white tee. Those arms... That chest... And his hair! So perfect... I've-Just-Got-Out-of-Bed messy hair, that made her want to run her hands through it, and touch him, and stroke him, and pull him close and smell him, and…

But Ryan represented everything that was dangerous to her emotional wellbeing. Ryan was a firefighter, and he had a child. He needed someone stable to be in his life. Someone who could give him future children. She was none of these things, and yet…

'We'll always be friends,' he said now. 'No matter what.'

He had a lovely voice. Soft. Gentle. Understanding.

*I want to kiss him. I want to kiss him so much!*

'I really do.'

'What?' Ryan frowned.

She felt her cheeks colour. Flush with heat. 'I mean thank you. Sorry. I was…er…thinking of two conversations at once. You know how your mind drifts sometimes?' She laughed nervously.

'Mine does it all the time,' he said sincerely, staring straight back at her.

'I ought to go. Say goodbye to Carys for me.'

'I will.'

He held open the door and let her step through.

'She's welcome to come and finish her jigsaw any time.'

'And…am I allowed to come with her? Stay?'

How would she be able to concentrate on anything with him there? But how could she say no, without being rude?

'It's okay if not. I could drop her off for an hour or two and then you could call me when you want her to be picked up.'

She was grateful that he'd given her a way out. 'Or I could just walk her back,' she told him. 'Seeing as we live so close to one another?'

'Sure! She's away this weekend, though, as I said, so maybe the weekend after that?'

'Great. Sounds great. I'd love that. I could do another fitting for her then as well.'

'Or take her with you to get a cat if you choose to. She'd love that. Though it might be dangerous for me, allowing her near all those animals that desperately need homes.'

He laughed good-naturedly.

'Yeah…anyway, I'd better go.'

She pointed at the pathway, as if it wasn't clear which direction she'd be taking as she moved away from him. It was wholly unnecessary, but her brain didn't seem to be functioning very well around him.

'Of course. I'll see you around.'

'Absolutely. Yes. At work.' She nodded.

'At work. Work only.'

'Mmm…'

She stared at him a moment longer, clinging to her last vestiges of hope that if she were just brave enough all it would take would be two steps towards him to plant a kiss on his lips. After all, what harm would that kiss, in that moment, do?

*Terrify him? Embarrass him? Send me down a path that I would regret afterwards?*

That last one was the reason that made her pause and reconsider. Because she didn't want any more regrets in her life. She had enough to deal with. She'd lost her boyfriend because she couldn't give him children. Lost her father and brother in a tragic accident. Did she really want to lose Ryan too?

By resisting—by not kissing him, not letting this attraction thing she had going on proceed any further—she could stop any more regrets right now. They could remain friends. And that was enough, right?

'Goodbye, Ryan.'

She gave a slight smile and, using all her strength, she walked away.

# CHAPTER TWELVE

WATER RUSHED FROM the hose towards the flames as Ryan held it steady, grimacing inside his helmet as his gaze took in the blackened walls, the blooms of soot, the curtains that seemed to dance as the fire consumed them from the floor upwards, the way some of the ornaments that had been in the window had either exploded from the heat or melted.

The source of the fire was the sofa. Someone had not noticed their cigarette falling from the ashtray that was perched on the arm, and it had fallen into the innards of the upholstery and started a fire.

Smoke had been the first sign. Luckily the owners had been in the kitchen when they'd noticed it, and had been able to get everybody out of the house before smoke inhalation had become a problem. But they would still need to be checked over by an ambulance crew, just in case.

There was no one to rescue here, which was great.

Their job was to extinguish the flames and stop

the fire spreading to the houses on either side, as this one was mid-terrace.

Paolo had made sure those homes had been evacuated, too, just to be safe.

Smoke billowed all around and another window shattered, allowing in more oxygen to fan any remaining embers.

The heat was incredible, but Ryan kept the hose aimed at the source until the flames began to die down and the living room became sodden.

Black licks of soot patterned the ceiling in a kaleidoscope of marks, and one part of the roof had begun to burn through. He kept an eye on it, aware of the possibility of collapse, but he had no reason to move further into the room from where he was. They had control now. They had it beaten.

Ryan grabbed the hose lock and turned off the water, bracing himself for the drop in pressure that would affect his balance. When only drips dropped from the hose-end he and his crewmate Jonno, who'd been behind him holding the hose too, began to make their way out of the devastated and ruined building.

'Fire origin was definitely the sofa in the lounge, boss,' he told Paolo.

Paolo nodded. 'At least everyone got out. That's the main thing. You can replace bricks and mortar; you can't replace people.'

Ryan nodded. Paolo was right. You couldn't replace people, even if you tried. Because everyone was different. When Angharad had first left him he'd never imagined wanting to replace her. He'd been too hurt. But lately he'd often thought about what it might be like to meet someone new.

Like Addalyn.

Carys adored her, and he did too. But she would never replace Angharad. He would always remember his wife. Always try to remember the good times they'd shared. Because life was too short to keep on remembering the pain.

Addy, in turn, could never replace her father or her brother. Or that guy she'd hoped to have babies with. In fact, she didn't seem interested in replacing anyone. Almost as if she was too scared to—which he understood. She was still in the scared phase. It would pass. One day. He hoped he would still be around when it happened. Because he believed that if she ever got brave enough, then his life with her could be something amazing!

But her fear, her hesitation, her need to flee… that worried him. Because if he was going to be with someone else—someone who would be part of his daughter's life—then he needed someone who was strong. Not someone who was a flight risk. He couldn't let Carys hope that Addy would be in their lives for good if Addy was going to run each time things got difficult or terrifying.

'Get the hoses back and pack up,' Paolo ordered.

'Will do.'

Ryan glanced over at the two ambulances that had turned up to treat the family in case of injury, hoping to see Addy. But she wasn't there. She only got sent to the really serious jobs. And even though this had been a potentially hazardous rescue, the information that had come in before the shout had told Control that there was no danger to human life. Everyone was out. A HART paramedic had not been needed on this occasion.

Maybe she was on a shout somewhere else? Maybe she was on a day off? Maybe she'd finally taken that holiday she'd said she would?

*I miss her.*

That was the pervading feeling. He'd got used to seeing her at work. He'd finish a job and look up to see her there. It always made him feel good, knowing that she was by his side. Knowing that she was safe. Taking care of her patients. But also knowing that she had one eye for him as well. For all of Blue Watch.

Her family.

The Tutbury cat rescue centre was practically overflowing with cats. Kittens, pregnant females, feral cats that had been captured and were being trained to get used to humans and, of course, the older, senior cats, which were kept in a different, quieter building. A retirement home of a kind.

That was where Addy had asked to go. She'd spent some time being interviewed at the front desk—about her home, her lifestyle and what sort of cat she was looking for. She'd told them about her job and her hours, and fully expected the manager to say *I'm sorry, but you're just not suitable.* But then Addy had explained that she'd got a couple of weeks' holiday booked soon, and she wasn't actually going to go away, but wanted to use that time to help a senior cat settle in. After that she'd be out for eight or nine hours each day. Sometimes more, if a job ran over, because accidents and emergencies didn't run to a neat schedule.

'But I grew up with cats,' she'd told the manager. 'My family always had them. Mostly moggies, but I do remember we once had a Russian Blue.'

'I think one of our senior cats will be perfect for you,' Letty, the manager, had said.

So she'd been escorted to the senior cats' housing unit and allowed to look around on her own. The majority of them were curled up fast asleep, as classical music played softly in the background. Each unit had a single cat in it, or sometimes two, if there was a brother and a sister, or a bonded pair that couldn't be split up. Cats of all colours. Of all types. One had an eye missing. The card attached to its cage said that Poppy had been injured in a fight with another cat and an infection had caused her to lose the eye.

There were so many sad stories. One cat had feline FIV. Another only had three legs after a traffic accident. One had been diagnosed as having cerebellar hypoplasia—a neurological condition that made it wobbly and have issues with its balance. This one was a black cat.

'Black cats are often not chosen for rehoming. People can be terribly superstitious,' Letty had said, as if apologising for the quantity of black cats she was about to see.

And there were a lot of black cats.

Addalyn was not superstitious, and as she perused the cards she also looked at the dates, wanting to know which cat had been there the longest.

And then she found him. In the last unit. Sitting in his soft bed, washing his face. Curly.

Curly had been born with anophthalmia, his card said. Which meant he'd been born with no eyes. And he'd been at the home the longest.

Seven years.

Addy couldn't imagine a cat being stuck inside this place for seven years. Seven years of classical music. Seven years of listening to people come and go, never being chosen.

He was a pure black cat, thirteen years old, and he'd come to the rescue centre after his previous owner had died.

It was a long time to be here.

A long time to go without someone to love.

A long time to go without affection.

Even though she felt sure the caretakers here

would have done their absolute best for him, she felt an affinity for Curly. She'd lost the person she loved too. She'd been left alone with no home until her father and brother had taken her in, and then she'd lost them too. And she had spent a few years without affection. Blind to love.

'We're made for each other, you and I,' she whispered, putting her fingers through the bars and making noises to try and entice Curly to the front of the cage.

Clearly he'd heard her. His other senses must be heightened because of his blindness. He came forward to sniff at her fingers, and then rubbed himself along her hand and the side of the cage, his tail in the air.

Addy smiled.

She'd found her cat.

'I'm going to take you home with me, Curly. Would you like that?'

Curly purred in response.

She spent some time with him in a special room along with Letty, who was thrilled that Curly had been chosen by her.

'He's such a special cat. We've all become so fond of him. In a way it'll be sad to see him go, but he's going for all the right reasons.'

'My time off doesn't start for another week,' said Addy. 'Can I collect him then?'

'Of course! And you're welcome to visit him as often as you'd like in the meantime.'

'Really? That's great. I'll try to pop in every day after work—if I have the time and you're still open.'

'Perfect. Shall we do the paperwork?'

'Let's do it.'

It was a mere formality. Addalyn had to promise to send the rescue centre pictures of Curly in his new home, and agree that if for any reason she couldn't keep Curly she would return him.

'I don't think that's ever going to happen, let me tell you now,' she said.

Letty smiled. 'I'm sure it won't, but it does happen on occasion, so we ask everyone.'

'Okay. I feel like he's mine already. It's going to be hard to walk away right now,' she said, stroking his soft fur. 'But I need to get the house ready for him. Get bowls and toys and a litter tray...'

'Exactly. You want to be ready when you invite someone new into your life.'

Addy looked up at Letty. She meant the cat, clearly, but she was right in other ways too. If you went into a new relationship without being ready then it was likely to fail at the first hurdle. Life was difficult enough without plunging headfirst into emotional turmoil.

She thought of Ryan and Carys. She missed them so much—which was crazy! Staying away was hard when you knew the person you'd like to spend time with was just around the corner. Literally two streets away.

When the paperwork was done, she gave Curly one last hug and then turned to leave the building. She pulled open the door and walked smack-bang into a man's chest.

'Oh! I'm so sorry! I…'

She looked up and saw Ryan. Of all the places… She'd never expected to find him *here*.

'Ryan! What are you doing here?'

He looked embarrassed, and shocked to find her there.

'Same thing as you, I'm guessing.'

'You're adopting a cat?'

'After you spoke about it Carys and I talked a lot, and we decided that it was something we both really wanted to do. Give a cat another chance at life. Give it something better than what it has right now.'

'You do have love to give,' she said with a smile, knowing the feelings he was talking about.

He stared her right in the eyes. 'Yeah… We do.'

She stared back. Taking in the beautiful darkness of his soft, chocolatey eyes. The intensity of his gaze.

'Have you chosen one, or…?'

He broke eye contact—reluctantly, she thought.

'Yeah! Curly. He's back there. Last cage on the left.' She pointed behind her.

'Mind if I take a look?'

'Sure!'

She walked with him over to the pen, smiling

at Curly as he settled himself back in his cat bed, plumping the soft pillow with his paws, purring away.

'He's cute.'

'He was born without eyes, so I think people might have overlooked him because of it.'

'Bless him… He looks sweet. He'll make you a very good pet. What other guys have we got in here?'

Addy decided to walk around with him as he considered the senior cats, even though she'd been on her way out. It seemed right to do so—and besides, Letty was still there, so it wasn't as is anything was going to happen.

'Who's this guy?'

'Girl,' Addy said, looking at the card. 'It's a female. Molly.'

Molly was a striped tabby cat. Twelve years of age.

'She has six toes on one front paw, it says here!'

'I can't see…'

Molly was curled up in her bed, slowly blinking at them. Probably wondering why there were suddenly so many people in the centre, looking at her.

'Perhaps she only shows them to people who are special?' Addy said with a smile, then laughed as Molly stood and stretched, front legs low, back end high in the air, showing off her six-toed foot after all.

'Hey, there…' Ryan put his finger though the

bars so that Molly could sniff him. 'What do you think, Addy? Will Carys like her?'

'She'll love her! She looks like a little tiger.'

'With huge feet.'

'With huge feet!' she echoed, laughing, letting Molly sniff her fingers too.

'Molly gets on very well with Curly, actually. We think they love one another,' said Letty, coming to stand behind them. 'When we let them out into the outdoor runs for some fresh air, they snuggle up all the time.'

Addy looked up at Ryan. 'That's sweet, isn't it?'

'It is.' He turned to Letty. 'Could I get Molly out to see how she reacts to me?'

'Sure.'

And so they sat on the floor and let Molly explore them. The cat sniffed here and there, intrigued by the other pens, but eventually she came over to Ryan and Addalyn, walking between them, tail held high, as they stroked her and she began to purr.

'She's perfect,' said Ryan.

'You're made for each other,' agreed Addy, feeling a mixture of emotions. She was happy for Ryan and Carys that they would have a cat so perfect for their home, but also strangely jealous of Molly. Because she would get to spend so much time with her favourite people. People she herself was trying to train herself to stay away from.

Ryan arranged with Letty that he would call

again when he knew his shift pattern and would have a decent break to help settle his new pet. He filled in the paperwork, and Addy listened as Letty asked him the same questions and had him agree to bring Molly back if she got too much for any reason.

As they left the centre, Ryan walked next to her through the car park towards her car.

'Well, this is me,' she said, pulling her car keys from her bag. 'Where's yours?'

'I walked.'

'You *walked*?'

He laughed. 'This is going to sound silly, but the house is so quiet without Carys there. It feels strange being there on my own.'

'I understand that feeling.'

'I thought it would take up more time if I walked.'

'Less time home alone?' she asked, smiling.

'Yeah!'

She knew, intimately, how that felt. It had been her life for years, and she could see he was struggling with it.

'Do you fancy going for ice cream?'

The question was out of her mouth before she could think about the dangers. And after she had asked it she told herself it would be fine. They would be in public. Nothing would happen. They were just friends. That was all.

'Oh!' he said. 'You don't have to…'

'No. I mean it. We're okay, aren't we? We can have an ice cream. A walk in the park. It doesn't have to mean anything. Besides, we're going to be like in-laws.'

'In-laws?'

'Because of our cats. They're in love. Or whatever,' she said, with a hint of embarrassment.

She could not quite believe what she had just said. She looked at him and shrugged, as if to say *You know what I mean.*

'That's as good a reason as any,' he said.

Addalyn drove them to the high street and parked near the fancy ice cream parlour that had opened up there. She'd been meaning to try it for ages. It was called One Scoop or Two? and as usual it had a queue out through the door, despite the time of the year.

Addy had heard nothing but good things about the place. Apparently it was owned by an Italian whose grandfather had begun a gelato shop in Naples. It had become two shops, then three, then four. She'd heard people say the flavours and the texture of the ice cream was out of this world!

She'd not had an ice cream for years. She'd used to go out for ice-cream all the time with Nathan. He'd loved nothing better than a raspberry ripple every weekend. More often than not she wouldn't have one herself, preferring a sorbet or nothing at all, but right now she wanted to have an ice cream with Ryan and go for a walk in the park. Spend time with him now that she'd run into him. It was as if this moment was an unexpected gift and she didn't want it to end. Not yet.

As they got closer, they spotted a board listing the flavours—all the usual suspects, but also butterscotch, cake batter, green tea, maple, watermelon and bubblegum. Lots of unexpected things.

'Do we try something new or stick with a favourite?' Ryan asked, turning to smile at her.

His smile made her feel special.

'Go for whatever you fancy,' she told him.

His look, with a raised eyebrow, made her blush slightly.

When they got to the front of the queue, Ryan ordered one scoop of matcha tea ice cream, with a second scoop of maple. Addy ordered cake batter and butterscotch.

They were delicious! Smooth, and not too overpowering in flavour. Sweet, without being sickly.

'Want to try mine?' Ryan offered his cone to her.

She looked directly into his eyes as she leaned in, took hold of the cone and licked it. The matcha was amazing! Slightly bitter, but sweetened enough that it wasn't off-putting. She offered her own cone and he tried her flavours, looking directly at her as he licked the ice cream.

There was something almost sexual about it. Almost hypnotic. Addy couldn't tear her eyes away from his gaze. And then he mentioned he liked the cake batter more than the butterscotch and she remembered they were sharing ice cream in a public space.

'It's good, isn't it?' she said.

'It can be scary, trying something new, but sometimes you can find something that you don't ever want to let go of,' he said.

She nodded. He was right. In, oh, so many ways. With food.

Experiences.

People.

Ryan was like a drug at this point. She wanted to be with him so much. To experience him. To taste him. Smell him. Envelop herself with him. But he was dangerous. He represented a threat to her mental and emotional wellbeing. He could hurt her. Not intentionally. But it might happen anyway.

Could you experience someone like that in moderation and not go mad?

People in the park were enjoying the last of the warm days. There were families, couples, people jogging or walking their dogs. Here in the park, surrounded by greenery, unable to see the town, it felt as if they were in a small bubble of peace and serenity. It was nice. Soothing. And she understood completely why people liked being surrounded by nature.

Here she could forget. For a moment, at least. Pretend that all was right with the world and that being here with Ryan was fine. Meant to be. A gift that she should cherish, because soon it would be over. Soon he would go home and she'd be alone again. Without him. But right now, at this moment, it was perfect—because he was here by her side.

'I love it here,' she said, as their steps carried them past the lake.

'It's very peaceful.'

'Makes a change from our jobs, doesn't it? We're so frenetic there. Running on adrenaline, with a million thoughts and possibilities and prospective dangers rushing through our heads…lives on the line…other people relying on our life-or-death decisions…'

'We can be like everyone else here. Normal.'

'Yeah…'

A dog raced past them and leapt into the lake, sending a group of ducks quacking in all directions as the owner bemoaned the fact that her dog was now wet and would stink up the car.

They both smiled as the dog came trotting out of the lake, pleased as punch, its tongue hanging out of its mouth.

'When does Carys get back?' she asked.

'Sunday evening.'

'Not long to go, then?'

He glanced at his watch. 'Too long. I always think it'll be good to have a break from being Dad. Nice for Carys to spend some dedicated time with her grandparents, being spoilt, but I always miss her when she's gone.'

'Do her other grandparents ever see her? Angharad's parents?'

Ryan shook his head. 'They did once. Had her for the day. But…it didn't work out. They said it was too stressful—that they were too old to look after a little one. Which didn't make any sense as they were only sixty-something, and in very good health. Maybe it was too stressful for Angharad? Having the daughter she gave up on spending time with her parents?'

'I'm sorry. Carys has lost more than a mother… she's lost grandparents too.'

'You can't change other people's decisions. If they've decided they can't have you in their lives, then that's how it's got to be.'

She pondered on his words. She had made a decision not to have Ryan in her life because of her deep growing feelings for him. Yet here she was. Walking through the park with him. Sharing ice creams and not yet ready to walk away.

*Because every time I walk away I think it won't hurt this way. But it does. It does.*

'Do you ever wonder if she thinks she made a mistake?'

'Angharad? No. If she did, I would have heard from her. Texts. Calls. Maybe even emails. But I get nothing—so, no, I don't think she has ever doubted herself.'

Addy doubted herself. She yearned to protect herself, but she also yearned to be with Ryan.

*What am I doing?*

'Hey, look, the boat place is still open! Fancy sharing a rowing boat with me? I'll row,' Ryan offered.

She'd finished her ice cream, so…

'Sure!'

She still wasn't ready to walk away. Today was a gift.

The rowing boats were all lined up alongside the small lake, and after they'd paid the boat guy took them over to one that had faded red paint on the hull, and held it steady as they both clambered in.

Ryan began rowing and took them out onto the water, dark green and cloudy. She tried not to notice the muscles flexing in his forearms as he rowed.

'Wow. This is so peaceful,' she said. 'I don't think I've been out on a rowing boat before.'

'You haven't?'

'No. I've been on a cruise ship, though.'

'Exactly the same.' He smiled. 'This is your captain speaking. We have just left port and we'll be making our way around the local lake today. Conditions are sunny and warm. Wind is blowing at a slow two knots and the onboard entertainment for today is…er…me.'

Addy laughed at him and he laughed back.

'You're silly.'

'I am. One hundred percent.'

'I like you, Ryan Baker.'

He paused as if to consider her. 'I like you, too. A lot.'

Her heart beat a little faster at his words and she felt her cheeks grow hot, so she looked away, at the people walking in the park, not knowing what to say next.

The fact that he liked her too…it meant something. It meant that what she was feeling wasn't stupid. She wasn't imagining this attraction between them. They both felt it. It was a war they were fighting, both not sure which tactic to use next to ensure they both survived and came out of it relatively unharmed.

Because being hurt was scary.

Being hurt was difficult and hard.

Painful.

The recovery process could be long and arduous, and she'd been injured so much already. She wasn't sure how many more injuries her heart could take. Which was why she tried to eke out small moments in which she could be happy.

Like today.

Like now.

With Ryan.

There was a small island in the centre of the lake, thickly populated with trees and bushes, and Ryan headed towards it. 'There's a folly on it somewhere. Want to go and find it?'

'Why not?'

He rowed their boat towards the island, looking for a small bay or inlet they could use, and on the far side of the lake they found one. A small nook, barely noticeable behind a weeping willow that overhung the shoreline. As they approached Ryan slowed, so that they could move aside the curtain of overhanging branches. It was like being transported into a new world. A hidden world. With the willow muffling the sounds from the lake. After he'd moored up, Ryan pulled the boat higher onto the shore and then proffered Addalyn a hand so she could disembark.

She took his hand delicately, her skin electrified by his touch and guidance as she stepped onto dry land.

It was quiet here. Darkened beneath the canopy of trees.

'Are we allowed to be here?'

'Probably not.'

'How do you know there's a folly?'

'I read about it once. When we moved here. This lake, and the land around it, used to belong to a duke or something.'

'I didn't know that. I've lived here all these years and never knew.'

He smiled at her and reached for her hand as they walked along the narrow path through greenery that was waist height.

'He built the folly for his wife. In remembrance of her.'

'Sounds like he loved her very much.'

'She died young, I think, and he pined for her for the rest of his life.'

Addy felt his pain.

'Can you imagine that?' he asked, stopping to turn to her.

'Which part?'

'Being so overwhelmed by grief that you couldn't enjoy life any more?'

She stared into his eyes. 'Perhaps he didn't know how to?'

'Perhaps he never met the right person who could help him.'

Addy didn't know what to say. She didn't have a folly for her father and Ricky, but there was kind of a shrine in the fire station. She didn't want to be like this duke! Pining for those she had lost for her entire life. Because what kind of life would that be? She still had to find happiness. She still had to find the thing or the person that would give her joy. And right now the people who did that for her were Carys and Ryan.

And what would her dad say if he could see her acting this way?

*Take the chance, love! You can't live a life alone.*

'Ryan, I...' Her voice faltered.

She wanted to tell him, to let him know that she hadn't walked away before because it was his fault in any way. But for some reason the words wouldn't come. They caught in her throat. She wanted to say how much he meant to her, how he made her feel, and just how she wished she could be what he needed her to be.

'It's okay. I know,' he said, smiling at her. 'You make me feel that way too.'

She sucked in a breath. What he was saying… what he was admitting… This was more than friendship. This was scary territory. But territory that she just might be brave enough to enter all the same. With him.

The folly emerged up ahead. A stone building once white, but now cobwebbed and grey, with moss, lichen and ivy creeping over its old bones. Parts of it had crumbled away, proving time was not a kind mistress to memories either.

Was Addy going to make a lifetime of grieving?

Or create something new?

Something to celebrate?

Ryan led her up the two stone steps and turned to face her. She held her breath. Afraid and terrified of what he might say or do. And yet at the same time eager and keen for something to happen. Because this was a magical place. She could feel it in her bones. In her blood. In her heart.

'Addalyn…'

'Yes?'

'You mean the world to me… I want you to know that.'

'You're important to me, too.'

'I think we could have something amazing together if we let it happen.'

She nodded, unable to speak now. He was saying all the right things. The things she'd dreamed of him saying. But it was scary stuff. Heady stuff.

'Will you let it happen?' he asked. 'I won't do it unless you want me to.'

Consent. He wanted her consent. He knew she'd be scared and, despite how much he wanted her, he needed to make sure that she was happy. Was determined that she should be the one to decide if this proceeded or not.

She'd tried walking away and it had hurt.

What would happen if she allowed him to take his pleasure with her?

Surely the world wouldn't be cruel enough to take away a *third* firefighter from her life?

She gazed deeply into his dark eyes. Stared intently at his lips. Imagined them on her own.

They were hidden from the rest of the world here. In this spot that symbolised a lost love. Maybe they could find love here? Change the significance of this place even if it was just for them?

'Kiss me, Ryan. Kiss me.'

A slight smile curved the edges of his lips as his head lowered to her hers and the rest of the world drifted away.

# CHAPTER THIRTEEN

HE'D NOT INTENDED to bring her to this island. He'd not intended to run into her at all! Discovering her at the Tutbury cat rescue centre had simply been lucky. Right place. Right time. And now they were both looking forward to rehoming Molly and Curly.

Getting to spend time with Addalyn was an unexpected bonus. First ice creams, then a rowing boat, and now this.

He knew she was scared, and he'd refused to kiss her without her consent. Because there was no way in hell he was going to do anything that would send her scurrying for safety again. He didn't want to represent danger to her. He didn't want her to view him as some sort of risk. He needed her to see him as who he was. Ryan Baker. A man who could offer her happiness and joy if she let him.

The kiss deepened.

He felt her sink against him, heard almost a purr or a growl of pleasure in her throat, and it was enough to stir his senses and make him giddy.

His hands sank into the hair at the nape of her neck as hers came to rest at his waist. He couldn't remember the last time he'd kissed a woman in this way. There'd been no one since Angharad, and their relationship had been dying a slow death since the birth of Carys. She'd not wanted him near her. He'd felt confused. Rejected. All he'd wanted to do was love her. Protect her. Revel in the tiny person that they had made together. But she'd pushed him away, and for a long time he'd felt unworthy. Unworthy of another's love. Unworthy of another's attraction.

Until Addalyn Snow had come into his life.

She loved his daughter almost as much as he did, and he had to be careful not to let that sway his feelings for her. But it was hard not to. She was sexy, brave, clever, beautiful, funny, loving… His desire for her was a powerful thing, and having been told once to stay away when he had feelings for her had been one of the most difficult things he'd had to deal with. And it had come just as he'd been beginning to accept that Angharad's behaviour and desertion from their marriage was more about Angharad than it had ever been about him.

*It wasn't my fault.*

That had been a huge thing for him to accept. To realise that he did have something to offer a woman, but it was about finding the right woman.

And Addalyn, he felt, could be the one.

He needed to let her know just how much she meant to him. This wasn't just a snog…this wasn't

a mere attraction. This was more. Ryan wasn't
playing games. He was serious. All his life was
serious. Personally and professionally. And Addalyn got that, because hers was too.

Maybe she was the only one who could ever
understood him?

When he came up for air, he gazed into her
eyes, noted her full, soft lips and knew he wanted
more.

'Are you all right?'

She shook her head. 'No.'

That startled him slightly. Had he misread the
signals? She'd wanted this, hadn't she?

'I don't understand…'

She smiled. 'I want more. I want all of you.
Here. Now. In this place.'

'I don't have protection.'

She turned her head, kissed his hand. 'I can't
get pregnant, and I haven't been with anyone since
Nathan.'

'I've not been with anyone since Angharad…
Are you sure about this?'

'I'm the most sure I've ever been about anything. *You* make me sure.'

He stared deeply into her eyes. Into her soul.
She wanted this as much as he did.

'All right then.'

He kissed her again, but this time he released
the chains and did not hold back the way he had
a moment before.

His fingertips found the buttons of her blouse and began to undo them.

One by one.

Until his fingertips found flesh and heat.

And after that…?

He wasn't sure he could think straight.

Being with Ryan was everything and more. Her senses were firing as if they were being electrocuted. Short-circuited. Her entire system was in a frenzy of pleasure and ecstasy. He was gentle, yet strong. With the right amount of rough and the perfect amount of dirty.

She'd never made love outside before. She would never have imagined that being out in the open, during the day, in the middle of a public park, with no soft beds or soft lighting, would be anything but uncomfortable. But in actuality she felt no discomfort at all. Because being with Ryan felt so right that it would never feel wrong.

Afterwards, she lay in his arms, feeling so relaxed, so sated, so happy… She found herself wondering what she'd been worrying about. Nothing this amazing could be bad. Her thoughts from before, her entire rationale for staying away from Ryan, were faulty.

They had to be.

She curled into him, her head upon his chest. 'I don't think I ever want to move from this space.'

She felt his smile. Heard it in his voice.

'Nor me. But we only get an hour on the boat, so...'

Addy laughed. 'They can bill us. I'll split the charge with you.'

'Let's stay out here all day, then.'

He gave her a small squeeze and pressed his lips to the top of her head. A little gesture, but it meant so much. Their relationship had taken a step forward and now they were on uncharted ground. But that little kiss told her that whatever waters they waded into next he would be by her side. That they would do it together.

'I wish we could...'

A small gentle breeze blew over her skin and she shivered.

'Cold?'

'It's getting cooler.'

They agreed to go and both stood up, straightening their clothes and making themselves presentable again. Ryan held her hand as they made their way back to the boat, and he helped her into it before pushing it back into the water and hopping in himself.

The boat rocked slightly, then settled as he rowed them out from beneath the weeping willow and back into the sunshine. The goosebumps on her arms dissipated beneath the last warming rays of the sun as he took them back to the boat house, apologising for being late. The guy was fine with it, and they soon got back onto dry land and headed towards the car park.

At her car, they got in together and looked at one another.

'Want me to drop you off at your place?' she asked.

Ryan smiled. 'You could. Or...'

'Or?' she asked with a smile.

'Or you could come back to mine and stay the night. Carys is away, so she won't know, and I rather like the idea of getting you into a hot shower. What do you say?'

Ryan. Naked and wet. In a shower.

'Sounds perfect.'

'Then let's go.'

Addalyn came padding downstairs in her bare feet, her hair wrapped in a towel, wearing his bathrobe. Never before had he ever considered his bathrobe sexy, but with a naked Addalyn in it... It sure the hell was!

He put down the knife that he was using to chop peppers and turned to greet her, pulling her into his arms and kissing her deeply. He simply could not get enough of her.

They'd made love all day. In the shower. In his bedroom. Once against the wall and a second time in the actual bed, where he'd taken his time to take her in and marvel at how she responded to his touch, how she tasted, how she felt... He'd almost forgotten about his own pleasure. He'd just wanted to see her enjoy hers—until she'd rolled him onto his back and trailed her lips down his body, and then he hadn't been able to think at all.

'Can we stay in this bubble?' she asked.

'At least until tomorrow we can. Carys comes back in the evening.'

'You want me to be gone by then?'

'Of course not! But I don't want to give Carys the wrong idea about us.'

'That's fair. I don't want to confuse her either. Best wait until there's something to tell her.'

'Do I tell her that I've seen you?'

'I don't mind that.' She smiled.

'Okay. I'll tell her we chose cats together. That's a cute story.'

'I'd miss out the island chapter, though,' she said.

'And the shower one? And the bedroom one?'

She laughed. 'Of course! Mmm…something smells good. What are you making?'

'A sauce to go with pasta.'

'You don't just use something out of a jar?'

'Carys isn't the biggest fan of tomatoes, so I usually make my own.'

'Can I help?'

They spent a merry hour in the kitchen. They nearly got derailed when he spoon-fed her a taste of his pasta sauce and his thoughts ran away with him slightly, but their hungry bellies kept them back on track and eventually they sat down to eat in front of the television and watched a movie. An adventure flick about art thieves and a heist.

When had he last sat down and watched a movie with a beautiful woman in his arms? Ryan wondered. When had he last felt this content? He couldn't remember. Even with Angharad there had always been an *edge*. A slight nervousness. A feeling of never being fully relaxed.

But with Addalyn he felt as if he could be himself. Totally. Wholeheartedly.

Why was that?

Actually, he didn't need to question why. He knew. His feelings for Addalyn ran deep. He cared for her. Adored her. Maybe he even loved her?

But he wouldn't say so. Not yet. Because he didn't want to scare her away—not when they'd just spent practically all day and evening in each other's arms. A declaration of love now might be too much!

He smiled to himself and laid his head against hers. 'Happy?'

'Very much so.'

Her answer was all he needed.

# CHAPTER FOURTEEN

ADDALYN WAS PACKING up the car, going through her checklist to ensure the vehicle was ready for her shift, when a call came over the radio—a fire at a four-storey building. Multiple casualties, residents trapped inside.

Her blood ran cold, as it always did, as she listened to Control reel off information. There was a possibility that the incident had begun after some kids had been found mucking about with fireworks in one of the flats. She recalled going to that building once before, as a fledgling paramedic. It was always overcrowded, meaning many lives could possibly be at risk.

'Roger, Control. ETA six minutes.'

She turned to look at the town and saw grey-black smoke beginning to billow up into the sky over on the western side. It was rush hour, too. So the roads would be busy. Already she'd calculated the fastest route in her head, and thought about any shortcuts she could take to maybe get there quicker to liaise with the fire crews and the police.

And to think she'd come to work this morning floating on cloud nine...

Her weekend with Ryan, though short, had been the most wonderful couple of days and the most amazing, mind-blowing night. When she'd left him she'd practically skipped away from his house, and for the first time ever had returned to her own home without that feeling of dread, that sense of isolation, she usually felt.

She'd gone home, taken a shower, sewn a bit more of Carys's costume and then spent the rest of Sunday evening retiling the backsplash in her kitchen. She'd changed so much in the house now and made it her own. The repairs and decorations had really helped with the sense of comfort she felt there now. It was as if she'd given the place a new lease of life. The way Ryan was making her feel like a new person. And Addy liked who he had helped her become.

But now they were back to reality—and their reality was that their jobs were to assist with the accidents and emergencies of life. Life or death situations.

Addalyn raced through the traffic, her lights flashing and her siren blaring as she weaved through parked cars and the vehicles that had come to a standstill to let her pass. She forged her way down the centre of one road as cars pulled over to each side, and had to perform an emergency stop when an old lady stepped off the kerb, thinking the traffic had stopped to let her cross.

Maybe the lady couldn't hear or see very well,

but she almost jumped out of her skin to see Addy sitting there, waiting in her car, lights circling red and blue.

And then she was going again—always aware, always on the lookout for dangers as she drove. It would be no good if she got into an accident herself when she was needed somewhere else. She glanced at the dashboard clock. Two minutes down. At least another four, maybe three, if the traffic lightened somewhat.

'Scene update. Fire services now on site. Police are cordoning off Bart Road.'

'Thanks, Control.'

Ryan was working today—she knew that. Day shift. He was probably already there, along with Paolo and the others.

She tried not to think about him having to go inside a building that was aflame. It was his job. He knew what he was doing. They all did. They were trained for these situations. They practised. People like Ryan and the rest of Blue Watch, they kept calm and steady. They knew what they had to do and how. Knew that fires were tackled in certain ways.

*'The best-known method is something we call direct attack,'* she remembered her brother saying. *'We aim to suffocate the flames at the base of the fire. To do this effectively we must have a clear line of sight to the fire. Then there's the combination attack method, where we use direct and*

*indirect attacks on the fire to help fight the over-head gases and the flames as well. Or we have the two-line-in method, when we have to deal with a fire in high winds. A solid stream and a fog nozzle work best with those.'*

She could see her brother now, sitting at the breakfast table, trying to show her using the salt and pepper shakers as props and the cereal boxes on the table to represent a building.

That very day he and her father had been killed. She remembered because afterwards, when she'd raged and screamed and cried, someone had patted her on the back, trying to soothe her with words.

*'They knew what they were doing. It was just an accident.'*

There were high winds today, so maybe the two-line-in method, then?

Traffic began to back up and clog as she got closer and closer to the site. She had to honk her horn a couple of times, to get people to move, and slowly but surely she crept her way up the road.

Bart Road sat at an intersection with Williams Street, and now she could see what she was responding to. One of the blocks of flats—a four-storey building called Nelson House—was billowing thick, black, choking smoke from almost every window. The outer walls were darkened with soot and orange flames roared furiously out of the ground-floor and second-floor flats, moving upwards.

'Holy hell…' she muttered, looking for a place to pull over and park.

Her gaze was caught by a couple of firemen helping two people away from the building. Probably residents, they were coughing and choking furiously, their skin smoke-stained, and one of them, she could see from her position, had burns to the back of one hand.

Addy leapt into action, slinging on her high-vis vest and getting the attention of two other paramedics to attend to the burn victims.

The fire crews behind her had many hoses pointed at the building, jets of water streaming in through the broken windows to the flames within. Around the site sat many people, shocked, stunned, coughing—residents who had escaped.

But how many were still left inside? Trapped? Terrified?

'Sit rep?' she asked Paolo as she reached his side.

They spoke a shorthand that might seem strange to others, but it was something they knew well, and he brought her up to speed.

There were still people trapped inside and he'd sent in some men to rescue them.

Addy looked at the building, at the fire that still seemed to be out of control and raging inside, and tried to imagine having to walk into that. How had her dad done it? Her brother? How did Ryan do that?

'Who have you sent in?'

'Ryan and George. White Watch have sent in two, as well.'

Ryan was inside.

She tried not to focus on that one piece of information. It would not do her any good to imagine him inside that hell on earth.

'How many do we think are still trapped?'

Paolo looked at her with a frown. 'Unknown.'

'So how will they know when to stop looking?' she asked with concern.

It was a question she had never asked before, and she'd only asked it because she knew Ryan was inside. She didn't want him in there any longer than was necessary. She wanted him *out*.

Paolo glanced at her with a raised eyebrow. In all the time they'd worked together she'd never sounded worried, because she'd always slip into work mode. Businesslike. Stoic. Calm. She'd never shown fear before, and he'd clearly heard it in her voice.

'When the fire gets too great or the building becomes unstable.'

*Unstable.*

Immediately she saw in her mind's eye the building that had collapsed right in front of her, killing her father and brother in an instant.

Addy felt sick.

'Right.'

Paolo turned to her. 'Addy? If this is too much, then maybe you should—'

'It's not. Too much. I'm fine. I have a job to do.'

And she walked away from him towards the gathering patients to assess and triage quickly, so that the other paramedics knew who to attend first, who were walking wounded and who were fine.

It was odd that even with something like this there were people who could walk away without a scratch. It had happened when Ricky and her father had died. People had lost their lives that day. Firefighters and residents alike. But some had escaped without even a cough.

She tried to concentrate. Tried to do her job. But with every shout, every yell, every call, she looked up, distracted, often needing to pull her focus back to her patients with grim determination and fight the desire to stand in front of the flames and yell Ryan's name.

Addy dealt with burns and smoke inhalation. A broken wrist from a fall. A fractured femur in someone who had leapt out of their second-storey window. And then she heard it. A rumble, a crash. And she turned to see a new cloud of thick, black smoke puff up into the air as the roof of the building collapsed and flames leapt into the air.

'*Ryan!*'

The heat was unbearable. Ryan was sweating non-stop, and he could barely see anything through the thick smoke as he emerged from the stairwell to check for anyone stranded on the top floor. People had told him there were others still up there. Residents trapped in their rooms. They'd heard the screams.

The stairwell was the safest place in the building. Made of concrete, it couldn't burn—not like the rest of the place, which had seemed to go up like dry tinder. It was an old building. Built during the sixties. No doubt with cheap materials and the work contracted out to save money. And this was the result. A highly flammable building, overflowing with families and children. Pets.

He'd already guided out three families. Saved over twenty lives.

'You must get Mustafa! He lives in flat forty-two. He's bed-bound and blind!' someone had told him.

He'd promised he would, sending the families down the stairwell and out into the fresh air to be treated whilst he remained and surged upwards. George trailed behind him. George was a seasoned firefighter and they worked well together. He trusted his life to him.

The fire was working its way up through the ceiling of each flat now, and when he emerged onto the fourth-floor corridor the smoke was thick and black and flames licked from beneath the doors of one or two flats. Yes, they would check flat forty-two—but they had to check *all* the flats, just in case.

He kicked down a door and called out to see if anyone could hear him over the noise of the consuming flames.

'Is there anyone in here?'

He looked in the narrow kitchen, the living space, the bedrooms, the tiny bathroom, edging along the sides, avoiding the gaping holes in the burnt-through floor. He knew lots of people would hide in bathtubs, after soaking themselves with water. But this flat was empty.

Eventually they got to number forty-two. Smoke poured out from beneath the door and Ryan burst it open, calling out.

And he heard a voice.

It was weak. Croaky. Scared. Coming from the bedroom.

'Stay where you are! We're coming for you!' he yelled, unsure if the old man would hear him.

Fire had burst through a hole in the floor in the main hall and the smoke was thick and dark, billowing like steam from a kettle.

George followed behind him.

'Let's maintain our exit!' Ryan shouted.

George nodded as he checked through a doorway to find a small storage area, cluttered with towels and cleaning equipment.

He watched as George grabbed the towels and took them into the bathroom to douse them with water. If they reached Mustafa in time, they might help in getting him out.

There was the sound of something breaking. They paused their advance long enough to check it was nothing in their immediate vicinity and then continued on down the hall to the bedroom at the end.

The hall was cluttered. Filled with newspapers and scientific journals. It would all go up like tinder if the flames reached them, effectively blocking their exit. They had no time to lose.

Ryan surged forward and checked the bedroom door, to make sure it wasn't hot before he opened it, and when he did he saw an old man, huddled in bed, coughing and afraid.

'Mustafa?'

'That's me.'

'I'm Ryan, and I've got my friend George with me. We're with the fire service and we're going to get you out of here, okay?'

'That would be wonderful, my friend.' He coughed again. 'COPD.'

'Or maybe just smoke.'

Ryan smiled as he wrapped Mustafa in the wet towels, apologising for how they might feel.

'I would rather be wet and cold than dry and burnt.'

'Good attitude. Right. Let's get out of here. Can you walk?'

'No.'

'Then we'll carry you—but we must be quick. We're losing flooring with every second.'

'Do what you must.'

Ryan hefted Mustafa into his arms. He barely weighed anything—all skin and bone. The wet towelling seemed to weigh more. He checked their exit, saw that it was still viable, and began to thunder his way back down the corridor. There was another crash behind him and he turned to check on George. He was right behind them, but the flames that had begun licking up through the floor had reached the pile of papers and magazines and was beginning to feed.

And that was when he saw it. Down at the bottom of the pile, leaning up against the wall, almost hidden by the journals, was the top of a gas canister. A canister of oxygen.

*Mustafa's COPD.*

'Damn. Let's go!'

He practically ran from the hall, out of flat forty two and into the stairwell, and then began running down the stairs as quickly as he could.

When the whole building was rocked by an explosion Ryan fell to his knees, rolling expertly to protect Mustafa from the concrete steps, and all around him the world went black. A high-pitched ringing noise was the only thing he could hear after he briefly banged his head against the floor and came to a stop.

And then all vision was lost as thick plumes of dust and dirt and soot filled the air.

# CHAPTER FIFTEEN

THE TOP FLOOR collapsed in on itself, it seemed, and Addy couldn't stop herself from screaming out Ryan's name.

'Ryan! *Ryan!*'

She surged forward, only to be held back by Paolo.

'No, Addy. You can't go in there!'

'But Ryan's in there. It can't happen again! It can't!'

Paolo wrenched her back and stood in front of her, staring into her eyes until she made eye contact with him.

'Stay. Out. Here. Let us deal with this.'

Addy began to shake, shudder and cry. She couldn't think. She couldn't deal with this. It was just so awful, so horrible...

Ryan could be in there—could be trapped. Maybe pinned down by a concrete pillar or a beam? Maybe knocked unconscious somewhere, unaware of the flames getting closer? Or maybe he was dead already? Killed by smoke inhalation so severe that he had been completely asphyxiated.

She sank to her knees, realising that she was

of no help now. She couldn't help anyone. That wasn't what she was there for. All she could do was stare at the building and feel such pain that...

She blinked. Were those figures coming out of the flames? Or were her eyes just so watery from her tears that she was imagining things?

It looked like two figures. One was misshapen and blackened...the other looked like a fireman...

And then the smoke cleared as they got closer and she realised it was two firemen, but one was carrying a man wrapped in towelling. He lowered the man to the ground, once they were clear, and pulled off his helmet.

*Ryan!*

Addy surged forward and ran to him, almost knocking him over when she reached him.

'You're safe!'

He was bleeding. Blood had trickled down his scalp and dried on his face, which was riddled with sweat and soot.

'This is Mustafa. Registered blind and with a history of COPD.'

Ryan staggered to his feet to give her room to treat him and she literally had to force her brain to go into medical mode. She didn't want to treat anyone. She wanted to make sure that Ryan was okay. He looked so pale...he looked as if he was going to pass out.

'Ryan, are you okay?'

'I'm fine. I'm just...' And then he sank down

to his knees and keeled over, his eyes rolling into the back of his head.

She wanted to go to him, but couldn't. Other paramedics rushed forward to treat Ryan as she dealt with Mustafa, getting him further away from the burning hazard that was his home and towards the ambulances.

She knew she couldn't give him full-flow oxygen as that might be damaging to someone with COPD and could cause hypoventilation. But Addy almost couldn't concentrate. Couldn't do her job. Her mind was focused on Ryan and whether he was okay. He had a head injury—that was clear.

She managed to get the attention of another paramedic and passed the care of Mustafa on to him. He deserved the best medical attention he could get and she was distracted. Couldn't think. Was panicking.

And that made her useless.

She could not do her job because of how she felt.

Addalyn sat in one of the horrible plastic chairs that hospitals always provided in their waiting areas. It was green, with a questionable bleaching stain on the seat, but that didn't matter. She sank into it gratefully, her mind awhirl, as she tried to gather her thoughts and think straight for the first time since the fire.

She had a decision to make. Maintain her relationship with Ryan or walk away. And, as much as

she loved him—for she knew now that she did—
she knew that being his girlfriend, or whatever
she'd be classed as, meant facing days like today.
Over and over again.

Did she have the strength?

Or she could walk away. End it now. Create distance between them. Go back to being just colleagues and try to forget the last couple of days of
bliss. Consider them a gift. A cherished memory.
Walk away to keep her sanity and what remained
of her heart intact.

But first she needed to know that he was all
right. His head injury meant that he'd been taken
to Accident and Emergency. He'd probably be
needing stitches or glue for his scalp laceration,
and maybe an X-ray to check for any skull fractures—though he hadn't shown any signs of anything as horrific as that.

He'd been lucky.

They'd been lucky.

But was it lucky to have gone through what
she had?

Because to her it had felt like hell. That building's top two floors had slowly collapsed, as if in
slow motion, and the horror of losing her dad and
her brother had come rushing back. The feeling
it had engendered in her—hopelessness…impo-
tence…pain—was not something she wished to
experience ever again.

A doctor holding a patient's file came into the waiting area. 'Addalyn Snow?'

She stood, felt her mouth dry. 'Yes?'

'I'm Dr Barclay. Come with me, please. Ryan is asking for you.'

That meant he was okay, right? Conscious. Capable of forming sensible sentences.

She followed Dr Barclay to a cubicle where a dirtied, smoke-stained Ryan sat on a bed, having a gauze patch taped to his head by a nurse.

'Eight stitches and no broken bones,' she explained as Addy looked at her in fear. 'He's got a tough skull, this one.'

'Numbskull, more like.' Ryan grimaced, giving a half-smile.

His eyes had lit up at seeing her approach, but she could see in his face that he didn't know what she was going to say.

'I'm sorry if I scared you.'

Sorry. He was sorry. But it wasn't his fault. He'd been doing his job, after all, and he'd saved that old man. Risked his own life for it. He didn't have to apologise.

She did.

'I've never been so scared in my life.'

She stared at him, wanting to say more, but the nurse was still there, and the doctor, so she turned to them.

'Would you mind if I have a moment alone with him, please?'

'He's all yours,' Dr Barclay said. 'He can go home. You're a hero,' he said to Ryan, turning and shaking his hand before he and the nurse left.

Alone in the cubicle with him, Addy felt terrified all over again. 'I'm glad you're all right.'

He smiled. 'So am I.'

He held out his hand to her, as if he wanted her to be nearer. To hold her. Touch her.

And she wanted that too... But she couldn't do it.

Addalyn took a step back—a hint at what was to come.

'I'm very glad that you're all right. More than you could ever know. But—'

'Addalyn, you don't have to do this.'

'Don't I? I had to stand there and watch again— *again, Ryan!*—as a building collapsed into itself with someone I love inside.' She laughed bitterly, feeling tears burn her eyes. 'Losing one person in a fire is a tragedy, two is ridiculous—but three? Do you know what it does to a person to stand there and feel helpless? To watch as their world crumbles before them, knowing that they can't do a thing about it?'

'It must have been awful.'

'It was. Words aren't enough to explain how I felt in that moment when I thought you might be dead. How much I hated Paolo for holding me back from running into a burning building. And how relieved I felt when I saw you emerge from the flames.'

'But I'm okay, Addy. I'm okay!'

'I know. And I'm glad. But I can't keep doing that to myself, Ryan. I can't keep putting myself through that. We work in the same field; we know the risks. I couldn't do my job!'

'What?'

'My job. I needed to help Mustafa and I *couldn't*—because you'd collapsed and my fear for you stopped me from doing the one thing in this life that I can do well! I love you. I do. But being in love with you is painful, Ryan. It hurts. It burns me. And I can't be burned any more.'

Ryan looked down at his shoes. 'I'm sorry.'

'Don't be. You did your job. As the doctor said, you're a hero. And I'm so glad that you get to go home to Carys tonight.'

'I'd love to come home to you too.'

She smiled sadly as tears dripped down her face. 'Me too. Goodbye, Ryan.'

And she turned and walked away, her heart breaking as she walked away from the man she loved.

The man who caused her too much pain to be with.

# CHAPTER SIXTEEN

LIFE WASN'T THE same after Addy walked away. At first he'd felt shock, then anger. He couldn't help what he was! He was a firefighter and she'd known that from the get-go. He was not going to change the job he loved. And with the anger had come the thought that maybe he and Carys were better off. His daughter had already experienced a flaky mother—she did not need to experience her dad's new girlfriend not being dependable either.

Because that was what he knew he needed. Someone he could rely on. Someone who would love him no matter what. Who would accept what he did for a living and not ask him to change. He'd never ask Addy to stop being a paramedic. Stop doing her job! He would be better off finding someone who was strong enough to be by his side for all of life's little foibles. Not someone who was going to run every time life got hard.

But even though he kept telling himself that he didn't need Addalyn in his life, and even managed—sometimes—to convince himself of this, every time he saw her at work it was hard. He tried to not be around when she was on the scene, avoided her as much as he could, but today was one occasion when he'd just got his timings wrong.

'Addalyn.'

He gave her a nod of acknowledgement, hardening his heart, telling himself that being polite was more than she deserved.

But ye gods, it was hard. Seeing her was a torture. He might have told himself he no longer needed her, but he wished somehow he could make his body and his heart understand that. He wanted to stand by her. Touch her. Let their fingers intertwine and share a smile with her. Just to see a smile on her face when she looked at him would be enough…

'Ryan! I didn't know you were on today.'

They'd been called to a small village where, after a particularly heavy amount of rain, there'd been a flood from the local river. It had broken its banks and flooded streets and homes and many people had had to be evacuated.

'I think most of us are here,' he managed to say, knowing that fire services from many local areas had sent in teams of rescuers.

'Of course. And…you're well?'

'Very.'

'No problems since the head injury?'

'No.'

'That's good.' She nodded, all businesslike. 'I'm

very pleased to hear it. Don't let me stop you. I'm sure there's plenty you need to be doing.'

'We've finished evacuations. I think we're going to try pumping some of the water out of the infant school.'

She nodded and turned away from him. Dismissing him? She was discussing her plans with Paolo, as she often did when she arrived on scene.

He hated it that she'd made him feel as if he was surplus to her requirements. That he was nothing.

'That's it?'

Addy turned to look at him, alarm showing on her face. She glanced at Paolo, before looking back at him. 'I'm sorry?'

'That's all you have to say to me?'

'I'm not sure there's anything else to say, Ryan. We've said everything.'

Paolo took a step between them. 'Baker. You're needed at the school.'

He gave Ryan a look that said *You don't want to do this*. And, no, he didn't. But he couldn't help himself.

'Did you ever think about *me*?'

She looked shocked.

'Did you ever think about how much *I* worry about *you*? *Your* job? You're a HART paramedic! You could be hurt! You could die! And I'd be the one left behind. Me and Carys. And I can't let my daughter be abandoned again.'

Ryan stalked away, feeling a fire in his blood

that took some time to douse. He occupied himself in pumping out the water from the school and focused hard on the job. By the time he'd done everything he could, Addalyn was gone.

He knew he should have handled it better, but things had still felt so tense between them.

When he got home he tried to be present for Carys, who was happily chatting about a project she was doing at school with her best friend Tiffany. Something about a poster… But it was hard to concentrate.

'Dad?'

'Huh?'

'I asked you a question and you didn't answer me.'

'Sorry, honey. I was miles away. What was the question?'

'When can we go back to Addy's house? I haven't finished my jigsaw,' she said.

'Um…that might be difficult for a little while. I think she's busy.'

'Oh. Can we knock on her door and ask?'

'Er…maybe. Not tonight, though.'

'Of course not! I'm in my jammies, silly.'

She began to giggle and carried on playing with a doll that appeared to be having a tea party with some teddy bears.

'But we can go and see her new cat when she gets it, can't we?'

He nodded. 'I'll have to ask. She'll want it to

have time to settle in, I should think, and get used to its new home before strangers can come in and cuddle it. It might be scared.'

'Like Molly might be when we get her?'

'That's right. She'll need time.'

He thought about what he'd said. Did Addy need time because *she* was scared? And, if so, time for what? To process? To understand? To change her mind? Had he been too hasty in judging her? She'd been through a lot.

He tried to imagine how she must have felt when he was trapped in that building. She'd lost her father and brother the same way. Watching from outside. And that day she'd known it could happen again, with him inside. No wonder she had panicked! She must have felt awful!

Guilt filled him at the way he'd raged at her earlier, and he wondered if it might be too much to give her a ring and ask for a chat? Clear the air a little? Maybe let her know that he would still be there for her if she needed him?

But he didn't get time to ring.

Because the doorbell did.

Addy stood on the doorstep and tried to calm down, her nerves doing nothing to still the trembling in her body. She'd thought long and hard about her decision back at home, sitting there and staring at Carys's completed Halloween costume. She wanted Ryan's little girl to have it. After all, a promise was a promise, and she would never, ever want to let Carys down. But also she felt she needed to talk to Ryan. Clear the air.

His lights were on, and she thought she could hear the TV, so they were definitely in.

She raised her hand and pressed the button for the bell again, hearing it ring inside.

*Oh, God, what am I doing?*

Through the patterned glass she saw Ryan walk towards the door. Her heart began to hammer even faster and her mouth went dry.

*I won't be able to speak.*

Ryan pulled the door open and stood there, looking gorgeous as he always did. He wore a black crew neck jumper and blue jeans. His feet were bare.

He stared at her in surprise. 'Addalyn. We were just talking about you.'

*Oh. Okay.*

'You were? Nice things, I hope?'

Her voice lilted upwards at the end of her question.

*I sound Australian.*

'Carys was asking about coming to see Curly and working on her jigsaw—but don't worry... I told her you were busy and that Curly would need time to settle in.'

'Oh. Right. Okay.'

He seemed calmer than earlier.

They stood there for a moment, staring at each other.

'What's that?' He pointed at the parcel under her arm, wrapped in rose-pink tissue paper and tied with a pretty bow.

'It's Carys's Halloween costume. I thought I'd bring it round. A promise is a promise, after all.'

He nodded. 'Want me to call her?'

'I would like to see her. I've missed her.'

He turned and shouted behind him. 'Carys! There's someone here for you.'

*Someone.*

'And I'd like the chance to talk to you also, if I may?' she added.

Now he turned back to look at her, confused, but he didn't get a moment to say anything because Carys barrelled past, straight into Addalyn's arms, and clung on like a limpet.

'Addy! I've missed you! Can I come round soon?'

Addy laughed and gave her a squeeze. 'Of course you can! You're always welcome in my house.'

'We're getting a cat called Molly!'

'I know you are.' She playfully tapped Carys on the nose and set her down on the ground. 'Listen, I need to talk to your dad. Why don't you take this?'

She passed Carys the now crumpled tissue-wrapped gift.

'For me?'

'For you,' she said with a smile, watching with

joy as Carys ripped it open to gasp in delight and awe at her tiger costume.

'It's got a tail, Dad—look! And teeth!'

'I can see! Carys, honey…why don't you head upstairs and try it on for size?'

'Okay!'

Carys dashed up the stairs, her little feet thudding so hard it sounded as if a herd of wildebeest was passing through.

Ryan stepped back and invited her in.

She passed by him and headed to the lounge, feeling apprehensive. The easy bit was done. The hard part might just be impossible…but she had to try.

'Thank you for letting me speak to you.'

'I wasn't sure you'd ever want to speak to me again.'

'Of course I would. I would always want you in my life. I've just had to deal with some pretty strong emotions. Ones that I wasn't ready for. Or didn't think I was ready for.'

He nodded and she took a seat, whilst he settled onto the couch opposite her.

From upstairs there came a thump.

'I'm okay!' they heard Carys yell, causing them both to smile.

Addy sucked in a breath. 'I panicked. Before. At the fire when I thought you were trapped, and then again afterwards when you made it out.'

'You panicked when I made it *out*?'

'Yes. Because I knew in that moment that if I stayed with you I would have to experience that feeling over and over again.'

'Right. Of course.'

He looked disappointed. But she needed to lay the groundwork before beginning her explanation. 'I've taken a long time to think about things. Work through my emotions. I even went to a couple of therapy sessions. And that stuff's not cheap.'

She tried to make a joke. Lighten the mood.

'We all could probably do with therapy,' said Ryan. 'No matter who we are. What did you learn?'

'That I felt like a nobody.'

'A nobody?'

'I don't like feeling helpless. Or out of control. I've had it all my life, Ryan. I couldn't have children, no matter what I tried, and I lost the chance of having the family I'd always dreamed of. I thought getting pregnant, having a baby, would be easy. Natural. It wasn't. And when Nathan left me for someone who could give him the family he craved, it made me feel like…'

Her emotions threatened to overwhelm her in that moment.

'A nobody?'

She nodded. 'Like I was worthless. Useless. That I had nothing to offer anyone. That's why my job has always been so important to me. Because I make a difference! I save lives!'

'So do I.'

'Yes. You do. And that's why I know I could never ask you to change who you are—because it's important. Very important. Both our jobs are.'

'I'm glad you agree.'

'When I lost my father and my brother I felt so incredibly alone. I felt so incredibly unseen. All I did was work. I told myself that I couldn't get close to anyone. That I couldn't love anyone. Because everyone I loved left me alone and hurting and in pain. It seemed simpler to be alone.'

'And then I came along...'

She smiled. 'You came along. You brought life and warmth back into my life. I was scared of it. Scared of what you'd made me feel for the first time in ages. I felt like I mattered. Like I wasn't alone. And you brought me so much joy! So when I thought I'd lost you, I felt like I was going to lose myself all over again...when I was just beginning to live.'

He reached across for her hand. Squeezed it.

'In that moment when I thought I'd lost you I felt like the world was trying to tell me that it would take everyone from me, and I stupidly thought that if I stayed with you then I would lose not only you, but Carys, too. That something horrible might befall you. And I didn't want to be responsible for that.'

'It wouldn't be your fault.'

'I know. The therapist said the same thing. She

made me realise that my life alone was more painful than my life with those I love. That I cannot control what might happen to anyone and that's okay. I'm not meant to be in control of that. But that doesn't mean I need to punish myself by staying away from people. I deserve love, and I deserve to feel like I matter. And, more than anything in the world, I really, really want to matter to you and Carys.'

'What are you saying, Addy?'

'I'm saying that... I love you. And that terrifies the hell out of me. But what terrifies me more is being alone. I feel we have something that could be amazing and beautiful if we let it. If you're willing to forgive me.'

She let out a shuddering breath. Had she said it the way she'd wanted to? No. Even though she'd practised her speech in the car, and at home, and on the walk over she'd forgotten bits. Missed bits out. Got confused. But she had spoken from her heart, and she hoped that he would appreciate that even if he sent her packing. Because she'd had to try. Had to say sorry. Even if he wouldn't allow them to be together.

'Thank you. For all you've said.'

He paused for a moment. Was he practising his own speech? she wondered.

'I was hurt when you walked away. Confused and angry. Which I want to apologise for. I should never have shouted at you like that. In front of

Paolo, too. I thought it might make me feel better to blurt it all out, and it did for about a second, but afterwards…?' He frowned. 'Every time I try to love a woman she walks away from me. So I know how you feel!'

He smiled ruefully, before his face grew serious again.

'I vowed to never bring a woman into my daughter's life unless I knew I could depend upon her—because it's not just me that's had someone walk away from them. It's Carys too. She had a mother who one day may make *her* need therapy. *Why wasn't I good enough for her to stay for?* I didn't want her to think that you'd done the same thing, so she doesn't actually know that we fell out.'

'Oh. Well, that's good. But I would never have stopped contact with Carys. I would have asked you to consider letting me stay in her life even if I couldn't be in yours.'

'Really?'

'Yes! Absolutely! I could never imagine walking away from her. Her mother doesn't know what she's missing…what a wonderful person she is.'

Ryan smiled. 'I knew in my heart that you would never abandon her, whatever happened. But I have to know you're serious, Addy. Because my job is going to continue to make you feel helpless, and I don't want to be the cause of any more emotional pain for you.'

'I am serious. Relationships aren't easy, Ryan. None of them. They're difficult and they're painful and they're upsetting at times. But people get through because they're a family. I've lost my family twice now, but being with you and Carys has shown me what it's like to be in one again, and I'd rather be there, in a family, loving one another and being terrified, than not be in one. Love is worth the risk. *You* are worth the risk. Carys is worth the risk. I want to love you both. I want to spend my days with you. My nights. I want to soak up every minute with you and enjoy it. Even the difficult parts. I won't run. I won't hide. Because I can't leave you. And even if you do one day have to leave me I will be there. For our daughter.'

He smiled. '*Our* daughter?'

'She feels like mine. I can't stop thinking about her. Worrying about her. This time away from her has been torture.'

Ryan moved from his seat opposite to the one next to her. He stroked away her tears and tucked a strand of hair behind her ear.

'You're amazingly strong—you know that?'

'I've been cowardly.'

'No.' He shook his head. 'You've been incredibly brave. All that you've been through… It would break some people.'

'It almost broke me.'

'But it didn't. You *fought*. For yourself. For us.'

'Us? Is there going to be an us? I can't give you any more children.'

He smiled again. Broadly. 'Yes. There is an us. There has *always* been an us. And there is more than one way to make a family.' He kissed her. Lightly. 'I have always loved you, Addalyn Snow. And I'm going to continue to love you until the end of our days.'

Her heart soared. 'I love you too.'

At that moment Carys jumped into the room with a roar, her tiger tail swinging behind her.

They both laughed, and Ryan swooped her up into his arms.

Addy moved to stand beside them. 'You look amazing. It fits perfectly.'

'We all fit perfectly,' said Ryan.

And he leant in and kissed Addalyn on the lips.

'You kissed! Does that mean you're my daddy's girlfriend now, Addy?'

'Only if you say it's okay,' she answered.

They both looked at Carys.

'Yay!'

And Carys pulled them both in for a hug.

# EPILOGUE

THIS WAS THE perfect place. Now was the perfect time. Addy stood waiting in the bathroom on the morning of her wedding day. Waiting and staring suspiciously and hopefully at a small piece of plastic perched on the back of the loo.

She'd never dared to hope. Never dared believe that the happiness she already had could actually *increase*. Because life with Ryan and Carys, making her new family, had been *everything*.

Of course there'd been moments. Scary moments every time she'd got called to a shout that she knew Ryan was on, knowing that at each job he would be running towards danger, whereas she and anyone who wasn't a fireman would be staying away from it.

But she'd dealt with it. Grown accustomed to the fear and now called it her *'old friend'*. Because that fear only existed because *love* existed. And she was going to hold on to that love for as long as she could. She trusted in Ryan's training. In his skills. He'd survived the army. He'd survive the fire service. And if he didn't—if he got injured or, worse, killed—then she would be devastated, of course. But she would still have had their love, she would still have the many memories that they'd made, and she would still have Carys.

And maybe—just maybe—if this pregnancy test confirmed what she already suspected, she would have someone else to love and care for, too.

The doctors had never found a reason for her infertility, but she'd just accepted that she was infertile. But these last few weeks she'd become tired…occasionally had some tension headaches. And she'd felt bloated, sometimes nauseous. But she had put all that down to the stress of planning her wedding. To sampling lots of cakes—red velvet, lemon and poppyseed, fruit, sponge, chocolate… They'd tried them all.

And then her period hadn't come. It had to be stress, right?

But her period had continued not to come, and yesterday she'd gone out and secretly bought a pregnancy testing kit to use today, on the morning of her wedding.

It seemed right.

It seemed perfect.

Only what if it was negative?

Would it spoil her day?

*Their* day?

Today was a day for unadulterated happiness, and she didn't want anything to mar that!

But she had to know. She couldn't wait another minute.

Addy picked up the test, squeezing her eyes shut and praying to whatever gods there were that this test would be positive. That just for once life would work out for her and give her every iota of happiness it could. That things would go right. That she might go from being no one to being a beloved girlfriend and a beloved fiancée, to being a stepmother, and then to an actual *real* mother to her own child.

It didn't matter that Carys wasn't hers. That she wasn't her biological child. Addy felt that she was hers and always would. She loved Ryan's daughter as if she was her own, and grieved for the fact that she'd never known Carys as a baby. Never held her in her arms and rocked her to sleep.

*Please. Please. Please!*

Her wedding dress was hanging from the shower rail, having been steamed the night before. Her make-up lay waiting for her to apply it. Her hair, wrapped in a towel on her head, awaited the stylist.

And Addy waited too. Fear lingered for one last moment, pausing her hand, before she finally found the strength to open her eyes and look at the result.

Addalyn gasped, putting her hand to her mouth in shocked disbelief.

*Pregnant.*

Laughing, crying, she looked at her reflection in the mirror. She was going to have a baby! Ryan's baby! A sister or brother for Carys! The family she had always longed for.

Everything was perfect.

Addalyn felt happy. Serene.

Not calm. But buzzing!

How to tell Ryan?

When to tell Ryan?

After the service?

At the wedding dinner?

As they danced their first dance?

She tried to imagine his face when she told him. When they told Carys.

They would have picnics. With their children chasing one another as Ryan and Addy sat on blankets on the grass and held hands, watching them.

Happiness and joy were now hers for the taking.

Life only got better and better.

\* \* \* \* \*

# A Baby To Change
# Their Lives

Rachel Dove

# MILLS & BOON

**Rachel Dove** is a writer and teacher living in West Yorkshire with her husband, their two sons and their animals. In July 2015, she won the *Prima* magazine and Mills & Boon Flirty Fiction Competition. She was the winner of the Writers Bureau Writer of the Year Award in 2016. She has had work published in the UK and overseas in various magazines and newspaper publications.

Visit the Author Profile page
at millsandboon.com.au.

Dear Reader,

Book seven—how did that happen?

I loved dreaming up this story—the core of this idea has been in my head for a long time. As ever, my editor Soraya and Harlequin believed in the tale and helped me to shape it to be the very best book for you all to enjoy. As ever, I wouldn't be able to write these stories without my readers, so thank you all!

I sincerely hope you love reading this book and enjoy escaping from the real world, if only for a few hours.

Happy reading!

*Rachel Dove*

# DEDICATION

In honor of the late, great and much-loved
Eric Bell

# CHAPTER ONE

THE IRONY OF meeting her work nemesis on an NHS 'team-building' day was not lost on Lucy Bakewell. She didn't want to be here in the first place and, given what she had just endured, she knew her gut, as ever, had been right on the money. She didn't 'do' people at the best of times, and enforced bonding such as this set her teeth on edge. The last hour had been particularly abysmal: mud, testosterone, stupid, cumbersome apparel and bullets pinging past her ears. It was her worst nightmare.

Well, it was right up there, anyway. Definitely top three, and she was no shrinking violet either. Lucy was used to high pressure situations—at work she thrived in them—but this? This was her idea of pure unadulterated torture, all in the great outdoors. What was even worse than the last hour was her current situation. She was doing something that she'd never thought she would in a million years. Instead of being at work, doing what she loved, she was here, *hiding*, sheepishly hanging out in the huts that masqueraded as toilets, praying for a miracle to get her out of there.

Just as she was wiping the last bit of thick mud off her face, there was a loud barrage of knocking at the door.

'Are you still in there, or did you fall down the pan?' *No way.* She knew that voice. She'd just listened to it howl in pain.

'Er…yeah! Still here.'

*Worst luck.*

She eyed the toilet bowl. If she'd thought she could crawl her way out Andy Dufresne style, she'd already have been long gone. 'I'll be right out!'

She used the last bit of toilet roll in the stall at least to try to look clean before reluctantly sliding back the lock and facing her aggressor. He didn't look amused.

'I wondered if you were in there trying to fake some kind of emergency.'

'Of course not,' she lied. 'Just…freshening up. What is it that you want, exactly?'

He frowned, leaning closer and plucking a glob of mud from her pinned-back light-blonde hair. The masked helmet thing they'd made them wear had destroyed her usual neat and functional look—another reason to detest the day. The guy in front of her looked right at home. He didn't look ruffled, which made her feel even worse.

'Yeah?' His voice was deep, masculine. The kind of voice that you took notice of. 'No mirror in there, I'm guessing?' He looked amused. She could tell he was suppressing a grin. His twitching lips gave him away. 'I just wanted to see if you were coming. They're waiting to start the next game.'

*Dear Lord in heaven, I'd rather deal with an outbreak of diarrhoea and vomiting on my ward than play again.*

She focused on keeping the look of pure revulsion from breaking out across her rather sweaty face. 'Oh, that's fine. I can sit it out.'

He was already moving her away from the hut back to the paint-balling area.

'Not a chance. All participation is compulsory, remember?' She did remember.

*All department heads are to attend. Cover has already been arranged.*

It was so annoying. Also, it wasn't true. Her future brother-in-law Ronnie wasn't here as Head of A&E! She was still salty about that too. Sure, he was only Acting Head, but he was a sure thing for the job. He'd been filling in for two months since the department head had left. He should have been here, if only to endure this so-called morale booster with her.

She didn't need a morale boost, she needed real funding for her department. She needed her nurses and support staff to get paid a decent wage so she could keep them on her team and not lose them to better paid private sector positions. What was running around in a muddy field in the middle of a chilly February going to achieve?

'Anyway,' her adversary continued, unaware of her snarky inner monologue, 'After the last game, I have a score to settle, Lucky Shot.' He pointed to his long, camo-clad legs where a very noticeable and brightly coloured paintball splat was glaring up from his crotch area. Lucy winced; he had her there, not that she'd ever let him know it.

She puffed up her indignation instead. 'I did apologise for that.' She huffed. 'And you didn't have to be such a baby about it. It's not like we're using live ammo, and I've never done this before. I'm not exactly the gun-toting type.'

'Yeah, more Calamity Jane than GI Jane, eh?' he scoffed, making her scowl deepen.

Having her flaws pointed out by anyone was not something she relished, never mind from a stranger who she'd almost maimed.

'You hit that neurosurgeon guy pretty hard in the coccyx,' he banged on, frog-marching her back to her fate. 'He's been icing his backside for the last ten minutes.'

They were almost back at the starting point, and Lucy's anxiety was growing with every step. She could see the other medical professionals all looking around, some brandishing paint guns as though they were extras in an action movie. A couple of them were eyeing her warily. Normally, she would have revelled in the fear she had produced. Today, she felt as if she might end up on the evening news for shooting an ear off a consultant or something. It did nothing to soothe her frazzled nerves, and if there was one thing on this planet Lucy hated it was the feeling of not being in total control.

'Well,' she retorted sulkily, tutting when her jailer jumped away from the business end of the weapon she was waving. 'Why did we need to do this anyway? I barely get time off from the hospital as it is, and now I have to spend an entire day off shooting at other stressed out department heads? I mean, who's running the hospitals while we're all here playing "shoot them up"?'

He chuckled at the side of her, pushing her gun down to aim at the floor as they walked. When she glanced his way, she could see he was almost…smiling. His groin and pride were obviously recovering. He looked as if he belonged here, dressed like a soldier in the woods. He was tall, dark, handsome and rugged with a five o'clock shadow that made him look as if he'd slept rough under the stars after a day wrangling wild horses.

He was different from the other, weedier men on the field today—almost too alpha male to be some department head in some hospital somewhere. Most of the doctors she'd encountered over the years were like Ronnie—softer; geeky, almost—less Bear Grylls and more teddy bear.

Most of them considered golfing a serious sport. This guy, in comparison, looked gruffer than that. He was wood-chopping burly. He probably loved these activities or even did them for fun.

He was kind of cute, she noticed reluctantly. If she ever decided to have a dating life other than a few scattered first dates, he would probably be her type. Not that she'd taken the time to consider what her type was beyond the odd passing thought.

'I mean, look at them all. Hardly the A-Team, are we?'

'Why don't you say what you really think?' he joked, his laugh deep, rich. Stopping short of meeting the others, he came to stand in front of her. 'I'm Jackson, by the way.'

He flashed her a smile that on impact disarmed any remaining snarkiness she felt. Sure, he'd not reacted in the best way to her assault, calling her a 'ridiculous woman', but she'd never been shot in the crown jewels. She decided to let it pass. Maybe her day would be tolerable after all.

'Lucy—Head of Paediatrics at Leeds General.' She shook the huge hand he held out, feeling it dwarf hers entirely.

He shot her one of those smiles again. It made the dimples in his cheeks stand out. Lucy had to look at her feet to stop herself from fawning over him. If her work colleagues back home saw her like this, she would never live it down. Being a ballbuster was something she prided herself on. 'Well, hello, Lucy! It's so weird I met you today, I'm actually—'

'Come on, you two!' The over-enthusiastic paintball instructor, who was ironically named Tag, came and shuffled them both over to the waiting teams. Lucy was on the red team, Jackson on the blue. 'Game two commences in two minutes! Get your masks back on, make sure your guns are reloaded.' He stared pointedly at Lucy. 'And remember, it's the torso you are aiming for. No below the belt shots. Team building, remember?'

Lucy shot him a sarcastic grin, thrusting her mask over her face to stop her from biting back with a retort. She was pretty sure she heard a rumbling laugh from Jackson's direction.

'Positions, people! Let's have some fun!'

Lucy's groan was drowned out by the others' loud whoops.

The second game was even worse. Released from their usual whitewashed, walled workplaces, and possibly hungry for lunch, the medical professionals were unrecognisable from their usual polished and pedantic selves. The second the whistle went, it was all out war between the reds and the blues.

'Let's do this!' one of the red women bellowed. 'For the win!'

'Come on, now!' Lucy tried to placate the baying masses. 'It's just a game!'

'I am not going back labelled a loser! Reds, we win this—we win or die!'

'Slightly dramatic,' Lucy countered, but someone shoved past her and she ended up knee-deep in the mud. 'Hey!' she yelled, her surprise turning to anger when she saw who'd pushed her.

'Blue team, with me!' Jackson growled, taking off for the tree line like some kind of Viking warrior. He turned to look at her when she shouted his name, and she was waiting for him to say sorry when he kept running and raised his gun, pointing it at her breast plate. 'Take the red scum down! Death to the reds!'

Lucy heard the pings and splats of his paintballs sail past as she rolled away. Jumping to her feet, she grappled for the gun slung from her waist.

*Okay, now it's on, jerk.*

'Reds!' she yelled. 'Get it together!'

A short bloke with a red sash ran to her side. 'We're outnumbered! We're never going to make it!'

Lucy grabbed his jacket as he babbled about targets and something about not being made for violence. 'Shut up and fire at something!' she chided, half-dragging him to the tree line further down. Their flag was in the hut near where Jackson had run, and she just knew he was going to try to get the win. Which would not only mean he would equalise, with her scrotum shot having secured their first win by slowing him down, but even worse than defeat it would go to best out of three. Which would mean another game with these hungry, half-crazed knuckleheads. It was getting very *Lord of the Flies*, and she wasn't about to endure this a third time. 'We can't lose this one!'

The man, an ENT specialist from somewhere in Scotland, whimpered as they made the trees and sank to the floor, out of sight. 'We only won the last one because you took out the sasquatch! We have no hope now; he'll be at the hut by now! Emmett won't be able to hold him off; he's only an orthopaedic surgeon, not Rambo!'

Lucy bit her lip. 'Seriously, this is the NHS's finest? We faced Covid, and the government dropping us right in it, and one big dude with a cheeky smile and a gung-ho attitude is enough to terrify you all?'

The woman who'd hollered earlier crawled across from the nearest crop of trees commando-style. 'Basically, yes. I told management that this would suck. I suggested a spa day…'

She suddenly stood up, firing off a volley of shots and punching the air when she heard a satisfying yelp from a distance.

'Yes! Got one!'

'Nice!' Lucy cheered, picking up on the woman's Scottish accent. Pointing at her quivering tree mate, she motioned to the woman. 'I'm Lucy. He one of yours?'

'John? Yeah. I'm Annie. Do you think he breached the hut yet? That Emmett dude is on his own up there. Bigfoot will snap him like a twig.'

Hmm; it seemed Jackson had made an impression on everyone, not just her. She rather liked his height...

*What? Concentrate! He's the enemy.*

If he got that flag, lunch would be even further away, which would mean more of this torture. Looking at John, who was now hugging the tree and reciting anatomically correct body parts like a mantra as the blues hollered in the distance, she knew they were never going to make it.

'I'll try to take him out before he gets to the flag,' she whispered, pointing to the break in the line of trees where their hut stood. 'Make sure our team goes for theirs. Cover me, okay?'

'God speed,' John urged, releasing the tree to hug her and take up position, gun aimed. 'Annie, watch my six!'

Annie was already picking off another blue player who'd popped up at the wrong time.

'Go, Lucy, now! I'll go for the blue flag!'

Lucy closed her eyes, took a deep breath and ran as fast as she could for the hut. 'Thank God I love the treadmill,' she huffed to herself, ducking as a blue player popped up from behind a bush and nearly took off her head. Springing back up, she popped a shot at his leg.

'Ow! I'm out!' he yelped, before slinking off towards the refreshments tent, his gun trailing along behind. Lucy didn't wait to see who he was talking to, nor to see what had happened to make John scream behind her like a banshee behind her. She had one goal: to take Jackson out. Annie was right: he was the real enemy on that team; the others were just following his lead. They would be no match for Annie. Lucy had a feeling she worked in microsurgery or radiology or something, judging by her crack shot. She'd ask her over lunch, she decided, spying the hut with a grin, when they were enjoying their winning feast.

She stopped by the closest barrier, a wooden fence covered in burlap and curved around the edge of the red hut. It was quiet—a little too quiet.

'Emmett?' she called out. Nothing. 'Emmett?'

Still nothing. He wasn't there yet! If Jackson had taken Emmett out, the game would be over. The blue team would be crowing over the rest of them for sure.

The background shots sped up. Annie was going for it, by the sounds of it. Lucy could hear the blues shouting to each other, 'Take her out!' When she heard a string of profanity in a thick Scottish accent, she knew that her number two was holding her own. She saw another barrier nearer the red hut and decided to move position.

The lack of blues heading for their red flag told her that they had a plan, and Jackson was no doubt near, waiting to pounce.

Before her foot hit the floor, she heard it—the snap of a tree root a few metres away. Ducking down, her eyes narrowing beneath the mask, she saw him. Even bent over at the other side of the opposite barrier, he was bigger than her, more noticeable. She waited for him to turn the gun on her, but his aim stayed focused on the hut. He hadn't seen her. She reached for her gun, aware of every little movement of her clothing, the placement of her feet on the forest floor. Even her breath, which was coming out in shallow, excited bursts of adrenaline, filled air.

'Lucy.' She jumped at the sound of her name being called out. 'You got some explaining to do! Where are you? You know the aim of the game is to get the opponent's flag, right?'

She had to bite down hard on her lip to avoid the retort she wanted to throw back at him. *Smug git*. He knew she was there and was trying to get into her head.

*Nice try...wrong woman.*

'Lucy!' he sang out again. The competitor in her was well and truly fired up by this Neanderthal. He'd really got under her skin for some reason. She wasn't used to it, and the fact he was good-looking was a distraction.

Behind them, a volley of shots rang out, raised

voices bouncing off the trees around them. Lucy couldn't make out the voices. She hoped it wasn't Annie getting taken down.

'Sounds like your team to me,' Jackson teased. 'Best of three, eh, Lucky Shot?'

*Not on your life*, she fumed inwardly.

She focused back on him, just in time to see him move from behind his cover. *Now or never*, she realised. *This is for lunch. For the red team. For women doctors everywhere.*

Holding in a jagged breath, she closed one eye, focused on the trigger and squeezed.

*Pop-pop-pop!*

'What the…? Son of a— Ow!'

She scrunched down tight as he came into the clearing with a jump, holding his backside. He pulled off his mask, his head scanning the terrain, and she could see the anger in his expression. 'Lucy! Where are you?'

She stood up, waggling her gloved fingers in his direction.

'Right here, my favourite yeti. I win again, it seems.'

'You didn't win! You shot me in the butt—what do you mean, "yeti"?'

The siren rang out in the distance. Lucy saw Jackson's scowl deepen, and she saw why when she followed his gaze. A huge plume of red smoke was floating above the trees. Turning back to him, pulling off her own mask and letting her blonde hair fly free, she grinned triumphantly. He was glaring at her, rubbing at a spot on his rump.

'Like I said, we win.'

She could hear the others laughing and celebrating a short distance away, and she turned to join them. She was already looking forward to her spoils—a good lunch and an early shower after this enforced activity day.

She was almost out of ear shot when Jackson's words stopped her in her tracks.

'I was telling you something earlier when we got interrupted.'

'Yeah,' she called out, not bothering to turn around.

'Yeah,' he half-growled back. 'I was telling you that I'm the new A&E department head.'

Turning on her heel, she looked him dead in the eye. It was intoxicating, all this winning. She felt as if she could take on the world right then. He was still rubbing at his backside, and she pushed away the pang of remorse she felt at shooting the man yet again—the first cute man she'd seen in a long time too, worse luck. Good job she didn't have time for all that romance anyway. Somehow, work always got in the way somehow or the other. Even winning today had become a bit of an obsession, she realised.

'Congratulations on the job,' she told him earnestly. 'Perhaps your new staff can patch you up when you get back. Just don't tell them a little bitty woman did it, eh?' She bit at her lip, realising she could be a little nicer in victory; Harriet, her sister, was always telling her that. 'Listen, it's just a game. I got carried away, you were being smug… Let's go get some—'

'Smug? You shot me—twice—in two very painful places! I know your type; you have to win, don't you, have to come on top? Seriously, you didn't even want to play the game!'

'Says you! You were acting like the SAS, all testosterone and macho pecs.'

'Macho pecs? Who do you think you are?'

'I think I know your type. Your fragile male ego can't take being outsmarted, with your big old manly chin, and your growly voice. It's paintballing, not war.'

'Oh, yeah, it is.' He snorted. 'You taking a shot at my posterior saw to that. We'll be seeing each other again, so it looks like you'll be seeing my *manly pecs* on a regular basis.'

Lucy rolled her eyes. 'I'm sure we can survive lunch without killing each other.'

'I don't mean that.' He laughed softly. 'A&E at your hospital, Lucy.' He half-limped over to her. 'I'm starting at Leeds General on Monday.'

She felt her jaw drop. 'My hospital?'

This time, it was Jackson doing the grinning. 'Yep. You're looking at the new Head of A&E.'

'I didn't know,' she admitted, her eyes wide with realisation.

'Yeah, well, that was obvious.'

'I thought Ronnie would get the job.' She said this half to herself, thinking about her sister's husband. She knew he'd gone for the job.

*Another reason to hate this dude.*

'So I don't deserve the job?'

'Well, no, but Ronnie is already there—part of the team.'

'I interviewed fair and square. Take it up with HR if you don't like it.' He folded his thick arms against his chest, still bristling with anger. 'It was Ronnie who told me about the job in the first place, if you must know.'

'You know Ronnie?'

He laughed. 'You could say that, yeah. I thought he was joking about you, but I can see now he underplayed his description.'

*What? Ronnie had told this jackass about her? Why was he telling people about her?*

Her defences were well and truly up now. She'd been up for flirting with this guy, and he'd already known who she was. She didn't like it. 'Yeah,' she countered. 'Well, Ronnie said nothing about you, and my world was better for it.'

She couldn't help but smirk, seeing him pout. He raised a dark brow when he saw her mocking expression. His eyes flashed bright, which made her smirk all the more. It was quite fun, sparring with him. At work, people tended to just do as she asked. She wasn't mean, but her need for perfection and absorption in her job often made her come across as curt, aloof. It was kind of nice to butt heads with someone. 'Don't pout, Jackie boy. With shoulders as big as those, I would have thought you could carry an insult a little better.'

He huffed out a laugh. 'Yeah, well, with little sparrow legs like yours, I would have thought you would be used to running to keep up with the crowd.' They both stood there, lips twitching with the need to suppress their laughter. She was enjoying this, but so was he, she realised when he grinned back at her wolfishly.

*What is going on here?* Why hadn't Ronnie told her about this guy, about him being here today? Was her sister matchmaking again?

'Yeah, well, good things come in small packages. I could run rings around you any day of the week. Don't think that I'll give you an easy ride when you come to General.' She fixed him with her sternest gaze. 'We don't play games at work, and if you got the job over Ronnie, well, you had better earn it.' Family was important to her, something to be protected. They didn't need a fox in their hen house, disturbing things, ruffling feathers. When was change ever good, other than in medicine?

'Earn it, eh?' His playful look was long gone now. He was closed off. She might have mourned it if she hadn't been so guarded. 'Well, time will tell, little lady.' He side-stepped her on his way to meet the others. 'I'm Ronnie's brother, by the way—Jackson Denning. I'm sure he mentioned me.'

Lucy almost fainted on the spot.

*His brother? Oh, my God.*

It clicked. Ronnie's older brother, Jackson, was a doctor, working overseas. Harriet had babbled on about him moving back to the UK. As usual, Lucy hadn't listened. 'You're...' She was stumbling over her own tongue now. 'You're his brother, Jackson.'

It was his turn to smirk now. He'd turned around and she could see it now—the Denning jawline, the chocolate hue of his eyes. 'Didn't I just say that?' The fact he was still nursing his bottom while pinning her with his gaze made her face flush for more reasons than one. 'See you at work. Enjoy the rest of your weekend, Trigger.'

He waggled his fingers behind him as if he was pressing a gun trigger, and for the first time in her life Lucy understood what people meant when they said their blood was boiling. Something about the big idiot currently walking away from her made her want to grind her teeth down to stumps.

'You're being childish,' she called after him. 'I didn't know who you were!'

'"You're being childish",' he mocked back in a squeaky voice. 'Be seeing ya, Lucy. Real soon.'

He disappeared out of sight, and she stood alone in the forest.

'Hell,' she muttered to herself. 'Well, you've done it now, Bakewell.'

She started her slow trudge towards camp. Ronnie and Harriet were going to have a field day when they heard.

# CHAPTER TWO

*Five years later*

'HARRIET, YOU KNOW I'll try.'

Lucy allowed her forehead to rest against the large glass window for a moment, listening to her little sister's trademark slow sigh. The one that told Lucy in no uncertain terms that her sister was disappointed. She'd been doing it since they'd been fresh-faced teenagers, taking very different paths despite there only being a couple of years between the pair.

'I know,' Harriet said down the line. 'I get it. I just wanted you there. You know it's just us.'

Lucy lifted her head when a nurse came to check a patient history with her. 'Just a sec, Harry.

'Yes,' she agreed with the nurse. 'Monitor her every hour and call the parents to update them. I sent them down to get something to eat while the tests were being done.' The nurse nodded, leaving Lucy alone again in front of the viewing window of the SCBU—Lucy's little haven, where she came to remind herself why she did the job in the first place. Why she was probably going to miss her niece's second birthday, and why she was currently getting the sigh from her younger sibling. To remind herself why she annoyed her family with the sacrifices she made again and again.

'I'm back, Harriet, but I have to get back to the ward. And you are not allowed to play the "dead parents" card—no other family guilt trip for another month at least. I promise, I will try my best to get there. I already changed my shift, but you know what it's like.'

But Harriet didn't, not really. She'd been a teaching assistant before having Zoe; now she was a full-time mum. She'd never been one for all-consuming careers and motherhood together. She was happy to have taken a few years off to raise Zoe full-time. She'd wanted family more than anything else, and now she was a mother herself—a great mum; the kind who used Pinterest and made handmade gifts and elaborate cupcakes every Christmas. The polar opposite of Lucy, who was a workaholic with half a cucumber and a bottle of vodka in her fridge as opposed to real food.

When their parents had passed away when they'd been younger, Lucy only just an adult, they'd both veered off in different directions. Lucy had devoted herself to medicine and looking after her teenage sister, and Harriet had grown up wanting family life more than ever. The one thing they had in common though, was their fierce love for each other. Trauma was a pretty strong glue, and it held people together.

'Well, Jackson's coming; he took the day off.'

Lucy turned to look back at the special care babies, feeling her irritation grow tenfold at the mention of Dr Perfect. She scowled at the floor, wishing he could feel her scorn through the layers of brick. Being an A&E doctor was hard—and, sure, running a department was hardly a doddle; she could attest to that herself. But still, did he have to make her feel like an idiot in front of her sister?

His Mr Wonderful routine over the last few years had really got on her nerves, if she was honest. He still insisted on calling her Trigger, which made her want to peel off her own skin. He pulled faces at her like a petulant toddler whenever she alone was looking, and he seemed to revel in the fact that he irritated the ever-living hell out of her just by existing in the same proximity. Sure, she did the same to him, but still—he was the jerk in this situation. Sometimes she even wished for a paintball gun, just so she could pop one off again. That day had set the tempo of their working relationship. They were like stagnant embers around each other, fired into life by the other's presence. Every time she crossed paths with him at the hospital, she had to consciously work on not strangling him with her stethoscope.

To make matters worse, he was liked by everyone else. Of all the people to be her sister's brother-in-law, of course it had to be the flashy doc who loved to wind her up at every opportunity. The one guy she secretly fancied even while he was the biggest pain in her butt.

They'd become family after that day. She'd been maid of honour at Ronnie's and Harriet's wedding and he'd been the best man. He was there every time they did something as a family. Family holidays were quite often torture, with Jackson in his bathing shorts, tanned and beautiful, being ogled by women around the pool, while Lucy stuck her head in a book and slathered herself in suntan lotion.

She knew he at her looked too; she could see him run his eyes over her sometimes. He'd make little comments about a new dress. He always seemed to notice when she had her hair cut or did something new with it. It had been five years of tension between them, sexual and otherwise, and it showed no sign of stopping. But he was family, her sister's brother-in-law, uncle to her niece, so she did what she usually did—she buried it. Focused on the fact that, despite the fact he made her pulse quicken, he also well and truly got on her wick.

'Yeah, well, he would.'

Of course Jackson was going. He never put a foot wrong, did he? *Jackass*. Whenever he worked late and missed a family occasion, he was given a free pass by her own sister.

'What was that?' Harriet said down the phone line.

'Nothing,' Lucy half-sang back. 'Listen, I have to go, but I'll see you there, okay?'

'Fine.' Harriet breathed. 'Love you, sis.'

'Love you too.' Lucy smiled back. 'Give Zoe a big hug from her favourite aunt.'

'You're her only aunt.' Harriet laughed. 'I will. See you soon.'

Lucy glanced at the time on her phone before going back to paediatrics. If she was going to try and get to that birthday party, she had to get going.


'Cute, aren't they?'

Jackson took in the little sleeping bundle in the back of his brother's car. Her hair was stuck up in little tufts, and she was sweaty from the afternoon's exertions. She was adorable.

'Yeah, but I couldn't eat a whole one.'

Ronnie chuckled, wiping a stray blob of chocolate off his daughter's cheek. She stirred, her eyelashes fluttering, before her head dropped again.

'You're the worst, you know that, right?'

'Of course. That's why I don't procreate like you.' Jackson leaned in, brushing Zoe's little warm hand. 'She is all your wife, though, right down to those baby blues.'

Ronnie wasn't offended in the slightest. 'I know.

Good genes.' Jackson watched his little brother's contented grin turn devilish. The pair of them were standing by Ronnie's car in the car park of the local soft play area where they'd just partied. Well, if he could call ten very enthusiastic tod-dlers screeching and whooping for two hours on a sugar high partying.

'Speaking of genes, here comes Auntie Lucy!'

Jackson's lip curled into a smile before he could stop himself, seeing Lucy turn into the car park. She practically screeched to a stop a few spaces away. Seconds later, the door was flung open to a chorus of, 'Sorry, sorry! I had an emergency at the last minute I couldn't hand off!'

Jackson watched her face fall when she took in the scene, Zoe tuckered out and sound asleep.

'Oh, no! I missed the whole thing? Really?'

She scooped a huge cellophane-trimmed bas-ket from the back seat and huffed her way over. Jackson saw the tension in her shoulders; she was wrapped up tighter than the over-the-top birth-day gift.

'Sis, I told you not to go mad!' Ronnie, as ever, was thrilled to see his sister-in-law, who looked like his pretty blonde wife. They had the same hair colour and cute little brows sitting over bright blue-green eyes.

That was where the similarities ended, however. Harriet was always calm, collected. The twisted-up pretzel stomping over to them was someone who played a whole different ball game. Even at a kid's party, her face looked pinched. Her eyes roved over the party goers leaving with their progeny, who were all either half-asleep in their parents' arms or still bouncing up and down from their cake and fun overload. Jackson watched her watching them and wondered what was going on in that pretty head of hers. It was kind of a hobby of his, working her out.

Ronnie took the gift basket from her, his eyes boggling at the array of clothes and toys stuffed into the gift. 'This is ridiculous. She's only two, you know, not leaving for uni with the need for a capsule wardrobe. Did you leave anything in the shop?'

She rolled her eyes with a good-natured smirk, and Jackson watched silently as her shoulders started to dip.

'Well, I don't see her as much as I'd like. I have to spoil my only niece, right?' The furrow between her brows returned with a vengeance when she spotted her in the back seat. 'She's asleep.' She looked…disappointed. Jackson could see it written all over her face, just before she hid it behind the expression he was most accustomed to seeing—that of the closed-up professional. The expression that had given her the nickname Medusa at work. Not that anyone dared say it in her proximity; that would be professional suicide. If her glare didn't turn them to stone first, her tongue lashings were strong enough to strip the hide from a rhino.

Personally, he preferred his pet name for her, Trigger. It suited her better. She even answered to it sometimes, when she wasn't thinking, which made it all the sweeter to Jackson. The fact it raised brows from the other terrified staff members cheered him up on the bad days. The irony of him watching her, figuring her out, while the rest of the hospital watched them never lost its sparkle. After working overseas in some of the hottest climates, their banter kept him warm. He couldn't help it. She got under her skin as much as he did hers. In different ways, he thought with a familiar pang that he brushed aside. She was family, and that was that.

'Yeah, sorry.' Ronnie winced. 'She wore herself out in there. She'll love waking up to this, though.' He dipped his head towards the huge gift.

'Yeah,' his sister-in-law murmured, the sadness weighing down her words. 'Sure. I'll just have to come and see her at the weekend—take her to the park or something. Where's my sister?'

Ronnie thumbed behind him. 'She's saying goodbye to the other nursery mums; you know what they are like when they get together.'

Jackson thought he saw another wince cross Lucy's features before she locked it back down under that prickly persona. She looked at him then, as though she'd only just realised he was there. Or, more likely, was only just deigning to acknowledge his presence.

'And I suppose you were here on time.'

Jackson held down the sarcastic smile he almost threw at her and kept it hidden. It would only inflame the fiery woman in front of him. Whilst he normally got a thrill out of it, especially at work, something about her expression made him hold back. He knew she was genuinely upset to have missed Zoe's party. Even he couldn't mock her for that; they both adored Zoe.

'I was. Day off.' He added unnecessarily, 'I'm not on call today either. Good result at work?'

'Tricky, but yeah.'

Jackson nodded back. 'I'm glad. Worth it, then.'

Her gaze slid back to Zoe, still tuckered out in the back seat. Her little blonde curls were ruffled from the breeze coming through the open door. Lucy didn't look too convinced. She was already chewing the inside of her cheek, a tell that she was working something out. He looked away when her eyes locked onto his. She stopped biting.

'Yeah, I guess. Well, I might as well go.' She didn't wait for her sister. She'd be mad, and they all silently acknowledged it. To Harriet, family was first over work, everything else in the world. That was one of the many ways the two women differed. Even being a doctor's wife hadn't softened Harriet on that. Work was the only thing that ever came between them. Jackson thought Harriet harsh at times, but of course he kept that to himself. Lucy wouldn't thank him for voicing it anyway, and he knew that Ronnie had never managed to get through to her on the topic. What Harriet didn't realise was, when they weren't home with Harriet and Zoe, they were saving other people's families. Allowing them to have more time together that otherwise they might never have had.

Ronnie put the gift away to give Lucy a good-bye hug. Jackson didn't step forward; they didn't hug. They clashed when she came down from her department in paediatric care and entered his realm in A&E. The nurses usually went running the second they started to lock horns.

Ronnie had even joked once that Jackson was Perseus. After witnessing one rather heated exchange in the stairwell, Ronnie had sent him a plastic sword and shield. He still had it above his desk at home. It made him laugh every time he saw it. Ronnie was definitely the referee between the two of them at work, and the glue that held the four of them together. He and Zoe, who'd been adored by all of them from the second they'd laid eyes on her.

'Well, thanks for coming. Harriet will understand. You know she just likes the family thing.'

Lucy's brows rose in line with the scepticism Jackson saw across her strained features.

'No, she won't.' Lucy smiled. It didn't meet her eyes, and Jackson busied himself with his phone as Lucy said goodbye to Ronnie, and said nothing as she pulled her car back onto the main road in the direction of her flat.

'Will Harriet really be that annoyed? I miss stuff; she never says anything to me.'

Ronnie shrugged. 'She tries to understand. She takes it different when Lucy's not there. She gets the job; I work enough hours myself. She just thinks differently. Losing their parents hardened one and softened the other.' Jackson had no need to ask which. 'They might be sisters, but DNA is about all they share. You know Harriet—she loves all this.' He waved a hand in the direction of the venue in which they'd just spent two eardrum-shattering hours. 'Lucy just wants different things. Harriet will be fine. I've got a babysitter for tomorrow night so I can take her out. You know, to celebrate the incoming terrible twos.'

Both men's eyes fell back on the sleeping baby nearby.

'I can't believe she's two already,' Jackson commented, marvelling as he always did at the tiny little person his brother had created. 'It doesn't seem like two minutes since you brought her home from the hospital.'

'I remember.' Ronnie laughed. 'It was the last day I got any sleep.'

'Ronnie!' Harriet appeared at the doorway, a bundle of gift bags hanging from her arms. 'Can I have a hand, love?'

Jackson took his leave. He was looking forward to the rest of his day off, away from the bustle of A&E. 'I'll let you get on. Have a good night tomorrow, okay? Send Harriet my love.'

Ronnie was already heading over to his wife, who was waddling towards him with the weight in her arms.

'Will do, bro. Pool next week?' he called out.

Jackson nodded with a grin. 'To take your money again? Try and stop me.'

He waited till the pair of them were heading back to their car before heading to his own, making sure Zoe wasn't alone. As he drove away, he saw Ronnie take the bags from his wife, encircling her in his arms. He looked away, focusing on the road ahead.

*It would be nice to have that one day.*

He pushed the thought away, not for the first time. He wasn't at that stage yet. He wasn't even dating, really. He hadn't met anyone he'd wanted to see beyond a couple of dates. He liked his easy life, working in a job he adored. He had the house, the car, financial stability. Sure, someone to sit on the couch with him would be great, but he couldn't really see what that would look like in real life. He didn't even have time for a pet, so how would he fit his life around a family? His thoughts turned to Lucy—her face when she'd realised she'd missed the party.

*Maybe people just weren't meant to have everything they wanted.*

He was doing fine on his own. The big life plan could wait, for now. There was no rush. He'd come home to put down roots after years of doctoring abroad, and he had plenty of time. In the past five years, he'd adjusted his expectations, that was all.

He headed home, looking forward to an afternoon of gym and rest. There was plenty of time for toddler parties and date nights, he told himself for the millionth time. He had family and friends; the rest could wait. Perhaps the pieces of his life didn't fit as he would like them to. But maybe it was enough that he had them in the first place.

# CHAPTER THREE

*The next day*

JACKSON COULDN'T HELP but smirk as he heard the curtain swish back.

'You called for a consultation?'

'Yeah, I did.'

Lucy looked at the empty bed, her eyes narrowing as she looked at him standing there.

'Well, where's the patient? Triage One, you paged.'

'I put them in bed five—but Trig, wait!'

She'd already turned on her heel, but his hand whipped out to still her. He felt a zap of electricity pulse through him.

*Huh; static of the uniform. Well, we are like repelling magnets.*

Her aqua eyes widened, as though she'd felt it too, before they fell to see where his fingers had wrapped around the flesh of her forearm.

'Don't call me Trig,' she chided as his hand pulled away. 'What's wrong?'

'I needed to talk to you first. I think the child has pica.'

'Okay.' She nodded. 'What was the reason for attending today?'

'The little fella, Tom, aged five—he was helping his grandmother in the garden. Ate a bulb they were planting, or part of it.'

'Did you check whether it was toxic?'

Jackson nodded. 'Dahlia bulb; his grandmother acted pretty quickly. She got most of the bulb out of his mouth, and gave him water. No treatment needed this time, but it's his fourth admission in three months. The last time it was a Lego brick. He passed it without surgery, but I think he needs checking over—there could be more than pica at play here. He presents with some rigid behaviours, sensitivity to some sensory input... He doesn't speak very much, gives minimal eye contact. His mother's on the way; she was at work. The grandmother's pretty upset.'

He pursed his lips, remembering how the little guy's grandparent had wrung her hands together, her eyes never leaving the boy in the bed. Kids had that effect on people. He saw it time and time again. It was also one of the reasons he wasn't in the quickest rush to join the parenting brigade himself. Having that much worry and responsibility on top of running A&E seemed like a step too far—something he was reminded of by his patients from time to time.

'I bet she is, but from what you said she shouldn't blame herself. I remember a kid in my primary school class who used to eat sand. Children do the oddest things; they have no sense of danger. If pica is the diagnosis, it's a compulsion. Sounds like we might need to refer on to the neurodiversity pathway. I can speak to my team.' Lucy took the clipboard from him, her eyes scanning the paperwork. 'Thanks for the heads up. I'll go speak to the family. Have you mentioned your suspicions to them yet?'

Jackson stretched out his aching back with a wince. He'd been in resus before this case, working on a patient who'd had a heart attack in his front garden. He'd been one of the lucky ones, his next-door neighbour being a nurse who'd administered help quickly. The ambulance had blue-lighted him to the A&E doors, but he'd flatlined on the way in and the CPR had been tough. Jackson's back had started to sing during his stint, but he'd ignored it until the man was breathing and safe from the circling drain.

'Jackson? Earth to Dr Denning!'

'Sorry,' he apologised, shaking his head to wake himself up. 'And no, I figured I'd leave that to the Goddess of Paediatrics.' She rolled her eyes, but the usual fire and snark didn't come. He felt a little cheated. She'd been almost genial. Her game was off. Usually when he was feeling a little tired, or off *his* game, sparring with her fired him up and gave him an energy boost better than anything he could get from the vending machines around here. 'Come on, Trig—nothing? No comment back?'

She held the clipboard tight to her chest.

'Nope, I've got to get on. Busy day.'

He came to stand in front of her. 'Every day around here is a busy day. Really, what's up? You weren't right yesterday.'

'You noticed that, eh?'

He raised a brow. 'Spill. Patients are waiting.'

The sigh that rattled through her rib cage ruffled the papers she clutched to her chest.

'Fine, if it will shut you up. I feel like Harriet's mad at me. I rang her last night, and she was okay with me, but…'

'She judged you for not getting to the party?'

Her mouth lifted on one side, making her look oddly vulnerable.

'Yeah, I think so. She bites her tongue most of the time, but…' She bit her lip, and his eyes tracked the movement.

*This is really getting to her.*

'I didn't tell her the full truth, but we did have an emergency. I couldn't tell her how bad it was, of course, I never do. Perhaps if I had, she'd understand finally. I couldn't just leave to get to Zoe's party. Zoe was happy, healthy, eating cake with her friends. Sure, her auntie wasn't there, but would she have noticed really? She's two. She won't even remember the party, but if I said that to Harriet she'd explode!'

She was pacing around the cubicle, Jackson tracking her rant around the small curtained space, letting her get it out before they both went back to work. He rather liked these moments. When it was just the two of them, she was different, less guarded. She let him in. Not for the first time, he wondered what their working relationship might have been like if they'd met in different circumstances. If the dye of his character hadn't been set so firmly in her mind that day. If their families weren't entwined together.

'I...' She trailed off. 'Never mind.'

Jackson didn't want her to stop. 'Go on,' he said, his voice soft, low. 'Tell me.'

She pinned him to the spot with her baby blues, nibbling at her lip. He waited.

'Sometimes I wish she'd trained in medicine, like us, like Ronnie. I wish I could show her some of the horrors we see. The tiny coffins we work hard to avoid for our patients. You get it, and Ron does. Hell, A&E isn't all cuts and scrapes. She doesn't get it. I mean, our parents died in a horrific accident.'

She stopped walking, her free hand covering her heart as though saying the words had produced an ache. 'She remembers that; I mean, it's not something you'd ever forget, right? You'd think she'd be proud of us all, saving people. It's why I...'

The words fell away when her eyes met his

again. He could see the mental shields click back up into place in her mind. Huffing out a breath, she straightened the already collated papers in her hands. 'Anyway, I just feel a bit off today. I hate feeling at odds with her. She's my—'

'Family,' he finished for her. 'I get it.'

The pair stood across from each other, the hospital continuing on behind the curtain, noisy and full of life.

'Yeah.' She shrugged. 'Nothing will mess you up quite like blood relatives, eh?'

He laughed, and she looked surprised.

'Been a while since I made you laugh, eh?'

'Intentionally, yeah,' he agreed. 'I laugh *at* you all the time.'

'And we're back to normal. I'm glad. Heart to hearts aren't our thing, frenemy.' She tapped the board. 'I'll go see the patient now. See you later, Denning.'

Jackson was pretty sure that, before she left, Lucy had a smile on her face.

Hours later, he was still thinking about their talk. The emergency alert on his pager went off, jolting him from his thoughts. The second he got there, took in the scene. He wanted nothing but her—Lucy. He needed her here. She didn't know it yet, but their lives had just changed for ever. Even when the chaos had died down, he thought of that time in the cubicle. He wished that they could go back there. Wished he had said more. They could never go back to being those people, not now. The people they'e been in that moment were gone for ever.

# CHAPTER FOUR

*HOW IS THIS HAPPENING? How did we get here?*

The voice in Lucy's head wasn't as clear as normal. Her usual sharp mind felt as if it had been dipped in treacle, the cogs gummed up with the slush and debris of the last week and a half.

*A week and a half. Ten measly days since she'd last been at work. Since her world had collapsed for the second time.*

This was all she had now: a treacly brain, regrets and the welcoming, numbing feeling of shock and disbelief. It had taken all she'd had to dress this morning and to put make-up on. She'd not trusted herself to drive and, given she didn't remember the taxi ride here, that was a good decision. Better than some of the others, which had been haunting her this past week. Since before the funerals, the two coffins, side by side. She willed the image out of her head, concentrating on something else, anything else. She picked up a magazine from the table next to her and pretended to flip through it.

*I should have been at the party. I never even*

*said goodbye. If I'd known that was the last time,
I would have done better—been a better sister,
a more attentive aunt. I thought there was more
time. Stupid, stupid, stupid.*

'Did the solicitor say what this was about?'

Giving up the pretence of magazine skimming,
she turned to look at her companion. He'd already
been waiting outside when she'd pulled up. The
waiting room of the law firm was roomy, but he'd
still taken the seat next to hers. Which was why
his deep brown eyes were so close, leaving her
feeling exposed under his scrutiny.

She'd caught him watching her a few times
since…that day…a look of concern and wariness
in his big dopey eyes. Those eyes almost seemed
to see right through her, as if he could see the
core of her, when no one else did. It had irked her
immensely. Now, after this, it was torture. She
wanted to tell him to leave, to go back to work
and deal with his own grief. The one person in the
world she had that knew both Ronnie and Harriet
had to be him.

*Ronnie and Harriet.*

Her heart stopped working for a second. She
felt the stutter in her chest when she thought of
them. Of her sister, bloodied and broken on that
gurney. RTA: three little letters that had taken
their brother and sister away. They'd been going
on a date and had ended up dead. The only saving grace was the fact that Zoe hadn't been with

them in the car. She hadn't been lost too. She hadn't seen any of the horror of the aftermath, unlike Jackson and her.

Now they were both here, sitting in this waiting room, once again linked by family...only this time that family was gone for ever.

'Lucy,' he pressed. 'You with me?'

She had to look at the floor to get the answer out.

'He has the will. He said he needed to get things rolling. Are your parents not coming?'

Jackson shook his head. 'No. I spoke to Mum this morning. She didn't know about the meeting.'

'That's weird, isn't it?'

He shrugged. 'This whole thing's weird.'

'Was Zoe okay?'

His face brightened at the mention of their niece. 'Yeah, she's good. Mum said she's been a bit fussy but she's good.' His expression sobered. 'To be honest I think her being there is helping them hold it together.'

Lucy managed a nod. Anything else was blocked by the lump in her throat.

Jackson went to stand by the window, and she took him in for the first time. He looked dishevelled in the early afternoon light. She could make out minute wisps of grey in his longer than usual stubble and dark circles under his ever-seeing eyes.

'What? I know you want to say something.' He

didn't move an inch, aside from moving his lips. 'Out with it, Trigger.'

'Lucy,' she corrected automatically, irritated that he'd caught her studying him. 'You always say things like that. You don't know me, Jackson. You think you do because we were forced to spend so much time together. The only good thing to come out of this will be getting rid of you, actually. We won't have to pretend to get on any longer.'

'Nice. "Forced" was right. You are the prickliest pear I have ever met.'

'Prickly pear? What are you, five?'

'Yep, that's right.' His tone changed. 'I'll be six soon. Gonna buy me a cake?'

'You can shove your cake up your— What the hell are you doing?'

He strode across the room and knelt at her feet in one angry motion. When she went to get up from her seat, he stopped her.

'No, Lucy. What are you doing? Do you see anyone else helping you? We're waiting to see Harriet and Ronnie's solicitor. Harriet and Ronnie are dead!' The flicker of pain across his taut features was hard to miss. 'I know you've decided to just power through this in your usual way, but I'm a human! My little brother died. Your little sister died, and their little girl is here in this world all alone. Why do you not get that? Do you really not see anyone else? The whole hospital is devastated. We lost one of our own. My team is crying in the locker room between patients. Do you not see that?'

His eyes were wide, even darker than normal. 'Do you really not see me? I stood by your side at the funeral. Did you even realise I was there, Luce?' He sprang up, pacing to the window and back. 'I can't take this!'

*There you go, you did it again—pushed too hard. He's right, who else have you got? You've chased everyone away. He has his parents. You have no one.*

She took a steadying breath, willing her heart to stop racing. Her cheeks were flushed with shame and embarrassment.

'I'm sorry. I forget you lost someone too. I do care. I care about the people at work, about Zoe. I care that Harriet and Ronnie are…gone. I just deal with things my way. Grief is different for everyone.'

His sigh rattled the windowpane. 'Your way is to bottle it up. It's not healthy.' Lucy's eye-roll produced an irritated growl. 'See? There you go again, being all snarky when I am trying to get through to you.'

'I didn't say a word!'

'You don't have to! Your poker face doesn't work on everyone. It doesn't work on me. I just want to help, to make sure you face this properly.'

'I don't need your help, Jackson. I never did.' She jabbed a finger at her chest.

'Fine,' he snapped back, sitting at the farthest corner of the room. 'But this is not over, Luce.'

'Don't call me Luce,' was all she could spit back. No one called her Luce. It was Lucy or Dr Bakewell. Trigger was bad enough; he knew it wound her up. 'I don't need help. I'm fine. I just want to get this over with. Get back to normal. Get back to work.' The fact her manager had insisted on her taking a leave of absence didn't help. She needed to work. Rattling around her place, alone with her thoughts, was making her climb the walls.

'Right,' he scoffed. 'Whatever you say, Dr Bakewell.'

She busied herself with the contents of her handbag for a while, Jackson flicking through old magazines so hard she thought she heard some of the pages rip beneath his fingertips. After the longest twenty minutes in recorded history, a secretary came through a set of imposing double doors, inviting them in.

The solicitor's office was just as she remembered it from when her parents had died. A bookcase wall stuffed with weighty tomes provided the backdrop for Mr Cohen's huge walnut desk. The air smelled the same—a mixture of old books, paper and peppermint.

He greeted them at the door, his hair a little

greyer, his stature a little shorter, but still the same comforting presence.

'Miss Bakewell, you're all grown up!'

Lucy couldn't help but laugh. 'I am. How are you?'

She could feel Jackson at her shoulder, hear his awkward cough.

Mr Cohen didn't miss a beat. 'I'm well, thank you. This is Mr Denning, I presume?'

'Jackson, please,' he replied, the smile on his face as broad as it was genuine. Lucy had to look away. Behind that easy welcoming grin, she could see the taut expression as he exchanged pleasantries, see the hollows under his usually annoyingly sparkly eyes.

*Stop it. You can't hold anyone else together. You are falling apart as it is.*

'Please, take a seat,' Mr Cohen instructed.

Jackson took the chair next to hers, flexing his hands on the plaid leather arms.

'So,' Mr Cohen started, tiny little glasses perched at the end of his nose. 'As we discussed on the telephone, Harriet and Ronald left a will.' He eyed them both above the rims, pausing at the delicate nature of the conversation. 'It's pretty simple.' He eyed Jackson. 'Your parents were well aware of the contents of the will when it was written, and I have their agreement.'

Lucy sneaked a glance at Jackson, who looked as surprised as she felt. Harriet had never mentioned a will to *her*. Mr Cohen focused back on the papers in his grasp.

'Now, as to the financial aspects… It is instructed that the house be sold and any monies made as a result of said sale are to be put into a trust for Zoe.'

Lucy nodded along, barely listening as he spoke about jewellery and some other items of Ronnie's that were left to Jackson. The wedding rings were to be kept for Zoe. The pieces of Harriet's jewellery were to be shared between Lucy and Zoe. The ring from her mother was to go to Lucy, to be passed down to Zoe or any daughter Lucy had. Lucy sniffed at this, thinking of how Harriet had thought of her daughter and her, wanting things to be right and passed down to the future generations.

She willed her tears to stay away, blinking hard to clear her field of vision. A movement at her side caught her eye. Jackson was gripping the chair arms so tightly, she could practically hear his nails scratch against the leather. Her own hands flexed, and she held them together on her lap to stop herself from reaching out to him.

*Stay strong.*

Mr Cohen's professional tones pierced through her rampant thoughts a second later.

'As for the care of Zoe, Lucy Bakewell and Jackson Denning are named as her guardians, and are to raise said child together in a home to be determined by the beneficiaries. This will be subject to an initial six-month review to ascertain that this arrangement is working for all parties and benefits all parties. Any monies left in the deceaseds' accounts after all debts are paid are to be used for the purposes of raising said child, and the trust can be accessed through myself if further financial assistance is required.'

The money stuff didn't even enter Lucy's head. She was still baulking at the first part. Jackson looked like a clenched-jawed waxwork.

'I'm sorry,' she spluttered eventually when the sentence that had just rocked the very axis of her world had absorbed into her already addled brain. 'What was that? Joint custody? Me?' She jabbed a finger to her right. 'With him? Not Ronnie's parents—us?'

*Joint custody? Is this a joke?*

Zoe had been with the Dennings since the night of the crash. They were parents already. She'd just assumed... Well, she hadn't thought about it. Ronnie's parents had had Zoe that night, as they'd been babysitting. It had made sense for her to stay there until things were sorted. Until after the funerals were over and until Lucy was back at work. She'd just assumed that was what would happen and what they would want. She'd thought she and Jackson would just be there, Zoe's aunt and uncle, like always.

'Mr Cohen, I might be being dumb here, but I don't get it. There must be a mistake.'

Mr Cohen didn't look surprised at her reaction. In fact, he almost looked as if he found it rather comical.

'There's no mistake, Miss Bakewell. The instructions are clear. They were made when Zoe was born.'

*Two years. Two years and no one had said a word.*

Rounding on Jackson, she poked him hard in the arm. 'I'm supposed to raise Zoe? Me? With him?' He didn't even flinch. Her finger almost snapped as it hit a solid wall of tensed muscle.

'Yes, Miss Bakewell.'

'Lucy, please. This can't be right.' She looked at Jackson again. 'Did you know about this?'

He shook his head, leaning forward and putting it into his hands. 'No, of course not. Mum was being weird, but—'

'But what?'

'But she's just lost her son.' His tone was sober, flat.

'Right.' Lucy nodded. 'Right, okay. Sorry.'

Mr Cohen shuffled some papers in his file. 'I assure you, both Harriet and Ronald—'

'Ronnie,' Jackson corrected.

Mr Cohen pressed his lips tightly together. 'Of course. Harriet and Ronnie were very clear in their instructions. We discussed it at some length.'

'Yeah, well, they didn't tell me!' She was spewing her thoughts out loud now. 'I mean, I thought I might be named. It crossed my mind: I'm Harriet's only family. But why Jackson?'

'Why not?' Jackson pressed back. 'He was my brother. I know Zoe.' His eyes were darting all over the room. Lucy realised he was processing the news too. She was watching his freak-out in real time, as he was hers. She was wringing her hands, still waiting for him to erupt when he let out a surprised little chuckle. 'Ronnie, man.' He kept laughing. 'Well played, man.'

Lucy was apoplectic. 'This is funny to you? Are you freaking kidding me? Mr Cohen, why are the grandparents not named?'

Mr Cohen steepled his fingers together. 'Mr and Mrs Denning are well into their retirement. It was felt that the best chance of long-term stability for Zoe was for her to be raised by the pair of you.'

Lucy took it in, remembering times she'd dealt with patients in situations like this, with injured children orphaned by catastrophe. She'd dealt with enough social workers to see the logic. She and Jackson were both young, financially secure. They owned property. It made sense, if one didn't know their relationship. They bickered and taunted each other. HR had made them sign a waiver due to their legendary spats. They were so sick of hearing about complaints one made about the other they'd drafted a 'friendship agreement', as if Lucy and Jackson were toddlers fighting over the same toy at playgroup. Now they were supposed to sign up for a child together?

*No. Not happening.*

'Fine.' She sighed, finding her shields and barracking herself behind them. She would do what she did when her parents had died. She'd be the mother figure. She'd raise Zoe. She'd helped raise her little sister; she could do this, but she wasn't a team player. 'I am Harriet's only living relative. Zoe's aunt by blood. I don't need a co-parent in this.'

'Oh, really?' Jackson's voice was a gravelly hum. 'I didn't even know you were thinking about taking Zoe on.'

'Taking her on? She's not some project, Jack!'

'And you can't do this alone, Luce!'

Her fist slammed down on the desk before them and made a loud thump.

'Don't call me Luce! You know that drives me crazy!'

Mr Cohen made a loud, 'Ahem,' silencing them both.

'Sorry,' they both mumbled in unison. They were toe to toe, in each other's faces. Slowly, they sheepishly returned to their seats.

Mr Cohen's sigh ruffled the papers in front of him.

'I know that this has been awful. For both of

you. I did try to insist that the pair of you were informed beforehand, in case this event did occur, but Harriet was…reluctant.' His lips thinned. 'I suppose they never thought this day would come. I wish it hadn't myself, but the instructions were clear. Ronnie and Harriet wanted the best for little Zoe, and they chose you—together.

'Now…' He turned over the paper, pushing his glasses back up his nose. 'If one or both of you wish to object to this, or relinquish your guardianship, then there are contingencies in place.'

Zoe went to open her mouth to yell, *hell, yes*. She couldn't live and raise a child with her work nemesis, but Mr Cohen beat her to the chase.

'Lucy,' he addressed her. 'I have seen you and your sister navigate hard times before, and make no mistake, Harriet was the driving force behind this. Ronnie was on board, of course, but your sister, as you know, was a very determined planner. Even in death, she wanted the best. To that end, she left you this.' He opened the file and Lucy's eyes took in her sister's neat script across the surface of a crisp, cream envelope. 'I'll give you a moment. Jackson, would you like to follow me? We have refreshments waiting.'

Lucy didn't take her eyes from the envelope as the two men shuffled out of the room and didn't take in their muted voices or their back and forth. As soon as the door clicked closed, she reached and tore open the thick paper, her eyes brimming as she saw her sister's final words laid bare before her.

*Dear Big Sis,*

*If you're reading this, then the worst has happened. I'm gone, and my Ronnie too. I'm sorry I had to leave you, dear Lucy, but I want you to know that I love you. Fiercely. Always have, despite our differences. When we lost our parents, you barely into adulthood yourself, it bonded us for ever, but divided us too. I might have been the little sister, but you were always much more than an annoying older sibling to me. When Mum and Dad died, you became my parent too. My role model.*

*When I fell apart, you were the one who told me to buck up. To get up and get on with it. To be strong, to face things head on. To never give up. To stop being stubborn.*

*So that's what I am asking...telling...you to do now. Buck up, big sister. Get up and get on with life. I mean this with the greatest affection, but you're not doing the best job of that now. I know you love your career, but somewhere along the way—between holding me together and sticking families back together—you lost a piece of yourself. That little girl who danced with me to the radio in*

*our mother's kitchen knew that life was fun.
I miss that girl, miss that part of you. I see it
in Zoe already, in her tiny, joyful little face.
I hope she keeps it.*

*I know we didn't always see things the
same way, but I know you love us. Love Zoe.
She's a beautiful baby and, writing this, I
just know that you will be there to watch
her grow. To give her strength and gump-
tion. You taught her mother the same things.*

*I also realise that right about now, you're
feeling pretty mad too. The control freak in
you will be fuming with me. Don't be mad
at Ronnie's parents. We asked them not to
say anything. They deserve to enjoy their retirement. To be grandparents and not parents again. It's too much for them. This is
the right thing and, one day, you'll see it too.*

*You're probably giving poor Jackson hell.
You two are more alike than you think. I'm
laughing from heaven right now at the rage
I know you're feeling at me too. Our solicitor wigged out when I told him this was to
be our little secret, but I knew, if I told you,
you would have gone mad—not see the plan
I have in my head. Be nice to Mr Cohen, he
was always good to us. He steered us through
our parents' deaths, and he'll see you all
through mine too.*

*Back to Jackson. While you are my ride or*

*die, don't forget that Jackson just lost his too. Try not to torture him so much. Ronnie was worried not telling you both would make it harder, like some cruel final trick played on the two of you, but I have never been more sure of anything since meeting Ronnie that this is the right thing. I had you, and only you. I don't want that for Zoe, or you. Putting the burden of raising our child solely on your shoulders wouldn't be right. Jackson and you will need each other, like it or not.*

*Zoe will need people. She's already lost too much. I know you can guide our daughter to be fierce and brave. Braver and fiercer than I ever was. Jackson can tell her stories about her dad, help his memory stay alive for Zoe, like your memory of me will. He can be the dad that we had for that short time. The man she'll compare all those after against—someone to fix her bike, tell her to drive safely. Check the tyres on her car before she drives to college. And yes, you did that for me, but we missed Dad more than ever in those moments.*

*Jackson will be the one to protect her, to look after you both. You deserve someone to take care of you, even though I know you'll struggle to let him. Ronnie knows he won't leave, but try not to break him or send him away. I don't want you to struggle in this world alone, like we had to.*

*So, darling sister, my rock, my heart, my best friend—for once in your life, listen to your little sister and do what I wish. Don't shut people out, don't lose the softer parts of you. Be kind to Jackson and, if he wants to help, let him. You can shout at me later. I hope it's much later, dear sis. No more wishing life away, or letting it pass you by. Look after Zoe for us, and each other.*

*Ronnie and I love you all so much. I'll say hi to our parents for you. I'll see you when you get here.*

*Be brave, Lucy. I love you for ever.*

*Harry*

Lucy jerked the letter away before her tears marred it. She read it twice more, the tears multiplying each time her eyes ran over the words.

'Oh, Harriet,' she said between shuddery breaths. She looked up to the ceiling, till the tears had dried on her cheeks. 'Way to play the sister card. You always, always knew how to pull a good guilt trip.' A sob escaped her. 'I can't even argue with you! Kind of hard to hash it out with you now.' She wiped at her face, wanting to pull herself back together. To get out of this room, this funk, and get back to doing.

*I'm better moving forward. If I wallow in this, stay still, I'll be done.*

She drew a deep, shuddery breath into her lungs. 'One more minute,' she said to her sister. 'One more minute, and then I'll get up.' Looking at the clock, she sobbed quietly as she watched the seconds on the clock tick down.

When she emerged from the room, the letter tucked into her bag, the two men were standing there. Jackson searched her face, as if he was looking for clues, and she scanned his.

*Can I do this? Can we really live together? Can I raise a child, with a man who irritates the hell out of me?*

All she could hear was her sister's voice in her head. The words from the letter were embedded in her brain for eternity. She thought back to when it had just been the two of them, parentless and alone, so much older, more aware, than poor Zoe. They had memories Zoe would never have, as painful sometimes as they were to recall.

*The moment we knew we were alone.*

She recalled vividly drying her sister's tears that day, telling her she would look after her, that everything was going to be okay. She knew just what to do then. She'd lived through this before. She could do it again and, as before, she would look after her niece. Her family. No matter what the personal cost.

'I don't want to contest the will,' she said, her voice a ghost of its usual self. 'Jackson?'

It suddenly occurred to her that *he* might want to. All this was new to him too. It didn't help that, for once, his usually very expressive face was like stone, immovable and impenetrable.

'Jackson what?' He also seemed to be playing dumb.

*Was he playing for time?*

She felt her heart thud in her chest.

*Do I want him to say yes?*

It was watching his stone-cold face that begged another question, one that she hadn't asked before.

*What if he doesn't, and I am going to be alone in this anyway? I've hardly been nice to him.*

She remembered what he'd said, about being by her side. He had been. He'd held her up at the funeral. He'd sorted out both their work leaves, though she'd chewed his ear off, even though he'd been right about them both needing the time off. He'd been there, every day, looking after Zoe, his parents and her. He'd rung her daily, offering to bring over food. She'd never said yes, but he'd tried.

As confused as he made her feel sometimes, he was always there—whether she wanted him to be or not. This was a big shock to both of them and, right now, he was so angry with her she couldn't tell which way the storm was blowing his sails.

His deep-brown eyes grabbed her the instant

she dared look him in the face. 'So, do you want to? Contest the will, I mean?'

She felt her face flush.

'No,' he said, his voice even, soft. 'I don't want to contest.' The bite of his lip gave his worry away. 'Unless you want me to.'

She thought back to her panic seconds earlier: the prospect of doing this on her own; the letter from her sister that felt like a burning hot poker in her bag. Whether she liked it or not, they were in this together. Zoe needed people who loved her, who understood her. A mother's last wish couldn't be ignored over her own barriers.

*Six months. Give it six months.*

'We'll have a lot to organise.'

A slight nod was all she got at first. The tension in the room was so palpable she could have cut it with a scalpel.

'We've got time,' he added with a sad little smile. 'We'll figure it out, right?'

# CHAPTER FIVE

AFTER SIGNING AWAY what felt like their whole lives, an hour later the pair of them stumbled out into the daylight. When Lucy reached for her phone, Jackson put his hand over the screen.

'Don't get a taxi. I'll drive you.' Before she could tell him to move his hand, he cut her off. 'Get in the car, Lucy.'

They headed towards Jackson's car in silence, her head full of all the things they had to consider. Mr Cohen had explained that a date would be set for six months' time to confirm that the arrangement was working. If both parties agreed, and everyone was satisfied that Zoe was well cared for, the arrangement would continue. Six months to figure out how to co-parent with the Head of A&E, a man who was the subject of her tongue lashings and was now going to play 'Mummy and Daddy' with her.

'Whoa!' She felt Jackson's hand around her waist, yanking her back, just as the honk of a car in front startled her. 'What the hell are you doing?'

She'd walked out into the road. The driver

wound his window down and shouted an obscenity in their direction.

'Get lost!' Jackson countered, his fist banging on the roof of the car. He spun her round, holding the tops of her arms tight. 'You okay?'

'Yeah. No. Not at all.' His concerned features softened; his gaze was fixed on hers as if he was checking her for injuries. He wouldn't find them. They were on the inside, buried so deep, no surgeon would be able to cut them away from the healthy flesh. 'This is not normal, right?'

His laugh surprised her, jolted her out of her melancholy.

'No, Luce, this is far from normal.' He put her arm through his and guided her to the car park. 'Come on; let's get out of here before you try to stop the traffic again.'

Lucy stared out of the window when the car came to a stop. She'd barely registered the car ride and, staring at the neat house in front of her, she wondered how long they'd been driving.

'Come on.' Jackson nudged her, coming to open her car door before she got a chance to object.

'Where are we? Shouldn't we get back?' Over the last ten days, the pair of them had spent most of their time at his parents' house or dealing with the funeral arrangements.

'Zoe's fine. I want to show you something.'

She shrank back into the passenger seat.

'You have to get out of the car for me to do that.'
He held out his hand and she gave in.

'Fine.' She huffed, getting out on her own and following him up the neat stone path. 'Whose house is this?'

He answered her with a key, which fit neatly into the front door.

'My house. I realised you've never actually been here.' He bent to pick up the post, stopping when he saw she was frozen on the doorstep. 'You can cross the threshold, you know. I disabled the booby traps and removed the garlic cloves, Elvira.'

She stepped over the threshold into a large, well-decorated hallway. He put the pile of post down on an end table near the door, rolling his eyes and pulling her in far enough to shut the door behind them both.

'And why are we here?'

His head snapped back at the question. 'Well, Zoe can't stay with my parents for ever. Now we know what's going on, we need to start making some decisions. Since you live in a one-bedroom flat, I thought we'd make this place our base.'

*Our base. Our...base...*

'What makes you think I'd want to live here?'

'The one bedroomed flat was the first clue. I have three bedrooms, a garden, space for all your and Zoe's stuff. It's not too far from work and... you're bugging out.'

Lucy closed the jaw she didn't know had been

gaping open, wrapping her arms tightly around herself as if she could shield herself from the lair of Jackson Denning.

'I'm not bugging out.'

'Did you tell your face that? You look like you're about to be sent to war.'

'Well…'

He headed down the hallway, pushing open a door at the end. She followed him into the kitchen which looked like a stainless-steel fortress. Jackson stuck his head in the fridge, pulling out various items, then moving over and lighting the stove.

'I thought we should eat, then I can show you around the place. The smallest bedroom is currently my office, but I can move things around. I can set up in the corner of the dining room or something.'

He cracked some eggs into a bowl, motioning for her to sit down at one of the stools set under the island. She looked around, trying to reconcile the man she knew with the one standing in front of her. 'Omelette okay?'

Her stomach grumbled. Sheila Denning was always trying to feed her, but she couldn't remember the last time she'd actually eaten anything substantial. 'Sure. Thanks.'

He shrugged his shoulders, getting to work cutting ham into little slices and grating cheese. She watched him work. For once, the silence wasn't entirely uncomfortable. The knives that usually cut through the air between them seemed to be resting in the drawer.

'I don't know why I've never been here before.' He chuckled, mixing the ingredients in a large glass bowl.

'I know. I did invite you to the house warming, and a few barbecues, but you always said you were washing your hair.' He flashed her a sarcastic grin. 'You seem to wash your hair a lot. Remember when Arron from the fracture clinic kept asking you out? I'm pretty sure you gave him that same excuse for two months before he gave up.'

*How did he know that?* She thought she'd been discreet in turning him down.

'I remember,' she muttered, still distracted by the sight of Jackson doing something domestic. She was used to seeing him on the A&E floor, in scrubs or covered in blood. Today he looked different with his sleeves rolled up, his corded forearms flexing as he spooned the mixture into a frying pan. 'So, you own this? It's pretty big.'

'I bought it as a long-term investment.' He shrugged. 'I thought I might have a family one day, you know? I hate flats. I spent too much time in temporary digs whilst working away to live like that again—no gardens, thin walls. A buddy of mine's a builder, and he updated it for me. I like having the space. When I had a flat, I felt like I was on top of people, you know? Being so busy at work all day, the chaos, the noise; it batters the senses after a while.'

He pushed a plate holding a folded-up omelette over to her, together with cutlery. 'It's quiet here. I sit in the garden sometimes and have a beer, or fire up the grill. It's nice.'

He spoke about living here as if it was a foregone conclusion, and that got her hackles up.

'So you want us to live here just like that?'

He took a seat next to her with his own food, tucking in. 'It makes sense. It's near to work, there's room for two cars. You can have your own room. Space for us all.'

He noticed she wasn't eating, gently nudging her arm with his. Cutting off a piece, she popped it into her mouth. 'Wow.' It was quite possibly the best omelette she'd ever had, fluffy and filling. 'This is good.'

His bashful grin told her he didn't do this a lot. 'I like to cook too.' He waved his fork around the kitchen. 'State of the art.'

'Bragger. Bet you tell that to all the conquests you bring here too.'

He almost choked on his omelette. 'Conquests?'

'Yeah; Ronnie told Harriet things.' His brows shot up into his hairline. 'Sisters talk too.'

'Nice!' He huffed. 'Cheers for that, brother.' He saluted the ceiling, and they both went quiet, reminded of their loss.

'That's a point, though—dating.'

She felt him stiffen at her side.

'I didn't realise you were seeing someone.'

'I'm not.' She laughed at the absurdity, snorting by accident.

'All right, Miss Piggy.'

'Shut up!' She jabbed him with an elbow. 'I didn't mean to!'

His shoulders were shaking with mirth. 'Oh, I know, but that was funny. I intend to make you snort more often.'

'Jerk,' she said, but she was laughing along with him.

'You're really not dating, at all?'

She shook her head, finishing off the last morsels of food on her plate. 'Nope. No time for all that.' She thought of Zoe. 'Guess that won't be changing any time soon either, but if you date anyone we'll have to come up with some kind of plan.'

Jackson stood, collecting their empty plates and stacking them neatly into the dishwasher.

'I won't,' he said simply, leaning back against one of the tall, shiny, steel cupboards. 'I didn't do it much anyway, and never here.'

*Wait, what?*

'Never?'

'Nope.' He chuckled as he came over and pulled her to her feet. 'You'll be the first woman to sleep over, believe it or not.' He yanked her up so fast that she wobbled on her feet. Steadying herself against his chest with her hands, she looked up at him and heard his surprised gasp before she stepped back a little. He licked his lips and withdrew. 'Er... I'll show you around, then we'd better get back.'

He strode away, and she saw his fists clench together at his sides.

*That was... They'd been...close.*

'You coming?' he asked from the doorway.

'Yep.' She shrugged herself out of...whatever that had been. The last couple of weeks were giving her whiplash. She thought of her sister's letter, looking around at Jackson's house. Could she really live here, give up her life? Taking a deep, galvanising breath, she went to find Jackson.

'I think it's only fair if you see my place,' she said when she found him in the living room. 'Before we make any firm decisions.'

To his credit, he readily agreed. 'Fine; we have time. I've shown you mine,' he said with a wink. 'Let's see what you've got.'

'You can't be serious.'

There was no mistaking his mocking tone and, now she was here, she couldn't blame him. Compared to his place, her flat was a little on the small side. She'd never needed a big home, and had never wanted the expense or felt the need to rattle around in some huge, posh abode. She didn't have the time for decorating, and she didn't entertain. She was barely at home—she usually took extra shifts, ended up at the gym or went out with friends or with her sister. Her days off at home were usually spent sleeping or doing laundry so she didn't have to wear the grungy undies at the back of her drawer on the next shift at work. Having Jackson standing in her kitchen, rooting through her fridge, she almost felt silly at feeling so stubborn.

'Smells like something died in here.' He pulled out an old pizza box, opening it and retching.

*Oh, yeah, I forgot about that tuna and sweet-corn pizza I had in there. When did I order that— last week?*

He looked around the neat, little unused kitchen. 'Bin?'

She shrugged, taking the box from him. 'I usually just use plastic bags and take them out daily.'

He raised a brow but said nothing. 'I'm not here a lot. I don't really eat here.'

'Zoe will, though.' He motioned around him. 'This place is nice, but my place is a house, with a garden—like she's used to. I know that you want to keep your life, but maybe… Oh, I don't know.' He seemed to shrink into himself. Even then she had to look up to meet his eye line. 'It's only been a couple of hours. I can't tell you what to do; I don't know myself.'

'I don't know either, that's the problem. It's a lot to take in.' She joined him in peering at the fridge innards. 'Wow, it does stink.' Leaning forward, she pulled out a takeaway box that was pretty much mush. She couldn't even remember what it *had* been, let alone when she'd ordered it. 'Oh, my Lord, it smells like medical waste.'

'Told ya,' he muttered and, when she caught his eye, she couldn't help but laugh. He dissolved into laughter along with her, and the two of them were laughing hysterically in seconds. 'I knew you usually ate at work. Now I know why. It's not like the canteen food is that good.'

She wanted to bite back at him but couldn't stop laughing long enough to get any words out. She laughed till her sides hurt, Jackson laughing along with her. He leaned against the counter when their laughter subsided, looking around him at her home. He was here, in her space. The fact it wasn't the weirdest thing that had happened that day didn't make it any less...odd.

'I can't believe you're standing in my kitchen and we were laughing again. Us laughing in kitchens is becoming a habit.' She pulled her hair back into a bun and fastened it with a couple of chopsticks she pulled from her cutlery drawer—her very spartan cutlery drawer. 'It's been a weird day.'

'A weird time,' he said with a rueful smile. 'It's not a bad place. I hope you don't think I was—'

'I don't.' Lucy pulled a large disposable bag from a stack in the drawer, getting to work on emptying the fridge. 'I'm kind of a slob, I get it.'

She looked around at the barely used utensils in the pot on the side. 'Harriet bought that for me. She said it would encourage me to cook more.' Her voice cracked, and she fell silent. Yesterday she'd had a different life, now she was barrelling blindly into a new one. Still, there was no time to stop. Stopping meant dwelling.

She threw more things into the bag, not even caring what the food was now, whether it was in date or spoiled. It didn't matter any more. She'd known the second she'd walked back into her flat that she wouldn't be bringing Zoe back here Her home was for her old life. She dumped the bag on the floor and walked over to Jackson. 'You knew what you were doing, didn't you, bringing me here after your place?'

Jackson folded his arms, watching her as if he was waiting for her to say more before he reacted. He had a tendency to do that, she noticed. She noticed more things about him these days. Probably because she couldn't exactly walk away from him, or pretend he was on the outskirts of her life any more, a bug to be swatted. She felt his hurt as keenly as her own.

'I'm not judging how you live, Lucy. I know how hard you work. Harriet told me you always looked after her. Living alone, it's different. Working long hours, those things are not as important.'

'I know, but you're right. Your house…well… it's a house, for a start. Zoe is used to having a garden to play in. She has that swing set at her house. I can't exactly hang it off the balcony, can I? I don't have a bedroom for her. I have one allocated car parking space; you have a driveway.' She picked up the bag of spoiled food, reaching for her handbag. 'Let's go see Zoe, okay? We have the six-month review to prepare for.' She lifted the food bag and waggled it at him. 'I think we might need to get a plan together.' As she walked to the door, his voice stilled her.

'Grab some clothes too.'

Her head snapped to look at him. 'Why?'

'I have a bottle of Scotch I've been saving.' His lips curled into a smile. 'I think our life-merging plans might need a two-drink minimum.'

She didn't argue with him on that one. Leaving the food bag by the front door, she headed to the bedroom to grab her overnight bag.

The sun was barely up in the sky when Lucy looked out of the large, decaled window. She'd sneaked out early from Jackson's, intending to go to her place and pick up some more of her stuff. After seeing Zoe and Sheila and Walt, Jackson's parents, they'd been too drained to talk much. His parents had been so apologetic about keeping the contents of the will a secret from them. The relief on both their faces was obvious, and Lucy hated that they'd had to shoulder that on top of burying their son and daughter-in-law.

When they'd got back to Jackson's house after putting Zoe to bed at his parents' house, the events of the day had felt enough. Instead of making plans, they'd opened the Scotch, put on some dumb action movie and ordered a takeaway. They'd talked about work, their patients; they'd swapped stories each had never heard before.

She'd headed to bed early, feeling awkward going up to the spare room. She'd spent half the night staring at the ceiling. In the end she'd tip-toed back downstairs, taking another full tumbler of the good stuff to bed to try and knock herself out for a few hours.

Instead of heading home, she got the cab to stop at the coffee shop near work. She needed something familiar, something that hadn't changed. Before work, she often met her colleague Amy for coffee. When she pushed through the steamed-up glass doors, seeing her friend there gave her a jolt of sorely needed comfort and she spilled her story.

'So that's it, you're a parent now?'

Amy, who worked with Lucy in Paediatrics, pushed her coffee closer to her. Lucy didn't reply for a moment, focusing on the pretty little leaf art on the surface. Picking up her spoon, she stirred the liquid, erasing the image, turning pretty perfection to swirling chaos.

'Not a parent, still an auntie. Just more…hands on.'

'Mmm-hmm.' When she finally met Amy's

eye, she could tell she wasn't buying it. 'That simple, eh? Any other person would be curled in a ball somewhere. I know you're tough, Lucy, but still; you must have so much to think about. It's been, what, two weeks? And Jackson—Daddy Denning? Mate, that's a lot.'

Lucy bit at her lip, buying time with a slow sip of her coffee. 'I know. I haven't even told work. The hospital gave us both time off, and we have to adjust to this new normal, I guess. Curling into a ball isn't going to get things sorted. Harriet left instructions for everything, but I still don't really know where to start.'

'And you have six months to get sorted before you make a final decision?' Amy was always a good listener, one of the few people Lucy trusted, other than Harriet. Seeing her confusion and shock brought home just how gargantuan her situation was. Perhaps she was still numb. Maybe curling into a sodden mess would come later. It hadn't with her parents' passing; she'd had to get on with things.

She ran her hands down her cheeks, realising that this time wouldn't be any different. She was glad that her autopilot button hadn't let her down again. She hadn't cried since being at the hospital. 'Seems like a short space of time for the rest of your life.'

'Yeah, but it's not like I'm going to walk away from Zoe.'

Amy sat listening with that look she always had: attentive, helpful. Ever since they'd started working together throughout early mornings, late nights and coffee shop breakfasts, Amy had been a good sounding board. Whenever they got to talking, she always got that look on her face, as if she was digesting everything and judging nothing. Lucy made a mental note to tell her one day how grateful she was for her friendship. She never really had, and the reminder that life was short had made her more aware of the few relationships she had and how important they were.

'I never said you would. Still, it's not like it's just for the six months. A kid takes eighteen years—minimum. My little brother Ben is twenty and still bringing his washing home from university for my mum to sort out. I swear, how that boy still doesn't know how to use a washing machine…'

Lucy laughed under her breath. 'I think it will be a while before we have to think about that.'

'Exactly!' Amy seized on her point. 'She's what, two? It's a long time to share your life with someone you don't even like, and what if you meet someone, or Jackson does?'

A couple of customers walked in, stopping their conversation. Lucy's phone buzzed in her pocket. Thinking it was work, she fished it out: *Jackson*. She'd left a note letting him know she'd gone out. It had felt weird, skulking out of a man's house. It was not something she usually did, not that any of this was usual.

Got your note. Everything okay?

It was weird to see him asking her that on a text. Normally they texted about work, the odd time about Harriet or Ron, but mostly they sent each other sarcastic memes or snippy comments. He was listed in her phone as 'Satan', for goodness' sake. She tried to remember her sister's letter, but still, the day to day was hard. How the hell were they going to navigate the next six months, let alone life beyond that?

Yeah. Is Zoe okay?

She's fine. My folks would have called us. Not why I was texting.

She texted back.

I went for a walk.

He knew Amy. Why hadn't she told him the truth? She'd slept over, not done the walk of shame! Looking around her, she envied the other customers, enjoying their morning pastries and coffees without the side of drama.

'Everything okay?' Amy asked, tapping her nails on the table top. 'You look guilty.'

Amy struck again, knowing how to read Lucy's usual poker face in an instant. She remembered Jackson's comment about how he could read her. Perhaps she trusted him more than she thought. She must do, for him to see through her defences.

'Jackson.' She waved the phone at Amy. 'He messaged me to see where I was.'

Amy's tattooed brows knitted together with the force of her frown.

'You didn't tell him? I thought you stayed over?'

Lucy's defences sprang up, along with her shoulder blades.

'I left a note!'

'Saying what?'

'Gone out?' Hearing it out loud made her wince. 'It's barely past seven; I didn't think he'd be up yet. I did nothing wrong.'

Amy checked her watch and began gathering her things. 'You did nothing wrong, but you can't just leave a note and go out early in the morning. You might have worried him, going off like that. You're going to be living together.'

Lucy opened her mouth to object, but Amy shut her down with a pointed finger. 'Before you say you have your own place, you're an independent woman, blah-blah-blah, the man opened his home to you. You live on salads, smoothies, caffeine and three hours' sleep. I've seen how you live and work, Lucy: laser-focused. You are more than capable of looking after yourself, but it's not about just you any more! Imagine if you were Jackson, just for a minute. You've hardly been yourself lately. Who would be?'

Amy got up to leave, pulling Lucy onto her feet for a hug. 'Take back some drinks and pastries with you and sort it out.' She winked. 'Go home, Lucy. For once, let someone in. Having someone to take care of you might not be so bad. That person being Jackson? It could be a lot worse.'

'I'm not sure about that,' Lucy whined. 'Take me to work with you instead!'

Amy laughed. 'No chance, Bakewell. Now, be the tough nut I know you are and face him. I think you might find things will work out better than you think.'

'You think?'

Amy grinned. 'I'd bet money on it.'

Jackson's front door was unlocked when she got back. It felt weird, just walking in without knocking, but she was laden down with the bribes Amy had suggested so she pushed through her nerves. He met her at the door, taking the coffee cups from her full hands.

'Thanks,' she muttered. 'I brought us some goodies. I thought I was going to drop the lot.' He walked off into the kitchen and she followed him sheepishly.

'You didn't need to go out for coffee.' He looked as if he'd just woken up, his usually perfect hair looking messed up. He was wearing a pair of grey tracksuit bottoms, his T-shirt one of some old band from their youth she'd never liked. She'd never had time for music growing up, other than to shut out her university cohorts in the library when she was studying. Even then it had been more emo-grunge-type stuff, rather than the hard rock Ronnie and Jackson had preferred to blast out. 'I have a pretty good coffee maker here.'

'I prefer the coffee shop.'

'Okay.' She put the box on the counter, and he opened it. 'Wow. I can see why.' He pulled an almond croissant out of the box and sank his teeth into it. 'Dear Lord of medicine, that's good.' He finished the whole thing in three bites.

'The coffee's decent too. I've been going there for years.' She side-eyed him. 'I'm sorry I slipped out.'

His cup was halfway to his lips but he paused. 'You don't have to answer to me; I'm not your parole officer. You left a note.'

'So why did you text me, then?'

'Because of the note.' He nodded to the fridge where her words sat, glaring at her like a beacon.

*Gone out. Lucy*

'Not exactly *War and Peace*, is it? I just wondered if you were okay, if you were somewhere safe.'

Lucy took a donut and ripped it in half. 'What did you want, GPS coordinates?'

'No, but we just lost… It would have been nice if you'd said where you'd gone, that's all.'

'Would you have done the same?'

He didn't hesitate. 'I will, yes. I know yesterday was a lot, but I do think that before we do this and go back to work we should make a few ground rules together, don't you? I know Zoe has a nursery to go to, but we should talk about when we are both on the same shifts, nights off…'

Thinking about the nursery reminded her of Harriet and a memory of when she'd first started there. On a rare day off, Lucy had been at the dry cleaner's in town when Harriet had called her, distraught. She'd managed to sob out a plea to meet her for coffee and Lucy had abandoned her pressed clothes on the counter and run the whole way.

'Thanks for coming.' Harriet had sniffed when Lucy got to her table, panting. 'I ordered for you.' She'd pointed to a large coffee, but Lucy didn't register it.

'What's wrong?' She'd been alone. 'Where's Zoe?'

'She's gone,' Harriet had croaked out.

'What?' Lucy had been about to have a full-blown panic attack when her sister had spoken again. 'She didn't even look back this morning. The nursery staff just took her and she went off, happy as a clam.'

Lucy sagged into her seat. 'Harriet, I thought something was wrong!'

'Something is wrong!' Harriet sniffed again. 'I wanted Zoe to go to nursery a couple of days a week to let her play with other kids, you know? I don't want her to feel different when she starts school, but...'

'She still very much needs you. You're her mother. Just because she goes to nursery doesn't mean that she's gone.'

'I know.' Harriet had glugged at her green tea. 'I just...didn't expect it to feel like that.' She'd wiped at her eyes, flashing a smile that told Lucy that she'd pulled herself together. Harriet had known how to do that. Lucy had always been a little jealous of that ability. Lucy did the opposite: she just pushed everything down. 'They grow so fast.'

'I know.' Lucy had taken her sister's hand in hers. 'You did the right thing. Zoe will make friends, learn new things. It's only two days a week. You have Zoe for the rest of your life. Years of holding her little hand.'

Harriet's returning smile had been dazzling that day.

'Thanks, sis, you always know the right thing to say to calm me down.'

'That's my job.'

Lucy remembered the warm feeling she'd felt from those words...

The memory faded, and she realised Jackson was looking at her expectantly.

'Yeah, we can do that—make a schedule. I really want to keep her at that nursery. Harriet would want that.'

'Then we keep it going,' Jackson agreed. 'I agree. Mum and Dad will help too. We can do it. Other people do, don't they?'

They were looking at each other just a little bit too intently when the silence was broken. Jackson's phone rang: *Mum* flashed up on the caller ID.

'I'll just grab a shower and let you get that.' She jumped off the stool and half-ran up the stairs, anything to avoid the domestic scene she'd just left.

'To be continued, Lucy!' he called up the stairs. She was pretty sure he heard her groan of anguish. *She* was pretty sure she heard him chuckling.

'This is going to be a nightmare,' she muttered under her breath.

# CHAPTER SIX

WHEN LUCY CAME down from her shower, Jackson was ready and waiting with an invitation from his mother for dinner.

'Sure, that sounds nice, actually. Has she said anything about us taking Zoe?'

Jackson shook his head. 'She just said she'd give us time. You know, to sort things out here. I don't know what you were thinking, but I get the feeling my folks are pretty tired. They've had her since—'

'Yeah.' Lucy shuffled her feet. 'I know. They need time to grieve too, to rest.'

'Yeah,' Jackson echoed. The silence hung around them at the bottom of the stairs. 'We need to get on with it, I guess.'

Heaving out a sigh, Lucy rolled up the sleeves of her long T-shirt. 'Right—so we bring her here tonight after dinner.'

Jackson's brows raised, but he said nothing to contradict her. 'Okay, I have some boxes in the garage. We'd better get the office cleaned out. I read somewhere that kids need to be settled in their own room, so...'

'Yeah,' Lucy agreed. 'It's best if she has her

own room from the start. Gets a routine.' She narrowed her eyes. 'You read that where, exactly?'

The blush on his face was unmissable. 'Er...a parenting blog.'

She didn't want to laugh at that moment—it wasn't a happy moment—but she couldn't stop the smirk on her face from erupting. 'Right.' An odd kind of burble sprang up from her chest. 'Read many of those lately?'

'Laughing.' He smirked. 'Nice.'

She'd reached out to pat his arm before she realised. 'No, no. It's cute.' She laughed again, not bothering to supress it. 'Are you planning to breastfeed too?'

He grabbed her arm as she pulled back, as if he missed the contact. 'Ha! Funny!'

'I think so.' She cackled. They both noticed how close they were at the same time, and their arms dropped to their sides. 'So, you want to get the boxes?'

He cleared his throat. 'Er...yeah. I'll...er...see you up there.'

She heard the garage door open just as she was pushing open the wooden office door.

'Wow.' She breathed, and it wasn't seeing his office that took her aback. She knew that they'd been in the same space, but the contact, his hand on her bare skin, was still something alien.

*Weird*: that was the word for all of this.

*Keep moving. Suck it up.*

The office was pure Jackson. His desk was super-neat, like the rest of the house. Running her hand along the wooden surface, she picked things up, taking it in: little pots of rubber bands, paperclips and staples. The files on the shelves were all colour-co-ordinated, the same as his files at the hospital. His writing was a perfect set of uniformed letters, bold and confident, unlike her scribbly scrawl. *Everything in its place*, she mused. *So organised.* On the back wall above the desk, the pin board was full of photos, all neatly placed. There were photos of work nights out, a picture of Zoe wearing her Elsa dress, back when she'd been obsessed about being a cute little ice queen. Lucy laughed when she saw it, tears brimming in her eyes.

'I remember that outfit,' Jackson said from the doorway. She hadn't even heard him come up the stairs. Putting the flat-packed boxes to one side, he came to stand beside her. 'Harriet had to prise that dress off her every night for weeks.'

Lucy smiled. 'Yeah?' Jackson's aftershave was nice. It matched the room, she thought—light, but woodsy, strong but gentle somehow. 'She definitely knows her own mind.'

His head dipped closer as he took the board off the wall. 'I'll put this in my room for now.'

She reached for it, seeing something. 'Is that… us?' Jackson's gaze followed her finger to the photo in the centre. 'From the paintballing day?'

It was a group photo, a crowd of blues and reds, paint- and mud-splattered.

'I don't know.' He went to leave but she stopped him.

'It is!' She took the board from his grasp, leaning in to peer at the sea of faces. Jackson was laughing, head tilted to another player. When she found her own face in the crowd, she knew why— there she was, bright-red cheeks and mud smeared face, flipping him off. 'How do you even have this? That's so funny.'

When she turned to look at him, he looked as if he wanted the ground to swallow him up. 'Jackson?'

'I asked for it.' He shrugged, but the action was too forced to be real. 'No biggie.'

She passed it back, watching as he left the room.

*What was that? He kept a photo of her where he could see it all the time?*

She was still looking at the door when he came back, busying himself with making up boxes. He didn't meet her eye as he started to pack away the coloured files. Taking a box, she got to work, not sure what, if anything, she'd done wrong.

'It's a nice photo,' she muttered when she couldn't stand the awkward pause in their conversation any longer. He side-eyed her, and she witnessed the sag in his tight shoulders.

'I like it.'

* * *

It didn't take long to clear everything away. Putting the boxes in a neat stack in the corner, they got to work on the furniture.

'Careful,' Jackson warned as they navigated the stairs. 'Don't drop this desk and flatten me.' She pretended to consider it, a playful look on her face that made him shake his head.

'And raise a kid on my own? Death by desk would be the easier option.'

She felt his deep laugh through the desk, and the tension slid away. They managed not to maim each other getting the rest of the furniture down, which surprised them both.

They had just brought the last of the boxes down to the corner of the dining room that was now an office nook when she noticed the time.

'We need to go. We're going to be late for your mother.'

Looking around the now empty third bedroom, Jackson sighed. 'I forgot about dinner. Least we got this done. The blinds will do for now, till we can decorate at least. What does she have in her room again?'

Lucy tried to remember what Zoe's room looked like. It felt as if she'd not been there for ever.

'I think it was still decorated as a nursery. Yellow, maybe?' She rubbed her forehead. 'I know she has a cot bed, a dresser and a toy chest.'

Jackson was looking around the room as if he could picture it all in place.

'Cool. It should all fit, I think.'

The longer they were in there, staring at the furniture marks in the carpet, the closer the air felt. Lucy pulled at her T-shirt, feeling as if the collar was tightening around her neck somehow.

'Is it hot in here? I feel hot.' She went to the window, opening it and gulping at the air. 'I can't get my breath.'

'Lucy? Are you okay?'

Her chest was so tight, she felt she couldn't breathe. 'I… No… I…'

She felt Jackson's arms around her. 'It's okay. You're okay.'

'How is this okay?' she managed to push out. 'This was your office, and now it's a kid's room! How are you just okay with this?'

'Breathe,' he kept saying over and over in an even voice. 'It's okay. We'll be okay.'

When the panic released her long enough to cry, she bawled, gut-wrenching, stomach-hurting sobs. 'It's not my house. It's not Zoe's house. It shouldn't be like this, and we're just playing house and pretending that the world's not on fire.'

'I know,' he mumbled, his arms holding her tight, which for once she didn't even think to object to. They were necessary to hold her up, hold her together. 'We can do this. I promise, Luce. Rent your place out, move in here and we'll bring Zoe home. Do this one day at a time, okay? Breathe. You're okay.'

Listening to his voice, she looked around the bare room.

'I'm rubbish at painting,' she muttered when her breathing was even. She felt his laughter jolt her as they stood squished together. 'Don't laugh.'

His hand rubbed circles along her back. She felt her skin warm from his heat, her muscles unclench.

'I'll get you a paint gun.' His deep voice was full of warmth too. 'I seem to remember you could handle that.' She huffed, squeezing him to her like a reflex, before stepping away. This touching thing was getting out of hand.

Wiping her tears, she widened the gap between them. 'Come on; your mother will be worried if we're late.'

She didn't see the expression on Jackson's face when she left the room but the deep, throaty 'I'll drive' sent an oddly familiar shiver down her spine.

*Keep it together*, she told herself for most of the car ride over. *Grief does strange things to us all.*

Sheila and Walt were happy to see them both, but the fatigue on their faces was evident. When Jackson said they'd like to take Zoe home, they didn't object. They had dinner, and before they knew it, the pair of them were driving away with Zoe in the back seat, a load of toddler paraphernalia and enough food in containers to feed them for a week.

A couple of hours later, Zoe was well and truly making her presence known. Sheila and Walt had packed a travel cot and some supplies for them but they'd barely had a chance to set it all up before Zoe started to scream the place down.

'I wonder if she's just unsettled,' Jackson tried to say over the noise of her ear-splitting screams. 'I read that kids pick up on things, even when really young. Emotions, changes, you know.'

'You think?' Lucy snapped back, panic overruling every sane thought in her body. 'I'm not stupid, Sasquatch. My medical speciality trumps your parenting blogs.'

'Never said you were stupid, Trigger.' His jaw tensed, making his whole cheek judder from the sudden tightening. 'I hate my nickname too, shorty!'

Zoe started to cry louder the second he raised his voice, and both of them stilled. She could see the tension in Jackson's jaw as he lifted her higher up in his arms. 'Hey, Zo-Zo, it's okay! You hungry?'

'We tried that.' She pointed to the spaghetti hoop stain on her hoodie. 'We've tried changing her, she won't go to sleep...' The wailing intensified the second Jackson tried to put her down on the floor.

'She had a nap earlier but Mum said it was barely twenty minutes.'

Jackson lifted Zoe onto the kitchen counter. 'Does she feel warm to you? She's not warm, is she?'

Lucy placed a cool palm on the little girl's forehead. 'A little. No fever, though, I already checked her temperature earlier and it's normal.'

Zoe was sobbing now, tears spilling down her cheeks as her whole face went beetroot-red.

'Is she thirsty? What about a drink?'

'She'd a beaker of milk at dinner, and she had—what?—sips of juice half an hour ago.'

'What?' Zoe's wails had drowned out her words.

'Sips of juice!' she repeated, retrieving the beaker of cold apple juice from the fridge and showing him the measuring scale. 'See? It was at the top before.'

Jackson frowned. 'Maybe we should take her into work.'

'For crying? I'm not going into work for that. We'd get laughed out of the place!' Lucy scoffed, picking a now screaming Zoe up and passing her the beaker. Zoe screeched harder and knocked the cup away. 'Have a drink, come on.' She tried again, and this time Zoe pelted the beaker across the kitchen. The ear-splitting decibels she emitted make them both jump. 'We don't need to take her in.'

'Well, I don't know what's wrong. It could be a stomach-ache.'

Lucy didn't answer. She was too busy running irrational scenarios in her head. Her training was lost to her as she ran through every possible condition from hand, foot and mouth to meningitis…and the screaming thought that Zoe knew she had been left to her aunt and uncle and was just distraught at their lack of parenting skills. Trying to stop her inner panicked monologue from giving her another panic attack with her niece in her arms, she took her through to the lounge and tried to lay her down on the sofa. Zoe's whole body went as rigid as an ironing board so she gave in and changed tack.

*You can do this*, she told herself. *You save babies on a daily basis. Heck, figure it out!*

'Will you just hold her a second? I'll check her tummy, but I don't think it's to do with her digestion.'

She tried to lift Zoe up to pass her off to Jackson, but she was screaming blue murder and rigid everywhere but her legs. Her legs were not stiff; they were quite the opposite, in fact. She was windmilling them, kicking both of them as she bellowed at the top of her lungs.

'Let me, just… Zo-Zo! You're okay, darling. Let Auntie Lucy have a look at you.'

Jackson finally managed to get a grip on her, holding her up and out as if she was a bomb and he was a rookie disposal expert. 'She's like an eel! Hurry up, Trig!'

Lucy was trying to lift up Zoe's little top, but it was like wrestling an anaconda in the midst of an air raid siren.

'Don't call me that! I'm trying; I don't want to hurt her!'

'Hurt her?' Jackson half-shouted over the ear-splitting wails. 'She's got more kick than a striker! I've treated easier drunks in A&E! Just pull her top up!'

'I'm trying!' She managed to do a quick examination, trying to remember her years of training and experience—and not get kicked in the face. 'Her stomach's normal, no blockage. She had a bowel movement earlier—that was normal too.'

Jackson went to put her down on the floor, but she lifted her legs away, clinging to his clothing.

'Well, what's left? Exorcism?'

'That's not funny,' she half-yelled back. 'And, for the record, you're a doctor too!'

'Yeah, well, I'm just waiting for her head to spin round.' He tried to soothe her in his embrace, his hand over one cheek. 'She's not hot, but her cheeks are.'

The pair of them looked at each other at the exact same time. 'Teething,' they said in unison.

Jackson pulled his car keys out of his pocket.

'The supermarket—they have a pharmacy that is open late.'

Lucy was already grabbing her bag.

'Good thinking.' She rubbed at her head where a bitter headache was beginning to form. 'I'll get her coat.'

\* \* \*

The coat didn't get closer to Zoe than the back seat. She turned purple when Lucy came near her with it, and Jackson turned a ghostly shade of white and muttered something about her throwing up in his back seat. It took them ten minutes to get Zoe to bend enough to fasten her into the car seat, and by then they were both so frazzled they just wanted to get to the local supermarket without driving the car into the nearest brick wall.

Jackson backed out of the driveway at a slow crawl.

'Jackson, the supermarket closes in three hours. Any chance you could drive faster?'

He pulled onto the main road, Zoe's wails now receding into shuddering sobs with the movement of the car. She loved the motion, Lucy remembered. Harriet and Ronnie used to drive her round together when she wouldn't sleep.

He made a throaty huffing noise. 'Last time I was in a car with you driving, I got whiplash. We have a kid on board.'

'Yeah, well, a toddler on a trike would beat you in a race. She's not a new-born.'

'Yeah, thanks for that, Mrs Paediatrician.'

'That's Ms Paediatrician, actually, and you're welcome.'

A car pipped its horn behind them. When they both looked, they were greeted by a pensioner behind the wheel who promptly mouthed, 'Put your foot down!' at Jackson.

Turning to face the front, Zoe now quiet in the back, cheeks aflame, Lucy pressed her lips together.

'Don't say it,' Jackson droned, putting his foot down. Lucy laughed all the way to the supermarket car park.

Zoe was like a different child the second they sat her in the trolley seat. Her cheeks were still flushed postbox-red, but she was happily looking around her as they strode down the aisles.

They both stopped dead when they came to the baby section the pharmacist had directed them to—very quickly, they noted, which probably had something to do with the people in the queue and the ear-splitting wails Zoe had produced in Lucy's arms. They reached two long rows of shelves filled with toys, equipment, toiletries and pregnancy gear.

'All this stuff? Really?' Jackson was clinging to the shopping trolley with white knuckles. Lucy arched a brow and charged forward. In that moment she had never been more grateful that she'd gone into paediatric medicine and not the cardiology specialism she'd once considered. Affairs of the heart she didn't know, but this, she knew. From watching Harriet and the parents of the patients she cared for, she'd picked up a few things along the way. For some reason, the fact that Jackson wasn't the polished A&E doctor he normally was helped too.

'Yep. It's a multi-million-pound industry, Jackson. You been living under a rock?'

'Nope, but that doesn't sound so bad about now. Ronnie didn't talk much about this side of things.'

Lucy headed straight for the teething gel, picking up a couple of boxes and chucking them into the trolley. Zoe was starting to grizzle again, the distraction of the bright lights and people wearing off in favour of her irritable gums. Sanitising her hands, Lucy ripped open one of the boxes and squeezed some of the gel out onto a finger.

'Er, shoplift much?' he teased.

Lucy jabbed him with her elbow and started to rub some of the gel onto Zoe's gums. The little girl pulled a face at first, but then settled down. The relief was evident, and Lucy felt a small frisson of achievement.

'Well, that worked,' Jackson said, a touch of wonder in his words. He went over to the shelf and picked up another five boxes. 'We need to stock up on that. What else can we get? I'm guessing that they don't have holy water in their range.'

He was looking up and down the products, and Lucy couldn't help but smile as she pushed the trolley and watched him taking everything in. He was quite funny as an uncle. She'd always known that he loved Zoe, but seeing him take such an interest made her think that perhaps Harriet and Ronnie had not been so far off the mark. If she'd been alone with Zoe screaming the place down in her little unkempt flat, would she have been here now, so calm, getting supplies? She knew the answer to that—*heck no*. She'd either have driven to work in a panic to get help or been on-line, desperately looking for same-day-delivery miracle purchases to help her out.

'Hey.' Jackson shook her out of her thoughts, waggling a teething ring at her. 'These things go in the fridge; the cold is supposed to help soothe the gums. What do you think?'

Lucy pushed the trolley closer. 'I think we should get some.' She pulled a pack of pull-ups off another shelf. 'Let's get stocked up.'

Jackson's dark-brown eyes locked onto hers for a moment longer than she was used to.

'Deal.' The corner of his mouth turned into that smile she secretly liked, the one he'd flashed the day they'd met all that time ago. 'I say we get some alcohol too.' He grinned. 'For the adults— we deserve a treat too.'

'Double deal!' She laughed, pulling another pack of pull-ups off the shelf. 'Fifty-fifty, though, right? Anything we spend has to be fifty-fifty.'

She could swear his eyes sparkled. Supermarket lighting, she told herself, blinking hard.

'Fifty-fifty all the way.'

# CHAPTER SEVEN

'ARE YOU SURE your parents didn't mind having her again? I feel like we're putting a lot on them. They've just had her for over two weeks solid.'

They were sitting in Jackson's car the next day, parked at the front of Harriet's and Ronnie's house. They were both exhausted after Zoe's first night in her new home. Her bedroom was a priority, now it was emptied. The travel cot looked sad in there all on its own. The poor little love had been unsettled, meaning that they'd each slept in fitful shifts. Over one of Sheila's lasagnes and a bottle of red, they'd also managed to sort out a rota system for who did what, and Lucy had ordered a wall calendar online for when they went back to work. They'd been so tired and distracted from Zoe that they hadn't even fought about any of it—progress.

'She can start back at nursery soon, help give them a break. Mum offered—she'll take Zoe to nursery when we're at work, and pick her up when we need her to. She has a key for my—*our*—place already. Trust me, they want to help. When I dropped Zoe off, Dad practically ripped her from my arms. I think they've missed her, but at least they got some sleep.' He sounded almost jealous and, given the fog of fatigue currently swirling around them, Lucy understood his tone. In her early days in the job, studying and working all hours, she'd thought she could never be so tired. Turned out, having a toddler thrust upon her was just as exhausting.

'I'm glad they were happy to have her. They're still grieving too. Zoe's their one and only grandchild, so no wonder. Especially after losing…' She cut herself off from forming the words she could never quite vocalise. 'I guess they'll want to cherish every minute.'

She felt him tense at her side.

'What makes you think Zoe's going to be an only grandchild? I've dated. I didn't buy the house to live alone in for ever.'

Lucy thought of her flat. She hadn't bought it to live alone for ever either. When their family home had been sold, and she and her sister had split the money, a flat had just seemed logical. Not quite a 'for ever' home, she realised now. She'd already played house, though, far before her time. 'When have you dated?' she asked, glossing over the house comment entirely. 'I never see you with anyone past the fortnight mark.'

'Well, yeah, not lately.' He fixed his dark eyes

on her, making her feel silly, on show. 'I'm not a monk, Luce.'

'Lucy,' she corrected automatically. 'And I didn't think you were, I just…'

'Since when have you followed my love life, anyway?'

'Since never. I don't care. Anyway, you can talk; I didn't know you knew about Aaron asking me out.'

His jaw clenched. 'You know what hospitals are like. Staff never have time to date; you hear things.'

'Yeah, well, I was just saying, it's good Zoe has your parents. I think it's nice your mum is able to help. She has someone that's maternal.'

Jackson's face fell. 'She has you.'

Fiddling with the strap of the handbag on her knee, Lucy looked away. 'Yeah, sure.'

'She does. You're her auntie, her mother figure, now. She'll be fine. You turned out all right, didn't you, without a mum around?'

'Oh, yeah, I'm a totally well-adjusted human being.'

His chest rumbled with a deep, free kind of laughter she'd never heard from anyone else. It always made her laugh but, as now, she'd always tried to suppress the laughter of her own that it caused. Usually, the rumble came after she'd mocked him, or been zinged by her with a clever one liner. Today was no different.

'You never thought about having a family one day?'

Until his question dropped. She didn't know how to answer—families to her meant pain, loss.

*Perhaps buying my place wasn't such an impulse purchase.*

'Hello!' The rapping on the car window startled them both. There was a man peering through the glass at them. 'You lost?'

'Saved by the bell,' Lucy muttered under her breath as she went to get out.

'Hey, Luce, wait!' Jackson tried to stop her, but she was already out.

'Hi,' she addressed her saviour stranger. 'No, we're not lost. My sister lives here.'

Jackson appeared at her shoulder, bumping it from coming in so hot. She looked up to give her clumsy giant companion a quick glare before addressing the man again. '*Lived* here, I mean. Can I help?'

The bloke was smartly dressed in a suit and tie. He fitted in well with the upmarket suburban backdrop. In comparison beside her, dressed like a swarthy lumberjack in his checked shirt and jeans, Jackson looked as if he'd just stepped off his country ranch. The fact the suited man had to look up at Jackson wasn't lost on her either.

'Oh, no, I actually live a couple of doors down. I'm sorry for ambushing you. I didn't realise who you were. New car?'

'No,' Jackson butted in. 'It's mine, actually.'

'Ah, right. I knew Harriet had a sister; I didn't realise you had a partner.'

'We're not together,' they replied in unison. Jackson moved a little closer. So close, in fact, he blocked her line of sight. Lucy stepped closer to the man.

'You sound like you knew Harriet.'

The neighbour thumbed towards his house. 'My wife did. We have a son the same age as Zoe. We were really sorry to hear about what happened.'

'Thanks.' Lucy's eyes flicked back to her sister's house. 'Me too.' Jackson stepped forward, putting an arm around her shoulder. She shrugged him off, flashing her best professionally honed smile at the man. 'That's very kind of you. We'll be coming back and forth for a while, so...'

'No problem; well, nice to meet you.' He put out his hand to shake Jackson's, but Jackson folded his arms in response. The man's smile dipped. 'Right, well, better go see the wife.' He patted Lucy's arm. For a second, she thought she heard Jackson growl, but when she flicked her gaze to him she saw him looking at the neighbour as if he was stuck in a boring business meeting. 'If you need anything, you know where we are.'

Lucy turned to walk towards the house when the man left. 'That was rude.'

'I know. Who is he? Neighbourhood watch?'

'No,' Lucy spat back, fumbling for the keys in

her bag. 'You jackass. You were rude then. He was only checking on the house.'

'No, he wasn't, he was being nosy.'

They got to the front porch at the same time. Lucy tried to sidestep him to get to the lock but she was met by a wall of muscle.

'Do you have to stand so close, you big oaf? I felt like you were my bodyguard back there. What did you think he was going to do—throttle me with his tie in broad daylight?'

He tutted, stepping to one side. 'No, but that's another thing.' He followed her into the house, shutting the door behind them both and looking out through the side window as if he was expecting a sniper assault. 'He knows my car; it's been parked outside enough times. The guy was just fishing. What kind of man do you know wears a suit and is home in the daytime?'

Lucy reached for the scattered letters on the mat, shuffling them into some kind of order as she rolled her eyes. Jackson was muttering to himself, his eyes glued to the window.

'I don't know, do I? We're not at work, are we? I've seen him around before, but usually I'm alone and in my own car. I don't know. I don't really care. The house is empty now. We could do worse than have a vigilant looky-loo watching over the place.'

Dumping the pile of post into her bag, she put it on a side table and turned to face him. He was still glued to the window. 'Why are you so squir-relly today? It was a neighbour. Can we please just get on with getting some stuff done here? We need to empty Zoe's room first.'

She was halfway up the carpeted stairs before he spoke again.

'I'll get the boxes from the car. Sorry, Luce. I guess I don't like being questioned.'

'Funny. You don't seem to mind asking them.'

She gripped the banister when her eyes met his. He looked so...confused, out of his depth. Something deep within her stirred, but she didn't poke at the feeling. His fear sparked hers. That surprised her more than anything that had hap-pened in the last few days.

'You see why I am so guarded now?' she of-fered. The curl of his lip encouraged her to say more. 'Sometimes, the more pieces of yourself you give to people, the harder it is to keep them to-gether yourself. You don't always get those pieces back, Jackie boy.'

He didn't reply at first, just pressed his lips to-gether. She was at the top of the staircase when she heard him say, 'I understand. Sometimes, though, the right people keep those pieces safe because they know just how precious they are.'

She spun round, but he'd already left the house.

*What did he mean by that?*

She stared at the closed front door for a long

moment, before turning back and walking across the landing towards Zoe's room.

Six hours and three car trips later, they were done. Everything of Zoe's had been moved from the house, and they'd made a huge dent on the other rooms. The sight of Jackson taking apart furniture with a set of tools she hadn't even known he owned had been an event. Not entirely an unwelcome one, either. It was the first time in her life Lucy had understood the attraction women could have to a muscly man brandishing a drill. She'd had to go and get a glass of water to cool down at one point and remind herself of the reason they were there in the first place. Looking around her late sister's house had soon refocused her attention.

The kitchen had been easy enough: anything that she or Jackson didn't have went to the car. They would sell everything else with the rest of the stuff…eventually. The 'For Sale' sign would soon go up, and they'd hired a company that morning to put the rest of the stuff into a storage unit. Jackson had sorted that; he had a mate who worked there, so it had been a lot less painful than she'd first thought. They could go through the stuff later, when they were both stronger. They'd keep everything they could for Zoe, when she was older.

Lucy had taken some of the photos that were

framed, and she'd packed one that she'd seen Jackson linger over in the dining room: one of the three of them together at work. They were all looking pretty tired in wrinkled, stained scrubs. They'd worked together on a particularly hard case involving a teenager who'd come off his brand-new motorbike.

She still remembered it: the smells and sounds in the room; Jackson frantically pumping the lad's heart while she and Ronnie had raced to stop the bleeding, stabilising him enough to get him to the operating room. Hours later, when the patient was in the clear, his parents had asked them for a photo, to remember the people who had saved his life on that dark day. They'd sent the photo of the three of them standing there, by his bedside, smiling, to the hospital later. Ronnie had asked for a copy. She'd not looked at it properly in years. She reckoned Jackson might want it, and it would be good for Zoe to see her dad in action, see how close they'd all been. The thought of it being in storage gave her a pain in the pit of her stomach.

'You ready?' Jackson called from the front door. 'I thought we could ring Mum on the way, see if she wanted some dinner picking up as a thank you.'

She grabbed her bag and went over to him. Balancing the photo in one hand and her bag in the other, she fumbled around, coming up empty. 'You got the keys? I can't seem to find them.'

He waggled them at her. 'You left them in the door, Little Miss Organised. You hungry?'

'Starving,' she admitted. The sandwiches they'd had at lunch were a distant memory. Reaching for the keys, she almost dropped the photo frame. Jackson caught it. 'Jeez, thanks. I'm all fingers and thumbs.' Jackson laughed.

'I know. You're a mess.' He tucked the frame under his arm and leaned in close...so close. Lucy tensed until his hand came up and pulled something out of her tied back hair.

'Spider web,' he muttered, but when his eyes locked onto hers she could see his pupils up close. They were dilated. 'You still don't trust me, eh, Trig?'

He was close enough to reach out and touch, but the look in his eyes made her wish she were an ocean away. It was all too familiar a feeling. She'd felt it the day they'd met. Before the snarking had started.

'I trust you. I just thought you were going to pull my hair or something, our usual playground games.'

She felt his fingers brush a lock of hair back from her face, his touch along the shell of her ear.

'I was thinking about that, actually.' His voice had dipped lower, more a rumble than a voice. A sound that a woman could get addicted to if she wasn't quite so dead inside.

'You were.' She breathed, suddenly feeling as

though the pair of them were in some kind of weird bubble. 'And?'

'And I think we're a little old for the playground now, Luce. Given that we now have a kid of our own who will soon be in an actual playground, I think we should try to get along better.' He reached for another lock of hair. 'For example, it would be nice to be able to get a cobweb out of your hair without you freaking out.'

'I didn't freak out.'

'Your muscles tensed up so fast you almost snapped a tendon.'

'That's not a thing!' She laughed.

'Sure is; seen it. We have to share a house for the next sixteen years at least, Lucy. I'm probably going to see you naked at some point.'

*Jackson naked? What an intriguing thought.*

'Yeah! Probably… I mean, probably not. You do have doors at your place.'

'*Our* place. My point is that, if you flinch every time I come anywhere near you, it's going to get weird. Zoe will pick up on it too.' She was trying to concentrate on what he was saying, but he was still playing with her hair between his fingers. When he'd reached for it the first time, she'd seen the look on his face—as if he'd been wanting to do it the whole time. As if he was answering an old question when he touched it. She'd wondered things about him too over the years. Now, the grief was playing tricks on her mind. Yeah, that was definitely it. Close proximity broke down barriers—totally explicable.

It wasn't the only thing his words made click in her head. Zoe was probably going to pick up on a lot of things, if she wasn't careful, and their new charge wouldn't be the only one either. She'd have given the game away for sure if her colleagues could have seen her now.

His voice washed over her. 'Can we just…drop the fighting?'

*That almost sounded like a plea from his lips.*

'Try the whole "being nice" thing?'

Her hair was coiled around his index finger. She couldn't pull back if she tried, not that she really wanted to. Not if she was honest with herself. It felt too nice to be near him. To be close to someone like this, feel that connection.

*Well, this is it, Lucy-Lu. You're going mad, acting like some kind of rescue puppy, starved for affection. If you're not careful, you'll start humping his leg.*

His hand stopped moving, slowly shifting back so the hair corkscrewed free. Her silence had been too long; he'd taken it as an answer.

'Okay,' she said a little too quickly. 'I'll really try this time.'

His brows raised; he studied her face.

*Why do his eyes have to be so piercing?* One of life's little twists, she told herself, to make something she avoided looking at most of the time so ruddy entrancing.

'Good.' There it was, that crooked smile of his. 'You got everything?'

'Er, yeah. I thought you might like this, too.'

He studied the photo behind the glass, giving her the excuse to keep watching him, as if she could work out the path forward in the few seconds he was distracted. 'I remember this. The motorbike kid—Danny something.'

'Kirk,' she supplied. 'Danny Kirk.'

Jackson's lip curled. 'Yeah, that's him. He's actually studying medicine now. He wrote to Ronnie a few months ago.'

'That's…crazy!' Lucy breathed, looking again at the boy in the hospital bed. 'I bet Ronnie was thrilled.'

'He was.' Jackson was staring intently at the three of them all smiling in the photo. 'He said that we all inspired him that day. Ronnie was really proud of that.'

He met her eye, and the two of them looked around the hallway at the marks on the walls where the photos had once hung.

'It's weird, being here with things in boxes again. I always thought that Zoe would be driving to college from this house, you know? Taking photos in this hallway.' She pointed to the white front door. 'Harriet would have taken one of those

annoying pictures, with Zoe in her school uniform—all hashtags and crying emojis.'

Jackson laughed. 'Yeah, she would.' His smile
faded. 'Guess that's down to us now, eh?'

Lucy groaned and he laughed again. Tucking
the photo under one arm, he took her bag with the
other and headed to the door.

'Come on; I'm starved.'

Jackson's mother wouldn't hear of them bringing dinner. When they got to her house, Lucy realised why.

'Come in!' Sheila practically dragged them
both through to the kitchen. Zoe was sitting in a
high chair tucking into a bowl of chicken and rice.
Well, she was flicking more rice on the floor than
getting it into her mouth, but Sheila didn't seem
to care a jot. 'I made you some dinner. Not much,
just chicken and a bit of rice, some fresh bread…
The fruit pies are not ready yet; I'll pack them up
for you to take home next time.'

Two place settings were set side by side on the
island next to Zoe. The smell of cherries and pas-
try filled the air. It looked as if Sheila had been
cooking the whole day. There were containers
stacked up on the counter, with a pile of labels
on the side. Lucy was taking in the scene of domestic bliss when Sheila grabbed her, pulling her
in for a hug.

Lucy had seen her quite a lot over the years at

birthday dinners she'd been dragged along to, and other family events for Zoe, or Harriet and Ronnie. She'd cried at their wedding and fussed over Jackson in his best man suit. Lucy always felt a warmth from her, an 'earth mother' vibe she'd normally baulk at. From Sheila, it hit differently.

Jackson's mother was something that she never teased him about. The love both men had for their parents had been tangible. The way the whole family spoke about each other made Lucy miss her parents all the more. Her mother and father had never seen their children as adults. Had never seen what they had become in life. Every event and rite of passage was celebrated with the usual Denning joy; she and Harriet had never really talked about it, but she knew her sister had felt it too. She had cherished being part of their clan. Their love for each other was easy even now, tinged with loss. She could see the way Sheila and Walt were caring for Zoe and Jackson—and Lucy, for that matter.

She'd never divulged it to Jackson, but Lucy always thought it was sort of cool that he cared so much about them, enjoying the time they spent together. She loved the way he hugged his mum when she reached for him next. After all, who said a man couldn't spend time with the woman who'd given him life? Daughters did it all the time and no one thought anything of it. She watched him chatting away as he grabbed a baby wipe from the pack on the island. This father thing looked natural to him, easy.

*Uncle,* she reminded herself. *He's always been involved with Zoe. He made more time for her than I ever seemed to be able to do.*

He was talking to his mother about the packing they'd got done, the arrangements for the movers and the storage. All while making funny faces at Zoe and picking the worst mushed bits of rice off her clothes and floor.

She didn't even realise she'd been gawping like an idiot until Sheila spoke to her.

'Sorry, what?'

Sheila shot her a knowing look. 'I was just going to say it's lovely to see you two getting along so well. Sit down—eat!'

Lucy obediently took a seat next to Jackson, her stomach gurgling as a plate piled up with food was placed in front of her. Jackson was busy tucking into his, and the pair of them sat in a comfortable silence. Sheila put even more food into various containers, checking the oven from time to time. She chatted away to Zoe, who was now de-riced and demolishing a yoghurt and some fruit.

'She's been as good as gold today; she helped me in the garden earlier. She liked baking, although some of the buns she helped with might not be fit for the bake sale at church. The flour made her sneeze on one of the batches.' She turned to Jackson. 'I saved that batch for you.'

Lucy suppressed a laugh; Jackson gave her a side-eye. 'Thanks, Mum. Glad you enjoyed it. We're back at work next week, so I'll expect more sneeze buns in my future.'

Sheila giggled. 'You do that, love. Are you sure it's not too soon for you both?'

Jackson did one of his trademark shrugs. 'We'll manage. We both have departments to run, and they're already stretched as it is.' He didn't need to mention the hole that Ronnie had left in A & E. Sheila nodded at them both and turned her attention to Lucy. 'I will look after her. I know Jackson said you were a little worried.'

Lucy wanted the ground to swallow her up. 'I never—'

'Yes, you did.' Jackson sold her out before she could finish. She kicked him under the breakfast bar. He jumped but acted as if nothing had happened. 'I told you, Mum will pick her up from nursery. She'll bring her to ours too, so that she can be in bed on time.'

*Ours. Still sounds weird.*

Sheila didn't show a flicker of awkwardness. It was as though everyone was just okay with it, as if they were just doing this.

*We are doing this, you fool.*

'If you're sure it's not too much.' Lucy tried to get back into the conversation. 'I… We…' Jackson turned his head to her, but she didn't dare look at him. 'We do appreciate all this, really.'

Sheila waved her off with a flick of her floral-patterned tea towel. 'Give over. It's what grand-parents are for. Retirement is boring at times, I can tell you. Zoe and the three of us will have some adventures.'

Lucy couldn't help but smile at the thought of that. If her grandparents had been around, her ad-olescence might have been easier to cope with. It was one of the reasons Harriet hadn't waited to have kids. Her parents having them later in life had meant that their own two sets of grandparents had already passed. Harriet had talked about it be-fore she'd got pregnant. She hadn't wanted to wait.

'Family is not something to wait for,' she used to say.

Zoe would be with family she knew when Lucy and Jackson were at the hospital. Thinking about work next week was stressing her out enough—worrying about what Zoe would be doing, whether she would be happy…how the heck she would juggle work with her new life and responsibili-ties. 'I bet you will,' she told her earnestly. 'Zoe will love that.'

By the time Jackson's mother let them go, laden with yet more food, Zoe was tired out. Jackson could see her head lolling in the car seat on the way home, and he drove at the speed limit for once. When they pulled up at the house, Lucy lifted her out. 'I'll go put her to bed.'

Jackson put the food away, glancing at the boxes stacked in the dining room with a tired sigh. Decorating could wait, Lucy had said. The office walls were cream, the glossed paintwork unchipped. They'd taken most of Zoe's stuff straight to her room and added the rest of the boxes to the piles in the dining room. They'd deal with putting the furniture together tomorrow, which would make a huge difference to the rooms. They'd clear the clutter and help Zoe feel more at home.

There was still a fair bit of stuff to sort before their shifts started again. Work had been great about the time off, but he knew without Ronnie *and* him A&E would be stretched. Lucy's department was strong, but he knew both the staff and Lucy would be glad to be reunited. Never mind with her patients, who Lucy loved dearly. Children never saw her snakes; they got the softer side every time. He'd seen it, and he witnessed it now, watching her with Zoe.

Once everything was in order in the kitchen, he went upstairs to take a shower and wash off the day. After throwing his things into the hamper in the bathroom, he stood under the shower until he felt the hot water knead out all the kinks in his muscles. He felt it wake him up after the last few days of rubbish sleep. He felt like a medical student again, with that hazy, adrenaline fuelled way of moving through the day. When he turned off the shower, he felt human again. Wrapping a towel around his waist, he walked out to his bedroom and crashed straight into Lucy.

'What the—?'

'Oh, my God!'

His wet chest smacked straight into her face as she collided against him. Without thinking, he brought his arms up to catch her, which made things ten times worse. The towel tucked into itself around his hips fell away, just as he wrapped her tightly into his strong hold. For a second, neither said anything. Zoe let out a little cry from his former office, and they didn't move a muscle. At some point during the tussle, Lucy grappled for purchase with her flailing legs and arms and grabbed for something to steady her.

'Shh!' they said together. Listening, they both heaved a sigh of relief when they heard nothing more but silence.

Under his chin, he felt her head move up to look at him and he lowered his. Her marble-like blue-green eyes were right there, up close, wide beneath her impossibly dark lashes. His bare arms were wrapped around her tight, but he didn't move an inch.

'Jackson,' she whispered. 'My hands are on your bottom.'

'I noticed that, yeah.'

*It's one of the reasons I didn't move.*

She nibbled her lip, a cute little movement that did nothing to help his current situation.

'You're naked.'

'I know. I did have a towel,' he said, his voice low. 'I think you ripped it off.'

'I did *not*!' she squeaked, and Zoe made a loud snuffling noise. He gripped her tighter, just as she tightened her grip on him. 'I did not,' she said again, whispering. 'Be quiet.'

'You were the one that squealed.' He paused. 'Luce, you can take your hands off my bare bum now, if you want. I got you.'

'Oh, my God, sorry!' She gasped, pulling back. He went to grab the towel, but not before she saw…well, everything. She'd never call him Yeti again, that was for sure. He was hairless, aside from a line of thick, dark hair that ran down to his…parts…which she definitely saw a flash of before he whipped the towel back around himself. He noticed with a frisson of a thrill that her voice was breathy, almost panting—the shock, obviously. The panic of waking the toddler in the next room, who seemingly hated sleep at the best of times.

*Still, a man can dream…*

'I was trying to stop myself falling.'

He smirked, his chest heaving too. His breath was as ragged as the fast little puffs of air from her luscious lips. A rivulet of water dripped down his chest, running down his abs like a raindrop down a window pane. She tracked its movement as he stole a long look at her.

'You grabbed me like a squirrel does a tree.' Her jaw dropped, but when she met his eye he could see he was flushed.

*This woman.* She'd been in his head for five years, one way or another, a swirling tornado in his logical brain. She was addictive, maddening, enchanting, challenging.

He wondered how much he could fluster her right now. He was tempted to push it, just to see. 'It's fine, Trig. I told you we'd see each other naked eventually.'

His lopsided smile was the last thing she saw as he walked past her to his room.

'So, we could unpack some more, if you want. My vote is for a movie and a drink, what do you think?'

Those choices were not the thing on her mind at this minute. Either way, both meant being close to him for the evening.

*I need a minute to recover.*

'Whatever you want,' she said, trying to shrug nonchalantly. 'I'll just get changed.'

She shut the bathroom door and sagged against it. On the opposite wall, she caught her reflection in the steamed-up mirror. She saw her flushed red cheeks, the sparkle of attraction in her eyes. On her top, she had an imprint of where his wet body had touched hers. She could almost make out the ab imprints. Pulling the damp hoodie over her head, she stuffed it into the hamper.

Looking up at the ceiling, she closed her eyes. 'Harriet, if this is part of your plan, girl—it's not happening.' Taking off the rest of her clothes, she turned the shower temperature to cold.

She had work to think about, boxes to unpack, her place to sort and Zoe to look after. As the cold water hit her, she resolved to stick to the plan, like she always did. Teeny moments of attraction had peppered their involvement for so long, she was surprised she still felt them so acutely. Of course, it was easier when she hadn't been up close and personal with his butt cheeks. Wondering what was under his scrubs when she was bored at work had paled into insignificance the second that towel had hit the deck.

It wasn't the only thing hitting it, either. Breakfast was going to be awkward with a capital A. A for abs—washboard ones. She was surprised the drop of water she'd tracked hadn't sizzled to nothing.

'No, Lucy. Focus!'

'You say something?' She froze under the spray when Jackson's voice came from the other side of the door.

'No, no! Be out in a minute!'

'Okay. Meet you downstairs?'

'Yeah!' she squealed, her voice sounding strangled. 'Coming!'

She waited until she heard him downstairs and scrambled to get out. 'Coming?' She chided her reflection after she wiped the steam off the glass. 'Coming, seriously?' She jabbed a finger at her mirror image. 'That's one thing you won't be doing. Get it together!'

She needed to get back to work. She had a lot to sort out and, last time she checked, a hot, glistening wet Jackson Denning was not on her to-do list. It would stay that way.

# CHAPTER EIGHT

'DO YOU THINK we should go in separately? I could hang back.' Jackson's incredulous look told her his answer. 'Okay, stupid question.'

'Yeah, pretty dumb.'

Since the naked body-bumping incident, they'd fallen into a pattern of sorts. By the time she'd settled her nerves enough to go downstairs, he'd poured out wine for them both and was sitting on the sofa, flicking through the streaming options as though nothing had happened, and that was good enough for her.

The cold shower and verbal telling off she'd given herself upstairs had strengthened her resolve a little. Her sister had just died, and her brother-in-law. She'd inherited a baby and had had to move house, one huge event after the other. He'd gone through it too, and had to watch his parents grieve for his brother to boot. Whatever tingle his touch produced was one-sided. Those long looks he'd thrown her were nothing, built up in her head, or by her surprisingly awakened libido. Whatever she'd felt in that moment, it was nothing on the scale of 'whoa' moments she'd endured. Although seeing Jackson naked, feeling his hard body up against hers, wasn't exactly something she'd 'endured' and it was not so much 'whoa' as 'wow'.

She'd been ever more aware of his presence since, in the proximity of him when they were cooking together. Passing on the landing when taking turns to settle Zoe back down to sleep. The smell of his aftershave in the bathroom, seeing his clothes in the washing machine along with hers and Zoe's.

He had looked after both Zoe and her. She'd watched them together. She'd never really bought into the whole 'man holding a child being sexy' thing. In her line of work, she saw it often, but seeing Zoe in Jackson's huge arms hit differently, put it that way.

No matter what she tried to tell herself to the contrary, she was seeing him in a new light. The trouble was, she couldn't find the switch to turn it off. She'd had a moment of what she could consider to be jealousy too, if she hadn't known better.

Over the years, she'd never cared about someone enough to feel the green-eyed monster's breath on her back. When it had happened, she hadn't cottoned on to what the sudden rush of emotion was at first, but it would have been pretty hard *not* to notice the way the nursery staff fawned over him. She was pretty sure they wouldn't be able to pick her out of a line up. They all but ignored her.

Either that or they were fluttering their lashes so fast, they missed her in their line of sight.

Making the most of being with Zoe before they went back to work had been kind of nice. She felt more at home in his house. The boxes were slowly getting sorted. The to-do list didn't feel so overwhelming. Zoe was settling down. They'd been to drop off Zoe at nursery together. They both agreed it was better to settle her back in before work schedules came into play, make things as normal as possible for her, or what was the new normal of her life now.

They'd planned to use the time she was at nursery to tackle another day of clearing Harriet's and her places out ready for the respective sale and rental ahead. She was keeping her mortgage on. She felt absurdly better with an escape plan, not that she could ever realistically use it. Still, that place was the first home she'd bought on her own. The inheritance from her parents was tied up in it. Something made her want to keep hold of it and cover the mortgage with a long-term tenant. It would even provide a little income.

Jackson had agreed it made sense and insisted that he would cover his own mortgage. She'd played the fifty-fifty card on him on that one. She didn't want to take half his house, and she wasn't going to live there without fully paying her way. He'd reluctantly given in, eventually. The compromises were getting easier as each day went by.

The easiest decision they'd come to was to take another two weeks off work together, to get things done and be there for Zoe.

Lucy found she didn't even mind that. Work was a huge part of her life, but for once she wasn't in such a hurry. The FOMO wasn't as sharp as it had been in the past. The hospital had agreed without issue, so that was that. Their time in their little bubble had been extended. Each day, the grief and feelings of being overwhelmed fell away, tiny pieces at a time.

Zoe was a source of joy for them both. Being so young, after a few weeks the calls for Mummy and Daddy had lessened, which gave them a lot of relief, but also broke their heart at the same time. Jackson's walls now held the photos from Harriet's and Ronnie's house, and he'd even come back from shopping one day with a few of the three of them together.

Lucy had barely managed to hold her poker face at seeing those. She wondered how many of them he had, how many more snaps she'd not been aware of. The paintball photo was one of them, now enlarged and framed. One was of Harriet and her on the day of their wedding, and she knew it wasn't one from the official wedding photographer. Harriet had made her look at those for weeks after the wedding, to the point where Lucy had begged her to stop.

It was a strange photo to put up, really. Harriet

wasn't even fully in the shot. Her face was hidden from view, hugging Lucy to her, and Lucy's eyes were shut tight. A tear glistened on her cheek. Why Jackson had taken that shot at that moment, she didn't understand.

She remembered the moment well. It had been after the first dance, and Lucy had stood on the sidelines and cried—not full on sobbing or ugly crying, of course, just silent little tears as she'd watched her little sister dance with her new husband. She remembered the emotions she'd had swirling through her. She could see them on her features in the photo, even with her eyes hidden behind tear-soaked lashes.

She'd felt like a proud parent, as if her child was being married off, that her job was done. She'd been beyond sad that her parents weren't there to see it. She'd wished she truly believed that they were watching from somewhere, happy that their children had turned out so well. She remembered Jackson had come to her side as she'd watched the newlyweds dance. She'd brushed her tears away quickly, folding her arms. The DJ had just called for the other couples to join the couple on the dance floor.

'Dance with me?' he'd asked, but she'd shaken her head the second the words had come out of his mouth. 'I'd rather stick pins in my eyeballs, thanks, Denning.'

'Yeah, I figured as much.' He'd laughed, passing her a handkerchief from his pocket and moving away. She'd seen a few of the guests cast admiring glances his way. She was pretty sure his dance card would get filled.

When the dance had finished, Harriet had come straight over, beauty radiating from her. She'd been a stunning bride, and when she'd hugged Lucy to her she'd whispered, 'Thank you', and Lucy had cried again.

Jackson must have taken the photo then, she realised. When he'd hung it up in the lounge, she'd lingered over it.

'Jackson, why this one?' she'd asked him. 'You can't even see Harriet's face.'

He'd just shrugged, muttering something vague and getting back to his hammering. It still hung on the wall, and she had to admit she did love it. She quite liked the house, too. They'd brought the swing set over from Zoe's old house. The more they moved around each other, cooking together, looking after Zoe, the more she felt at home—if she ignored the sizzling sexual tension she'd felt ever since Showergate.

Zoe was calmer, sleeping better than she ever had. It was nice, their little bubble. She didn't want to strangle Jackson nearly as much as she used to, and he called her Trig less and less—although Luce seemed to have stuck. She'd stopped bothering to correct him any more.

She'd started calling him Jack. Zoe's 'Jack-Jack'

was seemingly not so bad to share a life with. It was tolerable. When she caught a flash of his muscles, it was more than tolerable, in fact. She'd had a few more cold showers recently, that was for sure. She'd even taken them both to her special coffee shop after one very early morning wake-up call from Zoe.

Amy had just been leaving when they'd arrived. She'd texted, rapid-fire, seconds after leaving:

Call me! You look so cute together! OMG! It's so weird to see you getting on. We need to talk, boss!

Lucy had fobbed her off.

Whatever...see you at work!

That was going to be a conversation and a half when she got back on the ward. She still didn't know how to shut it down, either. Their worlds were merging fast and work had seemed a far-off concept at the time. Until now, when they were about to walk through the doors.

As they sat in the car, staring at their workplace, Lucy knew that the woman she'd been the last time she'd been in that building wasn't the one setting foot in there today.

'So,' she ventured, pushing her mindset back into the here and now. 'How are we going to handle this? People will ask questions.'

'Sure.' He nodded. 'HR know your change of address, though, right?'

'It's not about HR. What do we say when people ask about Zoe?'

Jackson chuckled, leaving the car without answering her question.

'Rude,' she muttered, about to get out when she realised he was walking round to open her door. 'Thanks.' He held out the crook of his arm. She shouldered her handbag, an airbag between them as they fell into step.

'People are not going to be interrogating us about the ins and outs. They'll just be happy to see us back.' His steps slowed. 'Are you wanting to keep it a secret or something?'

'No, no.' She wouldn't have Zoe be some secret. 'I'm not sure people will understand it, though. Liz in HR choked on her bagel when I called to change my address to yours.'

'Ours,' he corrected. 'I bet she did. Remember that dumb agreement we had to sign?'

Lucy smirked up at him. 'I have it framed in my office. Scares the newbies into line.'

Jackson's laugh was a loud, hearty rumble that she enjoyed just a little too much.

When they reached the foyer, he shot her a wink. 'If people dare ask, you tell them what you need to. It's our business, Trig.' Her nickname sounded almost affectionate. 'I won't say anything till you're ready. Deal?'

'Deal.'

'Have a good day.' He smirked. 'Play nice with the other children.'

Rolling her eyes, she headed to the ward.

She didn't have time to answer any questions, as it happened. The second she'd turned her pager on, she was back in A&E.

'What happened?' she asked Jackson as she panted at the nurses' station. 'I'd barely got changed.'

Seeing Jackson in his uniform was a jolt too.

*Had he looked that good in scrubs before?*

She never got the chance to think about it; seeing his expression had her following him to one of the trauma rooms.

'Glad you got the page. I know it was quick.' He paused behind the curtain. 'Tom Jefferson, eight years old. Partly unrestrained passenger.' His lips were tight, words clipped. 'RTA. Mother's gone to surgery already. Fractured pelvis, open femur fracture.' His jaw clenched. 'Looks like he took the top half of his belt off without his mum realising. Dad's on his way from work.'

He paused, as if he needed a minute to process his own words. 'He has a fractured clavicle, head lacerations. He had his brain and spine cleared before we got here, but he's pretty shaken up. Nurse is still digging glass out of his right side—superficial cuts, luckily. Breathe, Luce.'

She gasped, air inflating her lungs in one shuddery breath. 'Thanks,' she muttered. 'Didn't re-alise I wasn't.'

They gave each other a tiny little nod, as if ac-knowledging the moment, before they pulled back the curtain.

'Hi, Tom, I'm Dr Denning, and this is Dr Bake-well.'

Harriet stared back at her from the hospital bed, her blonde hair matted with blood. When Lucy blinked, she was gone. A young boy stared back, hair the colour of Zoe's, with wide, scared eyes. His legs only came halfway down the long bed. He looked lost, tiny against his stark white sur-roundings.

'Where's my mum?' he asked. His bottom lip was trembling from the effort of trying not to cry. It was enough to break Lucy out of her stupor. 'Is she okay?'

'She's going to be, Tom. Your dad's on his way.' She offered him an encouraging smile as she stepped closer, scanning his body and itemis-ing his injuries in her head as Jackson spoke to the nurse. She heard her telling him that the glass was all out now, him telling her they'd take it from here. 'In the meantime, your mum wants us to look after you. That okay?'

Once the nurse had brought back dressings and a sling, closing the curtain behind her, he gave a slow nod.

'Good work, pal.' Jackson pointed to the equipment. 'Now you've been checked out and cleaned up, I need to dress these little cuts. Your arm and shoulder are going to be pretty sore for a while.'

'It hurts.' Tom's voice was hoarse, pained. 'I'm not going to school today, am I?'

Jackson shook his head. 'No school for a few days, but that's okay.' He leaned in, giving Lucy a chance to blink her tears away as she prepared the suture kit for his head. 'Dr Bakewell here is my friend, and she runs the children's ward. We need to give you a little sleepover tonight, but the children's ward has all the good, fun stuff.' He looked around him, pretending to be bored. 'Not like down here.'

Lucy's heart warmed as the little boy smiled for the first time, colour returning to his cheeks.

'That's right,' she agreed. 'Tom, we have all the good stuff. So, while your mum has a little rest, you and your dad can come hang out with me.' She dropped her voice to a near whisper. 'I have so many video games, you won't believe it.'

His eyes lit up. When she looked at Jackson, he was watching her, that little crooked smile matching the sparkle in his deep-brown eyes.

'Me and Dad love video games!' His little nose scrunched up. 'Xbox or PlayStation?'

'Both,' she pretended to brag. 'Now, I'm going to put some little stitches just here.' Her gloved hands gently touched the skin near his head laceration. 'Dr Denning will put bandages on your other cuts, and then we will have to put a sling on your arm to support that pesky broken bone.' She pointed at his shoulder. 'Do you know what bone you broke?'

He gave a head-shake. 'Well, it's called your collarbone.' She pointed along her own, showing him the wing-like bone jutting from her shoulder. 'The medical name for it is a clavicle, so when your dad comes you can tell him you learned all about the human body, eh?'

Another little smile came, which felt like the best reward.

Jackson leaned in, meeting him at eye level. 'Now, we need to give you some medicine for your pain, buddy. We need you to be brave, because it's a little needle, and another one in your arm.'

The little boy gulped, but sat a tiny bit straighter. 'I'm brave. Dad said when I turn nine I'll get more brave too.' He went to shrug, but winced despite the pain relief he'd already been given. 'So it's okay. I'll get more.'

Jackson's laugh felt like a balm to Lucy's triggered grief.

'Exactly.' He thumbed a gloved hand at Lucy. 'And, once you get settled upstairs, Dr Bakewell has special treats for bravery.'

Tom flashed little white teeth, showing a gap where his two front teeth had been.

'Tom?' a frantic voice called, and the curtain

swished back to show a man who looked just like the boy in the bed. His Hi Vis jacket loomed bright-orange, throwing colour into the room as he started to cry. 'Oh, buddy!' He didn't even glance at the doctors as he went to his boy and kissed his forehead. 'Oh, mate. I'm so sorry, I got here as fast as I could. Are you okay?'

Tom raised his good arm and cupped his dad's cheek. 'I'm being brave, Dad.' He eyed Lucy. 'She has Xbox and PlayStation, and she said we could play later.'

Tom's dad laughed and Lucy watched them, noting the relief on his dad's face as he laughed, kissing his boy and looking at his injuries. When she had pushed down her emotion enough to look Jackson in the eye, she couldn't help but see the tear he was wiping away with his sleeve. Clearing her throat, she got back to work.

'Mr Jefferson? I'm Dr Bakewell. Do you have a couple of minutes to have a little chat while Dr Denning stays with Tom? Tom?' She smiled. 'I'll be back soon. I just need to tell your dad how brave you are. Dr Denning will give you something to make your head feel a little bit numb, so we can get you sorted. Okay?'

The father followed her out, and she moved him away from the cubicle far enough that she could no longer hear Jackson discuss video games with Tom as he dealt with his dressings.

'I can't believe this.' The father was drip-white.

The adrenaline fading with the happy relaxed façade he'd put up for his son. 'The police called me, said he'd not had his belt on properly. He was on the way to school with his mum.' He leaned against the wall. 'I could have lost them both. They're everything. Is my wife going to be okay? Is Tom?' For a second, Lucy saw a flash of bloodied blonde hair.

*It's never going to be okay. Not really.*

'Doctor?'

She took a deep breath. 'Mr Jefferson, your wife and son are going to be fine. We are all here to look after you. I promise you; your family is in good hands.' She pointed to an unoccupied row of chairs along the corridor. 'Come, take a seat. I'll get the nurses to get an update on your wife.' She pointed to the foyer. 'In fact, I'll do that now for you. Go get a coffee and, when you get back, I'll update you on everything. Tom needs to stay here overnight for observations, but we can make up a bed for you.'

'Thank you.' Mr Jefferson finally drew breath. 'Coffee sounds good at the moment.'

She watched him head away on shaky legs and, calling over a nurse, wondered if Mr Jefferson would ever truly know just how lucky he was.

She was back at the funeral, standing alone by the flower-adorned coffins. There was no minister, no mourners. She was alone, and then Harriet was there. She saw her, standing at a distance. She was speaking, her lips moving fast, forming words that didn't reach Lucy's ears.

'I can't hear you, Harry! Come here! Please!'

She'd begged her to step closer to her side, past the wooden boxes. Her legs wouldn't move. She tried everything, but the grass held her feet fast to the ground.

'Harry!' she shouted, over and over, begging her sister to come closer, knowing she was saying something but not hearing it. 'Harriet, I can't hear you!' she yelled, crying with frustration. She longed to run to her sister and hold her, hear what she had to say. 'Tell me, please! What are you telling me?'

Harriet didn't come. She just kept smiling as she spoke her silent message. Lucy kept shouting, the coffins standing between them fixed points. 'Tell me!' she screamed, wishing she could rip her body away from the turf. 'Please?' she cried. 'Tell me!'

'Luce, it's ok! Stop, it's okay!'

'No! No! He doesn't know how lucky he is!' she screamed as something grabbed her. The coffins disappeared and she was in the dark, blinking the water from her eyes as she tried to focus. 'Jackson?'

'Yeah.' He soothed her. 'It's me. You're okay.'

'Harriet,' she gulped out between gasps. 'Harry was here.'

'It was a dream. Deep breaths.' Her eyes adjusted to the dim light from the landing. She was in her room, her bed, in her new home.

*Home. Huh.*

Her racing mind, focusing on five things at once, almost skipped over the relief she felt that she was here. The lack of shock that it wasn't her flat's bedroom walls she could see in the dim light. Jackson was stroking her arms, his bare chest rising and falling at a tempo matching hers. 'Everything's okay.'

'No,' she pushed out, unable to breathe. Her heart was pulsing in her ears, a thudding drum beat. 'I—'

'You can.' He stopped her. 'You can breathe. It's okay. I've got you. Control it. In through the nose, doctor, out through the mouth. Focus on me, Look at me.'

She pushed away the image of the flower-strewn coffins, replacing them with the dark pull of his concerned gaze. She did as he asked until the burning in her chest subsided.

He'd sensed it, the looming panic attack. Moving closer, he ran his hands down her arms one more time. He reached for the shaking hand in her lap. 'I'm here, Luce,' he'd said softly, the breath pushed out from his words whispering over her skin as he kissed the back of her hand. 'I'm not going anywhere, ever. Okay?'

She looked back at him, and the strength of conviction in his expression almost felled her. It was as though the swirling brown of his eyes was more intense, boring into her soul to bring the words home. 'You believe me, right, Luce?'

'Yes.' She nodded, squeezing his hand tight with her own. 'I know you'll stay with me.'

His face relaxed, his furrowed brow easing. 'For ever,' he mumbled, pulling their entwined hands to rest against his chest. 'For ever, Lucy. You'll never be alone again. Not while I'm here.'

The tears came soon after. He soothed her and shushed her. He brought her into his huge, unyielding embrace and lay down with her. She rested her head on his chest and fell asleep, listening to the beat of his heart.

The sun was up when Zoe woke them with her shouts, still wrapped together, her hand still caged by his, his fingers wrapped around hers. As she roused from sleep, from the feeling of waking with someone for the first time in, well, a long time, she stilled her body. She knew she had to move, but delayed it anyway. His heartbeat was steady against the shell of her ear. Neither had moved an inch the whole night.

Zoe yelled louder. 'Jack-Jack!'

When she felt him stir beneath her, the night before sprang into her head. His whispered words in the dark: *for ever*.

*Oh, it was going to be another weird day.*

'Morning,' he mumbled. He lifted their entwined hands, brushing a stubbly kiss onto her skin. 'You okay?'

'Yeah,' she bluffed, before she pulled away. Reality was rising faster than the sun through her window, sending her scrambling from their embrace like a startled vampire. 'I'll go get Zoe.'

'Luce?' he tried, his hold lingering before she untwined her fingers.

'I'm fine. Honestly. First day back was tough, that's all.' She sprang away from him and tucked her hand out of sight. He didn't reach for it again. His words were few after that, clipped. They went through the motions, their morning routine awkwardly stilted.

Now they were here again, back out of the bubble. Back to the normality of work. She didn't know quite how to feel about it yet. They'd dropped Zoe off at his mother's house that morning, both of his parents meeting them at the door with a tender smile. Sheila had pulled her in for a hug while the men had taken Zoe indoors with her stuff.

'Have a good day, love,' Sheila had said softly into her ear. 'You look tired. Take it easy on yourself, okay? Juggling family and work are hard enough at the best of times.'

Jackson appeared behind her, so she didn't get the chance to reply. She didn't know what she would have said anyway.

*I had a nightmare? Your son is dreamy to wake up next to, and now I'm freaked out about it happening again—or not happening again?*

The way she'd woken in his arms wasn't normal; she knew that much. Even without Jackson's and her complicated relationship, and their arrangement, she'd never felt like that waking up with a man in her bed. She didn't have much to compare it to, sure, but she had the feeling waking up with Aaron from the fracture clinic would *not* have felt that good, that, safe, that good. She was running out of ways to categorise it, which frustrated her all the more. She was so turned around, she didn't know what to trust. Even her gut was an unreliable narrator around Jackson.

She pushed the scramble of thoughts away, focusing on the here and now, one foot in front of the other, allowing one of her other new emotions to push to the front. Parental guilt popped its head up first, begging to be acknowledged. It had felt strange, leaving Zoe there and going off to work again. She'd got pretty used to being home with Jackson and her. Was this what working parents experienced every day? She wasn't sure she liked it. Watching Jackson at home that morning, losing his keys, spilling his coffee down his shirt, she knew she wasn't the only one affected by things.

*Does he feel what I do, or is that just him being his usual caring self?*

Perhaps she should have chosen Neurology. Maybe then she'd know what was going in his head.

*Oh, shut up, you daft fool. Not even science can help you on this one.*

They'd spent the car ride in silence. Lucy had busied herself scrolling through her phone while Jackson had grumbled about pretty much every other driver in the morning traffic.

Now they were sitting in his car in the staff parking area, drive-through coffees in hand, neither making a move to leave.

She felt his hand cover hers. They moved closer in the car, his hand still holding hers.

'You look a little tired,' she murmured. He looked away, focusing on their entwined hands. She followed his gaze and, despite herself, gave him a little squeeze with her fingers. 'I slept like a baby,' he eventually offered. His eyes found hers again, his brows furrowing a little. 'I was a little worried about you, though. I've never seen you like that. It was worse than the panic attack before. What was on your mind?'

'Just a bad dream—the Jeffersons yesterday…'

'Definitely a baptism by fire,' he replied softly. 'It got to me too.'

'I'm okay,' she assured him. 'After a bit of sleep and coffee. It's all good.'

She saw his face change, relax, and felt the relief flowing through him.

*He's relieved it's not about him. He doesn't feel this tension*, she thought.

The pang was unexpected. Her shields jolted to life. 'I'm not made of stone, Jackson. I know I'm difficult at times, I push things down, but I'm a wreck too.' She nudged her head towards the building before them. 'I've been looking forward to work, to getting back to some kind of reality. Moving, Zoe…everything's been so different, hasn't it? I thought it would feel easier, coming here—comfortable—but I feel sick about it.' If he wasn't going to talk about them spending the night together, then neither was she.

'I get it, more than you know. I love having you both at home. I know it's been tough, and sad, but I like having you two to come home to. You're not as prickly as you think, you know.'

Her smile was genuine then; she felt his words wash over her and her heart swelled. It was a strange feeling, but one that was happening more and more. The more she was around him at their house, looking after Zoe, fighting over the remote, it felt sort of…nice…and sexy.

*Confusing! You mean confusing.*

She'd fallen asleep listening to his heart beating; that had been more than sexy. It had been… more than a long-buried sexual frisson.

'I like it too.'

'You do?'

'Yeah,' she told him earnestly. 'I don't think I

would have coped on my own. I like being home with you both. It feels…normal almost, or it's starting to feel that way.'

His thumb started to move up and down the skin on the back of her hand, slow circles that made her nerve endings sing.

'I'm not as bad as you thought, eh?'

His tone was teasing, but it didn't make her her blood boil as it usually did. In fact, it made her feel a heat she'd never expected to feel. *For ever*: those words in his gravelly voice kept playing on repeat in her head.

'No,' she admitted. 'Not at all.' He was closer now; their faces had gravitated together. She could smell his aftershave, the one she had grown accustomed to in the bathroom they shared, on his skin. Heck, on her sheets now. It was all around her.

'You're not so bad either.' He breathed, his eyes falling to her lips. She licked them, feeling the air change in the car and dry out around them. 'Luce, about last night. Do you want to…?'

Her mobile rang out and they both jumped. The spell broken, she went to get it and saw the time on the dashboard.

'We'd better get in,' she told him. 'I bet that's work.' She was desperate to hear what he was going to say but, either way he went, it felt as if pain wasn't far behind. If he felt it too, so what? He and Zoe were all she had left. If it failed, it would be unbearable.

*Even less bearable than knowing what could be, and not having it.*

'Listen, thanks for last night.' She licked her lips again, which had gone bone-dry. 'For being there…you know, for my panic attack. It…well, it won't happen again, I'm sure.' There it was—an out wrapped in an apologetic thank you.

When she looked at him again, he was running his hands through his hair, an odd expression on his face.

'Yeah, of course.' He huffed, picking up their coffees. 'If you're sure, let's go.'

# CHAPTER NINE

JACKSON DIDN'T TAKE a full breath until he got to the locker room to change into his scrubs.

*What the hell was that?*

Lucy had been on the phone on the walk in, giving him a coy little wave before dashing off to her department. His heart was still beating hard in his chest. A bit like the night before, when he'd lain in her bed listening to her soft little breaths as she'd slept against his bare chest. He'd lain there in the dark, cradling her and wishing he knew what was going on in that feisty, stubborn head. He'd been torn between wanting to wake her to ask if she felt a fraction of what he did and willing the sun not to rise so they could stay like that for ever.

It was harder to brush off how he felt about someone when he were in close proximity all the time. His toothbrush sat next to hers in the bathroom but she still felt like a stranger sometimes. They'd held hands until she'd woken up and shut herself away from him again, behind the snakes that had slumbered soundly in his embrace hours earlier. If he didn't know better, he and Lucy Bakewell, tormentor and tormentee, had just had a moment—a big moment. On top of many moments they'd had over the last few weeks. If that phone hadn't rung, he'd have finished that sentence.

*What the hell are you thinking?*

He knew what he'd been thinking. What he'd been thinking was that he wanted to ask Lucy out to dinner. He wanted to crack open those shields of hers and have her willing to let him in.

If he was honest with himself, having her at his house, their house, had been good. Since Ronnie had passed, he'd had to stop himself from feeling like it was a gift. He'd liked having her around. He fancied her, big time. She was unlike any other woman he'd ever met before, or since. She'd shot him in the nether regions on their very first encounter, and when he'd tackled her about it she'd riled him up in more ways than one.

After that day, when his pride was hurt, when it became obvious that not only did she not see him as a love interest but a rival, he'd forgotten about it. He shouldn't have entertained the thought anyway. He'd expected to meet the sister of the woman Ronnie was dating. He'd never expected to see her any other way. He shouldn't have, but he was addicted. He enjoyed the banter, the feelings she evoked within him when they locked horns. Then he'd become part of her world, her family, and it hadn't been possible. He'd brushed it off as a passing fancy, something not meant to be. The way it was possible to fancy someone one minute, and then realise it wasn't attraction at all, or something that might turn into something that would last longer than an angry, sexy, frantic screw.

He'd dated, but no one seemed to measure up. He'd thought it just wasn't his time. There'd been no deadline to meet. Then Ronnie and Harriet had passed, and he'd thought *that* was why they'd met. It was part of a cosmic plan somehow. He was meant to be there to raise Zoe, stop her being alone in the world—his brother's last wish. Lucy had just been part of the deal, and he was okay with that. Ronnie had known he could handle it, and Harriet too. He seemed to be the only one who wasn't terrified of her, who didn't step away when she pushed.

They pushed each other and made the other feel alive, passionate. The second he'd touched her hand, he'd known co-parenting wasn't the full story. This feeling wasn't a by-product of being so closely connected, or the grief. It was a primal need to have this woman. She was his. He was hooked, and he didn't even realise when his cravings had started. If her phone hadn't gone off, he'd have asked her out, told her he *wanted* to talk about last night.

Which couldn't happen, obviously. He thought he'd been more than a comfort blanket, but it was all in his addled head. They were raising a kid together, working together. If he stuffed this up,

made things awkward when they were just starting to get on, when she was just starting to let him
in, it would ruin everything. They had to solidify
this arrangement in a few short months. Even ac-
knowledging the logic of it all, he couldn't quite
quell the irritation he felt. Maybe he should have
got a clue when she'd been worried about people
finding out about their new situation.

He was pulling on his scrub top when Dr Josh
Fillion walked in, the doctor filling Ronnie's job.
Jackson had exchanged a few emails with him,
and had had an online meeting while he'd been
off to get the guy up to speed on the way he ran
his department. From what he'd been told by his
staff, Josh was doing a pretty good job.

'Hey, man, first week back? Sorry I missed you
yesterday—day off.'

'Yep.' He clipped his ID to his uniform. 'Everything still standing, that's a good start. Settling
in okay?'

Josh immediately launched into what was going
on and what patients they'd had in. Taking his
wallet and keys from his pockets, stashing them
in his locker, Jackson listened while he checked
his phone. On the screensaver was a photo of Lucy
and Zoe. He'd taken it when she hadn't been looking, at the local park near his house. Lucy had
taken Zoe down the big slide. They were both
laughing, faces happy, full of fun. He dashed off

an action snap as they'd zoomed down the steel slope. It had been a good afternoon, carefree.

'That your daughter? She's cute.' Josh cut through his thoughts, bringing him back to reality. He thought of Lucy, and decided, for now, work was work. Perhaps the more separate they kept things, the less likely he'd be to lose his damn mind.

'Er…yeah.' Jackson click-locked the phone, turning the screen black. 'I'd better get out there.'

'Sure, see you in a minute,' Josh replied, turning to his locker—Ronnie's old locker. Jackson had cleaned Ronnie's stuff out himself and taken it home. He knew it wasn't his any more, but it still hit hard, as if Ronnie had never been there. He pushed his way out of the door, suddenly finding the air thin.

He could see some of his staff at the nurses' station; they all stopped when they saw him approaching. Steeling himself, he shot them a strong smile he didn't feel.

*I should have addressed this yesterday.*

They didn't know how to act around him.

'Hey, everyone,' he addressed them together. 'I know you all probably have things you want to say. I spoke to some of you yesterday but, since most of us are here, I'd just like to say thanks for covering, and for all the cards and stuff for Zoe, but I'd like to concentrate on the work now.'

Their faces all had the same expressions: pity,

sorrow, understanding. A few nodded, and he was grateful more than ever for the team he had under him. 'I know we all miss Ronnie, but he'd want us to carry on, kicking butt and saving lives.' He folded his arms, holding himself together when he felt as if he might come apart. The wave of grief crashed against his sand walls. 'That okay with everyone?'

One of the nurses spoke first. 'Hell, yeah.' He nodded. 'For Ronnie, guys.'

He could tell the rest of them were on board. A couple wiped at tears.

'For Ronnie,' he echoed. 'Let's save some lives, eh, people?'

As his team got back to work, and he headed to his first patient of the day, he wondered if Lucy was okay. He'd check on her later and see if she wanted to grab lunch. If this was all that being in her life was going to be, he'd just have to take what he could get.

'It's okay, Emma. Just a little scratch.' The flushed seven-year-old made a little whimper as the nurse inserted the cannula. Lucy was standing at the other side of her bed, holding her hand and keeping her steady. She had a pretty nasty infection. If her mother hadn't brought her in when she had, it could have been a lot worse. Sepsis worked fast, but it had been caught early, and getting fluids into her would help, alongside antibiotics.

Emma nodded from under her oxygen mask. Her breathing had been shallow when she'd arrived, a bad chest infection causing an asthma attack. Lucy had seen it a hundred times, but watching a child struggle for breath was tough.

'That's it, all done! It might just feel a little cold down your arm for a minute, and then you should feel a little better.'

'Thank you,' her mother said from the back of the cubicle. 'She couldn't breathe in the car; I was so scared we wouldn't get here in time.'

Lucy turned to her. 'You got her here, and she's going to be fine. We'll keep her overnight, monitor her, but she's doing great. Her oxygen levels have improved already. We'll keep her on high-flow O2 for now till they increase over ninety percent. The liquid steroids we gave her act fast, and the fluids on IV will help to hydrate her.

'Emma,' she said gently. 'I need you to be really careful with your hand here, okay? Be careful not to pull the wires.'

She read through her notes again. 'So, your GP diagnosed asthma at four?' Her mother nodded. 'How is she doing with the inhalers? Did he explain about using them with the spacer and mask?'

'I don't like my spacer,' Emma's muffled voice retorted from under the mask covering her nose and mouth. 'It smells funny.'

'She doesn't like doing it.' Her mother blushed. 'I try my best, but...'

Lucy nodded gently. 'I'll tell you what, Emma, I'll make you a deal. I'll give you a couple of new spacers with some masks attached and we'll see if they are any better. That medicine is boring, I know, having to do it every day, but it helps your lungs to work better. Especially when you get a nasty cold.'

'You've been great, the A&E doctor too. He came running over to us when we got to the main doors. He just picked her up and carried her to a bed. Will you be able to thank him for us?'

'Sure, did you get his name?'

The mother looked pained. 'Oh, gosh, you know—I didn't. He was very tall, though—huge, actually.'

Lucy continued marking up the patient file, but she felt the smirk creeping out.

'I know who you mean. I'll pass on your thanks.'

Leaving the cubicle, she pulled out her phone.

Heard you've been all heroic this morning, carrying damsels in distress.

It pinged seconds later.

Just an average Wednesday. You eaten lunch yet?

Nope. Thought I would just grab something quick later.

'K. I'll be in the canteen at one if you fancy it. Lunch, I mean.

Lucy's eyes bugged out when she saw his reply. They'd never eaten together without Ronnie...and with a side of innuendo? She began to type back.

Pretty busy... *delete*

No time...*delete*

Maybe... *delete*

Your chest makes the best pillow... *delete*

I like what your thumb did in the car... *delete*delete*

Do you feel anyt...? *delete*delete*delete*

*What am I? Twelve?*
She tapped the phone against her lip, wondering what the heck was going on. It was like a switch had flipped, and suddenly Jackson wasn't maddening, frustrating Dr Denning any more. Well, he was, but he was also the guy who'd held her tightly last night while she'd fallen asleep. The guy

who always bought her favourite snacks from the supermarket without being asked. The huge, sexy guy who read to Zoe and make her laugh when he did the voices for all the characters. The guy who she shared a kitchen with, who whipped up more than omelettes in low-slung PJ bottoms and a bare chest she now preferred to any pillow she owned.

When they'd first started working together, she'd gone to bed particularly wound up about one of their little work disagreements and had eaten half a cheesecake before bed. She'd blamed the cheese, of course, but she'd woken up that night horny and sweaty, half-wishing it had been real. The next time it had happened, she hadn't been able to blame the dairy.

Now he was sleeping across the landing from her every night, looking all sexy in the morning in his PJ bottoms, that sexy line of dark hair disappearing under the waistband. How on earth was she supposed to bear the space across the landing now that she had the scent of him on her duvet? Something told her the cold showers and sex dreams were going to increase tenfold.

*His chest. Man, his chest.*

She got it now: the cliché of a body being sculpted from marble. Now she had to sit across the island from him with that chiselled temptation. All this craziness wasn't good for the environment.

How could she go for lunch with him, when

little freaky moments like that popped into her head? Zoe needed two parents, no matter what. She had to focus on that, and work; nothing else.

That call this morning, breaking up their moment in the car, bothered her. She couldn't stop thinking about what he had been about to say. Whether, if she knew, she'd be glad of the knowledge. She'd shut it down anyway, but the look on his face... It couldn't all be in her head. Surely two people would *have* to feel the chemistry between them, whether they wanted to or not?

The screensaver on her phone had come on, and she saw Jackson smiling back at her. It was a candid shot she'd taken on the sofa one night. She'd gone to clean the kitchen after he'd made dinner and bathed Zoe. She'd put the dishwasher on for the fourth time that day and had taken a bottle of wine into the lounge. They'd got into the habit of watching a TV series together, a glass of red as a reward for a busy day toddler-wrangling and sorting out the properties and paperwork of their new life.

She'd found them both asleep on the couch, Zoe laid on his chest in her little bunny onesie. Her freshly washed curls were fluffed up, her little face content. He had his arms around her, his head back, mouth wide open. She'd snapped it to tease him later, but when she'd looked at the image she'd made it her lock-screen photo instead.

'Damn it.' She huffed, bringing up his message.

'Stick to the plan,' she muttered under her breath. 'Co-parenting—no cheese.' A shiver ran down her spine, remembering his body wrapped around hers in the dark. 'Cold showers. Lots and lots of cold showers.' She started to form a brush-off text in her head, when a deep voice stopped her.

'Talking to yourself is a sign of madness you know.'

Her heart sped up as she looked straight into a pair of teasing brown eyes.

'Jackson…' She breathed far too breathily. 'What are you doing here?'

She tried for a scowl but it didn't take. His eyes dropped to the phone in her hands, his finger tilting the screen. 'I came to check on my patient. I see your phone's working.' She locked the screen, regretting it the instant the photo popped up. 'Nice photo.'

'Thanks.' She blushed. 'I thought Zoe looked cute.'

He tilted his head and gave a slow, knowing nod. 'Right. So…'

'So…' she stalled, wondering when she'd turned into a simpering idiot and how to stop it. 'About lunch,' she started, just as he finished mumbling,

'About last night…'

'Oh.' She couldn't get a full breath. 'Um… I know. It was… I…'

'All good sentence starters.' He smirked, and

she had to grip her phone tight to stop herself from kissing it off his face right there and then. 'You want to pick one?'

'I'm sorry.' She was rambling. 'I appreciate last night, but I'm fine. I... If Zoe had seen us, I think it might have been confusing for her.'

'Zoe was in her cot. Unless she learned back-flips overnight, she wouldn't have.'

'I know, but she's growing fast. Soon she'll be in a bed, and running into our rooms, so I don't think...'

The clench of his jaw told her she'd made her point.

'Got it. No more sleepovers.' He straightened up and she felt lost in the shadowy distance. 'I just came to check on Emma.'

She reached for his arm as he turned to leave. 'Jackson,' she tried.

His voice was as sharp as flint. 'I get it. Zoe comes first.' When she stared back at him, he raised his brows pointedly. 'The patient?'

*Oh, yeah. He is annoyed. That sign is loud and clear.*

Emma's mum was thrilled when Jackson walked in with her.

'Oh, it's you!' She rose, reaching for his hand to shake. 'Thanks for bringing him.' She grinned at Lucy before turning back to Jackson. 'I asked Dr Bakewell who you were, so I could thank you.'

Jackson shook her hand, putting his other on

top to give her a doctorly pat. 'It's my job, honestly.' He leaned down, smiling at Emma. 'Glad you're feeling better. You gave your poor mum a scare.'

'Kids, eh?' she joked, the emotion belying her easy-natured chat. 'Such a worry, but you do everything you can to keep them happy and healthy. I am grateful, to you both.'

'It's no trouble. I get it.' He sounded almost sad. 'When you have children to worry about, you have to put them first, at any cost. I have to be going, but I'm glad you're okay.'

He took his leave and Lucy checked Emma's vitals.

'She's responding well,' she told the mother. 'The nurses will monitor her closely. Excuse me.'

Jackson was halfway down the corridor when she looked. Sighing, she pulled her phone out of her pocket. The photo lit up the screen, and she fired back a message, watching as his steps slowed to read what she'd written.

See you at one.

He didn't look back, pushing the door-release button and disappearing from sight. Just as she was kicking herself for being such a chump, her phone beeped.

One it is, roomie.

# CHAPTER TEN

BY THEIR FOURTH week back, Lucy felt that things were getting back to normal at work. Sure, there had been questions. Her team had rallied smoothly, accustomed to her workaholic, 'say nothing' personal work style. Amy had been there for her; she went to the coffee shop before work when Jackson was on a late shift and had child duty. Jackson told her a few people had wondered about the pair of them getting along without HR intervention, but no one asked her. She secretly suspected that they didn't dare, and Jackson hadn't said much of anything that didn't involve patients and Zoe since that first awkward lunch.

The first week was hell. They were both so tired that they barely spoke. Other than work and Zoe, they slept, ordered in or lived on Sheila's cooking that she left stocked up in the fridge. Lucy had forgotten how knackering the job was, and now she had no gym time and couldn't sleep away her days off. Not that she needed a gym; she was on her feet all day at work, running around after Zoe the rest of the time. She and Jackson got into the habit of taking her places when they were both off:

the zoo, walks in the park or soft play. All of this was a lot of fun, but none of it was exactly sedentary—no time for awkward chats or hand holding.

She had a newfound respect for new mothers. She realised just how naive she'd been, even as a paediatrician, about how hard it was, job or no job. How people had more than one kid, she would never know.

When lunch time came round, she headed to the canteen. They fell into a pattern of eating together when they could. She automatically scanned the tables for his face whenever she walked in. Even when she knew he wasn't at work, she found herself scanning the people for him.

Jackson was already there today, sitting with another doctor she'd seen in passing. They were deep in conversation; Jackson didn't even spot her walking past. Getting her lunch, she went to sit with a couple of the nurses from her ward, leaving them to talk. Since that night in her bed, she'd learned to judge his silences. Sometimes he would be right next to her but feel miles away. New people picking up on their weird tension wasn't something she relished.

'Lucy,' Jackson called to her. She smiled at her staff and headed over, lunch tray in hand. 'Come sit. This is Josh. Josh, this is Dr Bakewell, Head of Paediatrics.'

She took a seat next to Jackson, shaking the

other man's hand across the table. 'Oh! Dr Fillion; new A&E doctor, right?'

He nodded, taking her hand in a cool palm and holding it for a second too long. He was younger than Lucy had expected. From Jackson's description, she'd imagined him as being over fifty. He was a good fit, Jackson had mentioned: reliable, old school and professional. None of that seemed to fit the rather handsome hazel-eyed man before her.

'Please, call me Josh.' His brows knitted together for a moment. 'Have we met before? I swear you look familiar.'

Lucy shook her head. 'No. Well, yes—I've seen you around.' She'd noticed him in the corridor a couple of times, mostly because Amy had shown her his picture on the hospital website. She'd had a bit of a crush since she'd picked up an extra shift in A&E. 'How are you liking it?' She flicked her head to Jackson. 'Boss is a piece of work, isn't he?'

Josh laughed, flashing white teeth against the olive tones of his skin. 'He's definitely got high standards.' Diplomacy laced his words. He suddenly clicked his fingers. 'Lucy Bakewell! Of course, I've heard a lot about you too. Apparently you're a bit of a stickler for being the best.' He looked between them. 'Probably why you get on, eh?' He ran a hand along his jaw. 'Still, I feel like I know you from somewhere. Where are you from?'

'Here,' she and Jackson said in unison.

'Where are you from?' she asked, tearing open

the vinaigrette sachet in her hands and drizzling it over her chicken salad.

'Manchester, the last few years. Sussex growing up.'

'Interesting. I always thought I'd move around and work in different hospitals.'

He leaned forward across the table. Jackson moved his chair a little closer to hers. When she glanced at him, he was staring at Josh, an odd look on his face. When he saw her watching, he returned to stabbing at his food with his fork. 'Really?' Josh said, oblivious. 'Why didn't you?'

She thought of Harriet and shrugged. 'Oh, you know, it just never happened. Timing always seemed wrong.'

Josh smiled, a cute little dimple-punctuated grin. 'Well, I for one am glad you didn't.'

Jackson cleared his throat loudly. 'Josh, we need to hurry up.' He tapped his watch. 'It's busy on the floor.'

Josh looked down at his half-eaten meal. 'Er, yeah. Sure.' He winked at Lucy. 'No rest for the wicked, eh?' Jackson mumbled something under his breath, but Lucy couldn't make it out. Within seconds, the two of them were on their feet. 'It was nice to meet you, Dr Bakewell.'

She stood up from her chair, aware of Jackson watching the pair of them with an odd look on his face. 'Lucy, please. Nice to meet you too.'

'I'll see you later, Luce,' Jackson cut in sharply,

before striding off. Josh started after him, but just as Lucy was finishing off her food he came back to stand in front of her.

'Er, I don't know if you are free, but…' He fished into his pocket and pulled out a business card. 'I'd love to take you to dinner one night, if you're available?'

*Wait, what?*

The grip on her fork tightened.

'Er…' The business card was still in his hand, in front of her nose.

'It's just that I don't know a lot of people. Jackson's nice, of course, but he's pretty busy with his family. I thought it might be nice to get to know you better—colleague to colleague.'

'Family?' she echoed.

*Oh, he didn't know. How had the gossip missed the newbie?*

'Yeah, wife and kid.' He smiled innocently. 'He's always going on about them. Even has a cute little nickname for his missus—Tigger or something. So, dinner?' When she didn't answer, his smile dipped. 'Or coffee?'

'Trigger?' she checked, his words ringing in her head.

'What?'

'Trigger. The nickname.'

'Yes.' He clicked his fingers again, pointing his index finger in her direction. 'That's the one.' He laughed. 'You think I'd get it right…he's told me enough times. I swear it's the only time he cracks a smile.'

He raised himself to his full height when Jackson half-bellowed, 'Dr Fillion?' from behind him, dropping his card onto the table.

'See?' He shrugged. 'Think about it,' he said. 'Give me a call.'

Staring at the card, Lucy realised that sometimes having snakes for hair was not half-bad. Except in situations like this, when she was asked out by Ronnie's unknowing replacement right in front of the man she secretly desired. It was getting harder and harder to keep a lid on everything when the lines kept blurring.

Jackson was waiting by her car when she finished her shift half an hour late. She walked up to him, pulling her jacket around her shoulders. He took her bags from her, as he always did, putting them on the back seat when she unlocked the car with a click of her key.

'Your car's a mess again,' he grumbled as they pulled their seat belts around them. 'Crumbs all over the footwell.'

'Yeah.' She laughed, pulling the car out of the space. 'Well, Zoe had some of those biscuits she loved the other day on the way back from the park.' He huffed in response. 'What's with you? Bad outcome?'

'No,' he snapped. 'I just think that, since you

insisted on taking turns with the cars, you would have cleaned up.' He pointed to the reusable coffee mugs filling the cup holders. 'Pretty sure Zoe doesn't drink double-shot lattes.'

Lucy breathed as she turned the wheel. 'Okay, Grumpy, I'll get it cleaned out. We can take yours instead next time. What's with you?'

They were almost out of the staff car park when Dr Fillion walked towards his car. He didn't look up from his keys as they drove by.

'What did he want today at lunch?'

*Awkward.*

'Lunch?'

'Yeah, Luce. At lunch, when he came back to the table.' She saw his fist clench and unclench on his lap, and tried to focus on the road. 'He doesn't know about our…living arrangements. I kept your wish. Did he ask you out?'

'No. Well, kind of.'

'Kind of?'

She pulled out of the hospital grounds onto the main road, straight into heavy traffic.

'Hell. This is going to take a while; you might want to ring your parents; tell them we'll be late.'

'Fine. Will you answer the question?'

He pulled out his phone and tapped a few keys. A few seconds later, it pinged. 'Mum says it's fine, and do we want them to give her a bath? She's at ours, and said Zoe was getting sleepy.' The traffic lights turned to green and Lucy quickly took the next left.

'Tell her thanks, she just saved us about half an hour in that jam. I don't mind bathing her, though; I've missed her today.'

He tapped away, shoving the phone back into his jacket.

'Done. Did he then, or not?'

'Yes,' she relented, feeling more than a little weird about the conversation. It wasn't as if she'd expected it or flirted. Heck, she didn't know how to flirt. 'He mentioned coffee.' She bit at her lip. 'Or dinner, colleague to colleague. Do people really not know about us raising Zoe together?'

'No. You didn't want that, so I kept it quiet. Your terms, remember? So this dinner—just the two of you, I'm guessing, since he never gave me an invite.'

'Er, yeah, I think so.'

'Wow, he works fast.' The words came out like gravel. 'He only met you today.'

'Yeah, I think he's just a bit bored. You know, new town, new faces.'

'Not once has he asked me to go for a beer after work, or any of the other doctors. He can't be that lonely.'

'Why are you so mad? I didn't ask him to ask me out.' She looked across at him. He was already looking at her, his eyes dark pools in close quarters. 'I didn't say I'd go, either.'

They were pulling into their drive when he finally answered.

'You didn't say you wouldn't, either. If we're going to play this game at work, you could at least do me the courtesy of not dating my team members.'

'Games? He thinks you have a wife and kid!'

'I never told him that!'

'Well, why would he think it, then? He said you talk about us.'

'Oh, great.' He scowled. 'So I can't talk about any part of my life now? Not all of us are emotionally stunted, Lucy.'

'Oh, and I am, right, because I don't want Leeds General to know every detail of our lives? Answer me, Jackson!'

He didn't wait for a reply before getting out of the car.

'Jackson!'

He ignored her.

'Hi, love.' Sheila met them at the door, Zoe toddling along behind.

Lucy nodded to Grandad Walt, who was sitting on the sofa watching the football. He muted the TV.

'Evening, Lucy, good day at work?'

'Yes, thanks.' She scooped Zoe up. 'How's my girl been?'

Zoe babbled away, laughing when she tickled her.

'Good as gold,' Walt said, getting to his feet. 'Come on, Sheila love. Let's let them get on.'

Jackson shrugged his shoes off and headed straight to the drinks cabinet in the corner of the lounge. Clicking off the child lock, he pulled out a bottle of whiskey and a glass. Lucy saw his dad's eyebrows knit together when he noticed. 'You all right, son? Bad shift?'

He turned to see all of them watching, and he stopped pouring. 'No, Dad, all good.' He put it back, heading over to Lucy and Zoe and dropping a kiss on Zoe's little cheek.

'Jack-Jack,' she said to him, reaching out to touch his face. He kissed her pudgy hand. His gaze shifted to meet Lucy's eye and he shot her a rueful smile.

'Bath time, Zo-Zo,' he said softly, turning to his parents. 'Thanks for having her guys; you know we appreciate it. I'll see you out.'

Lucy stayed back as he waved them off. He didn't meet her eye when he passed Zoe to her. When their car pulled away, she was already upstairs. She needed the distance to cool her temper and give herself a second to process his cheap shot. She'd just put Zoe in the bubble bath when he appeared at the doorway.

She sensed his brooding presence before she saw him and kept busy, washing Zoe with her frog-shaped bath mitt.

'I'm sorry.'

'So you should be; you acted like a jerk. What's your problem?'

'I…don't think it's a good idea that you go out with Josh, that's all. I don't like it. You said we needed to keep work separate from home.'

Her hand paused as she took in what he said. Zoe lined up a duck to go down the slide.

'And I never said that I would go out with him, did I? I hardly have time to manage everything now.'

'Is that the only reason?'

'No. We work together too.'

'Hardly; he's been there weeks and you've not crossed paths till today.'

'Still, work is work. Dating a colleague never goes well.'

'Right,' he replied, but he didn't sound convinced. She could feel his pensive mood from across the room. Rinsing Zoe off, she wrapped a towel around the tot and started to dry her off. When he didn't say anything else, she looked over her shoulder, but he'd gone. A few minutes later, she heard the front door go. When she'd got Zoe off to sleep, she came down to a note on the kitchen island.

*Gone out. Don't wait up. Phone is on if you need me. Jackson*

'Nice.' She sighed. After showering off the day, she dragged her tired body under the covers. She'd found the business card in her trouser pocket when she'd undressed. It sat on her dresser next to Jackson's note. Picking both up, she scrutinised them. She could be stupid and play dumb. She could say that she had no idea why Jackson was mad, why he'd questioned her, but she had a feeling she knew exactly why. If someone asked Jackson out, she knew she wouldn't like it. He'd talked about them at work—his family.

*His wife and kid.*

It would be sweet if it wasn't so wrapped up in a big ball of messy emotional angst in the pit of her stomach. Her phone was on charge, sitting on the dresser. Pulling out the cord, she brought up the message screen and started typing.

It's me. Don't be mad… *delete*

I'm not going out with him… *delete*

Come home… *delete*

She picked up one of her pillows and threw it at the far wall.

'This is ridiculous,' she said out loud. 'What am I doing?' She looked at the photo of Harriet and Ronnie on her dresser. 'You two have a lot to answer for.'

Turning in for the night. I'll take Zoe to nursery

tomorrow. Let you sleep in and enjoy your day
off. Lucy

It read a bit cold. She added a letter to soften
the words.

X *delete*

Should she?

X *delete*

She hit Send before she could debate the kiss
any longer. Shoving the phone, the business card
and the curt note in her top drawer, and turning
off the lamp, she tried to fall asleep.

When she left the house the next morning, Zoe
and her backpack in tow, Jackson's bedroom door
was closed. He'd read her message but not replied.
*Fine*, she thought to herself. *Awkward it is.*

It wasn't as though they'd never played *that*
game before. This morning, she found the whole
thing silly. Yeah, they'd been getting closer, but
it was just the bubble they'd been in. They'd both
said as much: Zoe needed stability.

It was lust, that was all. Sure, there were feelings too, but *wife and kid* kept haunting her. She
tried to tell herself it was just her libido talking
for the millionth time. She hadn't been near a man
in, oh…for ever…and now she was living with

an extra tall version of a near-perfect specimen who was good with kids, saved lives while rocking a set of scrubs and wasn't a total player. Any woman would have looked, she reasoned, and it would pass. The hand-holding tingle would stop. She'd get over the loss of her perfect night, the one where he'd held her tight and told her 'for ever'. 'For ever' was a fantasy—nothing lasted; people didn't stay. Perhaps she should say yes to the date with Josh just to put paid to this nonsense. It was easier somehow when he hated her.

'Tell me what to do, Zoe love,' she said to her niece as they pulled up to the nursery. 'Auntie Lucy is floundering here.'

'Jack-Jack,' she said with a toothy smile, and Lucy laughed.

'Well, you're a big help. Another female totally under his spell, eh?' She turned off the engine, checking her phone again. She'd texted him again that morning—for a valid co-parenting reason, of course, telling him they were low on milk and she'd pick some up after her shift. A nothing message. Still, she was sad to see that he'd not read it. Perhaps he was still asleep. She'd told him to lie in. Or maybe he was ignoring his phone because he was still mad. She'd not heard him come in the night before. Stuffing the phone back into her bag, she tried to focus on her day.

'Morning, Zoe!' an exuberant redhead said the second Zoe toddled through the secure doors.

*Maddison? Melanie? Something beginning with an* M.

She looked to see Lucy at her heels and the disappointment was evident. 'Oh.' She smiled, recovering too slowly to make it look realistic. 'Hi, Lucy! I thought you were Jackson. He dropped her off last week.'

'Mmm-hmm.' Lucy passed her Zoe's backpack. 'Different shifts every week. Just me today, sorry; Jackson's got the day off.'

'Aww.' She simpered, taking the bag. 'He deserves it, working so hard.' Lucy bent to give Zoe a kiss.

'Bye, darling, have fun.'

The redhead opened the interior doors and Zoe sped off to join the other kids on the carpet. One of the newer nursery staff members was reading a story to the other kids, and Zoe was a sucker for being read to. Once the door was closed, Lucy turned to leave.

'So, what's he doing today with his day off? Out with his girlfriend or something, I bet.' Lucy met her eye. Her name tag said 'Maddy'.

*One mystery solved—another person who didn't know their urgent situation either.*

Perhaps she should correct that on Zoe's records. They were still listed as aunt and uncle, though the manager was aware.

'Er...no,' Lucy replied, reaching for the high door handle.

'Fiancée, then?' Maddy pressed.

'Nope, not that either.' She let go of the handle, turning back to face the woman who was seriously starting to tick her off. She was too...perky.

*Was everyone in heat these days?*

'Can I pass on a message or something?'

Maddy's sculpted brows raised in surprise. 'Er...well, it's not exactly professional, but...'

Lucy smiled, cutting her off. 'Of course— you're right, it's not. I'll let you get on, then, Mary.' Maddy nodded, dumbstruck. Reaching for the door, she pushed it open and felt the morning air hit her flustered face. 'Have a good day!'

'Er...you too, Lucy,' Maddy called out weakly.

'Always do,' she trilled, heading back to her car. By the time she got to work after enduring the thick morning traffic, her mood was murderous.

'Hi!'

The second she walked through the hospital doors, she came face to face with Josh.

'Oh, hi, what are you doing here?'

*Idiot.*

Josh laughed awkwardly, pointing to his scrubs. 'Well, I work here.'

Lucy's cheeks exploded. 'Sorry, sorry! Of course you do!' She slapped her forehead with a palm. 'I haven't had my coffee yet; it's been a bit of a morning.'

'No problem,' he said with a sparkle. 'Perhaps

you should have that drink with me, tell me all about it.'

She bit her lip. She was still mad at perky Maddy, but it clicked when she saw Josh—now she understood Jackson's mood. She'd felt that way, knowing that someone was angling for a date with him. It was exactly how he'd felt at lunch the day before. She didn't like the feeling one bit.

'Listen…' She steeled herself for yet another awkward conversation. 'I'm flattered, but the reason why I'm frazzled this morning is because I had to take my…er…little girl to nursery. A little girl I share with Jackson.'

Josh's jaw dropped, his pallor at least two shades lighter. 'Oh, my God. I had no idea you were his wife.' He swore under his breath. 'Gosh, no wonder he was so moody yesterday. Why didn't he say something?'

Lucy put a hand on his shoulder. 'It's fine. You did nothing wrong. We're not married…or even together.' She took a deep breath. 'Jackson's brother, Ronnie—the other Dr Denning—he was married to my sister. She died when he did, and Zoe's their daughter.'

'Oh, my god.' Josh's face was a picture. 'I wondered why people were so weird about talking about him. Jackson's closed off, but I just thought he'd lost a brother…so it made sense. I reckoned the staff weren't talking about it out of respect for his grief, or because they were grieving too. I didn't know he even had a daughter. When I saw a photo of Zoe, he never corrected me.'

'Well, they were grieving,' she agreed. 'And it's my fault Jackson didn't say anything. He was trying to respect my wishes. But also, I'm… Trigger…and also Medusa, around here. Actually, only Jackson calls me Trigger, which annoys the ever-living hell out of me, but I'm a bit of a dragon here.' She laughed, realising that was no longer a hard fact. 'Well, I was. They call me Medusa because I'm a hard-faced tyrant—or I was.'

Josh shook his head, his cheeks reddening. 'So many things make sense now. I thought people just didn't like me or something.'

She waved him off. 'No. No, it's just a weird time. Jackson and I were sort of family, and very much work enemies. Then our siblings went and died and left their daughter for us to raise together.' She tried to wrap it up. 'So, in short—' she pointed at herself '—Medusa, Trigger. Not wife—co-carer. We live together and raise a kid.

'Listen, it's a long, very confusing story, but I'm just not dating anyone at the moment. I just needed to set the record straight. I don't want you to feel awkward at work because Jackson and I can't communicate. I'm really sorry for word-vomiting all over you, but I think it's about time people know the truth instead of skirting around me.'

'That's a lot,' he said when she'd finally stopped

to draw breath. 'Well, thanks for telling me. I'm sorry for your loss, too.'

'Thanks. And sorry again for dragging you into our drama.' She went to leave, turning back to him when something occurred to her. 'Thanks, though,' she said, meaning it. 'You helped me re-alise a few things. I'll see you around.'

'Does he know?' he called after her.

'Does he know what?' she asked, frowning at him.

'That you're not together,' he said, his voice low to avoid attention. 'I don't know what the deal is with you two, but I'm not sure he has the same way of looking at things you do. The way he spoke about you, that didn't sound like just a co-carer to me.' He dipped his head by way of goodbye and strode away.

She watched him leave, but didn't feel a pang of regret. His words turned over and over in her head. Lucy thought of Jackson's mood, of him being at home, all huffy. Thought of her behav-iour earlier, bristling at Maddy for daring to ask about her housemate. Pulling out her phone, she rang Sheila.

'Hi, Sheila, sorry for ringing early. I'm just going on shift. Yes, yes, everything's great. Zoe's at nursery. Listen, I hate to ask, but is there any chance you and Walt could possibly do me a fa-vour and collect her for me tonight and let her sleep over?'

# CHAPTER ELEVEN

LUCY FELT EVERY step her aching feet made towards her car. Her whole body was singing with both exhaustion and nervous energy. She didn't know whether to laugh, cry or vomit. Seeing Jackson leaning against the back of her car, she didn't get a chance to choose.

*What is he doing here?*

She'd planned to go home and ask him if they could talk. Tell him Zoe was away for the night to give them both time to hash this out once and for all. She'd banked on the extra time driving home to gather the bravery she needed to get her words out. Spewing words all over Josh earlier wasn't something she wanted to repeat, not when these next few hours would change their dynamic again, no matter what his reaction was when she finally managed to get her words into the order she needed them.

Her heart leapt even as her steps faltered. She had to make a conscious effort to put one foot in front of the other. He looked gorgeous, which made it worse. He was wearing the soft dove-grey sweater she loved on him, the one with the

V-neck that showed off his chest. The muscles in his broad back flexed noticeably beneath the wool when he moved. She'd thought about that chest so many times that she could draw it from memory. His long, thick legs were encased in a pair of midnight-black jeans, the ones that showed off his tight behind. The first time she'd seen him leaning over the dishwasher in them, she'd had to leave the room before he clocked her ogling.

He was looking in the other direction, checking his watch, ruffling his thick, dark locks between the fingers of one hand. Seeing the tension in his gait, she braced herself for what was about to happen.

'Hey, you.'

He pushed off the car, levelling her with one look.

*He's absolutely stunning. How the heck have I ever been around you and not been a gooey mess?*

'Hey. Hi.' He stepped forward, making her feel smaller as he stood close.

*Not smaller—dainty.*

He reached for her work bag, and she gave him it to him readily. 'Good shift?'

'Not bad.' She breathed, willing her body to stop feeling as if it was on fire. Her heart was thudding in her chest cavity, so loud she felt he must hear it. 'What are you doing here?'

He pointed to his car a few spaces away. She'd not even noticed it.

'I thought we could take a drive. Talk.'

'What about my car?'

'Leave it here. I can bring you back after.'

*Well, this is not my plan*, she thought, but he obviously had things to say too. It wasn't as if she'd expected anything different.

'Luce,' he mumbled, so close to her now she could have reached out and touched that legendary chest. 'You trust me, right?'

She almost laughed at him. It was such a daft question now. She trusted him more than anyone else in the world. 'Of course,' she said instead.

'Then come with me,' he urged, his voice deep, pleading. He held out a huge palm and she put her hand straight into its grasp.

He pulled out of the car park and headed away from the direction of Zoe's nursery.

'Where are we going?' she asked, looking at the buildings going past as he drove in the opposite direction from the city centre.

'That trust thing didn't last long.' He smirked. 'I spoke to my mum, by the way.'

'Oh, really?' she said nonchalantly. Her squeaky voice didn't get with the program. 'Is she okay?'

'Thrilled to have Zoe for the night, yeah, which is why I didn't drive to the nursery earlier to get her.' He turned to look at her as they hit the motorway turnoff. 'You didn't say why you wanted the night off, though.'

Zoe felt her cheeks get hot. 'Is that why you came to work—to check up on me?' Something else occurred to her. 'Did you think I might be going out with Josh?'

'It crossed my mind.' She didn't miss the clench of his jaw. 'But I spoke with Josh. He called me about a patient, mentioned he was going out with some of the team.' He cleared his throat. 'I might have suggested some of the work lads take him out for a drink—welcome him properly. You don't have any plans, do you.' It was a statement.

'No,' she replied.

'Thought so. I thought you might want to talk too, so I came to get you.'

'So you did all that and came to stalk me in the parking lot. Nice.' He laughed when he saw her knowing smirk.

'Well, I didn't want to risk the chance some other doctor asked you for a date before you got home. I didn't want to wait to see you.'

He took the next turnoff. They were on the outskirts of Leeds, she noticed, where a large retail park and some industrial units stood. 'And now you're taking me to the warehouse district. I know we sorted the joint life insurance, but I'm pretty sure murder voids the policy.'

'Hah-di-hah!' He headed to the bottom of the main industrial park, turning off just after a bathroom wholesaler. 'I just wanted to talk to you.

We've not spoken since yesterday, I wanted to clear the air.'

'You weren't talking, actually. I sent you messages.'

'I got them.'

'I know.'

He pulled into the car park of a grey warehouse. Neon lights lit up signage on top of a large set of double doors. 'I was mad.'

'Yeah, and you're weren't the only one, Jack.' She looked at the name of the place: *Axe Me Another.* 'Where are we, anyway?'

He turned off the engine, pinning her with a grin so cheeky and so sexy she wanted to slap him, then pull him in and snog his face off.

'Well, since you bagged us a night off, I thought that we should do something about being mad with each other once and for all.'

'You've got to be kidding me.'

Jackson was positively gleeful as he passed her a set of overalls. She looked up into his eyes and they were bright with excitement.

'Nope.'

'You're an A&E doctor. You put people back together after dumb accidents like this.' They were in a side room, having just signed a bunch of disclaimers and been shown where to change. Jackson shrugged, pulling off his sweater without warning. Lucy squeaked, turning to face the lockers on the other wall. 'Jackson! What are you doing?'

'Getting changed! Come on, don't be a priss. It's nothing you haven't had hold of before, remember?'

*Remember? Ha! It's etched onto my grey matter.*

'How could I forget?' She sighed, looking again at the bright-orange jumpsuit and goggles in her hands. 'Fine. If we must dress up like hardened convicts, at least turn around.'

She heard him behind her, closer than before. 'I promise not to peek.' He half growled; his voice sounded strained. She looked over her shoulder; he was standing with his back to her and his stance was taut. She turned round and got changed as quickly as she could. Then she tapped him on the shoulder and he turned round, goggles on the top of his head like a pair of shades.

'I look ridiculous,' she told him. 'Orange is definitely not the new black.'

He laughed with that low rumble that did things to her insides.

'I like that laugh.'

His brows raised in surprise. 'Thanks.' His smile was genuine, bashful even. She went to push a lock of hair away from her face and he beat her to it, curling it round his finger before sweeping it behind her ear. 'You look cute in orange.' He paused, and she stood there, looking up at him and prompting herself to breathe. 'Come on,' he muttered, breaking the spell. 'Let's go get that rage out.'

Half an hour later, Lucy was throwing axes like a pro. The whole place was a rage-relief experience. They had a rage room full of stuff such as china, bottles, old furniture and weapons like bats and golf clubs. She could hear people screaming and bellowing from the other rooms, and the smashes and crashes. Their space was like a shooting range with big targets on wooden walls, and axes laid out for throwing.

'There you go, Luce!' Jackson hollered as she sank another axe into the target, this time almost on the bull's-eye. 'You nailed it!' She turned to see his palm up, and high-fived him as he laughed. 'Feel better?'

'Well, I'm not mad any more.'

*I might have imagined Maddy on a couple of the throws, though.*

He chuckled. 'Good. We should come again.'

'We should join up to their loyalty scheme or it might get expensive.'

He laughed, that rumble giving her a tingle under her overalls. 'Hungry?' he asked.

'Starving,' she answered.

'Let's go get something to eat,' he said, putting his arm around her shoulder. They put down the axes and headed back to the changing room. They were the only ones there, and Jackson clicked the lock on the door. They stood behind the door for a moment, toes almost touching, suddenly feeling awkward after the chaos.

'Why did you come to meet me at work?' she asked him. 'Why didn't you just ring me?'

'I thought you might ignore me, after yesterday. When Mum said you'd asked her to have Zoe, I connected the dots. I found this place online a while ago and thought it would be good to have some fun for once.'

'It was.' She grinned. 'Especially after this morning.' Her eyes widened. She hadn't meant to say that.

He lowered his head closer to hers. 'This morning?'

'Er...yeah.' She shuffled from foot to foot. 'I spoke to Maddy.'

His expression was blank, which cheered her up to no end. 'Maddy who?'

'Maddy, from nursery?'

He shook his head, his lip curling into a 'so' motion. 'And?'

'And she wanted to know if you were spending the day with your girlfriend.'

She could have sworn on the medical textbooks she revered that his eyes lit up.

'Ah. Right.' He grinned, all lopsided smile and pearly white teeth. 'You were jealous.'

She flushed, the fear of being so close to him

scaring her. She didn't just mean body to body either. 'No, of course I wasn't.'

'Liar.'

'Jackson, come on.'

'No, you come on, Luce.' He sighed, thumbing towards the door. 'We did the rage. I'm not doing the denial thing any more. I was jealous.'

'Of Josh?'

'Yeah.' He huffed, taking a step closer. 'I swear, I wanted to fire the guy on the spot. I saw him hand you his card.' He bit down on his bottom lip and she tracked the movement. 'I didn't like it. I don't want you to date him.'

'Yeah.' She raised her chin a little. 'Well, I saw Josh this morning.'

*There it was again—that low, reverberating growl.*

'I set him straight—told him the truth and that I won't be accepting any invitations from him.'

'You did?'

'Yep. I will not be dating Josh, so I don't want you dating Maddy.'

'Done. I don't want you dating anyone.'

'Done,' she shot back. 'Same goes for you. What else did you want to talk about?'

They were both breathing a little faster now, moving infinitesimally closer.

'Why you arranged for Zoe to sleep over at my folks'.'

'Because I wanted us to talk without distractions. Why did you really come to meet me in the car park?'

'Because I couldn't wait to see you a minute longer.' His lip twitched. 'I meant it. I didn't want someone else hitting on you before you got home and I got the chance to tell you that you drive me crazy.'

'You drive me crazy.'

'I know.' He growled. 'But you drive me crazy more than when we fight, Luce. I...'

He sighed, a bone-shattering, deep sigh as his arms came up around her. She put her hands on his chest and he stilled, as though she was going to push him away. When she didn't, he went on.

'I can't lie to myself any more. I won't. Fighting with you is the most alive I have ever felt. You get under my skin so badly, I want to unzip it and tuck you in. Since the paintballing day, you were it. But I knew Ronnie and Harriet were end game; it was too complicated to even try. I thought you hated me, too. So, I told myself it was fun, sparring with each other, picking fights, and it was— but I can't sleep across the hall from you for much longer without losing my mind.

'I spent the night in your bed, and now I can't stop wanting it again. I just lay there, holding you, smelling your hair and wishing I could wake you and chase those bad dreams away *for ever*. I started using your conditioner just so I can smell that coconut smell you had that night; I need it

with me when I'm away from you and can't get
my fix. I can't afford the damn water bill any
more, with all the cold showers. That day, when
we crashed into each other, I barely got out of that
alive, Luce. I wanted to just pick you up and carry
you to my bedroom.'

She heard her breath hitch in her throat.

'I want your hands on my bare ass *for ever*. I
swear, it took everything I had in me not to wrap
your sexy legs around me and take you to my bed.'

'Why didn't you?'

Lucy was so turned on, she couldn't stand it.
His words were like caresses she'd wrap herself
in. *For ever...* Every time he said it, she wanted
more, wanted to tell him yes. To beg him to do
all that, and more.

'Because you weren't where I was. Because you
pretend to hate me. Sometimes, I think you really do.'

'I don't,' she rebutted. 'I've shampooed my hair
so much since we moved in together, I think my
hair might fall out. The other day you were taking the rubbish out and I wanted to wrap myself
in a bin bag just so you'd lift *me* up and throw me
over your shoulder. You wind me up so much, I
can't stand it. I don't hate you Jackson, I have cold
showers too, to stop myself from blurting out how
freaking gorgeous I think you are. Then I think
about you *in* the shower, and I forget I washed my
hair already, so I do it again. Then I smell your

shower gel on the shelf next to mine and the whole cycle starts again. Even when we're with Zoe, my mind wanders. I can't help but notice how sexy you are when you're being cute with her.'

At some point when she'd been talking, he'd tightened his grip on her; her feet were barely on the floor now as he held her to him. She could feel him breathing hard, almost panting beneath the orange jumpsuit.

'I'm not stupid, Jackson. I know I'm a mess, and stubborn and prickly, but I swear, when Maddy asked about you this morning, I got it. I know why you were angry about Josh.'

She bit her lip, afraid to say the final thing she had to tell him. She felt it would be too much, she'd be too exposed. And far too turned on to concentrate on the dull panic her rational brain was trying to convey down her frazzled nerve endings.

'Because…' Her voice gave out. 'Because it's not hate, or lust, it's…'

'Because you're mine,' he answered for her. When she nodded, he lifted her off the floor into his arms, and she wrapped herself around him as he leaned her against the door and pressed his lips to hers. 'Finally.'

*Oh…this man is going to be the end of me*, she thought as she tasted him for the first time.

His lips were soft at first, as if he was waiting for her to come to her senses. The second she moaned into his mouth, all doubts were gone. He kissed her like a starved man, as if he'd been waiting his whole life to caress her mouth. 'Lucy. You're…so…mine,' he rasped out, his voice all growly.

'Shh,' she said, threading her fingers through his hair and pulling his mouth back to meet hers. 'No more talking.'

She felt his little laugh and she wriggled closer to his body. The laughter stopped, replaced by a visceral rumble as he ground her against the door. Sexual tension years old was unleashed. She grabbed his zip, pulling it down. His torso was bare, and she pulled away from his mouth to marvel at it. 'I love your chest,' she murmured as his lips fell onto her neck, nipping and kissing along the length. She leaned down and took a nipple into her mouth, licking at it and feeling the sensations in her own groin.

'Are you trying to kill me?' he mumbled, lifting her higher as she reached for his zip.

'Yeah,' she panted. 'Death by sex.' The orange jumpsuits were getting hot; she felt her body roasting from the inside. 'Take it off,' she begged.

He met her eye, and she could see it was taking him everything to slow himself down. 'Are you sure? We haven't talked about…'

She was already pulling at her own zip. 'Jackson,' she begged. 'No talking.' If they started talking about this, what it meant, she'd sober up from her lust. She was drunk on him, and she didn't want to stop. 'Take off your clothes. Now.'

One minute she was pressed up against the door, the next she was on her feet, her breath ragged, loud, in the room. He undid his zip the rest of the way, leaving him standing there in black boxer shorts.

She shuffled out of her jumpsuit, leaving herself in her underwear. The dark hue of his eyes deepened as she looked back at him shyly.

'Oh, no, not the green…' she heard him mumble. Looking down at her matching jade underwear, she started to pull her clothes back up, but he stilled her with his hand, picking her up once more.

'Don't you dare,' he warned. 'I just meant I knew I'd be lost when I finally saw you in them.' His teeth found her nipple through the lace as his body covered hers once more, leaning against the wooden door, overalls discarded. 'Ever since I found them in the dryer, I've been obsessed with the colour green.' He sucked gently, and she gasped as her nipple hardened beneath the lace. Pulling his head back up to meet hers, she wrapped herself around him tighter. She was desperate for him to do more, touch her more, say more.

'Stop teasing me, Denning,' she begged. This time, when their lips met, neither of them spoke. The dam finally broke between them and they were all hot breath, fingers, pulling and pushing. She clawed at his back. He was everywhere all at once, tongues and teeth, skin on skin. He groaned when his fingers finally dipped below the lace, and then he shifted her in his arms.

'I'm about to get a condom…' He panted, his arms solid around her quivering body. 'Last chance to stop this, Luce. We need to…'

She pushed her finger to his lips. 'Get it,' she begged. 'Don't stop now.'

She ground against him. 'Sex now. Talk later.'

His eyes darkened and, when his lip curled up, she knew who the victor was. Not letting her loose, he grabbed a foil packet from his jeans and passed it to her, only releasing her to drop his pants. Hers followed suit. Rolling it on, she felt him stiffen in her grasp, and then she was back in his steel hold. He kissed her frantically, pinning her to the door and lifting her legs higher. He told her to hold on tight and then he was inside her, thrusting, teasing and hitting everything just right. She was flush against the wood, limbs clinging to him as he started kissing her.

*Why the hell weren't we doing this the whole time?* she thought as his hot length speared her harder, deeper, hitting the sweet spots she dimly remembered and some she'd never known she had.

She tried to be quiet, aware that she could hear shouts of rage coming from behind the door, so at odds with the sounds of pleasure from within. He took every moan she had and muffled it against his jaw, against his mouth.

'Lucy...' He breathed. 'You feel so good. Lucy, my Luce...'

His movements were faster, more erratic, as she tightened around him. When he whispered her name again, she was done for, toppling over the edge as the white-hot orgasm ripped through her body, but still he drove on. Thrusting and cradling her to him as if he couldn't bear not to touch every inch of her, he growled and she felt him come hard. His arms came up under her bare bottom like a muscular shelf, holding her steady as she felt him shake on his own legs. He kissed her again and then touched his forehead to hers. Coming back down to reality, they both looked into each other's eyes, still wrapped around each other, sweaty and glistening.

'I guess that's what they mean by make-up sex.' She giggled. He huffed out a laugh, kissing her forehead and flashing her a smile she'd never seen before.

'A few years in the making,' he mumbled, before his expression turned serious. 'I meant what I said—you're mine, Lucy.' He kissed the corner of her mouth, and she felt him tighten himself around her protectively, as if he was afraid she'd bolt from his embrace. 'If you'll let me, I promise to make you happy—you and Zoe. I can't bear to go back now. Not now I've had this.' His look turned positively feral. 'Had you. There's no other woman on this planet who drives me insane. No other woman I'd rather be with.'

He kissed the opposite corner, turning her in his arms as he carried her away from the door. She wrapped her arms around his broad, sexy shoulders. 'What do you say?' He looked so nervous, so utterly gorgeous, her mouth went dry just looking at him. 'I'm pretty good at reading you, Luce, but I need a clue here.'

She leaned forward, brushing her lips against his. 'I say I'm ravenous.' His hopeful grin dipped, and she couldn't bear it. The bubble they had was thicker now, and she didn't want to pop it. 'Take me home, Jackson. Feed me, and then you can take me to bed and show me just how much you mean all that.'

His face split into a devilish, delirious smile and he twirled her round as he spun on the spot. 'Jackson!' she squealed as he bellowed out a whoop. 'People will hear you!'

He put her back on her feet, reaching for his clothes. 'Let them,' he said, slapping her on the butt cheek as they both scrambled to get dressed.

That was the last night they slept in separate rooms. He kept good on his word. He drove her home right away and fed her appetites until she was satiated. He showed her how much he meant every word, more times than she could count.

Much, much later, he curled her into his arms, smelling her hair with a contented sigh as they cuddled in her bed. As she felt her heavy lids close, lulled by the sound of his heart under her, she smiled as he whispered more words to her.

'I want to sleep like this for ever, Luce. There's no getting rid of me now. I love you.'

Lifting her head, she saw the nervousness in his face as he stared back.

'I do. I love you.' His grip tightened, just a touch. 'Don't run. I haven't the energy to chase you right now.'

She laughed softly. 'Where would I run to?' she asked. 'I'm home.' She kissed him, wanting the little furrow in his brow banished as he waited to see her reaction. 'I love you too, Sasquatch.'

His returning grin was her new favourite thing, she decided, before sleep won.

# CHAPTER TWELVE

IT HAD BEEN going so well—*so well*. The sex was hot…more than hot. It was as if the pair of them were teenagers. Since the Axe Me Another frantic bonking incident, as Jackson affectionately referred to it, they'd never stopped. They'd christened all the rooms in the house bar Zoe's. The shower was Jackson's particular favourite. He loved to soap up her boobs while they stood under the spray, he turning the shower to cold to shock her just after they'd heated each other to the point of combustion. Name anywhere, they'd done it there: her car; his car, twice. There was even a stack of mops in the downstairs cleaning closet that was still blushing.

It wasn't just the sex, though. They were together in every sense of the word. Jackson was romantic, which she'd never expected but readily appreciated. He'd leave her little notes around the house, stuffed in her locker at work or in the lunches he made her take to work in case she forgot to eat—which she did, of course.

*I always called you Trig because it was our thing. A reminder of when we first met.*

*You're such a good auntie. Zoe and I heart you mucho.*

*See you tonight, baby, miss you already.*

*Eat your greens, Dr Bakewell.*

Their work colleagues were surprisingly un-shocked. When she'd told Amy, she'd just laughed. 'I knew it,' she'd said. 'About time mate. Man, it's so good to see you happy.' Lucy had laughed, wondering at how things had changed.

They'd had an offer on Harriet's and Ronnie's house; a young couple had offered the asking price. She'd even found a tenant for her place. She hadn't told Jackson yet, but she reckoned that, after the lease expired, she'd sell up too. There'd be no point in having the place, and she no longer thought of it as home.

Zoe was thriving too, growing every day. She talked more and more all the time. She loved living with Jack-Jack and 'Luby', as she called her. Lucy had worried about whether the pair of them together would confuse her, but she didn't seem affected. In fact, she seemed thrilled to see the pair of them together. Jackson told her it was because kids were smart, and happy parents meant happy children. It was true, she came to realise as the days went on: they were all really happy. She should have known it wouldn't last *for ever*.

It was a Friday like any other. They were both on the late shift, Zoe sleeping over with Sheila and Walt, who were doubly elated at the news that Lucy was now even more part of the family than before.

I can't wait to sleep in tomorrow...shattered. Then I'm going to do that thing that makes your toes curl. Then breakfast. I'm thinking of pancakes at that place we like after we pick Zoe up.

Lucy laughed to herself, tapping out a response as she sat in the break room, resting her tired feet. She had five minutes left on break, and a ton of paperwork to get through. There were also a couple of patients she wanted to check on before she left.

Sounds good. I love pancakes. And you.

He typed back almost instantly.

Don't play with me, woman. Or I'll do it twice. With more tongue. Love you too.

She almost choked on her coffee. It was criminal how sexually combustible this man made her. She couldn't get enough of him. Harriet and Ronnie wouldn't be in trouble when she finally saw them again, that was for sure.

Promises, promises. See you soon.

See you soon.

A second later, another message popped up.

I'm going to marry you, Luce. Real soon.

*What?*
She read the words again and saw that he was typing again. She held her breath, waiting for him to take it back.

*He wants to marry me? No. It's too soon. It's... too much. She was an aunt, a carer, a lover. She was his...but wife? Harriet had been a wife, their own mother too—look how they turned out.*

Her old shields, stiff from lack of use these last few months, clanged back into action, raising up around her with a rusty screech. She felt her heart race as she saw the three dots bounce in the corner. He was still writing.

Don't freak out. We can talk later.

*Talk later? Seriously?* He'd told her something like that on a text and then expected her to work the rest of her shift? Her head was an utter mess. She wished that she didn't react this way, that she didn't want to run, but the second she'd read that text with their six-month review looming… It was too much. It felt like too much. She needed things just to slow down. They were about to cement their care for Zoe, which was a formality, but still. Marriage was binding: *for ever.* That suddenly felt like a threat, not a promise.

She tapped back.

You bet your ass we will.

His reply was instant.

Are you annoyed? I'm sorry, I know I should have said it to your face, I just couldn't hold it in any more. We'll talk tonight, okay? I have to go. A&E is slammed. Trust me, Luce. You said you were done running. Love you.

Fine.

That was all she could bring herself to write back. It felt as if he'd dropped a bomb at her feet. What should she do—run, seek cover, throw it away? The old Lucy would have without a second thought with not so much as a glance over her shoulder. He knew that. He'd dropped a grenade, and she was standing there, left to stare at it, knowing in all probability it was going to detonate and take off her face. She *was* angry. He was ruining it, changing things. They were going well, doing okay. Surely they could just go on as they were? Why change anything?

In a couple of days, after the six-month review, they were going to tell Sheila and Walt they were thinking about adopting Zoe. That was spinning her head already. Yeah, she wanted it, but it felt so final. Marriage would mean something else to risk losing. She couldn't take any more pressure. He loved her—*loved her.* She should be happy, right? She loved him. That hadn't and wouldn't change, but things were good as they were.

She cared about him, a lot. She loved waking up with him every day, sharing a bed. Falling asleep listening to his heartbeat was one of her new life's pleasures. She finally understood what Harriet had been on about. She got it. She was in this, but it was still so new, so precious, so fragile. They were exclusive, raising a kid under the same roof. That was commitment, more than she'd ever given anyone. More than she'd ever thought she would. She didn't want to go back to sleeping across the hallway.

Then she thought of what came next after someone said the 'M' word. They already lived together, but that was part of the arrangement for Zoe. It had lessened the blow of their grief, and had been a necessity. It had been thrust upon them, but now—this was different. It would be on them. If this next step failed, if she couldn't give him what he wanted, what then? 'For ever' was a long time, and look where it had got her sister and her parents. The one thing she'd learned was that love did not conquer all.

She saw the time on her phone and cursed.

*Looks like my break is well and truly over.*

Putting her phone back on silent and shoving it into her pocket, she speed-walked back up to the ward.

When rounds were over, Lucy headed for her office.

*Nearly there*, she told herself as she reached for the handle. *You can hide out here, do your paperwork. Catch your breath.*

'Dr Bakewell?'

*So close.*

Amy fell into step alongside her, following her into the room and taking a seat opposite hers.

'Well.' Lucy huffed. 'Come right in.' She slumped down in her chair. Amy was glaring at her from across the desk. 'What?' she snapped.

'Exactly. That's what I want to know. What's up? You've been like Mary Poppins lately, and today you've been biting people's heads off.'

'I have not!'

'Yeah, you have. None of the other staff dare mention it, but you've been worse than your old self—Medusa with a side of mean. What's going on?'

Lucy clenched her jaw and started shuffling papers on her desk.

'I'm not going till you tell me.'

Lucy tried to stare her down, but Amy just laughed. 'Nice try, mate. Your snakes don't scare me.'

'Fine.' She put down the papers. 'First of all, Medusa is better than Mary Poppins, so that's a rubbish insult. Second, I'm okay.'

'No, you're not. So, what's going on? Is it the adoption thing?'

'No. Yes. I don't know.' She bit the bullet. 'Jackson just told me he wants to marry me—by text.'

Amy's eyes bugged out.

'Exactly—you get it. It's bad, right? I mean—what is he thinking?' When Amy didn't answer, Lucy looked at her expectantly. 'Seriously, tell me—what is he thinking?' Her friend smiled with a slow, knowing grin. 'Why are you smiling?'

Amy leaned forward, resting her elbows on the desk. 'I'm thinking that for a smart, driven woman, you're pretty dumb.'

'Oh, well, thanks! I—'

'He told you he loves you because he does. He told you he wants to marry you because he does.' Her eyes narrowed, a look of wonder crossing her features. 'You really don't see it, do you?'

'See what? How soon this is? How crazy?'

'Love is crazy, Lucy. What you have been through is nuts. Anyone else would have crumbled, but you two—you make each other stronger. That man has hankered after you ever since he came here. The whole hospital can see it, and you really can't?'

'No.'

'Still?' Amy's tone was incredulous.

'No, I mean I can see it.' To her horror, a tear slipped down her cheek. She stopped its descent with a shaky hand. 'That's the problem. It's not just my life—it's three lives. I don't know how to do this, Ames. I never wanted to be in something like this, something that I could stuff up. I could lose it all. Nothing good ever stays. We were fine as we were.'

They were interrupted by a sharp tap on the door. 'I'll get it,' Amy said softly. After talking to the nurse, she closed the door again.

'There's a consult in A&E. You want me to take it?'

Lucy was already on her feet. 'No, I'm good.' She wiped her eyes. 'Do I look okay?'

Amy took a tissue from her pocket and rubbed at Lucy's cheek. 'You're good.'

'Thanks.' She smoothed down her uniform and fixed her hair. 'Tell the staff I'll try to keep the hissing to a minimum but, if the name Poppins is used in the same sentence as my name again, all bets are off.'

She was halfway out of the door when Amy spoke again.

'Being scared of losing something is normal, you know. Not reaching for what you want in case the worst happens is all well and good, but it's not a life either. I don't want that for you, mate. Not now, when you've seen how great it can all be. You've lost enough already. You didn't have a choice then. You do now. Life is fleeting, just like happiness. You have to go for it while you can.'

'Hey!' Josh greeted her with a wide grin. The place was rammed, the staff rushed off their feet—a typical Friday afternoon. 'What brings you down here?'

'Paeds got paged. One of your patients?'

He shook his head, nodding to Triage Four. 'In there.'

Jackson was standing by the bed when she got there, suturing an arm laceration.

'Hey.' She didn't look at him for long, but she felt his eyes watching her as she introduced herself to the teenaged patient. 'Hi, I'm Dr Bakewell. How are you feeling?'

'Pretty rough,' the teenager croaked. Aside from his arm lac, he had two black eyes forming, an obviously broken nose and a rather nasty lump on the side of his head.

'This is Lachlan, fifteen.' Jackson told her. 'Came off his skateboard at the top of the slope at the skate park. Ambulance brought him in, parents are on the way. I sent his friend to go get a drink.'

'He's scared of blood!' Lachlan laughed. 'Ouch.'

'Try to stay still,' she urged, shining a torch into his eyes. 'Normal pupillary response; did he stay conscious at the scene?'

'Ambulance said he was when they arrived but his friend Joe said he did knock himself out.'

Lucy nodded, checking his chart. 'Let's get him a head CT. No broken bones.' She donned gloves, removing the gauze to check his nose. It was cut on the bridge, the skin split but intact. 'Landed on your face, eh? Did you land the trick?'

Lachlan grinned. 'Yeah, stacked it straight after, though. My board broke on the railing.'

'No helmet either,' she chided, inspecting his head. He had a cut in his hairline that had already been glued. 'Do I need to lecture you about being safe over looking cool?'

Lachlan groaned. 'No. My mum always tells me. She's going to go mental when she gets here.'

She locked eyes with Jackson. 'Parents worry. I'm pretty sure she'll just be happy to see you, know that you're doing okay.'

She saw his eyes soften, and returned to Lachlan's face. 'Let's get you up to CT; we'll make sure your head injury is okay. Your nose is going to need some TLC, and you'll feel bruised and battered for a while.' She applied fresh dressings as Jackson finished sewing up his arm. Noting her instructions on his chart, she motioned for a passing porter to come over. 'Once we've done that, we'll get you up on the children's ward.'

'I have to stay overnight? Aww, man! The footie's on tonight.'

Jackson cut in. 'Leeds fan, eh? Good man. Your room will have a TV. We have that channel.'

'Safe.' Lachlan held out a fist, and Jackson bumped it gently with his gloved hand.

'I'll see you soon, Lachlan.'

Jackson was hot on her heels when she left the cubicle.

'Lucy, wait.'

'It's busy, Jackson, we can talk later.'

He blocked her path, taking off his gloves and shoving them in the adjacent bin. 'Fine.' He headed to the sink to wash his hands. 'Whatever.'

'No.' She joined him. 'It's not "whatever". Just not now.'

They both reached for the same paper towel, ripping it in half. Jackson grabbed another, his jaw taut. 'You talking about our talk, or us? I knew I shouldn't have said it. I knew you'd do this.'

'Do what?' she countered. 'You told me you want to get married in a text. I deserve a minute to process it!'

'You're not processing it, Luce. You know how I feel. You've known for a while, and I know you feel the same. You're just going to use this to push me away. I'm not demanding we do it tomorrow, but it is something I want. I thought you might too.'

He dropped the used towels in the bin, and she blocked his exit.

'That kid, in there?' She dropped her voice. 'His mother waved him out of the door and he ended up in hospital. She got a call telling her that someone she loved, someone she tried to protect and loved, was hurt, despite everything she did to keep him safe, despite everything she taught him. He knew to wear a helmet. She taught him to be safe, to look both ways when crossing the road, to chew his food. She taught him to be out in the world, and he ended up here.'

'And he's fine. He's on his way upstairs; he's alive and being looked after.' He scanned her face, his eyes widening with realisation. As usual, he saw through her shields. 'That's what this is about? Harriet and Zoe? The adoption plan?'

'It's not the adoption. I want Zoe. I like our life. I just…'

'You don't want more? I'm in this with you. I'm scared too, but we love each other, Luce. I will never not want this, want more.'

'I'm not scared.' She breathed. 'I'm terrified!' They were drawing attention now, her raised voice turning people's heads. 'I have to go, Jackson. We're at work.'

He grabbed her hand and wound his fingers around hers, grounding her frantic feet.

'I love you.' His voice was low in tone but not conviction. 'I'm here. I'm not going anywhere. Nothing has changed since this morning. I get that you're stressed. I'm sorry I didn't tell you in a better way, but I'm here—*for ever*.'

'You can't know that. Don't promise me what you don't know.'

His expression was so sad, she could barely hold his gaze.

'Oh, darling.' He squeezed her hand. 'My brave, stubborn heart. Tomorrow, I can't promise. You've got me there, but all of my todays are yours— yours and Zoe's. I will love you today and today and today, for as long as we've got. But you have to let me. You have to trust me. I want you to be my wife. I want to shout from the rooftops that I'm your husband.'

'Jackson, we have incoming!' Josh hollered, coming round the corner on fast feet. 'Sorry.' He winced, seeing them together. He looked back at Jackson. 'Two minutes out.'

'I'm coming.' Jackson dropped a kiss on her forehead. 'Think about it, Lucy.' She stared up at him blankly, stunned by his words.

*He loves me. He wants me as his wife.*

The second he'd said it out loud, her heart had felt it. Felt the solidity of his truth. 'I'm yours, and you are mine. Don't shut that out, not when we're this close. Love trumps tomorrow.'

With a rueful smile, he left her there, standing by the sink, motionless in a sea of busyness.

*Love trumps tomorrow*, he'd said. She thought about it the whole way back to the ward. She allowed herself to digest the conversation.

*When I get back to the ward, that's it—back to work, snakes at the ready, shields up.*

Holding her ID badge to the admission panel, she shrugged her shoulders back and held up her chin.

The letter from Harriet was in her locked desk drawer. Pulling it out, she pushed her paperwork to one side, smoothing out the pages.

She'd read it a lot over the last few months. She used it to hear her sister's voice in her head and remind herself why she was doing this. Ronnie and Harriet had known just what they were doing. She'd kicked and scratched her way through things, but they knew. It seemed everyone knew. They'd known when Ronnie had been alive, even when they'd been tearing strips off each other, when she'd declared him to be the most annoying man on the planet.

Rereading the letter for the hundredth time, she longed for her sister. She wished she could talk to her now about Jackson, about how scared she was. If Harriet were here now, she'd tell her how proud of her she was. How jealous she was of her ability to have leaped to form a family after living through the loss of their parents.

'I thought I was the brave one,' she said to the photo of Harriet sitting on her desk. 'Look at me now, eh? I know you said in your letter I'd be mad, but I'm pretty sure you're raging up there, or wherever you are.' Her pager went off; Lachlan was there. 'Oh, what does it matter?' She huffed, locking the letter back up. 'Tomorrow comes, no matter what you do. Screw today.'

Heading to Lachlan's room, she shoved her head back in the game. Taking a deep breath, she knocked and went in.

'Hi,' she said to a woman sitting next to his bed. 'Lachlan's mother, I assume?'

'Yes—Julia. His dad's just gone to get us some coffees.'

'Nice to meet you. I'm Dr Bakewell. Have you been updated?'

His mother, a small, rather worried looking woman who was the double of Lachlan, nodded back. 'The nurse said something about a scan.'

'That's right.' She looked at Lachlan. 'Your head injury has been checked over and we're satisfied it's just a concussion. Your laceration was glued in A&E, the cut on your arm has been cleaned and stitched and your nose isn't broken, but it will be very bruised and sore for a while.'

'That's it?' his mother checked. 'Nothing's wrong with his head? He knocked himself out.'

'I know, but he's fine. We'll keep him over-night to observe him, but tomorrow he should be well enough to discharge. You'll need bed rest at home, and no skate…'

His mother burst into loud sobs.

'He's really okay?' She sobbed.

'He's going to be fine,' Lucy said softly. 'We will take excellent care of him, I promise. He'll be home tomorrow.'

'Oh, God!' she cried, tears rolling down her cheeks. 'Thank you, thank you.'

'Mum…' Lachlan groaned, trying to reach for her hand. 'Don't cry!'

'I can't help it,' she managed to get out. She saw him reaching for her and clasped his hand tight between hers. 'If I wasn't so happy, I would be really mad, Lachie.'

Lucy stepped back, watching the teenager's bottom lip wobble. 'I know, Mum, I'm sorry. I swear, I'll always wear my helmet from now on.'

She kissed his hand, cradling it in hers and reaching over to brush back his hair from his face.

'You'd better, my boy. I can't function without you, okay? You're my world. I need you around.'

Lachlan sniffed. 'Love you, Mum,' he croaked.

'Love you too.' She smiled, her watery eyes bright. 'You're a pain in the bum sometimes, but I need you.'

Lachlan laughed. 'I need you too.'

'I'll…er… I'll let you have some time.' Lucy left the room, her legs shaking with every step.

*I can't function without you.*

Her kid hadn't worn a helmet. Something so basic, ignoring a request that could have caused a different ending—an ending she'd experienced first-hand, four times over. Watching them together in that room, so happy and elated to have escaped that, all she could think of was her people, her family: Zoe and Jackson.

For most of her life, she'd not only worn a helmet, she'd been too scared to get on her skateboard. Lachlan's mum had taken all the precautions, had had all the worry. She'd taught her son and he'd still got hurt. But she didn't regret being his mother, did she? She'd run to him, told him how important he was to her. She'd run to his side and stayed there, just as Jackson had for Lucy. No matter what she did or said, he was there, not fearing tomorrow.

She stood outside the room, heart pounding, and asked herself a question she hadn't dared ask before: if Jackson was hurt, would she regret it? Would she run to him, or run the other way?

She remembered his promise to her.

*All of my todays.*

For once in her life, she let the tears fall freely. Because she finally realised, no matter what happened down the road, no matter when tomorrow dawned, she loved him. If he had to leave her and this world, it wouldn't matter to her whether they were wed or not. But it would matter to him.

Lifting her tear-streaked face to the ceiling, she smiled. 'Okay, guys. You win.' She went to pull out her phone. 'It's time to get on that freaking skateboard.'

'Lucy!' Amy shouted, running down the corridor towards her as the nurses' station buzzed into life. Her pager went off in her pocket. 'Emergency!'

The warning siren went off around them and both women took off running.

# CHAPTER THIRTEEN

THE SECOND LUCY got there, she knew something was really wrong.

There was a huge flurry of activity as her team gathered at the nurses' station. Her number three, Dr Adebi, was shouting orders at the rest of the staff, calling them out name by name. Once they got their instructions they rushed off, professional and nimble, eager to get on with their designated task.

'What's the emergency?' Lucy asked, running to his side. Dr Adebi turned to her once the last of the staff was sorted, but his words were half-drowned out when the lockdown alarm sounded again. An announcement asking people to stay calm and remain where they were rang out on repeat.

'We're getting reports of a man with a weapon in the hospital. A porter was injured in the back delivery bays. Security is trying to track the man down. Porter was stabbed in the stomach once, and once in the arm as he tried to stop the guy.'

'Lockdown procedures need to be initiated immediately, no one in or out.'

Dr Adebi nodded, pointing to the ward doors. 'We already locked it down, SCBU too.'

'Shutters on the windows facing the corridor?'

Dr Adebi shrugged, his eyes wide. 'I'm not one hundred percent. I told the nurses to take the children who could be moved to the day room at the end of the hall, as per your protocols. Lunch is done, so we should be able to hole up for a while.'

She patted his arm. 'Go and round on the patients, make sure all observations are carried out on time. Nothing gets missed.'

He gave her a solemn nod and got to it. She picked up the phone, checking with maternity and SCBU that everything was locked down and all people accounted for. She knew they'd already locked down A&E. She felt better, knowing Jackson was safe, somewhere close. She hoped his parents weren't seeing any of this on the news. They'd been through enough worry.

The ambulances would have been diverted to other hospitals already. The other staff were coping well, pulling together as a team. The wards worked in conjunction with each other, all following the protocols and procedures. Now all they had to do was reassure the parents, carers and patients they had with them on the ward. Heading to the TV room, she pushed down the feelings of worry she had for the hospital and its inhabitants. Ensuring her patients were calm and still getting the best care was paramount.

'Right,' she said with a broad smile, taking in the sight of children in chairs, their parents' laps and wheelchairs and closing the door behind her to help muffle the sounds outside. 'Who fancies a movie, eh? We have headphones!'

She didn't hear a thing for the next hour. All the updates were the same: no one in, no one out. All non-emergency surgeries were cancelled. One of her patients was locked down in the post-surgery recovery room after having had a hernia repaired, and young Ada's parents were distraught at not being able to be there for their cute little five-year-old. Lucy had allocated one of the healthcare assistants to keep an eye on them. She knew what it was like to wait for news, and she looked after the parents and guardians just as well as she did the children.

Amy came to find her just as she was going on her rounds again.

'Ada's fine. The OR nurses got one of the tablets. I put the parents in one of the side waiting rooms so they could talk to her in private.'

Lucy patted her hand gratefully. 'You're a star; they should feel so much better after seeing she's okay.'

'Yeah.' Amy smiled, but it didn't last. 'I'll be glad when this thing's over. I heard from one of the OR nurses that someone else has been stabbed.'

'Someone on the staff?' Lucy asked, appalled. Amy shrugged.

'I don't have the details; it was pretty hectic there. They were getting him up to Theatre; she didn't have time to stay on the line.'

'Right,' Lucy replied, pulling out her phone.

She typed out a message to Jackson at super-speed.

Are you okay?

Then she got back to work, Amy in tow.

'Hey, Nathan, how's the apocalypse going?'

Nathan was one of her older patients, at sixteen, and secretly one of her favourites.

'Not bad. I finally kicked that level's butt last night.'

'Yeah,' she teased, washing her hands in the little sink near his bed. 'The night staff told me. No wonder you look tired. Three a.m.?'

Nathan winced. 'Can't believe they grassed me up.'

'They didn't, I read it on your observation chart. My team don't sweat the small stuff, but you do need to get your rest. Can I check your sutures?'

Nathan groaned, putting his game on pause. 'Fine,' he droned. 'But...' His smile turned mischievous. 'Since my parents couldn't get in today, you can't tell them that I didn't do my homework yet. Deal?'

Lucy pretended to ponder his bribe. 'Is it biology?'

'No, English lit.' Lucy's eyes flicked to the small stack of paperbacks Nathan had brought with him when he'd come in for his small bowel surgery and nodded. She wouldn't have been able to concentrate in his shoes, with all the excitement going on around him. If killing some zombies distracted him from being in hospital on lockdown when he should have been at school, that was fine with her.

In a kinder world he'd have been hanging out with his mates and not dealing with Crohn's. This operation wasn't the first he'd had. He lived on a special diet and had to endure a colostomy bag. He was a happy teenager who worked hard. One bit of homework missed was hardly going to derail his life. He read in the evening; she'd seen him plenty of times. They'd even swapped books before, ones she'd loved at his age.

'Fine, deal. What do you say, Dr Ackles?'

Amy laughed as she wrote on his chart. 'A day off on doctor's orders? They can't be mad at that.'

Donning gloves, Lucy gently removed the dressings, checking over the operation site. 'Good, it's healing well. No sign of infection or swelling. The surgeon said it went well.'

Nathan smiled. 'Yeah, they managed to save more than they thought, which is good, because I am sick of seeing you guys.'

Lucy pretended to be wounded, miming the removal of an arrow from her heart. 'Ouch,' she laughed. 'Cheers, Nath. We love you too.'

'When do you think the hospital will be open for visitors?' he asked as she finished up.

'Tomorrow, I would have thought,' she said, making sure she didn't show how uncertain she was. 'You have your phone, right, to video call your parents?'

Nathan nodded. 'Yeah, I told them to stay at work. I think they were planning to stage a vigil outside at one point!' He huffed, his trademark teenage eye-roll evident. 'I heard Isaac say the police were here. They would have freaked.'

'Hey.' She laughed, getting his attention. 'Don't knock it. Believe me, having parents that care and fuss like yours do is not a bad thing. It's nice having someone that cares for you.'

One of the nurses knocked on the door and Amy went to see what they wanted. When she came back, her face was white.

'What?' Lucy asked, knowing instantly that something was wrong.

'Nothing.' She went to open the blinds she'd closed for the examination. 'Good news, actually—the lockdown is being lifted.' She let the light into the room, making Nathan squint and hiss theatrically. 'Dr Bakewell, I need a word outside, please.'

Lucy passed Nathan his controller. 'See you

later.' She followed her colleague outside. 'What's up?' she asked straight away. 'Did they get the guy?'

'Yeah.' Amy breathed. 'They got him, but you need to go to Jackson, Lucy.' She watched Amy's lips form more words, and then she was running.

*Not again*, her voice was screaming in her head. *Not again. Why us?*

She ran down corridor after corridor, barrelling past people, banging on doors, demanding that they let her through, screaming that the lockdown was over and to let her get past. Her phone was at her ear, but all it was doing when she called Jackson was ringing out, ringing out again and again.

Finally, she was there. Josh saw her running and came over. He took her to one side, towards Resus Two.

*God, no, not that room. That was the room they'd taken her sister and Ronnie to. That room meant death.*

Josh kept talking, his voice hushed, his arm around her shoulder as he laid out the details for her.

The guy with the knife had gone to A&E; he had walked right through the hospital and not been stopped. The security team had still been scrambling to get a description since the first alarm had been raised. In the chaos, he'd slipped by everyone. The loading bay doors had CCTV, but he'd been obscured by a delivery van. The bloke had walked right past people into A&E, where Jackson had been working. The lockdown between departments had still not been in full effect, the chaos still fresh. Jackson had blocked his path and challenged who he was. When he'd seen the blood on his clothes, he'd reacted.

*Jackson had tried to protect everyone.*

The attacker had lunged. Lucy couldn't get a breath big enough to fill her lungs as she listened, and it looked as if they were walking straight to the room she'd never wanted to set foot in again.

*Not Jackson*, she thought. *Not now. Please. It's not fair. Not that room.*

They were almost there, her steps slowing as Josh kept talking about how the man was in custody, how Jackson was a hero. How bad it could have been. She didn't want to hear any of that. She didn't want to hear that Jackson was a hero. He was already *her* hero. He was hurt, or worse, and life was changing again. She'd run from him, from his love, for so long. They could have had more todays. She had so much to say. She'd barely begun loving him.

Zoe… Zoe couldn't lose another person.

They were almost at the doors now, and she didn't hear or see anything else—not the lighting, not the patients or the staff, dealing with the aftermath of the last few hours. All she saw was those big wooden doors, the ones she'd pushed through half a year ago. She couldn't feel Josh's arms around her shoulders. She didn't hear him talking or see the faces they passed as she tried to put one numb body part in front of the other. Her phone was still in her hand, which was useless, because she couldn't reach whom she wanted to talk to. It was too late for him just to pick up the phone and for everything to be normal.

'I can't do this again,' she said. 'I can't. Not again.' When they passed the doors, her knees buckled. Josh took her over to a set of chairs and sat her down. He kneeled in front of her, calling a nurse to bring them some water.

It was then she truly understood. She loved him—today, tomorrow, for ever. She was completely in love with Jackson Denning. She loved him enough to run down that aisle, with him holding her hand. She'd walk through fire for him. She'd been over-the-top obsessed, to the point of losing her mind, with him since the day she'd seen the big lug howling and clutching his bruised nether regions.

He'd always been there—in the background, in her face, in her thoughts. Pushing her to be the best at work, if only to one-up him. They made each other better, and she didn't know another man walking the earth who could handle her like he could. Who could understand her and be part of her family. He was always challenging her, annoying the hell out of her. He made her feel alive, sexy. He saw her like no other did. He'd always seen her as if she was transparent under his gaze. He loved her, and she jolly well loved him too. Of course she should be his wife…in this life, in every life.

It was then she realised that Josh hadn't taken her to his side. He hadn't taken her to that room, the one she'd once barged into, looking for her sister, for Ronnie. Looking for proof that what she knew in her head wasn't true. She turned to look at the wooden barrier between Jackson and her. It was still. No one was coming or going. No one was barking orders or running in with crash trays.

'I never told him,' she said, her tears taking over. 'I know the answer now, and I'll never get to tell him. To see his stupid grin.'

'What?' Josh asked, his voice finally filtering through to her ears again. 'Lucy, I think you're in shock. Please drink this.' She pushed the cup away with a shaky hand. She felt sick and dizzy, so dizzy. Her head was spinning. She'd run again when he'd needed her. He'd spilled his guts and she'd left him hanging. It was too late. He was gone. He'd never know now.

'Lucy!' Josh boomed. 'She's passing out! Hold her head!' Arms scrambled around her as her sight turned to pinpricks, surrounded by black. 'Can we get some help here? Lucy,' she heard Josh say to her, 'we've got you.'

And then she let go and succumbed to the nothingness.

When she woke up, she was in a side cubicle in A&E, the curtains drawn around her. She sat up with a jerk when her memory slammed into action.

'Careful,' a deep voice said. Her head whipped to the side and she looked straight into Jackson's big, brown eyes. 'Take it slowly.'

He was lying in a bed next to hers, his bare chest sporting a dressing. He had a split lip, and a deep bruise was forming around his right eye.

'Jackson!' she squeaked, her voice strangled. She pulled her blanket back and went to him. He reached for her hand as she sank to the chair next to his gurney. He pulled it to his lips and kissed it, wincing when it touched his injury. 'I thought you were…were…'

She started to cry then. Relief and shock flowed out of her. He pulled her closer, his other hand coming up to grab her cheek.

'Trig, I'm fine. I'm okay, Luce.' He looked down at his chest. 'The guy stabbed me. I clocked him the second he walked in, but security was thin on the ground. He was looking for another patient. Some ridiculous gang territory thing.'

She didn't care about any of that, she just cared that he was there.

'Shh,' he soothed her. 'Don't cry, darling, please. It'll drive me crazy. I can't get to you properly like this.'

She laughed, and it sounded hysterical between the sobs.

'You're lying there and you're worried about me,' she keened, leaning forward and kissing him. He made a pained hissing sound but, when she pulled back, he leaned his head closer to keep the contact. He kissed her softly, one kiss on each corner of her mouth and the tip of her nose.

'That's how this works,' he said once he'd let her go enough to look her in the eye. 'I'm fine.' He winked at her with his good eye. 'You're not getting rid of me that easily.'

She got his double meaning, and she didn't need to think twice about anything now. She knew she would never run from this man again. Almost losing him had woken her up. Life was short and cruel. She didn't want to miss a minute of it, good or bad, light or dark.

'I love you and I want to be with you. Yes…in every single way!' she blurted. 'I panicked when you said it today. I wanted to run, but I will never do that again.'

'Luce, you don't have to say this. You don't have to pity me or feel bad.'

'I don't. I already knew the truth; I just didn't

want to face it. I thought I'd never get the chance to tell you. I thought I'd never get to say it.

'I love you. I love you, Jackson, body and soul. I swear, I would go through a lifetime of pain and lonely tomorrows for ten minutes being loved by you today. I'm sick of hiding in my half-life. I want us to be a family, a proper family. So, marry me, and yes—that's what I want to say. A question and an answer, no more time wasting.'

He didn't say anything at first. She studied his beautiful, broken face for clues.

*Was she too late? What if he'd realised she wasn't worth it after all?*

'Took you long enough,' his deep voice teased. 'Get in this bed, right now. I need you close.'

She scrambled in carefully, feeling the warmth of him against her. She kissed his cheek over and over when he tried to smile and whimpered at the pain it produced.

She held his face close to hers and said over and over, 'I love you…for ever.'

'Wow,' he mumbled from under her. 'I should get stabbed more often.'

'Not funny.' She scowled.

'I love you too, Luce,' he said in her ear as she held him tight. 'I always have.' His grin lit him up from the inside. 'We're getting married, Trig.'

'You bet your lanky behind we are, Sasquatch.'

# EPILOGUE

*Two and a half years later*

'HEY!' JACKSON MET them at the front door, taking her shopping bags out of her hands as he always did. They walked down the hall to the kitchen and he leaned down for a kiss on the way, as if he couldn't wait any longer. 'Missed you,' he mumbled into her ear. Even after all this time, she still shivered when he did that. She still found him as hot as the day they'd met. The late August weather was fine, the sun blazing high in the sky.

'Did you get everything you needed?'

Lucy puffed her fringe out of her eyes, heading straight to the fridge to get them both a cold drink.

'We sure did, eh, doodlebug?'

Zoe was trying to get up on one of the stools on the island, her face like thunder.

'Mummy made me go to loads of shops. It was so boring.' Jackson lifted her up, making her laugh as he blew raspberries on her cheek.

'Oh, no, not shopping!' he teased. 'Did you get your school uniform?'

'Yes.' She grinned, brushing her blonde hair

back with a little hand and reaching for the juice Lucy had put on the counter. She slurped when she drank, her eyes on the back door. 'Can I play outside now?'

Lucy was busy unpacking groceries from one of the bags. 'Till lunch, of course.'

'Yes!' Zoe punched the air, and it immediately reminded Lucy of Jackson. She was a Mini Me of him, all guns blazing, just like him. She wasn't one for shying away from things, and it thrilled Lucy to see it.

Jackson caught her mid-air as she shuffled off the stool, brandishing sun spray.

'Aww, Daddy!'

He laughed, putting her on her feet and getting down to her level to spray the sunscreen onto her skin.

'Aww, Daddy, nothing. It's hotter than Hades out there, and you're built like a child of the corn.'

'A what?' she asked, her little nose scrunching up in confusion as he lathered her up.

'Nothing. Have fun.' He dropped a kiss on her forehead and Zoe took off for the garden.

Just before she barrelled out to the swings she loved, she turned back to them. 'Don't forget to show Daddy your surprise!' She beamed, and then they were alone.

'Surprise, eh?' he fished, coming up behind her as she put the last of the food away. He tried to peek into one of the other bags but she swatted his hand away.

'Hey!' Lucy admonished. 'I wasn't going to show you till later. She snitched a tad early.'

He came round behind her, wrapping her in his arms, nuzzling at her neck. He knew that drove her crazy. Hell, one more rub of his stubble and she'd give away all her secrets.

'That's my girl. What is it? Come on, spill.'

She pretended to be annoyed with him, but she was too excited. She didn't keep a thing from him any more, not since that day when she'd thought she'd lost him.

The last couple of years had been amazing. It had been hard work, sure, and exhausting. Somewhere along the way, they'd gone from Jack-Jack and Luby to Mummy and Daddy. Zoe knew all about her parents. Their pictures still hung in pride of place in their home. She'd heard the stories and, when she'd started calling Jackson and Lucy 'Mummy' and 'Daddy', they knew that she'd decided that for herself.

Zoe was a mix of all four of them. She had her mother's looks and soft blonde hair and Ronnie's calmness. Jackson always ribbed Lucy that Zoe had inherited her stubborn streak, and Lucy saw his loyalty and open-hearted love shine out from their little girl. It had been a journey, but she loved where they were going. Living for today, it turned out, was a hell of a lot of fun.

'Come on, wifey, show me!' Jackson had started to tickle her sides and she yelped as she jumped away from him, grabbing one of the plain bags.

'Fine!' She pretended to huff. 'Before I show you, though, promise not to freak out.'

Jackson scoffed loudly. 'Pot…kettle…?'

'Shut up!' She giggled. 'Fine.' She came to stand in front of him, holding out the bag to him. He grabbed at it, a daft look on his face, like a little boy on Christmas morning. She pressed her lips together to keep the smile off her face as she observed his confused frown.

'What…?' His voice trailed off as he unfolded the small, white cotton garment. '"My big sister is…"'

'"Awesome",' she finished. 'Zoe picked it out.'

He held it up, the bag falling out of his grasp to the kitchen floor.

'This is a onesie,' he said.

'Yep.'

'For a baby.'

'Yep.'

'You—you let Zoe buy this?' he stammered, his gorgeous face a maelstrom of emotions.

'Yep.' She smirked. 'Well, I reckoned we'd need it.' She came round the island to stand in front of him. 'You know, in a few months.' His eyes bugged as his jaw dropped. 'Freaking out?' she teased.

'We're having a baby?' His voice cracked. 'For real?'

'For real.' She laughed. 'Just our timing, too. One kid goes to school full time, and we start all over again. Are you happy?' she asked, watching him look at the little outfit in his hand as if it might vanish.

'I'm not happy,' he said, lunging forward and picking her up in his huge, muscular arms. 'I'm freaking ecstatic! Zoe!' he shouted, and she appeared at the back door. 'We're having a baby!' He yelled, twirling Lucy round on the spot.

Zoe rolled her eyes, a classic Lucy move.

'I know, silly! I'm the big sister!' She put her hands on her hips, nodding to the clothing in his arms.

Jackson and Lucy laughed out loud. 'Good point. Get over here, smarty-pants!'

Zoe ran over with a giggle, and Jackson reached down and scooped her up.

'My girls.' He grinned, showering them both with kisses. 'I love you,' he told them both. 'So much.'

'We love you more,' Lucy told him. Hugging them both to her, she wondered at how life could change so much. How tragedy could rip people apart and change them. It could alter their landscape for ever, but sometimes lead to something new and unexpected—something great that might never have made them so happy without going through the deep, dark sorrow first.

That night, with Zoe fast asleep after their busy day, and Jackson kissing her still-flat tummy before carrying her to bed with love and lust written all over his gorgeous face, she reminded herself never to forget how lucky she was. She liked to think that, wherever they were, the people they had lost would be watching and be happy for them…at peace. It gave her the strength to enjoy every moment and take the rough with the smooth. Squeeze every drop out of life and follow her gut in her personal life as well as in her career.

Months later, she proved just that to herself, and to the love of her life. As she cradled Zachary Ronnie Denning, exhausted from labour and eager to show Zoe her little brother, she didn't hesitate to enjoy every single second. He was perfect, just like Zoe. A child she'd made from love with Dr Denning, the man whom she'd once jokingly threatened to sterilise to do the women of the world a favour.

'I love you.' Jackson beamed, that grin bowling her over.

'Pack that grin up, Denning. I just had your baby. You'll make me want another just to make you do it again.'

'Deal,' he retorted, making her laugh. 'We can

fill the whole house with kids.' He looked at Zachary. 'He's amazing, isn't he? He has the Denning chin.'

She rolled her eyes at him. 'Let's hope he doesn't go paintballing and fall in love with a stubborn woman, eh?'

His low, rumbling laugh surrounded her as he hugged them both to him. 'I hope he does. I'll tell him it's the best thing his dad ever did, being shot in the groin by his mother.'

'Worth all the todays?'

He bent to kiss her just as the door opened. Zoe ran in, followed by two very excited grandparents.

'All the todays for ever,' he whispered. 'Fighting and loving you is what makes life worth living.'

'Deal?' she joked.

'Hell, yeah.' He growled. 'Bring it on, Trig.'

\* \* \* \* \*

# MEDICAL

## Life and love in the world of modern medicine.

# NEW RELEASE

## BESTSELLING AUTHOR

# DELORES FOSSEN

*Even a real-life hero needs a little healing sometimes…*

After being injured during a routine test, Air Force pilot
Blue Donnelly must come to terms with what his future
holds if he can no longer fly, and whether that future
includes a beautiful horse whisperer who turns his life
upside down.

In stores and online June 2024.